Praise for Julie Anne Long's Previous Novels

TO LOVE A THIEF

"A wonderful story."
—Midwest Book Review

"A delightful read. The characters and their repartee sparkle with humor and charm."
—Rendezvous

"What an amazing book! I love a good romance story, but I love a book even more when it is well written. To Love a Thief may be one of the most wonderful Pygmalion stories yet to come out of the romance genre."
—Rakehell.com

"A perfect blend of romance and humor . . . magical and engaging, a treat for anyone who believes that fairy tales can come true."
—TheMysticCastle.com

"Compelling and highly entertaining . . . To Love a Thief is extremely well written, fast-paced, and entirely enjoyable."
—RoadtoRomance.com

more . . .

"Lily is a wonderful heroine, and To Love a Thief *is a fun read."*
—Bookloons.com

"An excellent historical novel . . . the relationship between Lily and Gideon is the very substance of every young woman's romantic dreams."
—RomanceJunkies.com

THE RUNAWAY DUKE

"Wonderful and charming . . . at the top of my list for best romance of the year . . . It is a delight in every way."
—LikesBooks.com

"Thoroughly enjoyable . . . A charming love story brimming with intrigue, witty dialogue, and warmth."
—Rendezvous

"Hilarious, heartrending, and tender . . . ample suspense . . . A guaranteed winner."
—CurledUp.com

"A must-read . . . Combining the ideal amount of romance, suspense, and mystery, Long gives us a marvelous and dazzling debut that overflows with intelligence, wit, and warmth."
—Romantic Times BOOKclub Magazine

"Two fantastic lead protagonists . . . Fans will want to run away with this delightful pair."
—Midwest Book Review

Beauty and the Spy

ALSO BY JULIE ANNE LONG

The Runaway Duke
To Love a Thief

Beauty
and
the Spy

JULIE ANNE LONG

WARNER

FOREVER

NEW YORK   BOSTON

Copyright © 2006 by Julie Anne Long
Excerpt from *Ways to Be Wicked* copyright 2006
by Julie Anne Long

Book design by Stratford Publishing Services, Inc.

Warner Forever and the Warner Forever Logo are registered trademarks of Time Warner Book Group Inc.

Warner Books

Time Warner Book Group
1271 Avenue of the Americas
New York, NY 10020
Visit our Web site at www.twbookmark.com

Printed in the United States of America

First Printing: March 2006

10 9 8 7 6 5 4 3 2 1

For Karen—for the times we nearly drove off the road because we were laughing so hard about something we could never, ever explain to anyone else; for Fritos on Christmas Eve; for the millions of little things that make up the language of sisters.

And I do not look like a yam.

Acknowledgments

My gratitude to Melanie Murray, an editor so completely wonderful that I killed off a (fictional) wife just to make her happy (teasing, M); to Diane Luger and Mimi Bark for yet another gorgeous cover; to Geoff Hancock for my new, daily view of hummingbirds and roses, which has done miraculous things for my peace of mind; to the Divas (http://www.fogcitydivas.com) for friendship, laughter, and advice about certain, shall we say, *intricacies* of publishing that have nothing to do with writing; to Elizabeth Pomada, for helping to launch me on this thrill ride in the first place; to Ken and Kevin and Melisa and Karen for being so brilliant at just being there; to all the readers who've sent warm, funny, touching notes or stopped by to say hello at signings—I'm so delighted and honored that you enjoy my stories, and I hope you always do.

Beauty and the Spy

Prologue

1803

Years later, Anna would remember how big the moon had been that night, swollen and slung low like a pregnant woman on the brink of birth. The hard white light of it penetrated the shutters in her bedroom and kept her tossing and turning, and there was too much room in the bed to thrash. For Richard had been to visit, and Richard had left, as he always did, and tonight the bed seemed emptier than ever for it.

She tried soothing herself with thoughts of mundane things: Susannah, just three years old, was getting the last of her teeth, and was fussy and feverish with it. *I must tell Richard,* Anna thought, so he could exclaim over it and make Susannah giggle, for she loved her papa. She was such a funny little thing, bubbling over with laughter so easily, already exhibiting a taste for luxuries. Yesterday she'd taken one bite from a cake and then handed it back to Anna. "It's broken, Mama," she'd said sadly, as though she couldn't possibly eat something that wasn't whole.

Then there was Sylvie, four years old now, who was

proving to have her mother's quick tongue and temper and her father's intelligence. "I'd really rather *not,*" she'd loftily said to Anna just this morning, when she'd been told to pick up her toys. Anna smiled, remembering. Sylvie would be a . . . *challenge.* And Sabrina, who leafed through books intently and couldn't keep her jam-sticky fingers away from the pianoforte; who always seemed to know when her mother was feeling sad, and brought her little offerings, flowers, and leaves. It unnerved Anna, how much Sabrina noticed. Her daughters were miracles, all beautiful, all made of the best of her and Richard. Her love for them frightened her with its exquisite, terrible totality. Like her love for Richard.

Ah, but thinking of Richard would not bring sleep; instead, her senses surged with a hunger that his absences kept honed. His light eyes with the lines raying from the corners, the way her body fit so perfectly against his—he still took her breath away. An arrangement born of economics and necessity—he'd needed a mistress, she'd needed money—had bloomed into a surprising, abiding love. Together they'd built a semblance of family life here in Gorringe, a town, legend had it, named by a duke who'd gone mad searching for a rhyme for "orange." It appealed to Richard's perhaps overly developed sense of the absurd and to Anna's desire for a quiet country home, and it was a mere few hours' coach ride from London where Richard, a much-beloved member of the House of Commons, spent most of his time.

There had never been talk of marriage; Anna had never expected it, or pressed him for it.

But lately she'd begun to suspect that Richard, having survived battlefields, had grown too accustomed to danger and was no longer capable of living without it. He'd told her over dinner once, while the girls slept, that he suspected one of the country's most influential politicians, Thaddeus Morley, had amassed his fortune by selling information to the French. And Richard, a patriot to the bone, intended to set out to prove it.

Anna had seen Morley precisely twice, and she had been struck by his stillness and sheer presence—he held himself like a man carrying a grenade in his pocket. The populace thought highly of him; he had risen from humble origins to a position of prominence. Anna knew a little something about what it took to rise so high from humble beginnings. She suspected he was a very dangerous man.

"If anything ever happens to us, Anna . . ." Richard had murmured against her mouth the other night, as his fingers had worked busily at the laces on her dress.

"Hush. Nothing will happen to us, except perhaps some marvelous lovemaking tonight."

He laughed a little, applied his lips to her neck. "If anything happens to us," he insisted, "I want the girls to have the miniatures of you. Promise me." He'd commissioned three exquisite miniatures of her, brought them with him during this all too short visit.

"Of me? Why not of their handsome father?"

"Of you, my love. Of their beautiful mother." He'd had her stays undone by then, and then his hands had covered her breasts—

Bam, bam, bam.

Anna shot upright, her heart clogging her throat. Someone was throwing a fist against the door downstairs.

In one motion she swept from her bed and thrust her arms through the sleeves of her robe; her trembling hands tried once, twice, three times before she finally managed to touch a light to a candle. Cupping the tiny flame with her hand, she moved into the hall. Susannah was whimpering, startled awake; Anna heard the whimpers become choking sobs.

The maid, a girl with eyes and a mouth too sultry for her own good, stood at the top of the stairs, dark hair spilling like two shadows down the front of her, hands twisting anxiously in her nightdress. She'd come highly recommended from the agency, and yet she'd proved nearly as hapless as she was handsome.

"Please go see to Susannah." Anna was amazed to hear her voice emerge so gently. The girl jerked as though shaken from a trance, then glided into the nursery. Anna heard murmuring, heard Susannah's sobs taper off into hiccups.

Somehow Anna's bare feet found each stair without stumbling, and then she was at the door. She threw the bolts and opened it.

A man stood heaving before her, hunched with exhaustion, breath bursting from him in harsh white puffs; a thick scarf coiled around his neck and a heavy overcoat protected him from the weather. Behind him Anna saw the dark outline of a coach against the star-spattered night; two spent horses bent their heads in their traces.

The man straightened: the white glare of the moon showed her the long nose, kind eyes, and small, ironic mouth of James Makepeace, Richard's friend from London. The whole of his message was written on his features.

"It's Richard." She said it before he could, as if doing so would somehow protect her from the blow.

"I'm so sorry, Anna." His voice was still a rasp, but it ached with truth.

Her chin went up. The deepest cuts, she knew, brought a blessed numbness before the agony set in. "How?"

"Murdered." He spat the word out, like the foul thing it was. "And Anna . . ." He paused, preparing her, it seemed. "They're coming to arrest you for it."

The words sank through her skin, cold as death.

"But . . . that's . . . *madness.*" Her own voice came faintly to her through a burgeoning fear.

"I know, Anna. I *know.*" Impatience and desperation rushed his words. "It's impossible. But witnesses claim to have seen you arguing with him at his town house yesterday; others have sworn they saw you leaving it shortly before he was . . . found. You can be certain clues will be discovered that point to you, as well. If he's gone this far, I'm sure he'll be thorough."

No word had ever sounded more bitterly ironic than that last one.

"Morley," she breathed. "It was Morley."

James's silence confirmed this. Then he made a strange, wild little sound. Almost a laugh.

Anna jumped at the crunch of approaching hooves and wheels, and the flame of her candle leaped tall, nearly flickering out. In that instant, Anna saw silvery tracks shining below James Makepeace's eyes.

His low, curt voice cut through her numbness. "The hackney you hear approaching is one I hired for you. Anna, please—you need to leave *now.* They know to look for you here. Take it anywhere but London—I've paid the driver well enough not to ask questions. But don't tell him your name, for God's sake."

"How . . . how was he . . ." She stopped, shook her head; she didn't want to know how Richard had been killed. She wanted to picture him in life, not death. "The girls—"

"I'll take them. I'll make sure they're cared for until . . . until it's safe for you to return, Anna. You've my vow."

"But I can't . . . they're . . . they're so small . . ." Such futile words, and not really what she meant to say. *Richard is dead.*

James Makepeace seized her cold, cold hand in his gloved fingers and squeezed it hard. She sensed that he wanted to shake her instead. "Anna . . . *listen to me*: a woman with three children . . . you'd be dangerously conspicuous. They'll find you, and who knows then what will become of the girls? You're a brilliant scapegoat; the public will tear you to pieces. I swear to you if there was some other way . . ." He threw a quick glance over his shoulder, turned back to her, and she could see him struggling for patience.

He'd risked his own life for her.

Would it be better to flee without her girls, if there was the slimmest chance to reunite with them later?

Or for her girls to grow up knowing their mother had hung for their father's murder?

Anna made the only sort of decision one could make in the frantic dark: she gave a quick shallow nod, acquiescing.

James exhaled in relief. "Good. I swear to you, Anna, if I could hide all of you, I would. I just . . . there wasn't time to make other plans."

"You've risked so much for us already, James. I would never ask it of you. I cannot thank you enough."

James ducked his head, acknowledging the gratitude he heard in her voice.

"How did you . . . how did you *know* this?"

He shook his head roughly. "It's best I not tell you. And forgive me, Anna, but I must ask one more thing: Did Richard say anything, *anything* to you about where he kept some very important"—he chose his next word with care—"documents?"

"I'm sorry?"

"Richard said he'd found the perfect hiding place for them, a place no one would think to look, particularly Morley. He said it had something to do with 'Christian virtues.' Richard was amused by it, actually. Found it ironic." James's mouth actually twitched. A grim little attempt at a smile. "Richard was . . . Richard was clever."

"Oh, yes. Richard was clever." Anna felt a helpless, selfish rush of anger. When would love become more important to men than glory? How could one woman and three little girls ever compete with the glamour and excitement of capturing a political traitor? The thought itself was probably traitorous. "I'm sorry, he said nothing to me of it."

They stood facing each other. Frozen on the brink of a life without Richard, and hating to move forward into it.

"I loved him, too, Anna," James said hoarsely.

Loved. Past tense.

Anna stepped aside to allow him into the house. And then she became a whirlwind in the predawn darkness.

James Makepeace waited while Anna dressed herself in dark mourning, covered herself in a heavy cloak, twisted up her hair, and pulled a shawl around her head. She woke the girls, Susannah and Sylvie and Sabrina, kissed and held their little bodies to her, breathed in their hair, felt the silky skin of their cheeks, murmured quick desperate promises they couldn't possibly understand. She bundled them with clothes and the miniatures.

Anna gazed down at those miniatures briefly and felt hot furious tears pushing at her eyes. Those miniatures meant he had known, damn him. He had known they were in danger. Had known that something might become of Anna, or of him.

She would love him for all time. She wondered if she would ever forgive him.

"For you," she said to James, thrusting a simple but very fine diamond necklace into his hands. "It should help with . . . well, it should help the girls."

James took it without question. Closed his fist over it, as though sealing a bargain.

"How will I . . ."

"Send a letter when you can, Anna, but wait a few months for the uproar to die. Leave the continent if you can; I doubt any place in England will be safe when word spreads. Godspeed."

And then Anna looked one last time at the house that only hours earlier had been the source of her greatest happiness, her greatest love, her only love.

She prayed for her girls. For Richard. For justice.

James helped her into the hackney. The driver cracked the ribbons over the backs of the horses and the hackney jerked forward and took Anna Holt away.

Chapter One

May 1820

Susannah Makepeace had a new dress, and Douglas was being particularly charming, and together these two things comprised the whole of her happiness.

She sat with her best friends on a low hillside at her father's country estate, the young ladies scattered like summer blooms over the grass, the young men sprawling as they plucked tiny daisies to make chains. The day was warm, but a frisky breeze snaked around them, lifting the ribbons of bonnets and fluttering the hems of dresses. Douglas cast a furtive eye toward Susannah's ankles and she drew them quickly under her skirt with a teasing frown. He winked at her. In two weeks' time, when he was her husband, Douglas would be privy to the sight of every inch of her. The thought made her heart jig a little.

Like the breeze, their conversation meandered: friends and balls and parties were touched on, laughed about, abandoned, taken up again. It was summer after all, or very nearly, and summer was about gaiety. And they were between London balls. God forbid there should be a lull between entertainments.

"Did you notice how George Percy dances?" Douglas mused. "His arms hang as though they're inserted on pins, and he rather . . . *flails* . . . like"—Douglas lurched to his feet—"like this." He flopped about like a marionette, and everyone laughed.

Behind them, their chaperone Mrs. Dalton *tsked* in disapproval.

"Oh, come now, Mrs. Dalton, you must admit it's a *little* funny," Douglas cajoled, which earned him a *hmmph* and a reluctant, tight-lipped smile from the matron, who was the latest in a series of Susannah's paid companions. She drove her needle back into her sampler, no doubt stitching something meant to be inspiring but that always sounded admonishing instead, such as THE MEEK SHALL INHERIT THE EARTH. Susannah often felt that Mrs. Dalton's samplers were a silent attempt to rein her in. *You'll have to try harder than that, Mrs. Dalton,* Susannah thought cheekily. Susannah Makepeace hadn't become the belle of the season because she was *meek*. Nor, for that matter, was meekness the reason Douglas Caswell, heir to a marquis, had proposed to her.

Amelia Henfrey, Susannah's best friend, clapped her hands together in sudden inspiration. "You're so funny, Douglas! Now do Mr. Erskine!"

Susannah cast a sharp glance at Amelia, wondering if she was flirting. Amelia had a head full of golden curls and blue eyes very nearly the size of dinner plates, both of which had been the subject of any number of amateur odes this season. She did a surreptitious count of the flounces on Amelia's dress, and was a little mollified to discover that it featured only *one,* while her own new dress boasted three.

As for her own eyes—to Susannah's knowledge, no poems had been written about them. They were hazel, a kaleidoscope of greens and golds that, Douglas had once declared in an ardent moment, "fair dizzied" him. He claimed her eyes had mesmerized him into proposing, that she'd given him no choice in the matter, really. Douglas could be very clever that way, which was part of the reason she loved him.

Amelia, despite the golden curls and limpid eyes, wasn't engaged to anyone at all. But as they were both heiresses, Susannah silently and magnanimously allowed that Amelia would likely make a match as spectacular as her own.

And besides, Amelia is good, Susannah conceded. She never said an unkind thing, she had a smile for everyone, she never misbehaved. *While I am . . .*

Not wicked, *precisely,* she confessed to herself. *But not* good, *either.* She charmed and sparkled and said witty things, but she knew very well she was being charming and sparkling and witty while she was doing it, which felt somehow wrong. She was often plagued with an indefinable restlessness, an ache really, that beautiful dresses and nonstop gaiety couldn't fully assuage. And she frequently secretly suffered from envy and entertained observations that she dared share with no one, since she was certain they would do nothing to add to her popularity.

She had one of those thoughts now: *Amelia is dull.*

She batted it away. Amelia was her best friend, for heaven's sake. Susannah reached for her sketchbook and began quickly charcoaling in the stand of trees at the edge of the park in an attempt to distract herself from any more heretical thoughts.

"Erskine?" Douglas was rubbing his chin in thought at Amelia's suggestion. "The chap who laughs too loud at everything, bends double when he does it?"

"Remember how foxed he was at Pemberton's ball?" Henry Clayson, one of the sprawling lads, contributed lazily.

"Pemberton's ball? Was that where I wore my blue satin?" Amelia categorized all of the events in her life by what she wore during them.

"Yes," Susannah confirmed, because, quite frankly, so did Susannah. "And where I wore the silk with the matching—"

"*Tell* me we aren't now discussing ball gowns," Henry Clayson groused.

Susannah playfully tossed a daisy at him. "Let's discuss horses, then. Have you seen my new mare, Henry?"

Douglas sat down proprietarily next to her, a silent message to Henry Clayson: *She might toss daisies at you, but she belongs to me.* Susannah smiled to herself.

"Susannah's father is forever buying her new *everything*," Amelia said wistfully. "My father buys *one* new gown and tells me I'm in grave danger of being spoiled. And my mother never can persuade him to loosen the purse strings."

And there it was, that unwelcome little tightening in Susannah's chest: envy. It seemed extraordinary to envy the fact that Amelia's father *refused* to buy her things. It was just that . . . well, Susannah's mother had died so long ago and James Makepeace had left the rearing of his daughter in the hands of governesses and housekeepers and redoubtable matrons like Mrs. Dalton, who were charged with ensuring that Susannah acquired a full complement of ladylike accomplishments. Susannah could play the pianoforte and sing; she could draw and paint better than passably; she could certainly dance; she could sew. And miraculously, she'd escaped becoming *too* spoiled and willful, primarily because it had always seemed more effort than it was worth to seriously misbehave.

But that was the very root of her envy: though Susannah had grown up in a beautiful house surrounded by beautiful things, she would have traded most of it—well, perhaps not her new mare, but maybe the pianoforte and a few pelisses—if her father had seemed to care even a little about how much she spent on clothing. Or, frankly, about what she did at all. Oh, he'd been pleased enough about her engagement to Douglas, as any sane father would. But he was so seldom home—his antiquities-importing business often took him away—and she rather suspected her father considered her part of the furnishings. He . . . *maintained* her the way he did the big clock in the library or his best musket. He was as distant and impersonal—and as necessary to her well-being—as the sun.

And so whenever Amelia and Douglas and her other friends spoke of their parents, Susannah felt a tiny clutch of panic. This talk of parents was a language she could never hope to share with them.

All Susannah had of her mother was a fuzzy memory—of being awakened in the middle of the night amidst frantic whispers and movement, of a woman's dark hair and dark eyes and soothing voice—and one tangible thing—a miniature portrait of a beautiful woman: curls, large pale eyes with a bit of a tilt to them, a soft, generous mouth, cheekbones delicately etched. Susannah's own face. On the back, written in a neat, swift hand, were the words: FOR SUSANNAH FAITH, HER MOTHER ANNA. The miniature was the only image of her anywhere in the house.

When Susannah was small, she'd wanted to keep the miniature on her night table, but her father had gently asked that she keep it in a drawer, out of sight. Susannah had decided then that her mother's death had shattered her father's heart so completely that any reminder of her— including his daughter—pained him.

But just last week she'd found him in her bedroom, holding that miniature in his hand. Susannah's breath had suspended; the hope had been piercing: perhaps they'd finally speak of her mother . . . perhaps, little by little, her father's heart would thaw, and they would become close, and then he would complain about how much she spent on pelisses.

But then she noticed he was looking at the *back* of the miniature. And he'd murmured "Of course." Not "Alas!" or "Oh, me!", which would have seemed more appropriate for someone with an irreparably broken heart, but "Of course." And those two low words had thrummed with a peculiar excitement. They had, in fact, sounded rather like "Eureka!"

James had looked up then, and Susannah watched a startling desolation skip across his features.

"I beg your pardon, my dear." And with that, he'd drifted out of her room.

Douglas leaned over her now to reach for the sketch-book. The sun had turned the back of his neck golden, and Susannah was sorely tempted to run her finger along the crisply cut line of his dark hair. *Soon I can touch every bit of him.* She wondered what sort of message Mrs. Dalton would have stitched if she'd known *that* particular sentiment. But the thought made the tightness in Susannah's chest ease; surely being the wife of a marquis-to-be would make envy and restlessness a thing of the past.

Douglas suddenly paused his sketchbook-leafing and frowned, shading his eyes with his head. "I say, Susannah, isn't that your housekeeper coming this way? At rather a fast clip?"

Mrs. Brown, a large woman who typically moved as if every step required careful deliberation, was indeed taking the green so quickly she'd gripped her skirts to free her ankles.

Later Susannah would remember how, little by little, everyone went very still, transfixed, as though the housekeeper's mission was apparent in her exposed ankles.

And as Mrs. Brown's grim face came into view, Susannah slowly rose to her feet, her heart beating swiftly and unevenly.

She knew before Mrs. Brown spoke the words.

The earl's pen continued to fly across the bottom of a sheet of foolscap when Kit appeared in his office doorway. "Good morning, Christopher." His tone was abstracted. "Please sit down."

If Kit hadn't already known the summons from his father meant trouble, the "Christopher" would have confirmed it. He settled resignedly—and a little gingerly, since he'd been out very, *very* late the night before, and it was very, *very* early now—into the tall chair situated in front of . . . the prow of his father's desk. The thought amused him. It was a bloody great ship of a desk, of oak so polished the earl could watch himself at his daily activities: Thinking profound thoughts. Affecting the course of history with signature.

Berating his son.

For the life of him, however, Kit could not come up with a reason for this particular summons.

"Good morning, sir."

His father looked up then, eyebrows aloft at his son's formal tone, and then he leaned back in his chair to study Kit, twirling his quill between two fingers. Outside his father's great office window, London went about its business on foot and horseback, in barges and hack—business his father, who oversaw the budget for intelligence affairs and was often the last word on the assignments of His Majesty's agents, so often indirectly, secretly influenced.

"Just because you think your superior officer is an idiot, Christopher," the earl began wearily, "doesn't mean you should *call* him one."

Ah, *now* he remembered.

"But Father, that idi—"

The earl moved his head in the slightest of shakes, and Kit stopped. Truthfully, though he'd *thought* "Chisholm is an idiot" any number of times, he'd never said the words aloud . . . until last night, apparently. Which was a bloody miracle, really, since Kit had an innate tendency to frankness that only years of militarily honed discipline had managed to keep in check. And frankly, Chisholm *was* an idiot.

But he was just as appalled as his father that he'd said the word. It must have been all that ale. Well, that, and the brandy. And . . . hadn't there been whiskey, too? Fragments of last night were returning to him now, out of sequence, but unfortunately all too clear. He recalled that the evening had begun at White's with a few fellow agents, his best friend John Carr among them. Naturally they had begun drinking, which they seemed to be doing more and more in the five years since the war had ended. It was boredom, he supposed; Kit had become accustomed to living his life at the fine edge of danger, to subtlety and strategy and purpose; life in the wake of war lacked a certain . . . piquancy.

At some point in the evening, his superior officer Chisholm had appeared at White's, and then . . .

His father idly tapped his quill against the blotter. *Tap, tap, tap.* The sound echoed in his head like cannonfire. Kit was tempted to lean over and seize the bloody instrument of torture out of his father's hand and snap it in two.

"Chisholm is *not* an idiot, Christopher."

"Of course not, sir," Kit agreed.

Mercifully, the tapping stopped. A silence.

"He is an *ass*," the earl clarified, finally.

"I stand corrected, sir. I should have cleared the word with you first."

And now his father was struggling not to smile. He sobered again quickly, however, and resumed studying Kit in a way that made him a little apprehensive. And after ten years in service to his country, after dozens of narrow escapes and heroic successes and employing his astonishing aim more times than he preferred to count, *very* few people could make Kit Whitelaw, Viscount Grantham and heir to the Earl of Westphall, apprehensive. He thought he'd better speak.

"Sir, I know what I said was inexcusable, and I hope you realize it was uncharacteristic—"

The earl snorted. "'Uncharacteristic?' Like the incident with Millview?"

Kit paused. There *had* been an incident with Millview, hadn't there? Lord Millview. An incident so . . . objectionable . . . the earl had in fact threatened to reassign Kit to a government post in Egypt as a result of it, a potent threat indeed, given Kit's passion for London. Kit had questioned Millview's, er . . . parentage.

"I apologized for that," Kit said stiffly. "We'd all been drinking, you see, and . . . Well, I apologized for that. And I intend to apologize to Chisholm, too."

"Don't you think you've been doing rather a *lot* of apologizing lately, Christopher?"

Kit knew better than to attempt to answer a rhetorical question. His father was about to answer it for him, anyway.

"*I* do," the earl said. "And you've acquired quite a reputation for womanizing, too."

Have I, really? Part of Kit was impressed. The other part was appalled that he actually had a "reputation," let alone one with a name.

"Notice, at least, it's *woman*izing, sir," he attempted feebly. "Not *women*izing. Just one woman."

"One woman at a *time*. And the latest is married."

"She *isn't!*" Kit feigned shock. Though he'd awakened in time for this meeting only because said married countess had been hissing at him to get dressed and leave *now,* before her husband came home from the bed of *his* mistress. The countess wasn't terribly interesting, but she *was* beautiful, spoiled and difficult, which had made the pursuit, at least, interesting.

The earl ignored this; for some reason, he began marking off a list of sorts with that deuced quill. "You've distinguished yourself in battle, Kit. *Tap*. You saved the life of your commanding officer while you were wounded. *Tap*. Served bravely and well by all accounts." *Tap*.

Kit listened, puzzled. He'd merely been himself on the battlefield and in assignments beyond; none of those things had ever seemed particularly heroic to him.

Ah. Then he grasped his father's point: *You aren't exactly making me proud lately, Christopher.*

Kit redefined heroism then and there as managing not to squirm while waiting for his father to reveal his bloody agenda.

"To the matter at hand. Though you've distinguished yourself in many ways, as you know, Kit, in the wake of the war, we've less and less call for the sort of work agents do. In fact, I was informed this morning that James Makepeace is dead, and we don't intend to replace him. So I've decided to—"

"James Makepeace is *dead*?" Nothing like a bit of startling news to burn away the fog of a pleasant debauch. Why Kit had seen James just last—

And suddenly all the little hairs on Kit's arms rose in portent.

"How did James die, father?" He managed to ask this calmly enough. He suspected he knew the answer.

"Cutthroats. He was robbed; pockets were empty. It's a shame, and I'm sorry for it. Now, on to the business at hand. As I said, there's less and less call for the work agents to do, so I've decided to send you to—"

"Sir, I think James was murdered because he was pursuing a suspicion about Thaddeus Morley."

It was a blurt, really. And once the words were out of his mouth, Kit realized how mad they sounded, particularly in the bright daylight of his father's office, instead of the soft lamp-and-smoke haze of White's, where James had first told Kit the tale. Certainly the expression on his father's face confirmed this.

But murder cast the tale in another light altogether.

A week ago, Kit had arrived at White's to find James Makepeace sitting alone, staring at a glass of whiskey as though wondering what one actually *did* with a glass of whiskey. The alone part wasn't unusual; James was often alone. The whiskey, however, struck Kit as odd; James was employed by the Alien Office, and on the occasions Kit had worked with him on matters of foreign intelligence he'd never before seen James take in anything more controversial than tea. In fact, James Makepeace's most striking characteristic had always seemed . . . well, his striking *lack* of characteristics, apart, that was, from quiet dignity, rare flashes of dry wit, and an unswerving competence that inspired trust, if not warmth. He owned a town house in London, Kit knew, and a country home; he had a daughter. That was the extent of Kit's knowledge of the man, but he had long ago decided he'd liked him, partly, he suspected, because James was difficult to know. This intrigued him, and so little else did anymore.

So Kit had wandered over, thinking perhaps if James didn't plan to drink his whiskey, he'd do the job for him. But when James greeted him with, "Tell me Grantham, what do you know of 'Christian virtues'?" Kit had, half-jokingly, smoothly turned on his heel and began walking back the way he'd come.

But then James had . . . laughed.

If one could call the bleak little sound he'd made a laugh. Which drew Kit back to him out of perverse curiosity.

"Don't worry, Grantham, I'm the very last person to lecture someone about morals," James had said then, which was interesting enough. But then he added, "I've a story to share concerning Christian virtues . . . and a certain Mr. Thaddeus Morley."

And James, who had lived in Barnstable so many years ago like Kit and his family, and knew a little of Kit's past, knew Kit could no more turn away from a discussion of Thaddeus Morley than a hound could from a hare.

So James had told his story, and Kit had listened, more entertained than convinced. And then John Carr and a few of his other friends had swept Kit away before James could finish his mad tale, but not before Kit could finish James's whiskey.

His father was grim-faced, displeased at the interruption. "James was pursuing a suspicion about Morley? The Whig MP? What *sort* of suspicion?"

"It was last week . . . James told me he believed Morley was involved in the murder of Richard Lockwood some years ago. He said . . ." Kit paused, willing the returning fog in his head to move aside so James's words could return accurately. "He said that Lockwood had been gathering evidence—documents, apparently—proving Morley had sold information to the French to finance his political career. And so Morley arranged to have him murdered."

For a moment, his father said nothing. And then, like a man slipping into a coat, he donned the expression of exaggerated patience that Kit had known and loathed deeply since he was a child.

"Christopher, you know full well that powerful men provoke jealousy, even myths, and Morley has perhaps drawn more than his share because of his humble beginnings."

Kit sucked in a long impatient breath. "Sir, James told me that Lockwood hid the evidence incriminating Morley in a place that had something to do with . . . Christian virtues. Some place . . . 'whimsical.' That was the word he used—'whimsical.' But Lockwood never told James precisely where. And he was murdered before this evidence came to light."

The earl burned a dark frown into his son. Kit met it levelly.

And then all at once the earl's face cleared, as though he'd reached some sort of satisfactory conclusion. "Was James drunk when he told you this? Were *you* drunk?" Fatherly suspicion lit the earl's face and he leaned forward, forehead furrowed in scrutiny, and gave a sniff. "Are you drunk *now*? Did you drink your breakfast, Christopher?"

"Oh, for God's sake, father. No, I did not drink my breakfast." At the moment, the very idea of food or drink, in fact, made Kit's stomach lurch beseechingly. "And I've never seen James drunk in my life."

"Hmmph" was the earl's grunted opinion of James's alleged sobriety.

"And the very last thing James told me, father," Kit continued doggedly, "was that he thought he finally knew where to find those documents incriminating Morley. And now he's dead. That's two deaths now. Two murders. Both former soldiers, both of whom were ostensibly investigating Morley."

"Two deaths seventeen years *apart*, Christopher." And then the earl slapped two exasperated palms down on his desk, which made Kit's brain shrivel in pain. One of his eyes rolled up into his head. *Shouldn't have had the bloody whiskey, too.* "I fail to see the connection. And James most certainly wasn't *authorized* to pursue any sort of suspicion about Morley, if indeed, that's what he was doing when he was murdered. *Furthermore . . .*" the earl drawled, "witnesses put Lockwood's mistress at the scene of his murder, and then his mistress disappeared—never to be seen again. London was in an uproar for months. Sketches of her in the newspapers, a mad search for her all over the country . . ." The earl gestured broadly, illustrating the mad search, perhaps. ". . . and then the whole thing inevitably died away. It's really a very simple, if somewhat sordid tale, *and* a testament," he concluded, in a return to what appeared to be the day's developing theme, "to the potential danger of mistresses."

The potential danger of mistresses? Kit was briefly distracted as he considered these. Last night, the countess had been in danger of wearing out his—

"And let me ask you this, son, Why would James Makepeace choose to confide his . . . delusion . . . in *you*, in particular?"

Bloody hell.

And as Kit knew he couldn't answer the question without incriminating himself, he remained stubbornly silent.

And finally his father leaned back in his chair and sighed a long-suffering sigh, the sound of confirmed suspicions. "Christopher, just a few days ago, Mr. Morley asked me—very delicately, mind you—whether he'd done something to earn your dislike."

This was a surprise, and yet not a surprise. "His impressions are unfortunate, father," Kit said stiffly, "but I can assure you I've done nothing to inspire them."

But Morley, Kit was certain, knew precisely what he'd done. It went back to an evening nearly two decades ago, to a party at his father's house in Barnstable, to a rivalry between two friends that had almost turned deadly. To a beautiful, reckless young woman. To the first time Kit had met Thaddeus Morley.

And the last time he'd seen Caroline Allston.

A stalemate's worth of quiet ensued, and a breeze nudged the curtains at his father's window into a languorous motion that set Kit's stomach pitching and rolling again. With effort, he kept his eyes focused on his father's face, rather than closing them, which is what he very much would have preferred to do. So like his own face, the earl's was, but gentler, its lines more harmonious and pleasing. Handsome, everyone said. His son, with his grandfather's arrogant arch of a nose and long angular jaw and his mother's disconcertingly vivid blue eyes, had never been directly accused of being handsome. 'Unforgettable,' however, applied.

Or so he'd been told by any number of women. In tones ranging from infuriated . . . to satiated.

"Father," he tried again quietly, because it simply wasn't in his nature to surrender, "What motive could James Makepeace have possibly had for telling me such a story? Doesn't this at least warrant—"

"Christopher." His father's voice was terse now. "Leave it."

"Why?" Kit almost snapped the word. "Because investigating Morley would be awkward for you politically?"

Oh, *that* was a risky question, and Kit immediately regretted asking it. His throbbing temples were allowing unfortunate words to get through. He seemed to recall champagne now, too. Hadn't the countess poured some into her navel, and then hadn't he—

"That *should* matter to you, son," the earl said quietly.

Kit fell silent, chastened. His father did deserve his loyalty; his father, in fact, unquestionably had his loyalty. And he knew he could never fully explain to his feelings about Morley to his father. Just as he would ever have the words to explain Caroline Allston.

"Well then," his father said crisply. "We've wasted enough time with this nonsense. To the business at hand, Christopher, in light of recent events, I've decided to send you to Egypt, as we previously discussed."

Kit's lungs froze. He parted his lips a little; nothing emerged.

His father stared back at him with a sort of detached interest. A scientist, awaiting the results of an experiment.

"You've . . ." Kit finally croaked. The rest was too horrible to repeat.

". . . decided to send you to Egypt?" his father completed gently. "Yes. Today. A ship leaves in two hours. I've arranged for your trunks to be packed."

Kit had lost use of all of his faculties. His limbs had turned to marble. He certainly couldn't form a sentence. He stared at his father, waiting for shock to ebb so he could strategize.

The earl was still watching his son, but his face had gone steadily more pensive.

"Or . . ." his father mused.

Kit clung to that 'or' the way a sailor clings to the splintered mast of a wrecked ship. He waited. He tried a bit of a smile, as though nothing had ever mattered to him less than what his father was about to say next.

". . . you may repair to Barnstable immediately to work on your folio."

The smile vanished. "My *what*?"

"Your folio. Your nature folio." Said with deceptive innocence. "Like the work undertaken by the recently departed Mr. Joseph Banks. There's a recognized need now to document the flora and fauna in the English countryside, and the Barnstable region has heretofore been neglected. We've been looking for just the man to do it, and I think that man is *you*. You will take notes, make sketches. And you'll live at The Roses while you do it. It was your mother's favorite of our homes, as you recall, and it's been all but neglected in recent years."

Had his father just suffered a stroke? "Banks was a *naturalist*," Kit explained slowly. "I'm a *spy*."

"Yes, well, that's what you became after you shot your friend over that wild girl years ago and I packed you off into the military—"

"It was a *duel*," Kit muttered. "I was *seventeen*."

"—but when you were a very young boy, Christopher, you wanted to be a naturalist."

Kit couldn't believe his ears. "Yes. For about five *minutes*."

But the earl appeared to have drifted into some kind of reverie. "Don't you remember? Up trees, following squirrels and deer, bringing home snakes, nests, things of that sort. Always observing. Swimming at the pond. Making little sketches. Your mother thought it was adorable. And wasn't there a rare mouse in the region?"

"Vole. There's a rare *vole* in the region," Kit said testily.

"You see? You know all about it." The earl said delightedly, as if this proved his point.

All at once, with a sinking feeling, Kit comprehended. "Ah," he said flatly. "I see. I'm to be exiled regardless."

The earl gave him a smile that managed to be sunny and evil all at once. "*Now* you're catching on."

"You can't . . . *exile* me simply because I called a man an idiot."

His father regarded him in placid silence.

"Or for calling a man . . . a bastard."

Serene as a lake, his father's silence.

"Or for . . . womanizing?" Kit faltered.

"Oh, I can," the earl disagreed cheerfully. "For all of them. I warned you once before, Christopher. You now have two choices: you may travel to Barnstable and begin work on the folio, or you can leave for Egypt. Choose."

His father, Kit realized, was deadly serious. And when his father was deadly serious, no amount of reasoning could penetrate his resolve, which was how Kit had found himself installed in a military academy with head-spinning speed after his duel so many years ago. Kit stared at the earl, and his mind's eyes drew him a painfully vivid picture of the hard-won countess, and all of the myriad, glorious pleasures and comforts of the *ton*, shrinking inexorably from view as his ship drifted from English shores.

And as for Barnstable and The Roses . . . well, Barnstable was just a few hours' hard ride from London, but it might as well have been Egypt, simply because it wasn't London.

"You *need* me here. I'm the best agent the crown has."

He was absurdly gratified when his father didn't disagree with this patently unprovable statement. But he also didn't relent.

"Egypt or Barnstable, Christopher. And if you choose Barnstable, I want you to make a thorough job of that folio. Every plant, every creature . . . I want them carefully, lovingly documented. You have one month in which to accomplish it, after which we shall review your continuance in his Majesty's Secret Service. If I hear of you womanizing, if I hear of you doing *anything* other than working on your assignment, if I see you in London during that time, if I hear of you being anywhere *near* London . . . I will personally escort you on to a ship bound for Egypt where you will then take up a quiet little government post. Do I make myself clear?"

Silence fell like a gavel.

Kit decided he could at least do this with a little dignity. "I choose Barnstable," he said quietly.

"Good. I should miss you if you went to Egypt."

And then his bloody father actually *smiled*.

Kit would not be softened by fatherly expressions of affection. "If I complete the assignment to your satisfaction before a month is over?"

"You may return," his father said placidly. "*If* you're confident you've completed it to my satisfaction. You can take a day to prepare for your journey. And now, you may go."

Kit pushed back his chair and stood—all gingerly, of course.

"And son . . ." his father's voice was idle in a way that told Kit his next words were in no way meant idly. "I don't need to tell you again to leave the issue of Morley alone, do I?"

His father knew him too well. "Of course not, sir. I thought it was understood."

"You always were a clever boy, Christopher."

Chapter Two

The large ormolu library clock measured off seconds of incredulity.

"With . . . without resources?" Susannah repeated, just in case she hadn't heard her father's solicitor correctly.

"Penniless." Mr. Dinwiddy mercilessly enunciated each syllable. "That's what 'without resources' means, Miss Makepeace."

Bewildered, Susannah swiveled her head about the library, as if searching for help, for some clue to the man her father had been.

His throat had been cut, they said. Such a violent, dramatic punctuation mark to a life so quietly led. And all morning Susannah had graciously accepted murmured condolences from mourners, wishing she could summon tears, or a smile—but there was only this dull grief that cast a strange haze over her senses. Grief over the loss of a man who had never been anything but kind to her. And grief over the fact that she would now never truly know him.

She doubted it was the sort of grief that a daughter ought to feel for a father, the kind that welled up out of a broken heart. And so mingling with the grief was guilt and, if she were being perfectly honest with herself, anger, too. She'd *wanted* to know him. She'd *wanted* to love him.

He hadn't allowed it.

"Miss Makepeace?" Mr. Dinwiddy's voice came to her.

She swiveled back to him. "Penniless? But . . . I don't understand. How—that is to say—"

"The goodwill of shopkeepers and merchants has enabled your father to purchase almost everything in this house—including your clothing—on credit for years now. The servants have been paid, but no other creditors have— and *I* will not be," he added ruefully. "Your father's properties and furnishings will be confiscated immediately to satisfy his debts. I suggest you vacate the premises as soon as possible."

Penniless. The word throbbed in her head, and she couldn't get a proper breath. She stared almost unseeingly at Mr. Dinwiddy, and her mourning gown—beautifully cut and very dear, and apparently unpaid for—suddenly seemed sewn from lead.

Somehow a fly had found its way into the library, and it was orbiting Mr. Dinwiddy's shiny head. Susannah watched, half-hypnotized.

Mr. Dinwiddy's face was impassive. And then his head creaked to a tilt, and his expression became oddly . . . considering.

"Have you any relatives who will take you in, Miss Makepeace? No others are mentioned in your father's will."

"I don't . . . I'm not . . ." A strange ringing in her ears frightened her. *Am I going to faint?* She had never before fainted in her life, though once or twice she'd feigned light-headedness at a ball in order to get a moment alone in a garden with Douglas. And because it clearly made Douglas feel manly.

The fly decided to settle above Mr. Dinwiddy's right ear. Mr. Dinwiddy swiped a palm over his perspiring dome, disturbing it; it resignedly resumed its lazy circling. The solicitor cleared his throat. "Perhaps, Miss Makepeace, you and I can come to . . . an arrangement."

"'Arrangement'?" Hope animated Susannah briefly. "Arrangement" seemed a better word than "penniless."

"I have a home in London in which you may live in exchange for . . ." He paused. "Entertaining me . . . once or twice a week."

Susannah frowned a little, puzzled.

Mr. Dinwiddy waited, his eyes tiny and bright behind his spectacles.

When the meaning of his words at last took hold, she leaped to her feet and backed away as though the solicitor had suddenly burst into flame.

"You—how—how *dare* you!" she choked out. Her face burned.

The solicitor shrugged. *Shrugged!*

Susannah drew a long shuddering breath and drew herself up to her full height. "I assure you I will be *well* cared for, Mr. Dinwiddy. My fiancé is the son of Marquis Graydon. And once I tell him of your . . . your . . . *suggestion,* no doubt he will call you out."

"Oh, *no* doubt." But the solicitor sounded more weary

than sarcastic. And then he rose from his chair with a leisureliness that shook Susannah's confidence to the core.

"Good day, Miss Makepeace. You may wish to keep my card"—he extended it; Susannah jerked her head away and balled her hands into fists, as though she feared one of them might betray her and reach for it—"in case you find your fiancé other than . . . gallant."

"But . . . but . . . Mama *said* you would understand, Susannah."

Douglas stood before her, his fingers curled whitely into his hat, his face drawn with distress. And usually when Douglas showed any signs of distress, Susannah would comfort him, place a soothing palm against his cheek, perhaps, for that was the sort of thing fiancés did for one another. But now—

"Pardon us, miss! Step lively, now!" boomed a cheerful cockney voice. Two stocky, booted men were staggering across the marble floors bent under the weight of the pianoforte. Susannah stepped aside; briefly she saw her own reflection, distorted and pale, in the instrument's polished surface, before it vanished out the door, forever.

Douglas threw a quick, longing look over his shoulder toward the door. He'd done that a few too many times in the last five minutes.

"Douglas—" She heard the plea in her voice and stopped. She was *damned* if she would beg. She'd never begged for anything in her life.

Damned. Now there was a word she had never before included in her vocabulary.

But one needed the fortification of such words when one has just been jilted.

Susannah's mind reeled with the sheer *speed* of the spread of the news—*Susannah Makepeace is penniless*—as if the fly orbiting Mr. Dinwiddy had in fact been a spy for all the mamas in the area. Douglas's own mama had leaped so quickly into action she might as well have been whisking him away from the plague.

"*Whoop!* Lift yer feet for me, miss, there ye are luv, my thanks." Two more men were rolling up the soft parlor carpet as merrily as if they were playing with a hoop and stick. They hoisted the great tube of it up under their arms and wended their way toward the door, and the carpet's heavy fringe trailed across the curve of a bulbous cream-and-blue Chinese vase, like fingers dragged against the cheek of a lover. The vase wobbled threateningly on its pedestal once, twice . . . it stilled. Susannah exhaled. She was glad it hadn't broken.

She might need to hurl it at Douglas.

"It's . . . it's for the best, Susannah." Quoting his mama again, no doubt.

"How, Douglas? Please explain to me *how* it can possibly be for the best? Or perhaps"—she added bitterly, and she could not recall saying *anything* bitterly before in her life—"you should have your mama come explain it to me."

They stared at one another wretchedly as cheerful cockney voices drifted in from the courtyard, where the crewmen were loading carts with the things she'd taken for granted since she was a girl. Carpets, chandeliers, candelabras, books, settees, beds.

Her life.

"Don't do this, Douglas," she cried softly, despising the hint of plea in her voice. "I love you. And you love me, I *know* you do."

Douglas made a little sound in his throat then, and took a sudden step toward her, his hand outstretched in . . . in what? Supplication? Comfort? Farewell? Whatever it was, he apparently thought better of it, for he dropped his hand and shook his head roughly, as though clearing his mind of her. And then he turned abruptly and went the way of the pianoforte and the parlor rug, smashing his hat down on his head as he went.

He never looked back.

Susannah stared after him. She could feel what surely must be the jagged edges of her heart clogging her throat, and her hand went up to touch it there.

"Make way, miss, thank ye kindly!"

A man was marching down the stairs, his arms piled high with her beautiful gowns. The silks and velvets and muslins slipped and slid in his grasp, and suddenly, to Susannah, they all seemed like kidnap victims struggling to escape.

"Put . . . those . . . down. *Now*."

The glacial ring of her own voice strengthened her—she hadn't know she'd had such a voice at her disposal, and it certainly seemed to give that big man pause. He froze midstep and stared at her wide-eyed.

"But miss, we've orders to take all of—"

She seized the heavy vase from its pedestal and hoisted it slowly, meaningfully, over her head. The man's eyes followed it up there warily.

"You have until the count of three." Every word chiseled from ice.

He raised a brow and took the tiniest step forward, daring her. Susannah brandished the vase warningly.

"One. . . " she hissed. "Two . . ."

"Susannah?"

Susannah turned her head swiftly. Amelia stood in the doorway, her dinner-plate eyes bulging with astonishment.

There was a rustle from the stairs.

Susannah swiveled. *"Three!"* She drew the vase back.

"All right, all right, no need to take on so, miss." Surrendering, the man lowered his bundle of dresses to the stairs; the fabrics settled there with a sound like a collective sigh of relief. "I'll just move on, shall I?" He lifted his hands placatingly.

Susannah lowered the vase and hugged it to her chest, and the man, seeing that whatever demon had possessed her a minute ago had now vacated, clambered confidently down the remainder of the stairs until he stood before her.

"And I'll just take that, too, shall I?" he said gently.

Susannah sighed and handed the vase to him, and he took it out the door, whistling, the very picture of no hard feelings.

She sank down on the stairs and covered her face in her hands, breathing hard, horrified and strangely exhilarated all at once. Her father's death had unleashed a veritable Pandora's box of emotions, all of them interesting, none of them pleasant.

She'd just threatened a man with a *vase* over *dresses*.

Amelia was silent, and at first Susannah thought she might have left. But then she saw the toes of her friend's shoes through cracks in between her fingers: blue kid walking boots.

"Do you suppose it was pride, Amelia?" she finally asked, pulling her hands away from her face.

"Pride?" Amelia was staring down at her, looking distinctly nervous.

"As in, 'goeth before a fall.'" Susannah quoted bitterly. It seemed as sensible a reason as any for the sudden collapse of her life.

Alarmed, Amelia unconsciously touched a hand to her blond curls. "*Were* you proud, Susannah?"

"Yes," Susannah said emphatically and a little cruelly, in case Amelia felt a little *too* proud of those blond curls and those blue kid walking boots. Amelia's hand flew from her hair and began to fuss with her skirt instead.

There was a silence. "What are you going to do?" Amelia all but whispered, finally.

"I—" Susannah stopped.

The servants had been tendering their notices for days now. Good servants were hard to come by, and they'd all found new jobs easily enough; one by one they'd bid her fond but pragmatic farewells. *They* were all on to new lives in new places. But as for Susannah . . .

Well, she knew how to run a large household. That was, she knew how to instruct *servants* how to run a big household. She wasn't qualified enough to be a governess, really, unless one wanted one's daughters tutored in dancing and the number of flounces considered most stylish in 1820. In short, she hadn't the faintest idea what she would do.

Of course, there was always Mr. Dinwiddy's offer.

Susannah was suffused with a fresh wave of hate.

Until a few days ago, her life had been one long sunny afternoon, a song in a major key. And now . . . soon she wouldn't even have a place to live. Her palms went clammy, and she rubbed them against her skirt. Pride might very well have led to her fall, but it was the only remaining timber of her life, and she clutched it to her. Damned if she would give Amelia any sort of reply.

Damned. She was growing fond of that word.

"And Douglas. . . ?" Amelia added carefully, when Susannah remained silent.

Something in Amelia's tone made Susannah look intently at her, and for the first time ever she found the face of the eminently transparent Amelia Henfrey . . . closed.

So this is why she came today. She knows. She just wanted to make certain. Susannah wondered if Douglas's mama had sent a note to Amelia's mama: *There's a position opening up . . .*

Before she could reply, Mrs. Dalton appeared, dressed for traveling in sensible dark clothing. She was the last of the current household members to leave and she, too, had acquired another young lady to oversee and plague with her dutifully judging presence. "This is for you, Miss Susannah, as a farewell," she said briskly, handing over a sampler.

Susannah read it: CHARITY BEGINS AT HOME. "Thank you, Mrs. Dalton," she said, with the irony the gift deserved.

Mrs. Dalton nodded modestly. "And this arrived for you, too, Miss Susannah, in the post. From a Mrs. Frances Perriman in Barnstable." She extended a gloved hand holding a letter.

Susannah had no idea who Mrs. Frances Perriman in Barnstable might be, but the letter was indeed addressed to Miss Susannah Makepeace. And Susannah felt so alone in the world that she decided that Mrs. Frances Perriman, whoever she was, was her new best friend.

She reminded herself that the last shining thing in Pandora's box was Hope.

She gave Amelia another deliberately enigmatic look, and split the seal on the letter.

Dear Miss Makepeace,

I hope you will forgive the presumption, as we
have met but once, and then when you were only
a little girl. But I am your poor deceased father's
cousin, and I have heard of your new circumstances.
I would like to invite you to stay with me, if you
haven't another situation, and I've enclosed enough
fare for a mail coach . . .

And so it appeared that she did have a family, of sorts.
"I shall be living with my aunt in Barnstable," she told
Amelia triumphantly.

Thaddeus Morley pushed aside a heavy velvet curtain and
gazed out onto St. James Square, watching for the hackney that would bring his visitor. He saw only a few pairs
of fashionable men and women promenading beneath a
sky sullied with the smut of London's daily life, and the
statue of William the III, snowcapped with bird droppings.

He dropped the curtain and let his hand fall to his side.
His cat immediately drifted over and bumped its head
against it. *Perhaps he smells the blood on them.* His mouth
twitched in self-mockery at the thought. *Such* melodrama.
In a moment he'd be muttering "Out, *out,* damned spot"
like that barmy Lady MacBeth.

Besides . . . there had only been *two* deaths.

Still, blackmail letters arrived nearly as often as ball
invitations lately.

He smiled again. Perhaps a good meal would steady
his thoughts; he seemed a trifle prone to hyperbole today.
There had only been *two* blackmail letters.

Nevertheless, one would have been too many.

"Puss, puss, puss," he crooned, running one of his broad, blunt-fingered hands—hands that betrayed to the world that he was but one generation away from the peasantry—over Fluff's silky body, to make him arch and purr. Something about the arching and purring suddenly brought to mind Caroline, the author of the first blackmail letter, and an unexpected sweep of regret and irritation stilled his hand.

One night, years ago, at a party held by the Earl of Westphall, he'd collected Caroline, much the way one might gather up useful things in preparation for a journey. He recognized darkness and weakness and need in other people, and sank into it, like a tree sinking roots deep, deep below the surface of the ground in search of water. He'd seen it in Caroline. It was, in fact almost integral to her astonishing beauty. And once . . . well, once he had felt a twinge of something when he was with Caroline. "Perhaps this is love," he'd thought wonderingly.

More likely it had only been gas.

But Caroline—perhaps inevitably—had left him almost two years ago. He hadn't kept her chained, after all, and any wild creature might venture out when the door is left open. She'd chosen to wander out of doors with a handsome American merchant.

Perhaps she'd left the merchant, too. Something had clearly gone wrong with him, or she wouldn't now be resorting to blackmail.

Morley thought she of all people would have understood why blackmailing him would be a terrible mistake. How ferociously, ruthlessly, quietly he had fought for everything he now had. How ferociously he would fight to preserve it.

But then again, Caroline wasn't clever, and rarely thought past a given moment. He'd run her aground soon enough.

The bell rang. He waited for Bob's heavy boots to come up the stairs to his sitting room. He called all of the men Bob; it seemed simpler; it reminded them of their place and imposed a sort of anonymity. This particular Bob had proved his competence and discretion for many years now.

Morley leaned hard on his cane for balance and turned from the window. He said nothing, simply looked a question at Bob.

"Nothing, sir. Searched every bloody cranny, opened all the upholstery, opened up every drawer, went through every bit of furniture. Went over the whole place, stables and outbuildings, too. And you *know* I'm a professional." He puffed out his chest a bit.

Relief was perhaps an overstatement for what Morley felt, because he'd been certain all along Makepeace had been bluffing. Blackmail was usually a desperate act; Makepeace had been crippled by debt. And he'd been neatly, thoroughly, remorselessly dealt with before he could become any more of a nuisance.

Plink. The sound of a chess piece knocked from the board. That was Makepeace.

"Very well"—he turned back toward the window—"thank you, Bob." A dismissal.

But Bob, irritatingly, cleared his throat. "Sir . . . there's something else you should know."

Morley turned around again, waited, grinding the tip of his cane into the plush carpet beneath his feet in impatience.

"The girl . . . Makepeace's daughter—"

"Yes?" He didn't like to spend more time than necessary in the presence of men like Bob; it reminded him too much of his own origins, which pulled at him, sometimes, like a great wave coming to take him back out to sea.

"She's the image of Anna Holt."

The jolt through his body was extraordinary. For a moment he couldn't breathe.

"Were like seein' a ghost," Bob added, with an illustrative shudder.

"Are you sure?" Morley hated the uncertainty in his own voice.

"I'm a *professional,* sir." Bob sounded wounded. "I've a memory like a trap, you know. And I saw Holt often enough when I was following Lock—"

Morley lifted a hand. He didn't like to be reminded of . . . well, he thought of them as previous chess moves. Maneuvers planned and executed, literally.

"And anyhow, there were letters."

"Letters?" Morley repeated sharply. "What do you mean?"

"Letters to James Makepeace. They all just said just one thing: " 'I beg news of the girls.' ' "

The girls. Morley had forgotten about the girls. He'd known about the daughters, of course, but they'd been so small, seemed so unimportant in the scheme of things. They'd disappeared along with their mother. Morley had always assumed they were together, Anna Holt and her daughters.

Apparently not.

His mind was moving quickly now. "Where did the letters originate?"

"Couldn't tell you, sir."

"Were they signed?"

"No, sir."

"And did you burn them?" Morley asked.

"Of course." Bob almost sounded wounded by the question. "Went right up in flames, sir."

Morley's thoughts tumbled through the past. "Where is she now? The girl? Susannah?"

"Barnstable, heard her say. She was going to stay with an aunt. Pretty thing. She tried to brain me with a vase," he added, half-awed, half-resentful. "Wanted her dresses, so I left her to them."

The girl *must* be one of Anna Holt's and Richard Lockwood's daughters. But how had she come to live with Makepeace? In his methodical fashion, Morley swiftly riffled through potential scenarios in his mind.

There were two possibilities that he could discern: Perhaps Makepeace had been bluffing in the letter he'd sent, and knew nothing at all about Morley's past or Richard Lockwood. Perhaps he'd adopted the girl. Perhaps the entire thing was a coincidence.

He dismissed this out of hand; he didn't believe in coincidences.

The other possibility was that Makepeace had known all along that the girl was Richard Lockwood's daughter, and very recently had come to some sort of conclusion, or come upon some clue, some exceedingly damning evidence.

But Makepeace had been an agent of the crown. And Morley found it difficult to believe that an agent of the crown would have resorted to blackmail if he'd truly uncovered any evidence. Although desperation and debt could play havoc with a man's sense of reason.

"Is she married? The girl?" he asked Bob. "Has she any other family?"

"No, sir. Watched her bloke jilt her outright, in fact, sir. Right there in the parlor. He can't marry a penniless girl—he's an heir. She went to live with an aunt."

"What a shame." Morley did feel an errant stab of sympathy. The horror of losing all he'd acquired woke him less and less often at night as the years went on, but Caroline's letter, and then Makepeace's letter, had introduced sleeplessness again. Blackmail was not a lullaby.

It was entirely possible James Makepeace had bequeathed the evidence to the girl, if the evidence did indeed exist, and she had managed to keep it about her person, which would explain, perhaps, why they had found nothing in Makepeace's homes. And now that Susannah Makepeace was penniless . . . perhaps she would resort to her father's means of obtaining an income.

Or, if she was feeling civic-minded, would somehow get the evidence into the hands of people who would know precisely what to do with it.

Morley began to concoct still more scenarios in his head, but stopped himself. He could truly make this complicated, if he liked, but he lacked the fervor for complications that characterized his youth. He was tired, and he rather intended to spend his dotage peacefully—in Sussex, gardening—rather than at the end of a rope, swinging. He'd discovered a passion for gardening, in fact, along with large houses and fine furniture. This was odd, since he'd once considered gardening a sort of farming. But wealthy men could afford to tenderly tend frivolous plants; in a way, cultivating roses was the ultimate expression of Morley's rise in the world.

Sometimes when he was gardening, he'd pull a weed out by its roots, only to watch it sprout again some weeks later, threatening to strangle all he'd carefully tended.

And he knew, suddenly, that the solution was elegantly simple. Susannah Makepeace was a weed. And if her sisters were to sprout up, too . . . well, they were also weeds.

"Mr. Morley? What should I do about Susannah Makepeace, sir?"

"Why, whatever you do, Bob . . . you should make it look like an accident."

And because Bob was a professional, he understood his orders. He puffed out his chest again. He did enjoy a new challenge, and Mr. Morley paid well to keep his own hands free of blood.

Chapter Three

Two days later, Susannah arrived at the door of Mrs. Frances Perriman's cottage. She would have arrived a good five hours earlier, except that the mail coach in which she had been traveling had tipped over. *Keeled* over, in fact, like a felled elephant, with a groan and a crash, just as everyone had finally tumbled out of it to go into the inn for a meal.

All the weary travelers, who by this time heartily loathed the sight and smell and sound of each other, had gazed back at it stupidly, almost unsurprised. Almost perversely pleased that this particular instrument of torture had been felled.

The horses had been alarmed but unhurt, and it had been determined that the wheel or something or other on the coach had broken. Susannah had heard faint murmurings about it, but she'd been too exhausted to care about the details. And besides, she'd needed all of her resources to locate another conveyance to Barnstable. Someone who would take her there out of sheer kindness, or in exchange for a pair of slippers or gloves. Which was really all she had in the form of currency, anyway.

As the coach driver refused to hire out his horses as mounts, the passengers descended en masse upon a poor farmer who had innocently arrived to fetch his nephew for a visit. A lot of frantic negotiation ensued among the passengers. Some waved bills, some plied charms, Susannah had nearly sprained her eyelashes in an attempt to beguile and disarm him.

In the end she'd been triumphant. The farmer agreed to take her a few miles out of his way to deposit her at the door of Mrs. Frances Perriman, and Susannah had needed to remove his nephew's hand from her thigh only once. Gently, but firmly.

The sheer, chaotic, exhausting indignity of it seemed rather a metaphor for her new life.

And now she stood at the threshold of a little cottage just after midnight, and Mrs. Frances Perriman held up her candle and gazed and gazed at Susannah with what could only be described as bemused wonder, as though a large exotic bird had flown off course into her parlor.

Finally, recovering herself, she flung open her arms. Susannah stepped into them, as that's what seemed required.

Frances was about Susannah's height, but considerably rounder, with the same mild brown eyes and the long nose that seemed to be Makepeace hallmarks, and she was soft and smelled of lavender. Susannah's vision blurred with fatigue and—for heaven's sake, *tears*. Astonished, she quickly dabbed them away, and lifted her head up to take in the softly lit room with a glance: small and worn, though some effort had gone into making it other than plain: wallpaper in a pattern fashionable more than a decade ago, a few pictures upon the wall, one small vase filled with flowers. Her beauty- and luxury-loving heart clenched.

"I'd begun to worry, Susannah, and Mr. Evers finally went home to his family when your coach never arrived at the inn."

"There was a bit of an accident, I'm afraid, hence the delay. I came in with a farmer who was kind enough to bring me."

"Well, I'm glad to find you sound, and there *is* kindness in the world, then. Anyhow, welcome, my dear. It's not the grand place you've no doubt been accustomed to, but I do hope you'll feel at home. Would you like some tea? Or shall we get acquainted in the morning?"

"I can't thank you enough for having me Mrs. Perri—"

"Aunt Frances," her aunt interrupted firmly. "Call me Aunt Frances. And say no more of it, my dear. I'm happy for your company."

Susannah managed a weary smile. "I think I'd make a better impression after a night's sleep, Aunt Frances."

"And you must by all means make a good impression," her aunt said with mock severity and a pat to reassure Susannah she was teasing. "Let's pack you off to bed, then."

Within minutes, Susannah found herself tucked into a small bed in small room up a flight of creaking wooden stairs, an ascent that couldn't be more different from the marble steps she'd taken to her rooms since she was a little girl. A single rose in a vase next to the bed breathed its fragrance into the room. It mingled with the smells of aging wood and clean linen. The sheets were worn, but deliciously soft from age; her quilt had a patch, she noticed, and smelled, like her new aunt Frances, of lavender.

The room was dense with summer heat, but she saw no fireplace. She parted the blinds to peek out, saw stars strewn thick as salt against the blue-black summer sky. Sleepily, Susannah decided she'd spent her life tripping gaily from star to glittering star; perhaps it had only been a matter of time before she slipped and fell into the blackness between. It was almost a relief to have finally done it.

Her first thought upon waking and looking about was: *Goodness. I must have drifted off in the servant's quarters.*

And then she recalled where she was. She sat bolt upright, sending her pillow cartwheeling to the floor.

Light was pushing through the blinds, and Susannah slipped out of the little brass bed to open them all the way. A wash of sun and green instantly swamped her eyes: the *country.* The country used to be a place to retreat to between parties and balls, a place to wait impatiently for the season to begin. She'd used the country much the way one used the withdrawing room at a ball, to sew up a trodden hem, or pat your hair into place before you reentered the festivities, refreshed.

It was to be her view every morning from now on, this endless green.

It was silent, apart from a bird trilling a maniacally cheerful scale over and over and over again.

She fished a dress out of one of her trunks and pulled it over her head: the three-flounced summer walking dress in blush-colored muslin. She dispensed with drawers for now, a nod to the heat and to the fact that no clucking maid was about to object. She rolled on stockings, however, because she liked her garters; they were pretty, and they cheered her.

She twisted her hair into a quick knot. Out of habit, she seized her sketchbook, and then all but tiptoed down the stairs, discovering that the third one from the top creaked. Soft, snuffling snores came in intervals from behind Aunt Frances's door, but the house was quiet otherwise: no maids about starting breakfast or getting in wood or coal for fires.

The house was so *tiny*. The sort of house a gardener would live in, she imagined, with its faded wallpaper and scrubbed wood floors, its plain, serviceable furniture. The settee in the parlor was a faded ruby and sagged in the center; there was a large nick in the surface of the small table, which supported the small vase of flowers, a vase lacking any sort of pedigree, no doubt, unlike the one she'd threatened to heave at a cockney workman.

Panic squeezed her lungs. She desperately needed to step outside, if only to remind herself that the world was indeed bigger than this little house.

So she pushed open the front door. It was just past dawn, and the roses lining the front of her aunt's cottage were in full exuberant bloom. They were the brightest things as far as Susannah's eye could see; they reminded her of young ladies in ball gowns, with their delicate flounces and rich color—everything else around her was green, green, green. That tiny pressure began somewhere in the center of her chest again, and she knew it might very well blossom into despair if left unchecked, so Susannah reflexively opened her sketchbook.

With sweeps of charcoal, she captured the roses, their contrasts in texture and color, the tiers of petals, the red shading into crimson at their tips; the tiny stalks topped in yellow fuzz springing from their hearts.

Finished with the roses, she lifted her head. Outside her aunt's gate, a tree-lined path wound tantalizingly off into two different directions; to the right, where it surely lead to the town of Barnstable; to the left, where it appeared to lead into a wood—the trees were taller there, the greenery denser.

Something reckless in her reared up. *I shouldn't walk alone.* Mrs. Dalton certainly would have frowned upon it, as would have all of the duennas who preceded her.

Which seemed an excellent reason to proceed.

Overhead, the birches and oaks and beeches had latticed together, creating a romantic sort of arch. It could hardly be dangerous, could it? She entered into it, hesitantly, and then more boldly, and followed it furtively, promising herself with each step that she'd turn back after just a few more. There was something about paths, however: they drew one forward as surely as a crooked finger, and on she went, over soft dirt and leaves crushed to a fine powder by the passage of other feet over the years.

And she thought, perhaps, if she kept moving, she could outpace the feeling of being dropped outside the comfortable confines of society. Of exile.

A hot spark of green, very like light glancing off an emerald, tugged her eyes off the path. She braved a few steps into the trees toward it.

The spark of green expanded into a pond as she approached, luminous as stained glass. Not an emerald, perhaps, but pretty enough, and the dense smell of wet dirt and green things was strangely agreeable. From where she stood, she could see the tip of what appeared to be a faded wood pier; something pale glared atop it. She squinted. It looked like—could it be—

Good heavens, it rather looked like a pair of feet.

She craned her head to the left, and stood on her toes, and—

Clapped a hand over her mouth to stifle a yelp as she ducked back against the nearest tree.

The feet were attached to a man.

More specifically: a rangy, breath-catchingly *nude* man.

Susannah peeped out from around the tree. Just, she told herself, to prove he wasn't an apparition.

He wasn't. His torso was a perfect "V" of golden skin and muscle; his slim hips, whiter than the rest of him, tapered to thighs and calves that could have been turned on a lathe, and these were dusted all over with fair hair that glinted in the low sunlight. The hair on his head was cropped short and beacon-bright, but the features of his face were nearly indistinct from where she watched. Given the glory of the rest of him, they scarcely seemed to matter. The man's beauty was, in fact, an *assault,* and a peculiar tangle of shock and delight and yearning began to beat inside her like a secret, second heart.

And then the man stretched his arms upward, arching his back indolently; exposing the dark fluffs under his arms, and this, somehow, seemed more erotic and intimate than the rest of his naked body combined. Susannah had seen paintings and statues of naked men, for heaven's sake, but none of them had ever sported fluffy hair beneath their arms. In fact, the sheer easiness with which this man wore all his raw beauty frightened her a little. He was like someone too casually wielding a weapon.

She fumbled her sketchbook open.

Quickly, roughly, she sketched him: the upraised arms, the curves of his biceps and legs and the planes of his

chest, and when he turned, the darker hair that curled between his legs and narrowed up to a frayed silvery-blond
line over his flat stomach. Nested right between his legs
were, of course, his . . . *male* parts . . . which looked entirely benign at the moment, really, at least from this distance. She sketched those, too, as she intended to be
thorough, hardly thinking of them as anything other than
part of her drawing.

A squirrel rippled by and stopped to stare at her, its
tiny bright eyes accusatory. It chirped once; Susannah
frowned at it and put a finger to her lips.

The man bounced lightly once on his toes and then
dove; the smooth water shattered.

He surfaced an instant later, sputtering happily, his
arms rising out of the pond in rhythmic long strokes that
took him away from the pier, and then he rolled over and
did it on his back, his pale toes kicking out of the water,
playful as an otter. And Susannah's knees locked; she toppled over with a little grunt.

She fumblingly righted herself again, and to avoid any
further toppling, braced a hand against the oak tree, and
while he swam the length of the pond she took the opportunity to refine her drawing, quickly roughing in the trees
behind him and the pier beneath his feet.

The man finally pulled himself from the water onto the
pier again. Dazzled, she watched water run in clean
rivulets down the muscles of his back and buttocks. He
shook himself like a great cheerful animal, diamond
droplets flying from him, exhaled a satisfied-sounding,
"Ahhhh!" and then strode off the pier and vanished from
her sight.

For a moment, Susannah remained very still, staring at

the place he'd been, feeling light-headed, oddly elated. *Perhaps he does this every morning.*

The thought filled her with an entirely improper hope.

The magic of the moment finally began to ebb a bit and sense seeped in; she worried about her aunt waking and finding her gone. She pushed herself upright, and found herself eye-level with a pale, heart-shaped scar gouged into the oak. Inside it, the words KIT AND CARO had been carved; they were now swollen with age. Susannah traced the heart with her finger, half enchanted by it, half sorry for the wound to the tree.

And this was when two hands—*smack, smack*—landed on either side of her face, flat against the tree's trunk.

Her heart turned over like a great boulder in her chest—*thunk*—and lay still.

There passed an intolerable moment, during which no one moved or said a thing. And then a masculine voice drawled virtually into her scalp, fluttering her hair and causing gooseflesh to sweep up her arms. "Do you think it's *fair* that you have seen every inch of me, and I have seen none of you?"

Oh no, oh no, oh no. Her heart had recovered. It was now drilling away inside her chest like a woodpecker.

The warmth of the man's body behind her was as penetrating as a sunbeam, though not one bit of him actually touched her—she pressed herself closer to the oak tree, to make bloody sure of that. But his scent immobilized her as surely as a net: sun-heated skin and the faintest tang of sweat, and something else, something rich and complicated and fundamental that started a primal buzz of recognition in her blood and made her peculiarly aware of how very *female* she happened to be.

This wasn't the groomed-for-a-ball brew of starch and soap with which she was familiar. This was stripped-to-the-essence *male*.

She lost her tenuous grip on the sketchbook; it flopped to her feet.

Susannah slid her eyes sideways. They saw long elegant fingers and a sinewy forearm covered in that silver-gold hair. When his hand shifted a bit she saw a small birthmark in the shape of a gull in flight on the vulnerable skin below his wrist.

She made the subtlest of attempts to crane her head to try to get a closer look at his face.

"Oh, I wouldn't turn around if I were you." Still amused. *Oh, God.*

And when, at last, her throat was able to release words, the ones that emerged appalled her even as she said them: "*You* were bloody quiet."

There was a shout of surprised laughter; the man's hands fell away.

And not being a fool, Susannah bolted around the tree, crashing through the young bushes for the path. She didn't dare look back.

Oh, it really had been too bad of him. For he was of course completely clothed; he would never creep up behind a young lady in any other state. Actually, he couldn't recall ever creeping up behind a young lady at *all;* he wasn't mad, just a rascal. But she *had* been spying, whoever she was. She'd thoroughly deserved to be shocked.

Kit had arrived in Barnstable, hot, sticky, and resentful from his long trip from London, his thoughts ricocheting between James Makepeace and Morley and the countess.

He'd decided to stop at the pond before he headed for the house and rousted all the servants, who would be flabbergasted by his presence and would need to be reminded of what they were actually paid to do. The thought hadn't improved his mood, but the swim had. It was odd; he hadn't known how heavily he carried his life until he plunged into the pond again, and emerged feeling as though years had been rinsed away.

His mother had called this estate "The Roses." Which had always amused him, because there might be all of ten rosebushes on the small property, and it didn't even boast a greenhouse. He'd been raised here, however, in Barnstable, and the orderly grounds surrounding the house always interested him much less than the woods bordering it, filled as they were with haphazard shadows and light and surprising wild things. They'd been wonderful for make-believe and exploration when he was very young; for trysts when he was a little older. And for duels.

Since his mother's death a few years ago, his father spent almost all of his time in London, visiting this particular estate only every now and then. Kit had visited it rarely since he'd disappeared from the town so many years ago so swiftly—and under a veil of mystery, to boot. The Roses didn't even have a bailiff, merely a small staff of servants charged with keeping the place from crumbling.

Kit smiled a little as he bent to retrieve the abandoned sketchbook; the irony of a spy being spied *upon* didn't escape him. He leafed through it idly.

Imagine that . . . she'd not only been spying . . . she'd been *documenting* her findings.

He bit back a laugh when he saw himself, arms stretched skyward, penis dangling modestly—he *had* been swimming, after all. But it was a beautiful drawing. She'd roughed in the pier beneath him and the trees behind it, too, and she'd caught him perfectly, the mindless contentment of the moment, the strength and confidence of his body, a hint of pleased-with-himself arrogance in the arch of his back. There was nothing tentative or missish about the drawing; it was, above all things, honest and surprisingly accomplished. He was flattered, but he felt oddly exposed, which had nothing to do with the fact that he was naked in the sketch. She'd captured something essential about him.

He slowed his leafing to examine the other drawings: a young man—this one fully clothed—stretched out on a spread of grass, the smile on his face soft and intimate. Irrationally, Kit felt a little pang of envy. The artist and her model clearly knew each other well, probably cared for each other. Another page was covered with roses, tenderly rendered in skillful strokes. A house filled another page, a great estate that looked somehow familiar; the view of it was distant. There was a simple stand of trees. A group of young ladies, the ribbons of their bonnets undone, their sweet faces bland and open.

There was an almost offhand passion, a skill and singularity to these sketches that mere drawing lessons could not impart. Much to his surprise, Kit found himself moved by them.

His father had been right: Kit *had* wanted to be a naturalist at one time. He'd been fascinated by Joseph Banks, his travels with Captain Cook, and his discoveries of flora and fauna. But he'd never been able to draw the things he saw in quite the way he saw or felt them, and he'd found it maddening. It was as though nature had gently manacled him in this way: *No, you shan't be allowed this gift along with all the others.* He'd been so accustomed to excelling at everything he tried; his attempts at drawing had humbled him. He supposed he'd *needed* humbling at that age.

He studied the drawings again, paging back to the beginning. Who was the artist? The line of her body was slim and softly feminine in a way that spoke to every one of his senses. Her hair, a rich mahogany had smelled wonderful, though he'd be hard-pressed to describe just exactly what it smelled *like* . . . fresh, he would have said. Or clean. Or sweet. But none of those words really seemed to apply, precisely. How he loved discovering the unique smell of a woman . . . a good place to start discovering it, he knew, was the nape of the neck. But there were other delightful places, too.

He smiled, a wicked, private smile, which faded when he remembered he was not to be discovering the smells of females while he was in Barnstable.

You were bloody quiet, she'd said. As though he'd *thwarted* her.

He gave a bark of delighted laughter. It rather sounded like something he would have said.

This is going to be fun.

Kit stabled his horse, badly startling the pair of lethargic stable boys who looked after four geldings, a beautiful, enormously pregnant mare, and a smug-looking stallion who lived here at The Roses. She would bear watching, that mare; she would foal any day, he was certain.

Then he crept around to the back of the house and entered very stealthily, pushing the kitchen door open only enough to allow his lean body through. The kitchen was empty; there wasn't a soul in sight. He imagined the maids were all out dallying with the footmen; he could hardly blame them, really, given the weather and the continued absence of the Whitelaw family, but he would have to impose some semblance of order today.

He stood still for a moment, listening for voices. And then he heard them, lifted in a lively cadence, coming from the large sitting room, the one dominated by an enormous portrait of the Whitelaws featuring a small, half-scowling Christopher, none too pleased at being forced to hold still long enough to be captured for posterity. Knowing from childhood where to find carpets to stifle his footfall, which tiles or patches of floor were likely to squeak, Kit crept toward the room, sidled against the wall, and peered in.

Mrs. Davies the housekeeper and Bullton the butler were sprawled on a pair of settees, their backs to him, teacups lifted to their lips.

"My *dear* Mrs. Davies, *will* you be attending the assembly tomorrow night?" Bullton's imitation of an aristocratic accent was cuttingly accurate. He thrust his pinky out sideways and took a sip.

"*Hooo* my, I jus' *cannot* decide 'ow to wear me 'air, or what *gown* to wear, Mr. Bullton. I must 'ave me *maid* choose it for me, the way she does everything *else* for me, as ye ken I canna think for meself."

They laughed merrily together and clinked teacups.

"Hello," Kit said pleasantly.

They both shot nearly straight up into the air in a blur of scrambling limbs. He watched with some regret as the china cups flew up with them, their contents arcing up in graceful streams and landing on the carpet.

It had been worth not writing ahead to warn them of his arrival, he decided.

"Yer . . . yer *lordship!*"

They bowed and curtsied and bowed and curtsied and then bowed and curtsied again, as if bowing and curtsying would make up for the fact that their feet had been up on his mother's ancient French furniture.

"'Tis I!" he said cheerily. "How goes it Mrs. Davies? Bullton?"

"It goes . . . it just . . . we were . . ." They stammered over each other.

"Just about to rally the staff to make ready for my visit?" he suggested politely.

"Our apologies, sir. If we'd known you'd be *paying* a visit, sir—" Bullton had admirably gathered his composure; he was dignified and apologetic now. *Good man.*

"Didn't know myself, Bullton, Mrs. Davies, and for that I apologize. But if you'd begin airing the rooms, getting some food in—well, you know your jobs. I needn't tell you."

"Yes, sir. No, sir. That is, of course, sir." Another jumble of overlapping words.

"You'll want to see to that stain straight away, Mrs. Davies," he said mildly.

"Y-yes, my lord." Her eyes rolled down to the carpet, and her expression went tragic. Ever since Kit could remember, Mrs. Davies had treated the carpets as though they were her own children. Even the best housekeepers become a little lax in the absence of any sort of lord of the manor, he suspected.

"And is there really an assembly tomorrow night in Barnstable, Mrs. Davies?"

"Y-yes, my lord."

"And where would that be held, if you please?"

"The town hall, sir. Everyone in the town is invited."

That is, everyone except *servants,* Kit knew.

"Well, then." He regarded them sternly, almost broodingly for a moment, long enough for them to begin fighting not to squirm. "I fully expect there to be an assembly of *servants* here tomorrow evening. And get in a little—what's your poison, again, Bullton?"

"Wh-whiskey, sir?" Bullton said a little faintly, hope beginning to glimmer around the corners of his mouth.

"I expect you to get in a little whiskey, then, for it. Mrs. Davies, I trust your household funds will cover it?"

"Oh, yes, sir." Mrs. Davies had relaxed a little, too. And then she hazarded a question. "Will *you* attend the assembly in town tomorrow evening, sir?"

"Of course, Mrs. Davies," he said breezily. It had been many, many years since Kit had set food in Barnstable, and with any luck, his legend would have grown.

The two servants smiled in earnest this time, and he grinned back at them. The villagers would be every bit as surprised to see the viscount as they had been, and Mrs. Davies and Bullton would almost prefer to witness *that* than have an assembly of their own.

"And will you be here long, sir?" Mrs. Davies asked.

"At least a month, Mrs. Davies. I've a special project here to complete, you see."

He could see her working out in her mind how to break the news to the maids and footmen, who would now actually need to behave as though they were working.

"I'll be out of the house much of the time," he assured

her, and she smiled sheepishly at him, knowing her thoughts had been read.

"And your father is well, sir?" Bullton asked carefully.

"He won't be coming, Bullton."

Bullton tried and failed not to look relieved. "Very good, sir. It is a pleasure to see you, sir," he said finally.

"I'm sure it is, Bullton." Kit was struggling not to laugh. "And that will be all for now, thank you. The stain, Mrs. Davies?"

"Oh!" she dropped as though shot down behind the settee to attend to it, and Kit strode up to his chambers, to see if spiders had knit coverlets over the entire room in his absence.

Susannah didn't stop running until she was at the very threshold of her aunt's garden, and then she stopped to compose herself and get her breath. Something savory was cooking, and the smell was winding its way out of the cottage and out into the yard invitingly. *Nothing like fleeing from the naked stranger you'd been spying on to build an appetite.*

Feeling tentative and a little embarrassed, she poked her head into the kitchen, which must also be the dining room, as there was no dining room to be seen. Whereas in her old home, the kitchen was an enormous galley beneath the house, and the dining room was a good acre or so away from it. And at her father's town house in London—

"Good morning, Susannah." Aunt Frances turned. "I thought perhaps you'd changed your mind and fled back to London."

Is that an option? But Aunt Frances seemed so kind, and so prepared to overlook the fact that her niece was wandering into the kitchen from *outside the house* just after dawn, that she smiled. "Good morning, Mrs.—Aunt—Frances."

"Do sophisticated young ladies take morning walks alone these days?"

The question seemed innocent enough, though Susannah suspected Aunt Frances was more shrewd than she was naive. "I . . . well, your garden was so pretty that I—" She was about to say, *wanted to sketch it,* but she realized with horror she'd dropped her sketchbook. *Damn.* "That I was drawn to it for the fresh country air."

She would desperately miss her sketchbook, for more than one reason. She almost squeezed her eyes closed with mortification, remembering: *You were bloody quiet.* What if he was a neighbor? What if he paid social calls? Would she recognize him *clothed*? Would he recognize *her*?

Her aunt turned then and looked more directly at her, gazed for a long disconcerting moment. "Aren't you pretty?" she concluded delightedly, with a tilted head. "And your dress . . ." The delighted expression slipped a little, and then became officially worried, complete with a furrow between her eyes.

"Oh, Susannah," she said impulsively, seizing her by the hands. "I'm terribly concerned you'll find it very dull here, a fashionable young lady like you. Perhaps it was impulsive and selfish of me to invite you to live with me. I just . . . well, I'm about all the family that James had, and though he seemed to do quite well for himself . . . well, word does travel, bad news rather more quickly than the good, it seems, the way a storm does. I heard about your . . . circumstances. And I know a bit about the . . . ways of the world." The last four words were delicately tart.

Susannah was both touched and a little startled by this effusiveness. "You knew I was engaged to be married," she guessed carefully.

"Yes, that's what I meant, my dear." She patted Susannah's cheek. "And as you came to me straight away, I must assume that you no longer are, which is what I feared might happen to you . . . well, mamas of marquises-to-be can be so devastatingly practical, can't they?" Again, acerbically delivered.

It was wonderful to have someone so completely, frankly on her side. An entirely new feeling, really. "Yes," Susannah managed, feelingly. *"Practical."*

"His loss, my dear," Aunt Frances said briskly. "More fool he. And life *does* goes on. As does breakfast. There's fried bread, and sausage in honor of your first full day here, and tea. Will you get the plates down for us?"

Susannah welcomed the subject change, but she twirled about, bewildered. She felt a little abashed. It seemed her aunt had actually *cooked* the meal. No one else was about to set the table, either, or to—

"They're in the cupboard, dear," her aunt said gently.

"Of course," Susannah said weakly. She reached up tentatively, and saw that "plates" meant exactly that: four plates. Plain stone crockery, the color of an old bone.

A flush of shame blazed over her skin. How many times had she seen a servant reach into a cupboard?

Suddenly, those four plates seemed bald evidence of her plummet from status, and the life ahead of her came rushing at Susannah the way the hard ground rushes up to meet someone falling from a great height.

With hands that shook a little, Susannah selected two

of the plates and laid them on the table, hoping her aunt thought the flush in her cheeks was due to the warm day.

"Thank you again, Aunt Frances, for inviting me to stay," she said bravely.

"I'm happy for your company, Susannah." Her aunt's tone was crisp. "Say no more of it, I beg of you. There's an assembly tomorrow night, and I don't mind telling you, you've made quite a celebrity of me, as a new face in the neighborhood *will* set everyone to talking. They're all dying to get a look at you. And you're welcome to come, if you feel up to it, my dear."

This cheered Susannah just a little. She didn't mind being looked at. Being looked at was one of the things she did best, in fact. And an assembly . . . well, gaiety and motion had always kept the restlessness that forever danced on the edge of her awareness at bay. Perhaps she could forget everything for an instant, the loss, the humiliation, the grief—

Wait.

"Do they . . . do they know how I came to live with you, Aunt Frances?" she ventured cautiously.

In other words: *Do they know I've been jilted? Do they know I'm penniless?* Susannah knew very well what it meant when *people* were "set to talking." She'd been one of those "people" not too long ago. Having a good laugh at the way George Percy danced, for instance. It occurred to her that she might wish to take a night . . . or a fortnight . . . or a year or two . . . to assimilate her new status here in the cottage, before she threw herself upon the mercy of the villagers. She knew precisely how juicy a piece of gossip she represented. They'd feast on her like a swarm of mosquitoes.

Aunt Frances's brown eyes were sharp and knowing and sympathetic. "They know that your father died, and that you came to live with me, and anything else they might know they learned from someone other than I. But I think a better question is . . . how much do you care, Susannah?"

A breeze kicked up the curtains at the window then, and the room, with its plain wood floors and whitewashed cupboards and fireplace, was suddenly awash with light, and a faint scent of roses came in to mingle with bread and sausage. It occurred to Susannah then that most anything could be beautiful when viewed in the proper light.

And so pride hiked her chin. "Why, I find that I don't care very much at all."

In that sunny, airy moment, it was almost true.

Chapter Four

Kit had forgotten what a miser the Grantham country manor was—it hoarded heat in the summer and cold in the winter, and by nightfall, stepping into his chambers had been like stepping off a ship docked in the East Indies. But he'd learned not to be fussy about where and how he slept; in the military, you took sleep when you could, the way you did food, grateful for any crumb of it. He stripped off all of his clothing and heaped it over a chair; his pistol, locked, went on the table next to his head. He cut a slice of cheese from a wedge on a plate and devoured it. And then he settled the knife down again, too, next to his head, because he rather liked having a buffet of weapons to choose from, should the need arise.

He flipped open his one indulgence brought from London—fine bedsheets, which were almost as good as a breeze on a night like this—and climbed beneath.

But before he doused the lamp, he impulsively reached for the sketchbook again, trying to piece together the story the drawings told. The artist had led a benign, genteel life, he concluded from the pages, filled with pretty houses and friends. But then, suddenly, like an exclamation point: a naked viscount!

He grinned and set the sketchbook aside, doused the lamp, and closed his eyes.

The light in the room hadn't changed when he opened his eyes again; clearly he hadn't been asleep long. But there was a different quality to the silence now . . . as though something new had been introduced into it.

His senses sang a warning. Holding his breath, he scanned the room through slit eyelids.

And saw a tall shadow next to the bureau.

In one swift motion, Kit seized the knife, rolled from the bed, and clamped his arm around the throat of the intruder from behind.

"Move and your blood will be *everywhere*," he murmured.

A male hand clawed vainly at Kit's arm. For a long moment, the two men stood locked together in a knot of tensed muscles, their breathing rasping the air.

"Ease up, Grantham," the intruder finally choked out.

Kit's grip slackened a fraction. *"John?"*

A silence.

"K-kit?" John Carr choked out.

"Ye-e-s," Kit confirmed incredulously.

Another silence.

"Are you *naked*?" John Carr sounded horrified.

Kit pushed John Carr away with a snort and jerked his trousers from his chair. He thrust his legs into them and then lit the lamp next to his bed, and the light swelling into the room revealed his best friend since childhood standing in the center of it, rubbing his throat ruefully.

"John Carr. Thought I smelled goat."

His friend gave a short hoarse laugh, hoarse because a powerful forearm clamped across the windpipe could do that to a voice. "Christ. So you're a pirate now, are you, Kit, with that bloody great cutlass or whatever that is? *'Move and your blood will be everywhere,'*" he imitated.

"It's a *cheese* knife, John. And it's a hot night. A man can sleep naked in his *own room.*" Apparently, he couldn't be privately naked anywhere in Barnstable today. "How did you get in?"

"Window open just a hair in the nursery, and you know that tree outside of it—"

"Ah." He nodded appreciatively. Kit did know the tree. Very cooperative tree, that one. He'd shinnied up and down it to go in and out of the nursery window numerous times as a boy when he was supposed to be sleeping, or being punished for some other childish transgression. John had come in and out of that window numerous times, too. In due time, they'd both been caught at it and thrashed, naturally, because Kit's father had always been one step ahead of him.

There was a silence.

"John, why the *hell*—?" Kit made a sweeping gesture, indicating the absurdity of the question.

John Carr, dressed in boots and dark trousers and a dark coat of light wool—the better to blend into shadows and scale trees, presumably—pulled out a chair and straddled it backward. "You weren't supposed to be here."

Kit didn't honor that with a reply, so John tried again. "I'm on assignment, Kit."

"You're on assignment. In my bedroom. In Barnstable."

"Yes."

Kit stared at his friend. John had always been the handsome one: tall and hard, dark-haired, dark-eyed. His features achieved that magical balance of rugged and refined guaranteed to set feminine hearts aflutter.

But most people began babbling when faced with a few moments of Kit's silent blue stare.

John stared levelly back at him.

And suddenly, foreboding prickled at the back of Kit's neck. "You'd better tell me."

John lowered his head briefly, deciding. Then he lifted it again, his expression carefully bland, which Kit disliked immensely. Kit and John never used their spy faces with each other. "I'll tell you what I can."

"Am I under investigation?" Kit heard the incredulous tension in his own voice. "Does my father know?"

"Why would he know? Because he's omnipotent?" A whiff of rivalry hung about those words. John's father was a baron who enjoyed gardening; he was *not* one of the most powerful peers in England.

"He'd definitely like us to think so," Kit said mildly.

John couldn't help but grin at that. "All right, I'll tell you why I'm here Kit, but I must ask you not to repeat it. To anyone, including your father. I could be seriously reprimanded. Or worse."

Kit shook his head impatiently. "Talk, John."

"It's about Morley."

Kit went very still; oddly, he was unsurprised. And then he padded over to his bureau, blew dust off a pair of glasses, which made John snort a laugh, and poured two brandies. He slid one across the table to John. "Go on."

"We've intercepted a letter to Thaddeus Morley written by a woman who says she will 'tell all I know, all you've done,' if he doesn't send money to her. In other words, she's blackmailing him. We need to find her, because she might very well be able to prove Morley sold information to the French. But so far, she's remained one step ahead of us."

"Who is 'we' John? And what the hell does this have to do with me? Apart from, shall we say, my 'interest' in Morley?"

John curled his fingers around his brandy a little too casually. "I can't tell you who 'we' is. But that woman is Caroline Allston."

The sound of her name after so many years wasn't quite as dramatic as a sword drawn from its sheath, but it wasn't comfortable, either. Kit watched John's hand go up almost absently to rub his shoulder, where a round scar marked his skin. Kit had put it there with a pistol shot when they were both just seventeen years old.

Caroline's legacy.

"Again, What does this have to do with me, John?"

John took another sip of brandy, and there was an odd lilt to his voice when he spoke. "She's sent a letter to you, too, Kit."

The muscles of Kit's stomach tightened. He was stunned. "Ah," he said.

John continued quickly. "To your London town house. I intercepted it. In the letter, she asked for your"—he paused, and cleared his throat; his voice had gone strangely husky—"for your help. Said she was in trouble, and she hoped to come to you. I suppose the letter was meant to prepare you for her . . . visit."

Help. Caroline needed his help.

"When was this letter sent?"

"A week ago."

"And you're here at The Roses because . . ."

"She never arrived at your town house. And The Roses would be the ideal place to meet her, or hide her . . ." John took a sip of his brandy, lowered the glass. "If you were inclined to do so, that is."

The lamplight guttered in a wayward breeze; the liquor glowed on the table between them, but their faces were momentarily cast in shadow.

"I haven't seen or heard from the woman in almost two decades, John," Kit said finally, managing the words blithely. "I've scarcely given her a thought. But you've only to ask me, not crawl about my bedroom. Or my town house, for that matter."

"Orders, Kit."

"From whom?" he demanded swiftly. A fruitless question, he suspected, but it was worth a try, anyhow.

John shook his head. "You know I can't tell you. And I didn't know you'd . . . that is, I wasn't told you'd be here. It's possible she would have come here without your knowledge, looking for you, if she didn't find you in London."

"Possible," Kit said, in such a way that made it sound *highly* improbable.

John said nothing; he merely looked about the room idly. He probably knew Kit's room as well as he knew his own. Kit considered whether to tell John about James Makepeace. Part of him resented the fact that he wasn't allowed to investigate Morley. He wondered, too, how it was that his father didn't know about the investigation. And it was maddening, God help him, to think that John might very well bring Morley down before Kit could have a chance to do it. The unworthy, competitive part of him was tempted to stay silent.

But this was John . . . his best friend since childhood, the brother of his heart, and Kit was a patriot. If Morley had sold information to the French . . .

"John . . . there's something I should tell you. You've heard that James Makepeace was killed?"

John ducked his head in somber confirmation.

"A few weeks ago, James told me the most extraordinary tale, which I took only half-seriously at the time, I confess. And Morley was . . . shall we say, the hero of it."

John raised his brows. "Go on."

"Do you remember a politician named Richard Lockwood? Murdered some years ago?"

"I believe it happened about the time we were . . ." John hesitated as he was much more of a diplomat than Kit ever was. "Sent off to the military academy."

"The year I shot you, you mean," Kit said with blunt mischief.

"The year you *missed* me," John countered, predictably.

Once started, the two of them could go on like this forever.

And so Kit told John the whole story: of Lockwood and Morley and Christian virtues, of the allegedly whimsical hiding place of the allegedly incriminating documents.

John drummed the table a few times in thought. "Are you sure James wasn't drunk when he told you all of this?"

"When have you ever seen James drunk?"

"Were *you* drunk when he told you this?"

"Why," Kit said irritably, "does everyone think I'm bound to be drunk?"

John smiled crookedly. "You often *are* bound to be.

But why do you think James told you? Was it a whim of the moment, or do you think he *planned* to tell you?"

"Difficult to say, really. Perhaps because he thought he was in danger. Perhaps because, of all the people he knew, I might be disinclined to let the matter rest, should anything become of him."

A diplomatic way of admitting he was dogged to a fault. To his credit, John didn't snort.

"Do you believe him, Kit?"

"He wasn't raving, if that's what you're asking."

"Do you suppose Caroline knows anything about the Lockwood murder? Her letter . . . it said, 'all we've done.'"

"It's why I told you about James. It might be a mad tale, then again, I can't help but think it's somehow related to Caroline and Morley. But I suppose it will be up to you to discover that."

John smiled crookedly, damn him, because he knew precisely how much it would bother Kit to not be able to pursue this particular mystery. "What would you have done if James hadn't been killed, Kit?"

"Press him for more information, of course. Tell me why you've begun investigating Morley," Kit demanded swiftly.

"Excellent try. But you know I can't."

Kit swore colorfully under his breath.

John laughed. "But you've helped, truly. This was worth crawling in the window. And I'm getting a little old for that sort of thing."

Kit twisted his mouth wryly. The brandy was warming the pit of his stomach, but his mind was uncomfortably alert now. "To James," Kit said, lifting his glass.

"To James."

They drank together, and for a moment indulged in separate thoughts.

"Kit . . ." John's voice was careful; Kit looked at him expectantly. "You do know that if Caroline helped Morley sell information to the French . . . that makes her as much a traitor as Morley. And now . . . she's attempting to find you."

But Kit had already arrived there in reasoning: If the Earl of Westphall's son was known to be consorting with a traitor, a political cataclysm would ensue. Lives would be ruined. His own, for instance. His father's, in particular.

No doubt, some people would like to see that happen.

He wondered, for a moment, if either he or his father were carefully being set up to take a devastating fall.

Kit leaned casually back in his chair, his well-trained features entirely neutral. He clasped his hands behind his head in a luxurious stretch, the picture of nonchalance. He suspected that John knew it was a performance, because it was precisely what John would have done in the same circumstances.

And then, instead of saying anything further, he tipped the brandy decanter again into John's glass, and then into his own, and raised the full glass to his friend. "So where did you end up when we parted ways the other night? Lady Barrington's town house?"

John's smug grin confirmed this. "More specifically, her bed."

"Congratulations," Kit said in all sincerity, and they lifted their glasses to each other again. Lady Barrington had been John's particular quest for some time now.

John bolted the last of his brandy and plunked it down, gestured with a jerk of his chin for Kit to fill it again.

"What *are* you doing here, Kit?" John asked, as if the

thought had just occurred to him. "I had no idea you'd even left town."

"Thought I'd work on my folio."

"Your *what*?"

It *was* rather amusing to spring that word on people. "I thought I'd take some time away from the noise and bustle of London to document the flora and fauna of Barnstable."

He was rewarded when John's jaw dropped.

Kit allowed his voice to drift philosophically. "Nature is endlessly exciting, John. All that death and sex and violence . . ."

John clapped his mouth closed. He looked worried. "But . . . you're a *spy*. And you . . . you *love* London. I mean . . . the countess."

Kit burst into laughter and gave the table a hearty slap.

John scowled at him. "Tell me the truth."

"All right. The truth is . . . my father sent me here to work on the folio project. Under threat of Egypt if I don't complete it in a month."

"So you've been exiled," John guessed.

"One might say that. In a manner of speaking."

"Hmmph."

"'*Hmmph*'?" Kit repeated indignantly. "What the devil do you mean by that?"

"Well . . . you have seemed a bit . . . off, Kit."

"*Off*? And what the devil do you mean by *that*?"

"You drink too much," John said, and it sounded unnervingly like the beginning of a list. "More than I've known you to in the past, anyhow. You're argumentative . . . more so than usual. You're irritable. You've spent an inordinate amount of time in pursuit of a married countess, which seems to me an elaborate way to avoid matrimony."

"'*Avoid matrimony*'?" Only John Carr could get away with saying such a thing. "And what about *you*?"

"*I* am saving myself."

"For *what*?"

John smiled enigmatically. He allowed Kit to glare at him for a moment.

"I suppose I've been a little . . . bored," Kit finally muttered.

"We've all been 'a little bored.' But only one of us called Chisholm an idiot, and that was you."

Kit admitted the truth of this with silence. For a man who prided himself on control, his behavior had reflected little of it lately. His restless mind craved challenges, his restless body craved action. *Purpose.* He took a deep breath, released it, confused, irritated. He was not, in other words, happy.

John looked up toward the ceiling. "I suppose the countess will be . . . lonely now that you've gone."

At this, Kit laughed an oath. "You wouldn't *dare*."

He wasn't terribly worried, however. John might very well be the handsome one, but they both also knew Kit was, and always had been, just slightly better at everything else—shooting and running and riding and swimming and . . . well, at *fascinating* people. Simply by virtue of being his own idiosyncratic, stubborn self. Perhaps it was because he tried a little harder.

No, he decided cheerfully. *I'm just better at everything else.*

Détente regained, another companionable quiet passed.

"You can trust me, John," Kit said, finally, a little gruffly. "I won't say anything to my father about what you've told me. Or to anyone else."

"I know," John said after a moment. His words were shaded with something peculiarly like sadness. "If you hear from Caroline . . ."

"I'll tell you straight away, John. And now that your glass is empty . . . you'll see yourself out?"

"You're tossing me out?" John Carr feigned incredulity.

"I want my sleep. And visit your mother while you're in Barnstable, or I'll tell her you were in the neighborhood and didn't stop by. And go out the door."

"Bastard," John muttered glumly. Kit laughed.

When John was gone, Kit resumed his chair, poured another brandy, then thought about what John had said and poured it back into the decanter. He stared out the window into the darkness, listening, thinking. How silent it seemed here; within a few nights, he knew he'd realize what a racket nature could make, birds, chittering squirrels, crickets. The sounds would come in through his flung-open windows, as lively as London, in its way. His chest was already sticky from the night's heat; he absently rubbed the back of his neck, where a bead of sweat trailed.

And then Kit crouched next to the bed and pulled out a chest he'd kept here since he was a boy. He lifted the lid, and ruffled through the strata of his past—rocks and bones and leaves and books, his first pistol—until he'd found the letter.

" 'I'm sorry,' " was all it said. But he would have known the writing anywhere. He'd exchanged secret notes with her for two feverish years; they'd hidden them in the trunk of a tree near the clearing where he'd aimed a pistol at his best friend. Caroline had been a terrible speller, Kit recalled. But "I'm sorry," *that* she'd spelled correctly.

He remembered the morning of the duel vividly: the bruised dawn sky, the tribunal of birds, a half dozen or so, clinging to the winter-stripped trees, staring down at them. John's white breath hanging in the air, a ghost of the words he had just spoken: "She's not worth it, Kit." It had been both a plea . . . and a taunt.

Oh, but she had been. At least from a seventeen-year-old's perspective. She'd encouraged Kit to touch her bare breast, and sometimes he thought it was the single most important experience of his life.

And so Kit, who had always been the better shot, had aimed for John's shoulder, and their fathers had packed them immediately off to the military, where their friendship and John's shoulder had recovered nicely in the absence of the fever that was Caroline.

The letter had been posted from a town called Gorringe about seventeen years ago, shortly after his duel with John. A town, legend had it, named by a poetry-minded duke who'd apparently gone mad from searching in vain for a rhyme for "orange."

And now she was in trouble. This was no surprise, really, as Caroline had *always* been in some kind of trouble. She'd *courted* trouble. And everyone in Barnstable had known and disapproved of her.

Or known and wanted her.

And she'd disappeared the night she'd met Thaddeus Morley at a party held by Kit's father.

Why had he kept the letter? Proof that he *had* won her, he supposed. At least insofar as Caroline could be won. And, he thought, no doubt John would have found it, if Kit hadn't been asleep in this room tonight.

In short, John might very well be keeping things from Kit. But Kit had also kept things from John.

Again, Caroline's legacy.

Caroline couldn't remember a time when she didn't . . . *want*. Like an itch she could never reach, like a word that lived forever on the tip of her tongue, like a burr clinging to her soul, an indefinable want had driven her from the cradle, and every decision she'd ever made had been in an attempt to appease it.

Consequently, her life had been anything but dull.

For instance, she was fairly certain that Thaddeus was trying to kill her, a result of . . . well, a perhaps not very good decision she'd made a little while ago. She'd needed money; Thaddeus had buckets full of the stuff, some of which one might fairly say she'd helped him acquire. So she'd dashed off a sentimentally worded letter of blackmail.

Shortly after that, someone had tried to stab her, and she'd just barely squeaked away with her life.

She'd moved on to another town, her money dwindling.

And then someone had *again* tried to stab her. Thank heaven she had good vision and reflexes. She'd been moving from town to town ever since.

Ah, well. She should have known that Thaddeus would never do anything by halves.

She peered at the teeming crowd in the coaching inn, awaiting her tea. She was dressed all in black as befitting the widow she wasn't, but the discreet little veil clinging to her hat only heightened her mystique, she knew. The veil bared only her lips. Those red, inviting lips.

And then, out of desperation, she'd even dashed off a letter to Kit Whitelaw, telling him she was in trouble.

Telling him she was coming to him. But she'd run out of money, and she hadn't been able to reach London, so she might never know if Kit had grown into the sort of man he'd promised to become when he was seventeen.

At eighteen, Caroline had raked up a rivalry between Kit and his best friend until it blazed like a cheery autumn bonfire, and she'd warmed herself over it. It had eased that everpresent want in her, much the way her father lifted his war-wounded legs up onto the stool in front of the fire every night to soothe the ache in them. That and a bottle or two each night had always seemed to take the edge off the pain for him. Swinging a heavy hand at his daughter seemed to help, too. She'd learned to dodge him.

And she'd been dodging most of her life, it seemed, from the results of her decision and impulses, which ensured that she didn't need to think or feel any one thing for very long, because that would be uncomfortable, indeed.

And now . . . and now she couldn't seem to stop moving.

When she was younger, Caroline would sometimes look in the mirror and wonder at the cruel joke of her face: that flawless white complexion, lips so naturally red, huge dark eyes like pools that might be either treacherously deep or innocently shallow; to find out, one would have to risk wading in. Waves and waves of silky dark hair. What was the use of such a face when her father was a drunkard who'd sold off all their belongings; when she hadn't any decent clothes; when she was trapped in Barnstable, wild with boredom, reminded daily of her social inadequacy. God knows she wasn't about to marry the son of a farmer or mill owner, and God knows she was never deemed fit to marry the sons of the gentry, let alone the son of an earl.

But oh, how willing they were to dally with her. Given

a little encouragement. Kit had needed a good deal of encouragement, he had a very defined sense of right and wrong. But not even Kit would resist her, in the end.

Kit's ardor in particular had been dangerous. She'd almost felt something in her thawing when she was with him, and it had hurt, hurt, as though she'd been clawing her way through ice to get to him. She'd enjoyed handsome John Carr's attentions, too, but he wasn't nearly as dangerous as Kit. In part, because his father was only a baron. But mostly because he'd never really come close to touching her in any way besides physically.

Oh, but Kit had. Kit was another one who never did anything by halves.

And then one evening, at the annual party the Earl of Westphall held to demonstrate his largesse to the locals, Thaddeus Morley had appeared. Twenty years her senior, powerful in a quiet way that gave her shivers, she'd made another of her decisions: She'd cast her fate into his hands. And for a time, life had been exciting and interesting. And oddly comfortable. They'd suited, she and Thaddeus.

"Thank you," Caroline said softly to the innkeeper, accepting that cup of tea, stealing another glance about.

Men either looked at her with awe, with fear, with desire, or some combination thereof. The ones who had tried to kill her hadn't really looked at all. This being hunted business wasn't pleasant, but then danger and controversy kept the want at bay, too.

But now she was out of money, because she'd spent the last of it on these widow's weeds—her disguise—and a small pistol. And she needed money, since her blackmail scheme had failed. Thaddy had loved her once, or as much as he could love anything besides a cat, but she should have known he wouldn't let something as impractical as love interfere with ambition. Especially given how he'd come to be who he was. The blood and sacrifice involved. His own, and that of others.

Often Caroline wanted things simply because other people had them. For instance, that handsome, fair-haired young man having supper with what must be his wife and her mother at the table in the corner, who'd glanced at her more than once—the last time lingeringly. The wife was a blond thing, bland as blancmange, and her mouth had moved almost continuously, yap yap yapping while the husband's eyes drifted . . . and found Caroline's.

He froze, stared. The way they always did. She allowed him a moment of feasting before she returned her attention to her tea.

He was probably bored with his wife. But he'd married her no doubt because she was respectable, and they no doubt enjoyed a comfortable life. Possibly he even loved his wife, or at least tolerated her.

Caroline decided then that she wanted him.

And since she also wanted some money rather desperately, perhaps she could kill two birds with one stone.

Luck was on her side; the young man rose, and walked in the general direction of her table, heading toward the bar. Caroline casually stood just as he passed her.

"Second room to the right. In five minutes. Five pounds," she murmured.

Before she turned to head up the stairs, she caught a glimpse of his expression: Shock and lust. Fear and fascination. One after the other. And this was how she knew she would soon have enough money to keep moving, which was all that mattered.

Chapter Five

The Assembly decorating committee had clearly undertaken their responsibilities with zeal, but not even a galaxy of candles or a meadow's worth of flowers could disguise the fact that the Barnstable Town Hall wasn't Almacks. A buffet stretched out along one end, ratafia and sandwiches; an orchestra sawed away in the corner, pianoforte and strings. Susannah wondered if they were capable of sawing out a waltz. Not that *she* would be waltzing, of course. She was in mourning, and besides, she doubted there was anyone in attendance with whom she *wished* to waltz.

She took in the room with an expert glance—dresses, fans, slippers, coats—and felt a moment of swooping disorientation: every dress on every maiden had last been fashionable just after Waterloo—five entire years ago. In her own beautifully made, utterly current dress, mourning shade though it was, she might as well have dropped into their midst from another planet. At the moment, a goodly number of Barnstable's denizens were caught up in the patterns of a quadrille; the rest of them would awake with cricks in their necks from pretending they weren't trying to get a look at Susannah—the young men, in particular. So as she stood at Aunt Frances's side she smiled, a general sort of smile, warm and dazzling, the kind that had begun so many friendships in her old life.

Odd, but she could have sworn that everyone in the hall took a tiny collective step back.

Aunt Frances gave her arm a bolstering little squeeze. "Here comes Mrs. Talbot," she whispered. "You will hate her." She smiled cheerily at the woman in a Turkey red dress and matching turban bustling toward them.

Once curtsies and introductions were exchanged, Mrs. Talbot lowered her voice confidingly. "I've had it on good authority that Viscount Grantham is here tonight. He's a thoroughly disreputable character, Miss Makepeace. Disappeared from Barnstable years ago under a cloud. Went on to make his fortune in smuggling. I can't think who might have invited him, but he *is* the local aristocracy, so of course he's welcome here. Perhaps he'll dance with my daughter. She's very pretty, you know." She mopped Susannah with an accusatory head-to-toe glance, her face anxious and hard, then snapped open her fan with a flourish, a warrior putting up a shield. "A pleasure to meet you, Miss Makepeace," she concluded, managing to make it sound as though she meant entirely the opposite, and away she sailed, the red turban listing perilously atop her head.

"She's only *one* person," her aunt whispered apologetically. "She despairs of getting her daughter married, and I fear the strain has begun to show. I assure you, the viscount isn't quite as—oh, look, here are Meredith and Bess

Carstairs," Susannah and her aunt smiled for the Carstairs sisters, a pair of pretty brunettes with almost perfectly spherical faces, on which their features were arranged neatly, symmetrically, like roses painted on china plates.

"Do be careful of the Viscount Grantham, Miss Makepeace," the sister named Bess urged in a low dramatic voice. "He's here tonight. There's a scandal in his past so terrible no one will speak of it. I hear he's wanted for piracy."

"You don't say!" Susannah beamed, happy to be included in gossip.

The Carstairs sisters reared back a little. One would have thought she'd thrust a lantern in their faces. Their uniformly pretty faces suddenly became wary, as though they'd begun to suspect she might be an alien species who'd dressed as a human in order to attend an assembly.

After a few more mild pleasantries, they made polite excuses and went in search of their partners for the next dance, a reel.

Susannah gazed after them, puzzled.

"Just give them time to know you, Susannah," her aunt soothed with a pat. "They are unaccustomed to your . . . polish. I'm certain you will all eventually be great friends."

Susannah was not. She looked out across the wooden floors of the hall, at the smiling dancers lining up for the reel, and despite their woefully outdated clothing, envied them their comfort with each other. The music began, sprightly if a trifle slipshod, and so did the familiar, almost soothing, rhythms of the reel: the dancers bowed and curtsied, they approached and parted—

Which was when she saw him.

Across the hall, hands clasped behind his back, eyes

slightly narrowed, as if to more clearly focus the beam of his gaze on his intended target: her. No one was speaking to him, perhaps because he was the sort of person whose mere physical presence enforced a respectful, perhaps nervous, distance. His clothes were beautifully made and clung to his body as though they felt privileged to do so, and much to her approval, they were utterly current. It was difficult to tell from this distance whether he was handsome, though he was certainly tall.

The scandalous viscount, she thought, with a little thrill.

The dancers approached each other again; he disappeared from view. When they parted once more, she noticed he hadn't moved an inch from his observational stance. It occurred to her then that he was gazing at her as though he had come to the assembly to do expressly that.

And . . . hmmm. Wasn't there something familiar—

Oh, no. Oh, no, oh, no, oh no.

Kit had seen her almost the moment he'd arrived with Frances Perriman. She was too well dressed to be a local, and the black of her mourning dress suited her; her face was a pearl in the gentle light of dozens of candles. The way she held herself spoke of sophistication and breeding, of confidence in her own appeal, and there was something restless about her . . . her foot was tapping—that was it. Interesting. He wondered why she would venture out to an assembly if she were in mourning, and considered that perhaps the locals of Barnstable had become more forgiving and welcoming since he'd left.

This, however, seemed unlikely.

He'd watched her address the two pretty Carstairs sisters, who all but radiated dislike. Then again, she did rather put them in the shade, even dressed like a crow, and London polish *could* seem a bit like glare here in the country.

Ah, here was Mr. Evers, the owner of the Barnstable mill and the font from which all local gossip sprang. He was attempting to skirt Kit the way a cat might a sleeping watchdog—on his way to the punchbowl, no doubt. His vivid berry-colored nose told Kit it wouldn't be Mr. Evers's first trip to the punch bowl this evening.

"Evers!" Kit said quickly, politely. He stifled a laugh when Mr. Evers came to an almost guilty stop and bowed, the flap of hair remaining on his head flopping forward with him. Kit's reputation had never really recovered from the events of seventeen years ago; it had, in fact, blossomed luridly since then. In truth, this didn't bother him. He found it afforded a sort of camouflage, and he was not adverse to camouflage.

"Hello Grantham. You're in the neighborhood, then?"

Kit regarded him in friendly, but utter, silence.

"Of *course* you're in the neighborhood," Evers muttered, catching on. "Why, here you are."

"That I am, Mr. Evers!" Kit said cheerfully. He knew he was being a rogue, but he wasn't in the mood to make anything easy for anyone today. "And how do you fare? Your wife? The mill? All in good repair?"

"Good, good, all good, can't complain."

Evers looked hopeful that this would be the end of their exchange. Which, given the mood Kit was in, all but guaranteed that it would not be. "And the punch, this evening, Mr. Evers?"

This topic Evers warmed to. "Very good batch, Grantham," he confided. "Might want to get some yourself before I—before it's gone, that is."

"I might, at that," Kit agreed. He dropped a confiding arm over the man's shoulder. "Mr. Evers, I wonder if you would mind enlightening me about something."

Evers looked a little flattered. "I will try, sir."

"Who is the young woman with Mrs. Perriman?"

Evers lit up, and Kit knew his question would be spread to everyone in the assembly hall within the hour. Not that he minded, terribly. It would rather add to his legend here in Barnstable.

"Her name is Miss Susannah Makepeace, Grantham."

Kit could have sworn time stopped the moment the words left Evers's mouth. All the little hairs on his arms rose in attention.

"Seems her father died—James, hailed from Barnstable, don't know if you recall—and now here she is in the country, living with her aunt," Evers continued. "Quite the London miss, ain't she? All the lads are quite terrified of her. Been gawking all night, but won't asked to be introduced."

So the minx with the sketchbook *was* James Makepeace's daughter, though nothing at all about her suggested him; she must favor her mother in looks. Kit was almost sorry to find her here: Barnstable wasn't the place for such a vivid creature.

Then again, he was inclined to believe that fate had played a hand in exiling both he and Susannah Makepeace in Barnstable. For he was now certain of one reason James Makepeace had chosen to share his tale with him.

No matter what, Kit was unlikely to ever, as his father had so tersely suggested, "leave it."

"Thank you, Evers," Kit said distantly. "You've been very helpful."

* * *

Susannah's charm continued to glance off the denizens of Barnstable much the way an unsuspecting bird glances off a clean windowpane. They visited for introductions, eyed her with wariness, wandered off again.

"Give them time," Aunt Frances soothed. "You are the most interesting thing to happen to Barnstable in a good long while, and it makes them feel important to pretend that you are not."

Susannah offered up a weak smile, wondering how long Aunt Frances intended to remain at the assembly. She'd been in constant motion since her father had died, buffeted by events, too proud to allow the weight of them to drag her under. But she suddenly pictured that patched quilt on her bed, and wondered how it might feel to crawl beneath it, close her eyes, and linger for days.

Another dance concluded; dancers milled about in search of new partners. Susannah glanced across the room, half in hope, half in terror. The scandalous viscount was no longer watching her.

Relief mingled with a peculiarly acute disappointment. Perhaps she would never retrieve her sketchbook, but then again, perhaps she would never need to revisit her humiliation: *"You were bloody quiet."*

Remarkably the orchestra began to scrape out . . . could it be a *waltz*?

Susannah succumbed to the temptation to close her eyes briefly, imagining her life hadn't changed at all, that this was Almacks and not a town hall, that everyone sought rather than shunned her company. When she opened them again, she was eye level with a white shirtfront.

Slowly, slowly, she tilted her head back.

And her heart bounced into her throat.

"Good evening, Mrs. Perriman," the scandalous viscount bent his long frame into a bow. "I just paid this bloody awful orchestra to attempt a waltz so that I may dance with your niece. Do you mind?"

Oh, God. His voice was a lovely thing, refined, low and confiding. A *London* voice.

And it was the voice that had mused into the nape of her neck yesterday.

Aunt Frances's mouth dropped open; for a moment it hung that way, as if the hinges had snapped.

Shock iced Susannah's hands. Up close the man was imposingly tall. Imposingly . . . *male.* The ice gave way to heat, which begin at Susannah's collar and slowly spread upward. Two competing desires began a violent tussle inside her.

Spinning on her heel and fleeing was one of them.

"We thank you for the offer, but Miss Makepeace is in mourning, Lord Grantham." Aunt Frances had gotten her mouth closed, and this was very elegantly, and not impolitely, said.

The viscount's eyes—blue eyes, *unreasonably* blue eyes—glinted down at Susannah with an unholy and decidedly ungentlemanly amusement. "But you'd *very* much like to dance, wouldn't you, Miss Makepeace?"

And God help her: that was the other desire.

Later, much later, she would admit to herself that there really had been no contest.

"Please forgive me, Aunt Frances. I'm sorry, so sorry, *truly* sorry . . ."

The grinning viscount quickly proffered his arm, and he led Susannah, still trailing abject apologies, out to the floor.

* * *

She lifted her hand to fit into his, the most familiar gesture she'd made in days, comforting somehow even as she reeled in shock at what she'd just done. As she did, the sleeve of his coat slid back, and Susannah saw it. Between the start of his glove and the cuff of his shirt: a birthmark in the shape of a gull.

She promptly stumbled.

The viscount placed his other hand on her waist just in time, effortlessly steadying her, and eased her into the dance. "Yes, 'tis I, Miss Makepeace. The last time we met, I believe you said . . . what was it . . . what was it. . . . oh yes: *'You were bloody quiet.'* And then you went bounding off like a deer through the underbrush. Do I look different in my evening clothes? I imagine I do." His eyes glinted an almost intolerable amusement down at her.

Speechless. Then the words staggered out of her mouth. "You—how *dare*—you are—"

"Your sketches of me are quite good, by the way," he added. "Unflatteringly *accurate,* in some respects, but quite good. And I've always been a strong proponent of accuracy."

"I—" she choked. Her face, from the feel of things, was the color of Mrs. Talbot's turban.

"The way I see it is this, Miss Makepeace: you can either pretend to be horrified and make a scene—but I *do* know you'd be pretending—or you can laugh, which is what you'd prefer to do. Either way you'll still be the talk of the assembly, and the good people of Barnstable won't like you any more than they do now."

"How *dare*—" she began again, her tone indignant, because of course she knew she ought to feel indignant.

His eyes widened in mock fear.

Dash it, anyway. "No, I suppose they don't like me," she admitted, genuinely puzzled. "And people usually do, you know."

He laughed then, surprised, a rich sound that unfortunately made heads all over the room swivel toward them. And there they remained, riveted by the sight of Susannah Makepeace in her mourning gown waltzing with the scandalous viscount. "Do they, now? I suppose you make certain of it."

"It's easy, you see," she confessed. "Or, it usually is." This conversation was rapidly running away with her, and it was both terrifying and exhilarating.

"For you, I suppose it is. But perhaps you needn't try so hard."

"I wasn't *'trying,'*" she objected.

"No?" He sounded as though he didn't believe her at all. "Well, perhaps they don't like you because you're more handsome than the lot of them."

Finally the viscount seemed to be doing the sort of flirting she recognized. She dimpled a little.

"Comparatively, anyway," he added, sweeping the room with a dispassionate gaze, as if to ascertain the truth of that statement.

Her dimples vanished.

"And you've a certain amount of sophistication," he assessed thoughtfully.

Tentatively, her lips began to lift again.

"A modicum." He said it firmly, as though correcting himself. He glanced at her. "Why are you glowering at me?"

Accuracy, indeed. Flirtation wasn't about *accuracy,* for heaven's sake. *Everyone* knew that.

Her silence didn't seem to bother him. "Your drawings are brilliant Miss Makepeace. You're quite talented."

"My *drawings* are brilliant?" *What about my smile? What about my eyes?*

"Yes," he said. "Detailed, accurate, yet still singular and strangely . . . he looked upward for a moment, seeking a clean slate for his thought, then returned his eyes to her. ". . . . passionate."

He all but purred that last word, his eyes dancing with mirth, and for the life of her, she didn't know what to say. Susannah studied him warily instead, since his face was the one part of his body she hadn't yet sketched in vivid detail. His features were too strong, perhaps, to be considered classically handsome; his face a bit too long and angular, like a diamond, his nose slightly arched. Light brows, light lashes, and those disconcerting eyes. But in the midst of all those angles, his mouth was a work of art, wide, sensitively curved, indisputably masculine.

And of course, the rest of him was beautifully made, too. Almost overwhelmingly so.

God help her, she could feel color setting fresh fire to her cheeks at the memory.

"I'd like to make you an offer, Miss Makepeace."

Her head went back and her eyes flew open wide; on the heels of her last thought, his words were genuinely shocking. "I *beg* your pardon, sir?"

"Of *employment*. Don't look so hopeful." He was laughing silently again.

This man was absolutely, dizzyingly, *maddeningly*—

"Employment?" She said the word as though she'd found a tiny sharp bone in her soup.

"Yes. I'm a naturalist by avocation, and I've been

commissioned to complete a folio—a study of the flora and fauna of this region. I've need of an accomplished artist to assist me with it. I'll pay you well. Good heavens, you should see your face. You'd best change your expression quickly or everyone here will think I've gravely insulted you."

Humiliation had so completely snarled Susannah's thoughts she simply couldn't transform them into words. He wanted her to *work* for him. Like a maid, like a governess, a cook, a—

"How, Miss Makepeace, do you suppose your aunt accommodates one more person in her cottage? She isn't rich. And yet you don't look underfed."

He might as well have kicked her in the ribs.

Susannah thought of the patched quilt that covered her at night, her aunt's faded, sagging furnishings, the humble breakfast, the lack of a maid to poke up the fires.

Shame pooled, molten, in the pit of her stomach. She turned her face away from the viscount's direct blue gaze and swallowed hard.

For a moment, mercifully, he didn't speak.

"Forgive my gruff ways, Miss Makepeace," his voice was gentle, conciliatory; it curled deliciously around her, like rich smoke. "I lack experience with the tender sensibilities of young ladies."

Susannah cautiously returned her eyes to his face and narrowed them little, not certain she wished her sensibilities to be considered tender. He seemed to enjoy that, for his eyes glinted at her again. Such a blue, his eyes were. Like the center of a flame, as though some internal furnace lit them. She was tempted to hold her hand up to them, to see if she could feel heat.

He must have considered himself forgiven, because he kept talking. "Talent is like . . . money in the bank. You should spend it wisely, of course, but not to spend it at all is simply foolish. I have need of your assistance; your aunt, I'm certain, would be happy for the money. We can be of use to each other. Will you help me?"

"But . . . work?" she repeated faintly.

"Perhaps you'd prefer to cast about for other employment, Miss Makepeace?"

There it was, that word again. "No," she said vehemently.

"No? Good. I'll speak to your aunt, then, assure her of your safety, and make everything proper, etcetera."

"But—" she began. She gave up. "What is your name?" she asked suddenly, instead. "Your full name?"

"Christopher Whitelaw, Viscount Grantham. Kit, to *you*, Miss Makepeace."

And then he smiled a smile that made Susannah remember that he'd made a fortune in smuggling, and was wanted for piracy. Perhaps he'd also had an affair with the queen. For it was just that sort of smile: crooked, slow, unnervingly inclusive and intimate. It knew things, that smile. She felt shy suddenly; she was acutely aware of how substantial he was, how hard the muscles under his shirt and trousers were. Douglas seemed unfinished in comparison, a sapling.

Though she of course had never seen beneath Douglas's clothes.

"My aunt—" she faltered suddenly.

"Is not anywhere near as shocked as she seemed, I assure you. She's known me since I was in short pants, and I doubt I've truly surprised her. She's sturdier than you might think."

Susannah couldn't help but smile at that, thinking of him in short pants. "Did . . . did you know my father, then? He hailed from this region as well."

"He was older than I, so we didn't spend much time together when I was growing up in Barnstable," he said easily. "But I knew him in London. We were both soldiers at one time, and we shared a common acquaintance, a Mr. Morley. Perhaps you've met him?"

"No, sir, I am afraid I haven't. Are you involved in imports and exports, too?"

"We did have some business together, your father and I. Which is how I came to know him."

She almost said, "I wish *I'd* known him." She was quiet, instead, and focused on the row of buttons climbing up the viscount's dazzlingly white shirt, thinking about the quiet enigma that had been James Makepeace. His kindness, his detached bemusement. His violent end, which had, in a way, violently ended a way of life for her, too.

And suddenly her feet were heavier, and the waltz was an effort.

Susannah looked up again to find the viscount watching her, those vivid eyes softer. "He was a good man, Miss Makepeace. I'm sorry for your loss." Almost excruciatingly gentle, his voice.

"Thank you." And she felt tears burning the backs of her eyes for her father. "Am I horrible to dance?"

"A little," the viscount said lightly, which instead of making her *feel* horrible, comforted her somehow.

"I intend to get roaring drunk in his honor at first opportunity," he added after a moment.

She wasn't at all sure what to say about this, although it did sound like something of a tribute.

The dance ended then, and she was certain the orchestra all but mopped their brows in relief. The viscount released her hand.

"It's settled then? As of this moment, you are in my employ?"

"I—"

But she said the word to his retreating back, because his question had only been rhetorical, after all. It was clear he'd been certain all along of getting precisely what he wanted.

Chapter Six

"It . . . did what?" Morley fixed Bob with a pleasant gaze.

Bob flinched. He knew from experience that Morley was at his least pleasant when he . . . seemed pleasant. "Tipped over, sir."

"Tipped . . . over . . ." Morley repeated musingly. He knelt to waggle his fingers at Fluff, who trotted over urgently, as if it had been far too long since he'd been petted. It had been about five minutes.

He scooped the cat up.

"In the yard of the coaching inn," Bob explained hurriedly. "I replaced the linchpin with a short 'un, ye see, which works a treat nearly every time. When the coach came to the turn on the road just past West Crumley, it *should* have made a right nice accident—arms, legs, trunks, everywhere." Bob's mouth twisted wistfully. "Why, just last year a mail coach on the way to . . . on the way to . . ."

He trailed off at the look of frozen politeness on Morley's face.

"I'm a *professional*, Mr. Morley," Bob muttered defensively. "Deuced timing, is all."

"You also aren't the *only* professional in your . . . field, Bob."

Bob said nothing. He shifted his sturdy legs, one then the other, as though attempting to extricate himself from something sticky.

Morley sighed. "She's in the country now. Surely there are any number of ways one can . . . experience misfortune in the country? I can think of dozens. But I pay *you* to do the thinking, Bob."

"I'll see to it, sir."

The viscount had been efficient: he'd spoken to her aunt; somehow managing to explain his need for artistic assistance without mentioning how she'd demonstrated her skill. This proved that he had at least *some* diplomatic skills. And now Susannah was to meet him at eight in the morning. It seemed a barbarically early hour, but she'd heard before how everyone who lived permanently ("permanently" rather sounded like one has been sentenced) in the country was up with the light.

And so had she been. She'd rubbed the kernels of sleep from her eyes and splashed water over her face, managed to butter a slice of bread for breakfast, and then dosed herself with strong tea (her aunt's one indulgence seemed to be excellent tea). The night before, Aunt Frances had been kind enough to pack her a lunch, too, in a basket, in case the viscount neglected to feed her. She found the basket on the shelf leading out on to a mud porch, hooked it over her arm, and plunged into the bright, uncompromisingly green, birdsong-filled day.

If Aunt Frances was aware that going out to "work" constituted a cataclysm for Susannah, she'd said nothing of it—she in fact seemed so pleased about the whole thing that Susannah entertained a fleeting suspicion that she had conspired to get her to Barnstable precisely because she'd needed a wage earner under her roof. She *had* mentioned something about extra sausages and beef for meals, now that there would be a little more money.

Susannah dismissed that unworthy thought. Aunt Frances couldn't possibly have known that her niece harbored any particular income-producing talent.

Beautiful clothing had always been her battle gear, so she'd dressed with particular care this morning. Laying her mourning dress aside, since it was her only one and she had no wish to ruin it, she'd chosen the soft pink muslin trimmed in an even paler shade of ribbon, with two flounces, as it suited the weather as well as her complexion. An admiring glance or two from the intriguing viscount would at least make the day more tolerable.

She found him waiting for her at the end of the path that led to the pond, wearing snug fawn breeches, Hessians, a white shirt open at the throat, and an impatient expression. He, in other words, had *not* taken particular care with his dress. But still, somehow, he managed to look as though he had. The man seemed to confer elegance upon his clothes, rather than the other way around.

"Good morning, Miss Makepeace," he began pleasantly enough. But then he paused and swiftly appraised her, from her bonnet to her boot toes. "Your gown . . ." he began, and stopped, seeming at a loss. And then for some reason an amused furrow appeared between his brows. ". . . suits your coloring."

Susannah decided she might as well treat this as a compliment. She dipped her head demurely and looked up at him through her lashes, which had never failed to disarm any male within five feet of her. "Thank you, sir." Soft as a dropped handkerchief, her voice.

The amused furrow deepened and became *be*musement, as though she hailed from some exotic land and her customs were foreign to him. "That wasn't a compliment, Miss Makepeace. It was an *observation*. A demonstration, if you will, of the sort of thing we'll be doing today. Observing. Now show me your shoes."

Grrrr. While irritation and chagrin wrestled for control of her tongue, she lifted one foot out in front of her. Like a bloody child. Or a high-stepping horse. She couldn't seem to help it: he had that sort of voice. A taken-for-granted-that-no-objections-would-be-brooked sort of voice:

The viscount examined her brown-kid, rosette-topped half boots critically. "Not Wellingtons, by any means, but sensible enough for traipsing through the woods. Good choice."

Good *choice*? Did he really think she would wear dancing slippers out to the wood?

"Are you quite certain about that, Lord Grantham? Perhaps you need to inspect the *rosette* more closely, to ensure it meets your approval."

She dropped her foot again, stared up at him.

Well. She could tell from his crooked smile that her sarcasm, for some reason, met with his approval.

"As much as I would enjoy inspecting your . . . *rosette* more closely, Miss Makepeace—" and the smile spread, becoming that intimating, preternaturally confident smile of the night before "—I'll forego that pleasure for the moment. And I suppose we can avoid the water today. In honor of the rosette."

The wit-scrambling smile had her staring back at him blankly. Still, she had a concern.

"Water?" The word came out a little more faintly than she would have preferred. But really: did he intend to drag her through a *swamp?*

He was laughing again, silently. "Let's get started, shall we?" He made a startlingly fast turn and began covering the ground with strides so long she had to scramble after him to keep up. "And mind the snake," he called over his shoulder.

"Sna—"

A bright, slender *S* of a creature whipped across her path and vanished into the grass. She bit her lip against a shriek.

"Don't worry, Miss Makepeace," came the viscount's voice again. "It was only a little grass snake. *Those,* at least, aren't poisonous."

Somehow, she could tell he was smiling from the back of his head.

Kit wondered whether he was taking his resentment toward his folio assignment out on Miss Makepeace, and forgave himself if that was the case. He was enjoying keeping her off balance; it was like idly prodding a pianoforte in different places just to hear what sounds would emerge. He knew from experience that surprising people was the quickest way to take their measure, for they had no choice but to respond with their true natures.

So far, he admitted to himself, the sounds she made weren't entirely boring.

Wicked of him to tempt her to waltz—he'd seen the

longing all but vibrating in her posture from across the room last night—but then, he'd been feeling more wicked than usual all day. And besides, he'd seen so much of death in war that the very ritual of mourning—the clothing, the sequestering, the denial of pleasures—struck him now as shockingly extravagant, given how capriciously, terrifyingly short life could be, and how splendid it often was to be alive. The impulse to waltz struck him as infinitely braver and saner than the inclination to languish. Better to celebrate the lives of the dead by living thoroughly.

He suspected Susannah Makepeace might even become truly interesting . . . given a little encouragement.

She was pretty. Not in the usual way, the way the Carstairs sisters were pretty, the sort of beauty that would become indistinct with age. But . . . well, Miss Makepeace's eyes seemed filled with colors, and with a spy's impulse toward investigation, he had an urge to get a look at them in the full light so he could see how many and which ones. And her mouth . . . it was plush, her mouth. Pink as the inside of a seashell.

The softest, softest shade of pink imaginable.

The sort of mouth that made him feel restless and ill tempered, given that Susannah Makepeace was no doubt the veriest babe when it came to matters of passion, naked sketches notwithstanding, and that a dalliance with her would take unfair advantage of her status, which was no status at all, really.

Egyptian sand dunes undulated threateningly in his imagination, and Kit lengthened his stride: the sooner he completed some sort of folio, the sooner he could resume his life in London and return to the countess's practiced lips and arms.

A wedge-shaped shadow floated across the ground at his feet then; he looked up for its source.

High overhead, against the brilliant blue sky, a small kestrel was circling, wings tipping into the wind. Kit dropped his gaze, swept it along the trunks of trees, and saw the telltale signs: bark nibbled away in rings at the base of young trees. Circling kestrels plus nibbled bark usually equaled voles. Voles ate the bark; kestrels ate the voles. It was a very sensible, no-nonsense arrangement, but then nature was like that.

And damned if the thrill of discovery, of tracking, didn't stir in him. Just a yawn and a stretch, really . . . but a stir, nevertheless.

If he didn't know better, he would have sworn he was excited over *voles*.

Unfortunately, the dreamlike—or was it nightmare-like?—sensation hadn't yet ebbed. Susannah was accustomed to music, and comfort, and the company of gorgeous friends. Instead she was kneeling in a meadow next to a small hole in the ground, and a tall viscount, who by all the laws of nature, should be admiring *her* . . . seemed enthralled by what appeared to be a nest of baby mice.

He had a dent of concentration between his eyes, a pencil between his fingers, and he was scratching things into a small bound book.

The sun was seeping through Susannah's bonnet, baking her head; she could almost imagine it swelling, swelling atop her neck, like a great loaf of bread. She now regretted wearing the blush colored muslin, as she was certain perspiration was darkening it even now.

She gazed down at the little creatures. Again: mice were

as shriek-worthy as snakes. Or so she'd once thought. Certainly, if she'd encountered one in the presence of Douglas, she would have shrieked a little for his benefit. But these lot, six or so, were scarcely the size of the first joint of her thumb. Vulnerable babies, and, astonishing though it was to think it . . . charming. They were sleeping in a little heap. Her impulse was to apologize for staring and leave them to it.

"Voles," Kit whispered. "*Long*-tailed voles." He sounded as though he were sharing an exquisite confidence.

Susannah looked at them a moment longer, indulging him. And then:

"I heard you made a fortune in smuggling," she whispered. Which to her, seemed a much more pressing topic than voles.

"Did you?" he murmured. Still looking at the voles. Still writing in his book.

She'd wanted an affronted objection. She'd wanted to startle him the way he so excelled at startling her. Perhaps he *had* been a smuggler, then. Perhaps he still *was*. Perhaps this was how Aunt Frances managed to acquire her marvelous tea.

She tried again: "I also heard that you are wanted for piracy."

He stopped writing then, but only to look out across the meadow with a pleased, contemplative half-smile on his lips, as though he was imagining what it would be like to be a pirate, or fondly remembering a piratical moment.

He never did comment; silence went by, and he bent his head over his book again. He'd missed a few whiskers when he'd shaved this morning, she saw; they glinted gold on the underside of his sharp jaw. He wasn't wearing a hat. By the end of the day, his face would be darker than the pale gold skin that covered the rest of his body.

"Did you happen to hear the one about the opium dens?" he whispered.

"No!" She started guiltily from her thoughts of the rest of his body.

He looked mildly disappointed. "I was fairly certain that one wouldn't take."

Her mouth dropped open; she closed it hard again. "Why do they—why do you—"

He was laughing silently now. "Draw the voles, Miss Makepeace. You're in my employ now, or have you forgotten?"

She *had* forgotten. She felt the heat of a blush layering over her already sun-warmed cheeks; she really wasn't sure how employed artists were supposed to behave. Like a governess? Like a cook? No doubt deference was involved, not questions and flirtation.

She lowered her head to the task, and was soon enough submerged in it, in the strange deliciousness of drawing. She sketched the textures of their fur, shaded in the soft shifting colors of their overlapping bodies, their tiny toes and noses. And those tails, of course, where they showed. For these were, after all, special, rare, long-tailed voles.

She put the finishing touches on a vole toe and looked up from her drawing; she was surprised to find his eyes fixed on her hands. He was frowning in concentration.

A shadow, like a flying platter, darkened them briefly, and was gone.

"A kestrel. Looking for a meal," the viscount murmured.

Susannah was tempted to throw her body over the nest.

He looked up from her drawing into her face then, his expression thoughtful. For a brief, giddy moment she thought he was about to compliment her bonnet, or at the very least, her drawing. She smiled softly, in case he needed a little encouragement.

"You don't appear to be terribly grief-stricken over your father's death, Miss Makepeace," he said.

Susannah's breath left her in a cough of shock.

But the viscount's eyes remained on her levelly, for all the world as though it had been a perfectly reasonable thing to say. Granted, there hadn't been a shred of accusation in his words; he simply wanted to *know,* and so he had asked.

She supposed she could be missish and protest the question. But again, she found it oddly liberating, this forthright way of his. This . . . reckless . . . brand of honesty. She *wanted* to answer his questions. She wanted to know the answers to them as much as he did.

"I grieve for my father," she kept the words cool, because he deserved the coolness, she decided. Her voice was still a little unsteady from shock. "But we weren't close, Lord Grantham."

He said nothing for a moment. And then:

"Kit," he corrected. With a crooked half-smile.

Susannah frowned at that, which made his smile complete. He waited, his blue gaze steady. Confident she would say more.

And she couldn't help but say more into that silence. "I saw him seldom, as he was away so often for his business. I wanted very much to know him, but he was nearly a stranger to me, which I shall always regret deeply. So, yes, I do grieve him. But perhaps not to the degree I would have should we have enjoyed a warmer relationship. And perhaps not to the degree *you* find appropriate."

A droplet of sweat made the meandering journey from the back of her neck to the crevice of her bosom while the viscount took this in. She watched something shift in his expression, something difficult to interpret.

And then he gave a short nod, as though she'd given the correct answer.

Susannah felt pique. Both for him, for what seemed to be condescension. And for herself, for feeling gratified by his approval.

"He was difficult to know, your father," Kit offered mildly, surprising her. "I liked him, but I believe he invited very few people into his inner world. So he wasn't a stranger only to you, Miss Makepeace. It was, in fact, difficult for me to imagine how he acquired a daughter at all."

What a fascinating thing to say. "Do you suppose he had an inner world? My father?"

"Don't we all?" The viscount sounded surprised.

She glanced around them, at the little tree-ringed meadow they occupied, home to the voles. No houses were visible from where they crouched, nor was the pond. It occurred to her that they were very alone, she and the viscount, and yet she'd been far too absorbed in work to worry about impropriety. What on earth would Mrs. Dalton say?

"What of your mother, Miss Makepeace? What became of her?"

Susannah was still feeling lightheaded from the abrupt questions and her own ascent into bold honesty. But this conversation seemed to have acquired its own momentum. "My mother died when I was very young, Lord Grantham. I remember only . . ."

She stopped. She'd never before told anyone of that night. Partly because the memory was so faint, like something from a dream rather than an actual memory; she'd jealously guarded it, as though sharing it would somehow wear it away further. And partly out of pride: she didn't want to be pitied for having only one paltry memory.

But his voice and demeanor were easy. Not probing, or demanding, or sympathetic; rather, conversational, as though nothing she could say or do would ever shock him.

And suddenly it seemed safe to tell him.

She took a deep bracing breath; oddly, her heart was knocking. She turned away from him to speak. "I remember . . . oh . . . waking in the dark. A lot of rushing about and whispering. Someone . . . crying. A woman leaning over me . . . she had long black hair that tickled my cheeks." Susannah gave a short laugh; self-conscious, and rubbed the back of her hand against her cheek. "Her eyes were dark. Her voice was . . ." she cleared her throat. "Her voice was soft."

Susannah risked a glance back at the viscount. His expression was abstracted; he seemed to be picturing this along with her. "This woman with the dark hair was your mother?"

"This may seem odd, but . . ." Susannah hesitated. "I'm not certain it was. I have a miniature of her, and she didn't look like that at all. She looks like me. I look like *her,* that is."

"What was your mother's name, Miss Makepeace?"

"Anna."

"Anna," he repeated softly. "Rather like Susannah, isn't it? Perhaps you'll show the miniature to me one day."

This suggestion puzzled Susannah. Was he flirting, now? It was entirely possible, since the viscount didn't seem to flirt in any of the ways she recognized. "Perhaps," she agreed, cautiously.

His mouth twitched a little at that. And then, abruptly, he lowered his head to the voles again.

Finished with one specimen and on to another, Susannah thought acerbically.

She found, however, that she wasn't through with the conversation.

"Did . . . did my father ever speak of her to you? My mother?" She tried to make the question sound casual, yet she could hear the faint note of hunger in it.

The viscount looked up, surprised. "No." The word was gentle. "Did he never speak of her to you?"

Susannah paused. And then she gave her head a co-quettish toss, as if nothing had ever mattered to her less. "Apparently my father never spoke to anyone of anything, Lord Grantham."

The viscount didn't smile. "And no one else spoke of your mother to you, either?" Still gentle.

The lightness proved difficult to sustain. "No." Odd how the admission shamed her.

Pride kept her gaze even with his.

He watched her a moment longer, his expression diffi-cult to read. Then he inhaled deeply, exhaled, and ducked his chin briefly into his chest in thought. And raised his head again, eyes glinting.

"I thought we'd address the White Oak next, Miss

Makepeace, since you ignored it a few days ago favor of sketching *another* magnificent specimen."

Susannah gave a start, and blushed, and wanted to shake him, and all of this was somehow easier than the gentleness and the honesty. She felt her equilibrium restored, somehow. Oddly, Susannah suspected this was why he'd said it.

"May I see your work?" he asked, laughing silently at her flustered face. Mutely, she handed the sketchbook to him.

He studied her sketch of the voles. And for a time, a long time, it seemed, his face revealed nothing at all, which in itself seemed revealing. And then steadily, slowly, she watched his expression go sterner. A wall going up, over-compensating for some softer feeling.

At last, as welcome and startling as sun breaking through clouds: awe struggled through.

"How do you do it?" he demanded brusquely. It sounded like an accusation.

"'It'?" She repeated, afraid she sounded stupid. Still, she didn't know he meant.

"Capture them so . . . precisely the way they are. Their . . . *vole*ness." He rapped the drawing with the back of his hand and looked intently into her eyes. As though much hinged on her answer to this question.

"I . . ." she hesitated. "I've never really thought about it," she admitted almost shyly, hating to disappoint him, because he clearly considered this significant. "It's as though . . ."

He waited. So she thought about it. She didn't know quite *how* she did it—captured voleness, that is. But she did know she'd always turned to her sketchbook in order to escape from or capture something, whether it was a thought or an impulse she needed to stifle, or something she needed to understand, or . . . Perhaps it was because—

Oh, but this was going to sound foolish.

"It's as though I can stop being *me* for just a moment, and I feel what it feels like . . . to be a vole. Or a rose. Or—"

She was going to say, "or you."

She wouldn't presume to know what it felt like to be him. But she thought of him on the pier, gloriously nude, stretching his arms toward the sky . . . and it had been as though his own pleasure in the moment had become her own pleasure. As if every bit of his pleasure, his abandon, his beauty, had infused her drawing.

"No," he said suddenly. Softly but firmly. As though he'd just had a revelation of his own.

"No?" She was crushed. And here she'd really given it some thought.

"No, I don't think you ever stop being *you* when you draw, Miss Makepeace . . . not even for a moment. I suspect you are entirely yourself when you draw." One of his fair brows went up along with the corners of his mouth, daring her to challenge his conclusion.

And his eyes still held hers relentlessly. His fair lashes darkened to gold at the tips, she could see now, and a trio of lines rayed from the corner of each of his eyes; they deepened when he smiled. There was a tiny divot, a scar, near the corner of his mouth; fair whiskers sparked in the hollows of his high-planed cheeks. The terrain of his face seemed utterly suited to the man, with its unforgiving angles and unexpected softness combined. She had an impulse to trace a finger over the slopes and corners of it, the way one would follow a map to see where it lead.

"Oh," she said faintly, at last. Imagine, she, who could always effortlessly talk of small things, could only say "Oh."

She suspected no talk was small for this man.

But the questions and challenges he'd hailed upon her like a shower of bright, sharp jewels since they'd met had ceased long enough to allow her an insight of her own: he hailed those questions and challenges so she would *not* be able to see into him. So that she would forever be dodging, rather than looking.

Oh, but that's a mistake, Viscount Grantham, she thought. It only made her desperate to know what he was so determined to hide . . . or protect.

Her eyes lowered then to his softly smiling mouth, drawn to it as though his secrets could be found there, or perhaps because it was the most forgiving aspect of his face; certainly at the moment it was easier to bear than his searching eyes. And there her gaze lingered . . . a little longer perhaps, than it should have. Because she *was* a woman, after all. And it was a splendid mouth.

She watched the smile fade from it.

Cautiously, she returned her eyes to his. What she saw there landed as cleanly as a lightning strike at the base of her spine.

The blue had darkened nearly to black. There was a thrilling tension in his face; his eyes skimmed her mouth, hovered . . . considering. A delicious, breath-stealing heat unfurled through her limbs.

And then his face changed abruptly: hard, slit-eyed and predatory, he sprang to his feet with such shocking speed that she stumbled backward.

* * *

Someone had been watching them.

He'd sensed it like a shift in the wind; even after years away from this land, anything that didn't belong rippled his awareness. And so when instincts had tugged his eyes away from Susannah Makepeace's . . . promising . . . mouth . . .

He'd seen on the outskirts of the wood . . . a man.

Who'd run when Kit sprang to his feet. Disappearing from view with remarkable speed.

Frustration bit into him now like a tether. He supposed he could give chase, for he could run like a bloody deer, and he knew this terrain better than anyone; he'd have the advantage over the intruder.

But he suddenly felt distinctly uneasy about leaving Susannah alone.

Kit lowered his pistol; he'd retrieved it from his boot without thinking, a reflex. He swiftly scanned the perimeter of his property, the place where the man had been standing. He saw nothing else untoward. Trees, grasses, flowers, squirrels. No men.

Poachers weren't entirely out of the question, but everyone in the region by now would know the lord was back in his manor, and he sincerely doubted even a desperate poacher would risk a daylight foray—though a stupid one might. He hadn't seen the long dark shadow of a musket in the man's hand, but he'd investigate the area later, look for footprints in the earth, for traps, any clues to the man.

For if someone had wandered innocently on to his land . . . they wouldn't have run.

He thought of John Carr; dismissed that possibility. And then he wondered whether his father was actually having him watched. Now, *that* seemed possible.

Bloody hell. And there he was, naturally, gazing into the eyes of a female.

He turned to find Susannah still on the ground, leaning back on her hands. Frowning a little. Not as rattled as she might be, given the fact that that he'd just leaped up and drawn a pistol.

"I didn't know naturalists took pistols out with them. Did you intend to challenge the voles, then?"

He couldn't have said it more dryly himself, and for a moment, he wasn't sure what to say, which was a rare enough occurrence. Point to Miss Makepeace.

"It's not a dueling pistol," he said, before realized too late how absurd a defense this was.

"Ah."

"I thought I saw a poacher," he clarified coolly.

"I've never known anyone to hide a pistol in his boot. While he was out drawing voles."

"Haven't you?" he said absently. And then, remembering his manners, he extended his hand to help her to her feet. She accepted it with alacrity. She'd removed her gloves to sketch, and what a soft little paw she had; he was tempted to linger over it for a moment, as he would any small pleasure, and allow his imagination to complete for him how soft the rest of her would be. In fact, a moment ago . . . a mad, mad moment ago . . .

Well, it was probably a very good thing he'd seen the man when he'd had.

Irritated with himself, his father, Miss Makepeace and the world, Kit released her hand abruptly. She wasn't a siren. He wasn't a boy. He was just a bored, restless spy.

"No," she replied firmly. "I haven't."

One didn't really expect such a display of spine from a

young woman in blush-colored muslin. He wondered if she understood just how narrowly she'd escaped being kissed.

"And how would you know what a naturalist would choose to take out with him, Miss Makepeace? Odd, but I don't recall seeing any voles in your sketchbook before today. Naked viscounts, however, I *do* recall."

His words painted her face red as surely as if he'd dipped her in the color, and effectively silenced her, which had been his intent. He wanted to be able to look at her for a moment with a spy's eyes, and not a man's eyes.

For not only did she not in the least resemble James Makepeace—but the mother whom she presumably *did* resemble was entirely a mystery to her, if she was to be believed.

And he did believe her. It ached in her, he'd heard it in her voice: this void where her parents should have been. The twinge of guilt he felt about interrogating her was nicely fought back by his desire to get at the truth. It was all too odd, the deaths, the watching man, the mystery of James Makepeace's life.

"Perhaps," he suggested casually, "you should ask your aunt whether she thinks you inherited your talent for drawing from your father or your mother."

He probably couldn't overtly interview Frances Perriman about James Makepeace, however desperately he wanted to do it. But he could subtly urge her niece to do it for him.

Susannah still looked becomingly flustered; she fumbled her sketchbook closed. "It would be interesting to know." Polite and cool.

He preferred her sarcastic, or blushing, or proud, he

decided. Anything other than polite. "Do you ride, Miss Makepeace?" he found himself asking suddenly.

"Yes, quite well." Then, as an afterthought: "Thank you." Chin angled high, like a flag carried into battle.

Ah, that was better. "Please meet me at my stables tomorrow morning. We shall ride out in search of ferns."

She did brighten a little at that. And oddly, though it was a small thing, it pleased him to please her.

Chapter Seven

The day's heat gave way to a cool evening, and Susannah watched as her aunt swiftly and capably stacked wood in the fireplace, as competent and unself-conscious as a chambermaid. Susannah recalled the years of mornings she'd awakened to the familiar sound of a maid lighting the fires, of rolling over to see a white mobcap bobbing atop a girl busy with the coals, of waiting until the heat filled the room before she left the cocoon of whatever soft bed in whatever great house she'd been visiting.

As Aunt Frances stooped lower to arrange the logs, her knees against the hearth, she reached a hand behind her to touch the small of her back. An increasingly familiar dual shame swept through Susannah. Shame that no servant was about to do something as simple as light a fire for the two of them.

Shame that she didn't know the first *thing* about lighting a fire.

She felt . . . useless. This was another new sensation; it had never been necessary to be strictly useful before.

"I'll do it," she faltered. "I'll . . . I'll take care of the fire."

Her aunt turned around, surprised. "Well, it's done, my dear. But you can do it tomorrow night, if that would make you happy."

Aunt Frances was a wry one.

"Ecstatic," Susannah confirmed. They laughed a little together, less shy then they had been.

"Perhaps we can divide up the chores. I'll do the budget . . ."

There was a budget?

". . . And you can light the fires. Your back is better for it, no doubt, Susannah." Her aunt was teasing, she could tell, but . . . *was* her back better for it? What sort of back would she have if she knelt to stack wood morning and night, and cleaned, and cooked? Broad as a horse's? What sort of hands would she have? She'd always been so careful with hers, keeping them smooth and white, her nails tidy and pink and even. And yet she supposed hands were *meant* to be used. To lift and carry and build. Knit things. Wield firearms, steer plows.

A basket of knitting and mending sat next to a chair near the fire; the beginnings of a scarf spilled out of it. Aunt Frances clearly made thorough use of her hands. Susannah discreetly looked down at her own. At least she *could* sketch with hers—well enough to bring extra sausages and beef into the house.

The evening yawned, intimidating as a chasm, and they couldn't very well go to bed right after supper . . . or could they? She wondered what the Carstairs sisters and the rest of Barnstable's denizens were doing this evening. No one had come to call or sent an invitation since the evening of the assembly.

"They won't be able to stay away forever," her aunt had said, "as you are the most interesting thing to arrive in Barnstable in ages." Until they *did* come calling, what did one *do* with an aging aunt before one went to bed?

She could stitch a sampler, she supposed. Her needle-work was better than passable. What would the sampler say? I'M BORED! Perhaps, or: SAVE ME, PLEASE! The thought amused her darkly. She could create a whole gallery of frustration, hang it in frames across these bare walls to cover the fading wallpaper.

She watched Aunt Frances moving about the little room, lighting a lamp here and there, and together with the fire the lamps conspired to fill the room with a comforting glow, casting the shabby furnishings into a more flattering light.

Douglas had always admired her hair by firelight.

That thought would get her *nowhere*.

Still, her mind began to worry the image of Douglas like a tongue searching out the space once occupied by a tooth. Oddly, Douglas drifted out of focus; a more vivid, more complicated man usurped him tonight. And even though Douglas had betrayed her, Susannah felt a bit of a traitor for this.

"There you are my dear—now we can see each other, and we shan't freeze," Aunt Frances said as she settled her comfortable girth on the settee. "Do you sew? Or perhaps you'd like to read to me while I do finish my scarf?"

"What do you enjoy reading, Aunt Frances?"

"Oh, novels, my dear. And nothing but. All sorts, but I particularly like horrid novels."

"Do you?" Susannah had always been too busy social-izing and sleeping off the effects of the socializing to do very much reading, but *horrid* novels sounded intriguing. "What are they like?"

"They all have a ghost, and include dark and stormy nights, and secrets and the like. They're delicious, actually. Oh, and I'm a great admirer of Miss Austen, too. Very funny and romantic, Miss Austen is. All about lost love, and found love, and betrayal, and unrequited love, and such. And everyone lives happily ever after." She pronounced those last three words weightily, and gave Susannah a meaningful look.

Aunt Frances wasn't terribly subtle.

Odd to think of her as a romantic, this stout matron with the long face and merry eyes.

"Were you ever married, Aunt Frances?" Susannah broached tentatively. She hoped it wasn't a sensitive question. Perhaps Aunt Frances knew firsthand of unrequited love, which was how she'd guessed Susannah's own circumstances.

"Was I ever married?" Aunt Frances gave her thigh a gleeful little slap. "Good heavens, look at your sympathetic face, my dear. Of course I've been married. I've been *thoroughly* married. Wore three good husbands out, Susannah. Put the last one in the ground a year or so ago. Rather liked having this little place all to myself for a time, but then it does get to feeling a bit lonely come the winter evenings. I suppose I could acquire another husband, but in truth, Miss Austen's stories are all I need in the way of romance these days. And I suppose *you'll* have to do for company."

She winked at Susannah, and plucked up her knitting. "Will you sew and chat with me, or will you read aloud?"

"Perhaps we can do both. Chat *and* read."

"We've many dozens of evenings ahead of us in which to do both, Susannah. I think you might enjoy a little tale to take your mind off of things, for just this evening."

Those "many dozens of evenings" ahead of her sounded a bit like an advancing enemy army. Then again, her aunt had spoken of acquiring husbands as though one bought them at the milliner's shop. It should take at least a few of those evenings to discuss all of those husbands.

"Very well. Do you have a favorite novel?"

"Oh . . . let's start with *Pride and Prejudice*, shall we? If Mr. Darcy doesn't make you forget all about that young fool you left behind, my dear, I'll eat my knitting."

Miss Austen was funny and romantic, her aunt said. Why did the viscount suddenly spring to mind? He was funny, perhaps. Irritating, certainly. But romantic? Not in the way Douglas had been, all charm and compliments and calculated grace. Though his *gaze* had been somehow more intimate, more physical, than the one kiss she'd shared with Douglas. That was certainly romantic in another way.

And then there was the heart carved into the tree. That heart was virtually branded upon her imagination now.

Susannah opened *Pride and Prejudice* a little tentatively, and read the first sentence to herself. "'It is a truth universally acknowledged, that a single man in possession of a good fortune, must be in want of a wife.'"

Susannah blinked. Those words were fairly *embossed* in irony.

She thoroughly approved.

So she read that sentence aloud, and the one that followed it, and the one that followed that, while her aunt's clicking knitting needles and chuckles marked off the time. Aunt Frances had a way of kicking her ankles a bit when she heard something she enjoyed. Susannah would see them flying up out of the corner of her eye each time she read a particularly acerbic line.

And before she knew it, she'd turned more than a dozen pages, the lamps had burned low, and an entire evening had passed.

She couldn't truthfully say she'd been bored.

Only dozens and dozens and dozens more evenings to go.

Two diffident stable boys, gangly with youth, cast furtive glances up at Susannah from beneath their caps when she arrived at the stables, then quickly turned and pretended to be busy pitchforking straw into stalls. The viscount, towering and impatience in his shirtsleeves, turned, saw her . . . and slowly took in her willow green riding habit and the hat with the plume in it. Beginning at the top, with the hat.

All right: She knew she was a little late this morning, but the riding habit she'd finally chosen brought out the green in her eyes, made them *glow,* in fact, subduing the golds and blues in them. And she knew the plume of her hat was a little worse for wear ever since the carriage had tipped over in the yard of the coaching inn, taking her trunk down with it, but it was still pert enough. And she was virtually certain the lunch basket she'd hooked over her arm was a fetching addition to her ensemble.

Why, then, did the man look so bloody *amused*?

He turned away from her again. "We had a choice of four geldings or a stallion, Miss Makepeace, and I've saddled a fine gelding for you, because I'm afraid the mare is ready to burst. She should be foaling any day now." He outlined the star between the horse's eyes with his finger; his voice, and the gesture, gruffly tender. For some reason it made Susannah's breath catch.

"She's lovely." Susannah tugged off one of her gloves to touch the mare's velvety nose. She'd left her own mare behind.

Thank goodness, then, she'd threatened a man with a vase, in part to rescue her riding habits.

It occurred to her that evenings full of Jane Austen were only going to encourage her predilection for irony.

"Come," the viscount said, and cupped his hands for her boot and boosted her up on to the saddled gray gelding as if she weighed no more than the plume in her hat. Happiness surged; Susannah intended to enjoy this ride even if it *was* the name of employment, and she did ride beautifully. He swept his eyes over her posture and apparently approved, because he swung himself swiftly into the saddle of his gelding and kneed it into a slow trot out of the stableyard. Susannah adjusted her basket over her arm and urged her own mount to follow.

The gelding lurched forward for a few bizarre little hopping steps, then gave its head a dramatic toss and stopped so abruptly she nearly toppled from the saddle. Susannah was thrown forward; she pulled the reins tight in her fists, balanced herself by gripping the saddle.

She was mortified. Any casual observer would have thought she'd never before sat a horse. She murmured to the gelding and soothed him with little pats, and though its ears switched wildly too and fro, and its haunches twitched, she managed, through the sheer force of her charm, to persuade him to break into some semblance of a trot.

Dear God, it was as though an invisible rope was tugging him forward.

What on earth was troubling the poor creature?

The viscount glanced over his shoulder; Susannah saw the quick bright flash of his blue eyes as he took in her scarlet face—Susannah suspected her face was destined to be scarlet anytime she was in the vicinity of the viscount—and his fair brows leaping upward in a question. She gave him a winning unconcerned smile. The gelding danced sideways like a drunk staggering out of a pub and nearly bounced her from the saddle again.

The viscount was out of his own saddle and next to her in just a few long strides, and his hand went to her horse's bridle. Good lord, but the man was quick.

"I'd like you to dismount, Miss Makepeace."

Disappointment roiling sickly in the pit of her stomach, her face hot, Susannah swung her leg around the calf block, and the viscount lifted her down from the gelding as swiftly and matter-of-factly as if she were a stack of plates on a high shelf and set her aside.

"Lord Grantham, I assure you I—"

He put up a hand. His face was distant; he was as tense as a cocked pistol.

The gelding, on the other hand, was considerably calmer now. Its ears continued to switch forward and back like a weathervane in a breeze; it rolled its eyes at Susannah one more time, then hastily ambled over to join Kit's horse, its gait perfectly smooth, as if it couldn't *wait* to get away from her. As if she were a bloody *wolf*, for heaven's sake.

Puzzled, Kit took Susannah in: chin up, fair cheeks flushed in embarrassment, the very fetching riding habit—

he did like the green—the plume, the basket on her arm, the—

He could have sworn that the lid of the basket had just . . . bumped up. Just a little.

He hadn't been drinking the night before, he'd had a decent night's sleep . . . there was nothing, really, he could point to that might cause him to hallucinate.

It happened again: the lid . . . bumped up. As though something alive was inside it . . . and trying to escape. A leather loop loosely latched the basket.

"Put the basket down, Susannah." He said it quietly.

"I thought we were going to—"

"Put the basket *down*. Do it very carefully. But do it now."

What she saw in his face made the high color leave her own. She did it: she lowered the basket to the ground; he could see her hands trembling now.

"Now come stand next to me. Quickly."

She took a tentative step forward, clearly not eager to get closer to his stern expression. His arm shot out impatiently curled her swiftly the rest of the way into his side, and he held her fast. To her credit, she didn't even gasp.

"What—"

"Hush," he said abruptly. He kept his arm tightly around her.

Kit didn't see a long stick anywhere within reaching distance, and swore softly. It would have made a useful tool in this circumstance. And for God's sake, it might only be a squirrel or a mouse, something benign or inconsequential, and then wouldn't he look foolish?

The lid of the basket bumped up a little again.

Kit wasn't conditioned to think things might be "benign" or "inconsequential." They so seldom were, at least in his world.

So he lashed out a foot and toppled the basket over.

And an adder nearly as thick as Susannah's arm darted out.

Kit swiftly lifted Susannah up into his arms as it whipped past; she ducked her head in his chest.

Fortunately the adder's retreat was hasty and complete.

"It's all right," he said softly. "You're all right. It's gone."

Susannah said nothing for a time; just breathed swiftly in and out. She was warm and lithe in his arms; the faintest scent of lavender, and that mysterious sweetness of her own, the scent he'd discovered at the nape of her neck the day he'd caught her spying on him, rose up to him, released by the heat of her skin.

"It was a snake." Her voice, a trifle unsteady, was muffled against his shirt.

"It was, indeed," he said softly. Her breath had found a gap between the buttons of his shirt; it washed over his skin in a very nearly hypnotic rhythm. In . . . and out. In . . . and out. In . . . and—

He put her down so quickly she nearly staggered.

"Thoughtful of you to bring a specimen along *with* you to sketch, Miss Makepeace," he said abruptly, to disguise the fact that he felt a little unsteady, too.

To his astonishment, she actually managed a weak smile.

Surprise: again, a useful way to take the measure of a person.

He looked at her carefully. Her eyes were a little too bright, and her face was a little pale, but she wasn't wobbling on her legs, or shrieking. And the sheer surprise of that adder could have stopped the heart of many a stout man.

"Was *that* one poisonous?" she wanted to know. Her voice was a little threadbare.

"Yes," he told her, gently. "It was. Not very poisonous, but . . . yes, it was. And that's what was troubling your horse." Both horses had wandered a few feet away from them, and were now nipping contentedly at the short meadow grass. "Did you perhaps put that basket down outside, Susannah, or open it before you left the house this morning? Did you ever leave it unattended?"

"No, I never did. Aunt Frances packed my lunch last night, and put it on the shelf on the mud porch, just as she did yesterday. Perhaps . . . perhaps the adder found its way in last night, somehow?"

"I suppose it's possible . . ." *Not bloody likely, however.* "But . . . well, adders are very shy. They—" A cascade of boyhood memories crowded into his mind, and he knew that taking the mystery out of something could take away the fear of it. "Shall I tell you about them?"

Susannah nodded, albeit cautiously.

"Well, this one looked like a female adder—she was a little brighter in color than a male. Almost green." Almost *too* green, in fact, he realized suddenly. The ones in the Barnstable region tended to be lighter in color.

"She was pretty," Susannah said bravely. "Very shiny. Lovely marks."

"She *was* pretty, wasn't she?" he agreed enthusiastically. "*Big* for an adder, too."

"W-was she?"

"Oh, yes! And you'll notice she blended quite well into the grass, as adders are designed specifically *not* to be seen. When I was a boy, I eventually became quite good at spotting them," he added proudly. "And adders are not any fonder of people than people are of adders, which is why it would be unusual for her to enter your house. And did you know adders have their young this time of year? And adder venom can make you quite ill, but in most cases, it won't kill you, unless you're already frail, or you're a dog. And as you are neither . . ."

He trailed off when he realized Susannah was watching. Head tilted, wearing a slight smile. In his experience, women did that sort of thing when they were about to say something disconcerting.

"This makes you happy, doesn't it? Adders and voles and . . ." She swept her hand about, indicating the universe of greenery surrounding them. "Studying them. Knowing about them."

He stared at her. *No,* he wanted to bark incredulously. *Are you mad? This is exile.*

Except . . . he was a proponent of accuracy.

He turned abruptly and walked a few paces away from her and gathered the reins of their horses. Susannah's mount, a considerably calmer beast now, came docilely. He led them to where she stood.

"Will we need to draw adders as part of this folio?" she wanted to know, when he still didn't speak.

The devil in him made him say it. "To be thorough, it would be nice to have at least one proper adder in the folio."

There was an eloquent pause.

"Perhaps I can draw it from memory," Susannah suggested testily.

"Perhaps we'll be lucky enough to see another."

She scowled, which made him laugh, which teased her scowl into a smile again. "If I must, I must," she said dramatically. "After all, you do keep Aunt Frances and I in sausages. But I seem to be having rather a run of *luck* lately."

"A run?" Kit gave the basket another nudge with his foot; nothing else slithered out; he picked it up, inspected the inside more closely. Finding no other living things, only lunch and a sketchbook, he presented it to her. She took it very, very gingerly. "Did something else happen, Miss Makepeace?"

"Well, there was . . . my father dying, you see. That was rather a significant something." Said with admirable dryness. "And then there was—" she stopped, and he had the distinct sense she was skipping over something. "And then there was the mail coach tipping over in the inn yard—"

Kit frowned. "The mail coach *tipped over* in the inn yard?"

"As I was traveling to Barnstable. Something to do with the wheels, I believe? I was too tired to pay much attention to the cause."

A peculiar apprehension crawled up Kit's spine. Mail coaches didn't typically just . . . *tip over.* The idea of it was as discordant as an adder in a basket. A linchpin would have had to come loose enough for a wheel to shake off completely, or an axel would have had to snap. And the roads weren't rough enough at this time of year to snap an axel, unless the axel was already severely compromised.

Oh, bloody hell. Perhaps he simply saw patterns of nefariousness everywhere now; the price—the reward?—of life as an agent of the crown. But an adder in a picnic basket? A tipped coach? A watching man? He'd found crushed twigs yesterday when he'd investigated the place he'd seen the man standing; he'd seen part of a footprint pressed into some old leaves. And that was all.

A chilly little wind of suspicion ruffled his instincts. And his instincts had kept him alive again and again in situations that rightly should have finished him off. Well, instincts, and his impressive complement of practical skills with weapons.

But thirty days and a folio were all that stood between him and Egypt.

Again: *bloody hell.* Surrendering to his instincts might very well get him exiled for good. They had work to do. He drew in a deep breath, exhaled his exasperation.

"Well, they say bad luck comes in threes, Miss Makepeace, so I think you've had your run of it."

"*Do* they say that about bad luck?"

"Well, *I'm* saying it now."

She pondered this, head tilted back. "Because I'm not certain whether to count my father's death and the loss of my home as one thing, or two."

How on earth to respond? "Fives, then," he amended. "Bad luck comes in *fives.*"

This inanity, remarkably, made her smile again. And granted, it was just a slow, wry curve of that lovely mouth. But for some reason it pleased him beyond all proportion.

Which led him to this swift and startling realization: he rather liked Susannah Makepeace. It shifted his balance, a little, this realization: he couldn't recall the last time he'd simply . . . liked a woman. For years he'd seen them only in terms of . . . challenge. They were a necessity, a palliative, a diversion. Not something simply to enjoy, the way

one enjoyed . . . well, a summer day. The kind with a soft
breeze and something cool to drink.

"Do you feel equal to drawing today?" he asked, uncomfortable, suddenly, with the fact that he was comfortable.

"Oh, for heaven's sake. It was only an adder."

It was a passing good imitation of nonchalance. They
smiled at each other, both enjoying her bravado, and then
he cupped his hands for her boot and lifted her up to the
gelding again. *Ferns,* he told himself.

Chapter Eight

Morley cradled Fluff in the crook of one arm and combed his fingers through the soft hair on his belly. Fluff regarded Bob through sleepy, contemptuous gold eyes.

"When I said 'make it look like an accident,' Bob, I meant of the *permanent* variety. I didn't mean make her a little *ill* for a little while." Two days he'd waited for news of Susannah Makepeace's demise. And now *this*?

"T'was a right large adder, Mr. Morley—"

"Which would have been splendid, had it been possible to *frighten* the girl to death. You might as well say, 'it was a right large *apple*, Mr. Morley,' for how much true danger an adder presents."

This blisteringly icy stream of sarcasm made Bob blink. "I'm a London man born and bred, sir. What would I know of the country? And it was right difficult finding that bloody snake, too," he added on a mutter. He'd needed to buy the adder, in fact, from an odd old woman, a witch, some whispered, who specialized in the sales of crawling things. Bob was proud of the snake, the basket, creeping in at dawn to do it, the whole plan, in fact. Proud of the mail coach. Timing and stealth and skill had been required, knowledge and expertise gained only through years of experience.

Bloody difficult to make things look like an accident.

"And Caroline? What of her?" Morley demanded.

"Can't be everywhere at once, sir."

Bob was getting cheeky. Then again, he wasn't accustomed to failing, and perhaps it was taking a toll on both of them.

"Caroline Allston is not inconspicuous, Bob."

"But she *is* clever, Mr. Morley."

"No, Bob," Morley explained, strained patience weighting his words like lead. "She is *not* clever."

Beautiful, wily, unpredictable as an animal. All instinct. But *not* clever. Not his Caroline.

His Caroline. Odd, but it was how he used to think of her. How he still thought of her, even as they now attempted to hunt her down.

There was a long silence, during which Morley consulted his watch and Bob scuffed his feet nervously on the carpet.

"Sir, you know I'm a *profess*—"

"Then get it *done,* Bob."

Morley turned and lowered Fluff to the ground. The cat stretched and flicked his tail, unhappy at the interruption in attention.

Morley realized Bob was still standing there, when in essence his words had been a dismissal. "Yes?" he made the word a hiss of impatience.

"*Must* it be an accident, Mr. Morley?"

"Lost faith in your own repertoire of nefarious skills, Bob?"

Bob looked at him blankly.

"Can't do it?" Morley translated, keeping his sarcasm checked with some difficulty.

"It's just that she's never alone, sir. Always with that great fair-headed geezer."

This was new. "And who would this 'great fair-headed geezer' be, Bob?"

"Not certain, sir. They appear to be wandering about and . . . and"—his brow wrinkled—"*drawing* things." His tone said everything about how he felt about the peculiar habits of the gentry. "Looks like a farmer," he further illuminated. "Dresses like one, anyhow."

"Bob. Just go ahead and get it done. In your own inimitable, skillful, professional manner. And find out who the 'geezer' is, if you would. It might be important."

"Really, sir? It needn't be an accident?" Bob had brightened; his eyes were alight with new plans. "Because you see, after one too many accidents . . ."

"Accidents cease to look like accidents. I understand. Use your own excellent judgment, Bob. Please report back only when you've succeeded . . . or if you've new information."

Bob clicked his heels, his confidence restored now that his options had expanded. "You can count on me, sir. I'm a professional."

A little more than a week of riding through meadows and trudging about the woods had yielded sketches of the White Oak, some squirrels, and a few ferns, but the woods were filled with wild medicinal herbs, too, Kit knew, and it would take days to document them.

One month, his father had said. *Thorough,* his father had said. As if Kit would ever do any other kind of job of it. Every sketch in that book kept Egypt at bay.

He led their saddled geldings from the stable. "Today we go in search of Hellebore," he announced to Susannah.

Her vivacity instantly dropped several degrees. "Tell me 'Hellebore' isn't what it sounds like."

He grinned at that. "Fear not, Mis Makepeace. Hellebore will never creep into your picnic basket. It's an herb. A medicinal—some would say poisonous herb—that grows wild in this area. It's been used as a purgative and to bless cattle, among other things. And in . . . magic spells."

Speaking of magic spells, she was wearing the green hat again, which made her eyes glow a nearly mesmerizing shade. He knew now that her eyes were in fact hazel, which wasn't in and of itself a magical thing, but he couldn't help be fascinated by their ability to take on the color of things near them.

He cupped his hands for her boot and lifted her into the saddle, and Susannah hooked her leg over the calf block, settling into the saddle, taking the reins up in her hands. "Perhaps we should cast a spell upon—"

The gelding beneath her reared with a scream, his forelegs flailing the air. He heard Susannah gasp as she pulled the reins tightly in her fists. The horse came down hard and bucked out twice.

And launched into a headlong run.

Sweet Lucifer.

Kit vaulted into the saddle of his own horse and kicked it into a gallop. That gelding intended to unseat Susannah, and in single-minded horse fashion was heading straight for a tree branch in order to accomplish it.

Her hat flew from her head, a bright disk of green hurtling through the air, and she was leaning over the pommel now, clinging to the horse's neck, struggling to regain her balance and losing the battle for it. He saw her slip, and his heart flew into his throat. Bloody *sidesaddles*.

Kit kicked harder, harder, urging his horse to stretch out in punishingly long swift strides until he finally drew flush with Susannah.

To his horror, Kit saw her saddle slip roughly sideways, as though the girth had loosened. Susannah looped her arms around the frenzied horse's neck, clinging desperately now; the reins had become nearly useless to her.

Harder. He kicked his poor horse harder, goading it and goading it, cursing the fact that he couldn't bloody *fly*, until he finally drew past Susannah's gelding. And then he yanked his horse up short to a rearing halt and threw himself out of the saddle just as Susannah began to fall. He lunged for her, pulled her into his arms the moment the sidesaddle slid completely beneath the gelding's belly.

But the shift in gravity and the weight of their two falling bodies was too much for her gelding; it lost its footing. Kit flung Susannah aside just as the horse came down on him.

Blinding pain in his shoulder.

Blackness as his breath left him.

And then mercifully, quickly, the horse righted itself, thrashing its way to its feet.

Kit lay stunned, flat against the earth. He struggled to inhale, and couldn't. He choked, wheezing; in a moment there was breath in his lungs again. With great difficulty, he levered his torso upright.

Pain.

"Susannah. . . ," he gasped, turned his head, which sent a cloud of tiny dots swaying and bobbing before his eyes. He saw her through them, whole, sound, her face stark white above the green of her habit, the sky oddly brilliant behind her, her shoulders heaving with terrified breathing.

Pride and masculinity forced him to get all the way up on his feet as she rushed for him.

I am not going to faint. He took a step, but moving made him nauseous.

Now, vomit, on other hand—that *I might just do.*

He knew more than a little about pain; so he closed his eyes, took a deep breaths, exhaled, did it again, to steady himself.

"*Kit.*" She was next to him now. "God, please don't move. Are you—"

Well, then. At last she'd called him Kit. "You're all right?" His voice was a little wheezy, barely a voice. He opened his eyes; those black dots were still everywhere.

She squeaked. "Am *I* all right?" Am *I*? A *horse* fell on you."

He winced. "Only part of a horse," he voice was steadier now. "His shoulder and foreleg. Not the entire horse. Your voice hurts," he added absurdly. "Too squeaky."

"But are you—" Still squeaky. She stopped, adjusted her tone. "You're hurt, you *must* be." Her hand reached out reflexively.

"Careful of the shoulder," he heard himself say calmly. "Best not touch it."

Those black dots were floating like a flock of tiny birds

before his eyes. His voice sounded distant in his own ears. *I am not going to faint.*

"Your face . . ."

"Was already like that before the horse fell on me, Miss Makepeace."

"Don't jest," she said curtly. "I can see it hurts. Breathe through it, through the pain. Deep breaths. Is anything broken?"

Kit wiggled his fingers, then raised his elbow a little, all of which hurt like the very devil, but the fact that all of those parts still functioned was a very good sign indeed. Tomorrow was going to be *deeply* unpleasant.

"Just sprained and bruised, I think. I hope. My arm took the brunt of it. And . . . my ribs might be a little bruised. I'm bloody lucky. He wasn't on me long."

"Lucky?" Susannah repeated incredulously. "I would say you've inherited *my* sort of luck." And then she looked at him closely; he saw her face go worried at what she saw. "Kit . . . are you sure . . ."

He could only imagine how white his face must be. He felt bleached clear through, strangely hollow. "It's just . . . my body seems to want to go into shock. Struck my elbow in just the right place. Or wrong place. Happens that way."

"Breathe," she said gently. "I'll catch you if you fall, if you insist on standing."

He gave a faint laugh. But it was sensible advice, and somehow, he liked hearing her give it. So he did it, took more deep breaths, exhaling the pain with each one. A fine cold sweat gathered on his brow and over his back, but the black dots slowed their frantic dance before his eyes. He was more certain now that he wasn't going to faint in front of her. He thought he might like to lie down, however. And he was *positive* he was going to drink quite a bit the moment he returned to the house. Bloody hell, but he'd need a sling, at the very least.

What on earth had possessed a perfectly amiable horse to try to kill its rider? It couldn't possibly be another adder.

Kit's curiosity overcame his pain. He held his injured arm close to his side, gingerly, and slowly went to the gelding. The animal was still a little wild-eyed, and he tossed his head at Kit's approach, but he didn't try to bolt. He was clearly much happier with Susannah out of the saddle. Feeling much more himself.

"Ho, my lad," Kit said soothingly, reaching his good arm up to touch him. "What's got into you, eh? Shall we take a look?"

Susannah touched the horse, too, gently, calmingly on the flank.

"Poor beast. It was the saddle, I think. The moment I settled into it, he desperately wanted me *out* of it. And then the saddle itself . . . it felt as though it came loose. I tried to hold on, I did, and you . . ." She paused. "Thank you," she said simply. "You saved my—"

Kit gave a short, nonchalant, heroic shrug, which hurt, but it cut off her words. And then he used his good arm to try to pull the saddle from the horse, but the hefty leather of it was awkward. Susannah quickly took the other end of it. They deposited it on the ground, and Kit flipped it over with the toe of his boot. Then he slowly knelt, mindful of his throbbing limbs. While Susannah watched, he ran his hand across over the underside of the saddle skirt, searching carefully, feeling over every inch of where it might touch the horse.

He stopped when something pricked his finger.

It was a small twig with an end so sharp it nearly looked deliberately sharpened, and it had somehow lodged between the panel and the skirt of the sidesaddle. The added weight of a rider would have driven it right into the haunch of the horse. Not deeply enough to cause much damage, or a great wound . . . just deeply enough to cause great pain to the horse.

And possibly kill the rider, should the horse have succeeded in bucking the rider off.

A horrible little coincidence, perhaps. Any number of odd little things could find their way into a stable. Perhaps a saddle had been dropped to the floor of it, and the twig had become lodged there, or . . .

"Here's the culprit," he said lightly, holding the twig up. But he didn't drop it to the ground; he pocketed it.

Kit was having a difficult time stringing his thoughts together; pain had set up an annoying buzz in his mind. He took in another breath. He'd need a drink *soon*.

He examined the girth of the saddle, and saw that it had snapped entirely where it joined the leather beneath the flap, a place one wouldn't normally notice as they cinched the saddle around the belly of the horse. He supposed he could shout at the stable boys, but it wasn't entirely their fault. He ran the girth through his fingers; the leather was somewhat brittle with age.

Brittle enough to break?

Susannah had been using this sidesaddle for days.

He looked closely at the snapped ends. The break looked almost . . . too clean.

A chill settled into his gut. He couldn't shake the unreal sense that a knife had assisted the girth in breaking.

The watching man.

The mail coach, the adder . . .

The twig, the girth . . .

And this was a sidesaddle. No man was about to get into a sidesaddle.

Only a woman.

He looked up at Susannah, who was still quietly watching him. Behind her he could see the woefully crumpled green plume of her hat on the ground, fluttering in a breeze, and her hair was a little wild from her ride, spilling about her face. He'd never before seen it down, and his gut clutched in response. Lovely hair. So many subtle colors in the strands. Mahogany, and chestnut, and sable, and . . .

She suddenly seemed so . . . crushable standing there. Eminently fragile. How easily she could have been gravely injured today. What a near thing, what a very near thing, it had been.

An irrational fury, almost a panic, made his breath come short again.

How do you tell a woman who has just lost everything in her life that he suspected someone was trying to kill her?

You didn't say anything of the sort until you were entirely sure.

Susannah's gelding was nosing about for grass now next to his own mount, who was doing the same thing. Their reins trailed the ground. Susannah's poor gelding looked considerably more sound than Kit felt. *Glad I provided a soft place to land,* Kit thought mordantly.

"You're not in the army now. You don't have to endure the pain if you don't want to. There's a little something called laudanum that might help."

Susannah was trying a joke, but it didn't register, as his thoughts were elsewhere entirely. He would begin, he decided, by inspecting the saddles and having a chat with the stable boys.

"Yes." His voice was distant. "Or whiskey."

He wasn't certain whether walking or riding back to the stables would jar his body more, then decided it wouldn't make a difference; it would hurt like the very devil regardless.

"Thank you again for saving my life," she said gravely.

For some reason the tone made him smile. "It's the least I can do for a valuable employee, Miss Makepeace. You're certain you're sound?"

"The horse," she emphasized, "fell on *you*. Not me. You flung me out of the way."

He couldn't smile at that. *But it could have been you,* he thought. *It could have been you.*

The thought kept him from speaking.

He gathered the reins of his horse in his hand, and Susannah followed suit. He'd decided to walk, and slowly at that. Out of the corner of his eye he saw the hat again, a shade that had never grown in nature. "Willow," he knew it was called; fashionable in London just now, or so he'd heard. No actual willow tree was ever this color, but it did make Susannah's eyes glow that remarkable, mesmerizing shade of green. And for that he would forgive it anything.

"Your hat," he said.

"Oh." Susannah strolled over and plucked it up, gave the irreparably crushed feather a disconsolate stroke. "I did like this hat," she said.

"So did I," he said, unthinkingly.

Her eyebrows arced with astonishment. "A *compliment*, my lord?"

"An observation, Miss Makepeace," he corrected hurriedly.

But for some reason his answer made her give him a slow, softly radiant smile, as though he were her prize pupil. And oddly, for a moment, just that moment, nothing hurt at all.

Chapter Nine

Pettishaw, a relatively new MP, was droning on and on about the need for parliamentary reform. The faces around him were arranged in varying expressions of attention; some were even nodding. In agreement? Morley wondered. Or fighting off sleep? Difficult to know, really. The beauty of the House of Commons, Morley thought, was that someone would ultimately say something hopelessly rude and direct to shut Pettishaw up. A man was given but few opportunities to prove his oratory talents, and if he demonstrated that he had none, he was heartily discouraged from then on from orating at all. They could be an unruly crew, the Commons.

Morley's own voice was deep and pleasant; it carried enough warmth and inflection to keep the listener awake, and he had a knack for eloquently persuading while never veering into floridity or drama. In other words, he'd never been told in rude and uncertain terms to shut up. His political talents, in fact, had been compared to those of Charles

Fox, only Morley was better looking and he hadn't Fox's bad, if colorful, habits of gambling and womanizing.

Morley's leg ached; it often did in session, because these rooms seemed to hold the damp and release it just to plague him. He was grateful, in a way, because the ache reminded him of how he'd come to be here. He was grateful, too, for the scars that scored the length of it—great, ugly rippling scars, like calcified flame. Women often mistook the limp and the scars for a war wound, and he never disabused them of the notion. It *was* a war wound, as far as he was concerned. At least of a sort.

And he'd seduced more than a few of them based on that alone.

For some reason, however, he'd told Caroline the truth of it.

It had become useful, another tool. Morley was accustomed to thinking of everything in terms of how it served him.

Like Bob. Who was hopefully serving him by spending the day in Barnstable finishing the job he'd been assigned, so Morley could continue to sit in the Commons, taking for granted voluble politicians and the faultless reputation he'd earned.

His father had been a farmer. More truthfully, a peasant. His family had been large, and they'd eked out a living on a patch of land scarcely the size of four handkerchiefs sewn together, or so it seemed now from a perspective of years. But then industry had moved in, and the spinners and button-makers and poor farmers like his father had lost their livelihoods to machines that did the work faster if not better, and to landowners who built factories on all of the handkerchief-sized patches of land. His father had taken his family—his mother and brothers and sisters—into London to look for work.

Unfortunately, *everyone* who had lost their livelihoods—and they were legion—had migrated to London from the country, looking for work. Or to other factory towns. Consequently, no work was to be had. The Morley family then set out to slowly starve in St. Giles, which is where Thaddeus had made so many interesting and ultimately useful friends.

And then came the fire.

It killed everyone in the Morley family's lodging house—his entire family, in fact—except for himself, for some reason known only to the fates. He'd been gravely injured, his leg blackened and blistered, but the wealthy building owner, stricken with conscience, perhaps—the building had been a disaster, after all—or perhaps wishing to buy his way into heaven, paid for Thaddeus's care, and then, discovering he was a bright boy, paid for him to go to Eton.

And then he'd grown bored of the largesse, and completely forgot about Thaddeus Morley. Leaving Morley floundering.

But only briefly.

Because he had wit, intelligence, charm, a handsome face, a sympathy-eliciting limp, and a great, helpful, deeply buried seam of rage that ran like lava through his soul and fueled his enormous ambition. He wasn't overly burdened with scruples; living in St. Giles taught one the frivolousness of scruples. He used them selectively. A connection with a few old friends involved him briefly in the distribution of smuggled goods, and he invested his earnings wisely, and earned his way into Oxford.

And after Oxford, nothing would satisfy him other than a parliamentary seat. Where he would set out to attempt justice for people like his family.

And . . . well, perhaps exact just a little revenge, as well.

But getting there had been like climbing the face of a cliff with bare hands. To be elected to the House of Commons, he desperately needed money to campaign. And he'd thought he'd found the support he needed when the Earl of Westphall invited him to a party over the winter holidays. The earl had, for reasons of his own, regretfully declined to contribute any funds to Morley's election. However, the Westphall party *had* yielded Caroline Allston. And so, in retrospect, Morley did have the Earl of Westphall to thank for his entire political career.

He remembered his first sight of Caroline Allston—he'd been astounded to find such a creature in a town like Barnstable—and knew instantly she was another person who would need to scale the faces of rock cliffs with her bare hands. Her beauty was wasted in the country town; Morley knew how to make *excellent* use of it.

He remembered those blue eyes of the earl son's, Kit Whitelaw, Viscount Grantham, burning into him that evening. Even at seventeen, the boy had possessed an unnerving intensity. The hurt and longing in them as he'd watched Morley and Caroline. Clever boy. He'd known.

His leg twitched violently, suddenly. Morley covered it with his hand, soothing it like a restless pet, willing the pain to subside. He remembered a time when Caroline could tell from a glance at his face when the pain in his leg became unbearable. Without saying a word, she would knead the pain away, and chatter to him about something else as she did it.

Pettishaw was still droning on. Morley glanced about the room; Groves, an MP who hailed from Leeds, intercepted the glance and rolled his eyes. Morley gave him a faint, commiserating smile.

His arrangement with Caroline had at first been simple: She warmed his bed in endlessly original ways, he paid for her keep. She was grateful and young and excited by him; they both recognized the value of their alliance.

But Morley saw everyone and everything as useful or not useful; sentiment (for people, anyhow, cats were another story) had been burned out of him in the fire.

So when Morley saw Caroline's effect on other men, his busy mind went to work. At a private dinner he'd strategically introduced her to a naval captain he'd met socially, who, as it turned out, became garrulous after he'd made love, as most men did. Garrulous, and particularly careless after too much wine, and hence, helpful beyond words.

Soon after that, Caroline had gleefully gifted Morley with the most marvelous information. Numbers and types and names of ships, and the numbers and types of guns they carried. Where and how they would be deployed. The officers who commanded them, and the names of other officers aboard. Snippets of information, mostly, and a document here, and a document there, things Caroline purloined when the captain was sleeping. But useful and very *valuable*—to the right people.

French people.

And the sale of this information was how he'd financed his campaign. And how he'd been elected. And how he'd built his wealth. And why he still sat here today, with a reputation for calmly crusading for the rights of children and workers, for tasteful dress and a moderate lifestyle. He'd been faultless ever since.

Almost faultless.

He glanced around the chambers now, and thought: *Surely these men are plagued by more ghosts than I? Surely they have more blood on their hands, having aimed rifles and cannons at flesh-and-blood men during war, with the goal of taking as many lives as they possibly could?*

And his own hands might even have remained entirely clean, if bloody nosey fellow MP Richard Lockwood hadn't happened to meet that particular naval captain socially, too. Or if the naval captain hadn't innocently, and with great enthusiasm, told Lockwood all about his encounters with a beautiful woman introduced to him by Thaddeus Morley. The topic had been mistresses, apparently, and the naval captain had been eager to brag, since Lockwood had such a splendid mistress of his own in Anna Holt, who had just been installed in her own home in the town of Gorringe and now needed a household staff.

"Asked a lot of questions about you and the girl, Lockwood did," the naval captain had told Morley cheerily. "Perhaps he's casting about for a new mistress. What became of her, by the way?" he asked hopefully.

"Found a wealthier protector," Morley had lied mournfully. Caroline hadn't yet left him at the time; her departure with the handsome American merchant was still two years away. But he'd tucked her back into her quiver, to be used again when the time came, and made certain she wasn't seen publicly.

Perhaps Lockwood hadn't reckoned on the strength of Morley's sense for things dark, for self-preservation.

It had almost been child's play to discover what Lockwood had been about, and to put a stop to it. It wasn't a pleasant business; he hadn't taken pleasure in it, but it had needed to be done, and he'd undertaken it like a job, planned it and executed it. And he'd thought it *had* been done . . . certainly, he'd begun to ease into complacency in the ensuing years.

And then Makepeace's letter had arrived.

Well, if his political career was to be bookended by murders, perhaps it couldn't be helped. He'd been seeing more of Bob lately than he preferred, but he was looking forward to their next visit more anxiously than he preferred.

By the time he saw Susannah home and returned to the house, Kit felt . . . well, exactly as though a horse had fallen upon him. Pain sang a nasty chorus all up and down his nerve endings. He could scarcely tell where it began and ended.

Bullton stopped in his tracks when he saw him enter the house.

"Sir?" Bullton's face was eloquent with the question.

"A horse fell on me, Bullton."

"Ah. Whiskey, sir?"

Good man. "If you can spare yours, Bullton."

"And a doctor?"

"I don't think so. But I'll let you know. If you'd help me with the stairs?"

"Of course, sir."

"And I need a pen and foolscap, if you will."

"You'll be writing your will, sir?"

"I do appreciate the attempt at wit, Bullton, and rest assured I am laughing on the inside. Laughing on the *outside* rather jars everything at the moment. No, I'll be writing . . . some important correspondence." He knew just how to word it, too, to avoid arousing the suspicions of anyone who might want to intercept it—particularly his father.

"Very good, sir. Foolscap and a pen it is."

The two of them, Kit and Bullton, got Kit's aching body up the stairs, and then they got him out of his shirt and into a sling. The arm felt better when the muscles and tendons were relieved of the need to move at all. Some bolted whiskey, helped with the rest of the pain; Bullton imbibed, too, as Kit hated to drink alone. Kit gingerly prodded his ribs, took in a few deep testing breaths. They weren't broken, he warranted. He knew from experience that broken ribs were excruciating and unmistakable. If he could move without stifling screams, no doubt he was only severely bruised.

"How is your penmanship, Bullton?"

"Fair, sir."

"Fair as in 'maiden fair,' or fair as in, 'only passable'?" Kit was feeling a little drunk now, and it wasn't unpleasant.

"The former, sir. If you don't mind my saying so."

"Not at all, Bullton, not at all. I admire a man who isn't afraid to admit to his talents. Take a letter for me, if you would then, and let's have a little more of that whiskey while we write it, shall we?"

A bottle of whiskey later, the letter read:

Dear sirs,
   I am writing on behalf of my neighbor, who was traveling your coach line en route to visit her aunt in the town of Barnstable when your conveyance apparently "tipped over" in the yard of the coaching

inn, leading to a ride with a randy farmer, irreparable damage to her favorite hat (a very fine green one), and immeasurable overall distress. I am tempted to bring my considerable influence to bear in order to exact retribution and to discourage other passengers from riding your line, but I may settle for a full accounting of the precise cause of the accident and an assurance that it will not happen again. Rest assured, the information you impart will remain confidential. Your hasty reply is appreciated.

    Christopher Whitelaw, Viscount Grantham

"Terrible thing, about the hat, sir." Bullton hiccuped mournfully. They were at the stage in their second bottle of whiskey where everything seemed either beautiful or tragic, or some combination thereof.

"It was, oh, it was, Bullton." Kit's voice sounded a little despairing. "It was a fine hat. Had a plume . . . Made her eyes *so* green . . ."

"Very good color—green," Bullton agreed wistfully.

"Particularly for eyes," Kit mused. "But I'm partial to hazel. Hazel is green with blue and bits of gold in it," he explained to Bullton.

"Are you, sir? Are you really partial to hazel?" Bullton solemnly wanted to know.

"Very, very partial," Kit said dreamily.

"I'm an admirer of brown eyes," Bullton confessed.

"Doesn't Mrs. Davies have brown eyes, Bullton?"

"Brown as a spaniel's." It was Bullton's turn to sound wistfully dreamy.

This struck Kit as very funny, and he laughed, which turned out to be a mistake, because the whiskey hadn't entirely vanquished the pain in his ribs. And then he groaned, but groaning also hurt.

"All right, sir, time to rest," Bullton ordered. "No traipsing about in the woods tomorrow."

"You are very strict, Bullton. But you are no doubt correct. Get my boots off, will you, good man?"

Bullton tugged and tugged and tugged, then staggered backward and toppled to the floor with a Hessian in his arms as though it had been shot out of a cannon, which struck Kit as very funny again. He laughed, forgetting what happened the last time he laughed, and as a result, was soon groaning again.

"*Christ.* You really must stop being funny, Bullton."

"I will try sir, but there's another boot, yet."

Bullton got the other boot off, and Kit laughed again, then groaned, and then laughed because he was groaning again, which made him groan some more. Finally, the whole business wore him out.

"Thank you, Bullton. Good night. Dream of spaniel eyes," Kit murmured.

"Good night, sir. Dream of hazel."

Chapter Ten

It was Aunt Frances's turn to read this evening, so Susannah settled into her chair near the fire and took up her sketchbook, idly drawing while she listened. Aunt Frances had a habit of licking her finger before she turned a page, which had definitely taken getting used to. But now the little smacking noise measured off their evenings as surely as a ticking clock, and Susannah had begun to find it soothing. They were both deeply involved in the story; Susannah vicariously enjoyed proud Elizabeth Bennett's heartbreaks, the sweet idiocy and hope of love.

Behind her, a fire she had built—she'd stacked the wood and lit it—crackled away. She was bloody proud of that fire.

The viscount had vigorously rebounded from being fallen upon by a gelding, and apart from a sling and a tendency to wince a little when he moved too quickly, showed no signs of permanent damage, either to his wits or his person. She'd trailed him as usual—on foot—for the past few days, adding a new fern and several more trees to her

sketchbook, and nothing at all to her storehouse of knowledge about his past. But he *did* talk: about squirrels and
birds and ferns and trees and the like, with an enthusiasm
and reverence and a sort of abstracted, increasing delight,
as though he was discovering something he already knew. It
was contagious, this joy; it found its way into her drawings.

"With the Gardiners they were always on the most inti-
mate terms. Darcy, as well as Elizabeth, really loved them;
and they were both ever sensible of the warmest gratitude
toward the persons who, by bringing her into Derbyshire,
had been the means of uniting them."

Aunt Frances sighed with pleasure. "I always hate to
read the last sentence of a wonderful book, don't you?"

Susannah gave a start. She hadn't heard that last sentence at all, truthfully.

"Everything is wrapped up rather neatly, isn't it?" she
said, diplomatically. She would peek at it when Aunt
Frances wasn't looking.

Susannah glanced down at her sketchbook and discovered, with some surprise, the reason she hadn't heard the
last sentence: the viscount's face, rendered in pencil, now
occupied the corner of the page. He looked amused in her
drawing, but there was something wistful in the lines around
his eyes, and his mouth, that lovely mouth, was somewhat
tentative, quirked into a smile at the corner. She ran her
thumb lightly across the face, gently traced his lips with
the edge of her fingernail.

Then feeling a little abashed, she turned the pages
quickly to the safer-looking ferns and trees.

"How goes the traipsing about with the viscount,
Susannah?"

She wondered if it was a coincidence that her aunt had transitioned from talk of a happy ending to the viscount.

"Oh, it goes very well. He is all that is . . . gentlemanly." She tried to keep the regret from her voice.

"Oh, I sincerely doubt *that*," he aunt said, amused. "I'm certain he is *some* that is gentlemanly. But I also know he wouldn't lay a hand upon you, Susannah, no matter what some of the neighbors might say. His father bred him too well."

Odd, but she found her aunt's firmness of conviction along those lines a little disappointing.

"Is there really a scandal in his past, Aunt Frances?" she asked it tentatively. She wasn't positive she wanted to know, since the wondering about it had been both such a pleasure and a torment.

"Well . . . there *was* a little something, when he was a boy. His father packed him off into the army rather abruptly one day, as I recall. Or perhaps it was the military academy. Just a lad at the time, he was. One day he was here—the next, or very near it—poof! Gone! There was something about a girl, too, I believe, but I can't recall her name."

Caro, Susannah almost supplied. She was surprised when she stopped herself. Odd, but somehow, it would have seemed almost like . . . like a betrayal of him.

"It's too long ago, and it scarcely matters now, does it?" her aunt continued. "He's served his country, which in my book redeems him, more or less, no matter what he's done. But you know how rumors are . . . people *will* cling to one, and tend it until it grows like a great weed in all directions. He was a good lad for the most part, even if he was full of oats. He's a good man, too, I warrant. I know, because it's in the eyes," her aunt said sagely, pointing with two fingers to her own brown ones. "And he's in Barnstable so seldom, but he never fails to call upon me when he is. And as far as I'm concerned, that is the mark of a gentleman."

Susannah rather thought so, too, and it warmed her heart to think of Kit sitting in the parlor with Aunt Frances, gripping a cup of tea, having a chat about—

About what? Horrid novels?

"The viscount thinks I'm very talented at drawing." Susannah offered this almost shyly. She'd never discussed her "talent" with anyone else before.

"Well, how about that?" Aunt Frances looked pleased. "Talented, are you? Not just a young lady who draws like any other young lady?"

"That's what he says. Do you suppose I got my talent from my father?" She remembered Kit suggesting this question; it had seemed important to him.

"Well, you might very well have at that, Susannah. Lord knows no one in the Makepeace family has a whit of artistic talent."

Susannah frowned a little. That sentence hadn't made a whit of *sense.*

"But . . . you *do* think I might very well have gotten my talent from my father?" She said it almost gingerly, in case this was the first sign that Aunt Frances was actually losing her mind, and she would have to begin making plans to live somewhere else.

"Well . . . yes, dear." Her aunt, for her part, looked a little troubled now, too. "That *is* what I said."

They stared at each with wary politeness.

Aunt Frances's knitting needles slowed.

An uneasy silence slunk by.

And it had started out as such a *benign* discussion.

"James," Susannah tried carefully, "my *father*. I might have gotten my talent from *him*? Is that what you meant?"

Her aunt's needles froze completely. "Oh—oh my. Oh my *goodness*."

Aunt Frances sat straight up and pushed her spectacles up on her nose. Susannah paused in her lunging, sat back in her chair again. She didn't look ill; on the contrary, she looked alarmingly lucid.

"Aunt Frances? Are you—"

"Good heavens. Susannah—surely you know?"

Susannah almost closed her eyes. *No more revelations, please.* But she had to ask.

"Know *what*, Aunt Frances?

"That James wasn't your father, dear."

It was Susannah's turn to go perfectly, perfectly still. "I beg your pardon?" She said it so faintly they were barely words.

"I said, James wasn't your—"

"I heard you," Susannah said abruptly. "I'm sorry. That is to say . . ." She shook her head roughly. "I *beg* your pardon?"

"Oh, my dear. My poor dear." Aunt Frances sounded truly distressed; she had her hands fisted against her cheeks now. "I'm so sorry to startle you. I had no idea you didn't know."

Susannah couldn't move, or think properly. *James wasn't your father.* Those four words had become the entire contents of her mind.

"But surely . . . surely that's the sort of thing a solicitor would at least mention, Susannah? As he read the will to you?" Aunt Frances peered with frowning concern into

Susannah's face. "I suppose not," she concluded after a moment, from Susannah's dumbstruck expression.

"But *how* . . . why . . . I mean, *what*. . . ?" But no question seemed quite adequate or appropriate at the moment, so Susannah stopped trying to ask one.

Fortunately, Aunt Frances was able to collect herself enough to launch into a coherent tale. "My dear, I will tell you all I know, which I heard from another member of the family, so it's third hand, my dear. Almost twenty years ago now James went to a town called Gorringe. And apparently he returned with a little girl, who *may* have come from Gorringe, but no one knows, really."

"*I* was that little girl?"

"Perhaps. There was speculation in the family that perhaps James had a mistress who died, and this was her child, which in truth cheered his mother no end. Because, you see, James wasn't one to take much notice of women . . . he rather liked vases and art, I hear."

"Yes," Susannah said softly, remembering all of the vases and carpets and art coming in, and then going out, of the door. "He did. But . . . why? I just don't understand."

"I'm sorry, dear, but I've told you all I know. And I honestly don't know anyone who can tell you anything further, either. James was always the family's enigma. He seemed to prefer it that way. He kept *everyone* at a distance."

"But . . . what about my mother? I've a miniature of her, and I look just like her, I *do*! They weren't . . . weren't they . . . were they married? Wasn't he *ever* married?"

"Married? Good heavens, I don't think so dear. Well, I suppose anything's possible, really, but no one knew of a marriage, if he in fact was. But perhaps your mother was married to someone *else*," she added, hating to shock Susannah any further, perhaps, with the suggestion her mother had been a fallen woman.

"Someone who would have been my father."

"Well, undoubtedly, dear," Aunt Frances said hurriedly, reassuringly. "Perhaps you were orphaned, and James took you in."

"Then . . ." Susannah felt the world slipping out from beneath her yet again, as another realization took hold. "You . . . you . . . aren't really my aunt, then, are you?"

She dropped her eyes to her lap.

There was a silence.

"Oh!" Aunt Frances said softly. There was a moment of quiet, and then Susannah heard Aunt Frances pat the settee. "Come here, my dear."

She lifted her eyes, struggling to maintain a stoic expression. She raised up and went to the settee, curling her feet up underneath her.

And then Aunt Frances gestured coaxingly to her own plump shoulder with a tilt of her head and a lift of her brows. Hesitating an instant, Susannah gingerly laid her head down upon on the curve of it. She was a woman grown, but this was the sort of solace she'd never before known, this leaning her cheek against another woman's shoulder. It was so curiously comforting she felt again the tears pushing against the back of her eyes.

Aunt Frances stroked her brow soothingly, with a cool, rough hand. "There now. I am sorry to shock you after such a pleasant evening, my dear. But isn't it better that you know, somehow?"

"I suppose it is. It explains a good deal, Aunt Frances. There were never any pictures of my mother about the house. I thought perhaps . . . perhaps her death wounded him too grievously to think of her. A romantic notion, I know."

Aunt Frances nodded, approving of the romantic notion.

"And he . . ." Susannah swallowed over a knot in her throat. "Well, he never really seemed to care for me. Oh, he was kind enough," she said swiftly. "But . . . not fatherly. He was so seldom home, and didn't seem to have need of my company."

I sound pathetic, she thought, and despised the sound of it. She'd never before indulged in being pathetic. It involved relinquishing one's pride for a moment, and admitting to herself that she liked the stroking hand on her brow. *Just this once,* she thought. *And then I shall buck up.*

"Oh, I'm certain he cared for you," Aunt Frances said stoutly.

"Do you really think so?"

"He did keep you very well all of these years, Susannah, did he not? And made certain you were raised not wanting for anything."

Except a mother and a father, Susannah thought, traitorously. "He did." She couldn't deny it. But the sense of unreality was profound. She'd thought she'd lost everything but her sense of self: she'd at least known, despite the defection of the rest of her life, that she was Susannah Makepeace, daughter of James.

And as it turned out, she'd lost that, too.

"I wonder why James never told you," her aunt mused.

"Perhaps he never thought it . . . important." It seemed inconceivable to her that someone wouldn't think family was important. It was the only thing she'd ever really lacked, and, as it turned out, the only thing she'd ever really wanted. Perhaps he'd meant to tell her, some day. *No one really intends to get one's throat cut,* she thought. "Perhaps he thought keeping it a secret would ensure my good marriage."

"Or perhaps he was hiding something," her aunt added with acerbic practicality.

Susannah thought about this, about the gentle cipher who had been her father.

And then she thought of the adder hiding in the benign-looking picnic basket. What did one ever really know about anyone?

But then . . . something twitched inside her . . . it felt like hope again. And little by little, whatever it was began to blossom.

She'd always thought she'd had no family, no mother or brothers or sisters or cousins.

But now . . . her family could be anyone at all; she could be related to dozens of people, or none. Her life, her future, which had just a few minutes ago seemed as limited as this little house, now seemed as large as all the possibility in the world. She didn't know at all where to begin investigating it, but her imagination had already gone to work on it. She might be the bastard daughter of a prince. She might be . . . a peasant. She might be—

"Perhaps I have a family after all," she said to Aunt Frances.

"You do in me, Susannah. One can be an aunt in spirit, you know."

Susannah was moved, too overwhelmed with impressions and revelations to speak. She hadn't done a thing to warrant such kindness, such warmth or acceptance, from Aunt Frances. She hadn't charmed her way into Aunt

Frances's graces, or earned them with her status or money. She simply had to *be,* and Aunt Frances had taken her in, without question.

"Thank you, Aunt Frances." It was really all she could say. She quietly vowed to endeavor to live up to such acceptance. "One can be a niece in spirit, too."

Aunt Frances chuckled, her shoulder shifting up and down with it.

But maybe that was the point of acceptance: one didn't have to live up to it, or earn it. Susannah sensed that her entire life, she had tried a little too hard, no matter what she did.

Possibly because she hadn't a family, she'd needed everyone else to love her.

Perhaps you needn't try so hard, Kit had said to her. He'd seen it in her from the very beginning, her need to dazzle. And so, it seemed, had the denizens of Barnstable.

"Well, the Bennett girls went through their trials, didn't they dear, but it ended well for all of them, didn't it? Even, in a way, for that Lydia chit, isn't that so?"

"It did, at that," Susannah smiled a little. Miss Jane Austen certainly knew how to end a story.

The next morning, Susannah arrived at the stables to find the viscount stroking and murmuring to the pregnant mare.

The mare jerked her head away from him, tossing it high. And then a low moan came from her, a sound so very nearly human the breath froze in Susannah's lungs.

Kit turned and saw Susannah. His face was granite-colored with a terrifyingly contained anger. She took an unconscious step back.

"Go home." He bit the words off, turned back to the mare.

Susannah's hand flew up to cover her stomach with shock; his words had entered there, two swift darts.

"Something's wrong with the mare . . . she's . . . tell me what is wrong." Her voice was a shred of sound; it had taken all of her courage to speak to the cold wall of his back.

The mare groaned again and jerked her head high then her eyes rolled whitely in pain. And then the horse shifted and leaned into Kit, who pushed back, attempting to keep her upright, murmuring soothing words that contrasted starkly with his expression.

He finally looked again at Susannah.

"She's in foal, but she should have dropped it by now, which means the foal is presenting wrong. She's in tremendous pain. And the stable boys who should be caring for her are . . ." He stopped. "Nowhere to be seen."

He drawled these last words, and the hairs rose on Susannah's neck. Kit's fury was nearly acrid; she could feel it in her own throat. She imagined it blackening and curling the leaves on the trees black for miles around. The stable boys would be hung, drawn, and quartered when they returned, she was certain. If they dared return.

"What will happen to her?"

"She will die. And the foal will certainly die. Painfully and slowly, unless I shoot her." He tossed the words out casually, hard as little rocks.

"But . . . can't you do something?" Helplessness swelled in her, and oh *God,* she was tired of feeling helpless.

The mare's legs began to fold; Kit threw his body against her again. He seemed determined to keep her upright.

And then he turned again and something he saw in Susannah's face made his angry mask slip.

"It's . . . it's my arm . . . I can't turn the foal and brace the mare with just one arm. She could crush me, or the foal. I need to keep her upright."

Susannah understood now: His own helplessness in this circumstance was killing him.

"I'll help. Let me do it. Please." The words sprung from some place deep and instinctive; she was just as astonished that she meant them.

Kit made a short disdainful sound. "You'll thrust your hand into the womb of a horse and turn a foal, Miss Makepeace? Because that's what's required. And we might not save her, even then."

His fury was contagious; she'd caught it now. She yanked the sleeve of her riding habit up and held her arm out, glared at him, breathing hard now. "Tell me what to do."

He began to turn away from her again.

"Tell. Me. What. To. *Do*. Damn you," she added, fervently.

His head went back at that, as though she'd struck him with a glove. A mere instant later, the hard white mask was gone, and the Kit she knew glimmered through. "Hold out your arm," he demanded.

She did, as her reflexes always seemed to obey him unquestioningly. He scooped a handful of lanolin from a bucket, vigorously rubbed it up past her elbow and guided her arm toward the mare's uplifted tail. His voice was even, clipped, the voice of someone accustomed to issuing orders and hearing them unquestioningly obeyed.

"You'll need to insert your arm into the mare. I'll

steady her, and tell you what to do. And she might kick, and I'll try to protect you from it. But mind yourself."

She pushed her hand, slowly, tentatively, into the darkness of the mare, felt the straining muscles close around her arm as the mare shifted her legs, saw her elbow vanish. Somewhere above her, Kit murmured reassurances to the mare, leaned his body against her when she moved her haunches and tossed her head again, with a sound that was half-groan, half-whicker.

And then for Susannah the sounds of the mare faded, and the stable around her faded, and her world was the wet heat of the horse and Kit's calm voice from above. Her fingers, with scant room to maneuver, fumbled, carefully fanned out, attempting to translate what she felt. Her breath caught.

"A muzzle," she breathed. "I feel a muzzle." She moved her fingers over the dip of a nostril, a pointed ear, a lip.

The foal *nipped at her finger.*

"Oh! It's trying to bite me!" She half-laughed, half-gasped.

"It's alive, then." Kit's voice came to her, even, nearly emotionless. "Do you feel the legs?"

Susannah moved her hand up around the face of the little foal, felt knobby little legs pushed up there, too.

"Yes. I feel a leg . . . near the foal's face."

"Now feel carefully . . . is it a foreleg, or a back leg? Is the joint above the ankle a knee, or a hock?"

Susannah felt a knobby knee, not a hock. "Foreleg."

"Good. Very good. Now we need to turn its head so that it faces us, and its legs need to be toward us, too, which is how a foal is normally presented in the womb. Feel up around its head, if you can, and . . . guide it toward you."

"Will it hurt the mare?" Stupid question. Everything was hurting the mare now. Susannah shook her head once abruptly, as if to retract the words, and Kit didn't respond.

She did as told, fumbled up over the length and curves of the foal's head, felt bristly little eyelashes, a short coarse mane. Gently, gently, she pulled it toward her.

It wouldn't budge.

"Try harder, Susannah," Kit said from above, his voice a little taut. "You won't hurt it."

Susannah drew in a deep breath, closed her eyes, prayed, and gave a harder pull, put her muscle into it.

"Kit, she—he—oh, it's *moving* . . ."

"All right." She felt Kit's voice as surely as a steadying hand on her back. "She'll push, Susannah—you'll feel her push—and when she does, we hope to see the foal's forelegs."

Susannah waited, and then the mare pushed.

A small hoof emerged. And then another . . . and then the forelegs, up to the knees.

The mare pushed again: most miraculously of all, the small muzzle began to emerge.

"Kit—"

Kit dropped his control as if it scalded him.

"Bloody fantastic, yes, *yes,* you've done it Susannah, that's exactly right, we have it now . . . we need to grasp the legs, and tug now . . . I'll tell you when . . ."

Susannah slowly, carefully withdrew her arm, and gently seized a hoof scarcely larger than a teacup. When the mare heaved again, she pulled, along with Kit, inexorably, guiding, guiding—another heave—

An entire little foal fell into her arms, wet and warm,

all legs and nose and wriggling life, and Susannah tumbled back with it into the straw.

"By *God*, Susannah!" Kit sounded ecstatically.

It was only then that Susannah became fully aware of her body and her surroundings again, the tang of straw, the powerful earthy smell of blood and horse, her aching arm and shoulder and back. Sweat glued her hair to her face, her riding habit to her spine. She released the little foal gently, it struggled to its feet, collapsed again, wobbled up onto its four new legs. The mare turned around to nose it, welcoming her baby into the world.

Susannah felt wobbly herself; she straightened with some effort to her feet, feeling Kit's arm beneath her elbow guiding her.

Kit knelt to do a quick examination, the little foal tripped and righted itself a few more times, getting accustomed to the fact that the world was hard and flat and large, not close and warm and wet.

"She's sound . . . a beautiful little filly." And then Kit rose to his feet, too, and turned to Susannah. The corner of his mouth tilted.

Susannah rubbed her sleeve against her cheek. She felt dazed and light and unaccountably happy. A peaceful sort of happiness, as though she'd finally momentarily satisfied an appetite she hadn't known existed.

They heard voices then, boy voices laughing and swearing, the sounds of scuffling feet.

The stable boys had returned.

When they saw Kit they froze, turned into stone as surely if he were Medusa.

Kit regarded them for a time, expressionless, terrifyingly expressionless, and Susannah felt her own heart knot.

"You *did* know this mare was due to give birth any day?" Kit asked almost pleasantly.

Eyes bugging with fear, they remained silent. One of them darted a look toward the bonnie little foal.

"Answer me."

Susannah risked a sideways glance at Kit. How could one person imbue so much menace into two little words?

"Y-y-es, sir." One of them was brave enough to get the words out.

There was another long silence, broken by the slap of the mare's tail against her rump, the rustle of little hooves in the straw.

"They could have died," Kit said, almost musingly, "while you were gone. This mare, and her foal. Alone. And it's your responsibility to care for the horses, is it not?"

Susannah was certain the expressions the two boys wore were similar to those turned up to the executioner's ax. They said nothing; no doubt their vocal cords had turned to stone.

"Go," Kit finally said, his voice low and contemptuous. "And don't come back."

They spun on their heels and ran.

Behind Susannah, the mare nudged the little filly, a twin of her mother down to the star between her eyes. She was twitching her miniature tail, learning all about balancing on four legs, and breathing air, and her mother's teats.

Kit stared after the stable boys for a moment, silently, then turned back to the mare and foal. He watched them, quietly, and Susannah watched him.

"I'll have to keep an eye on them for a few days." Kit

ran his hand thoughtfully along the sweat-darkened flank of the mare. "But I think they'll do well enough." She could hear the relief in his voice. The warmth.

He turned back toward her and his expression was . . . tentative, almost awkward. As though he couldn't decide what to say.

Susannah doubted *that* happened very often.

"It was a brave thing you did, Susannah."

Something unfamiliar in his eyes warmed Susannah clear through, and at the same time made her feel strangely bare. "I wasn't trying to be brave."

Kit's lovely mouth lifted at the corner. "Which is what *makes* it brave." His expression was still difficult to read. He seemed so somber, almost shy, if she didn't know better. Humble? No, *that* couldn't be. But the warmth in it was unmistakable. "You'll be a little sore tomorrow." He absently reached out and kneaded her upper arm.

Susannah closed her eyes to slits; the kneading felt wonderful. It was almost more intimate than a kiss, but then again, almost nothing seemed intimate in comparison to having one one's hand thrust up a horse, and Susannah, at the moment, didn't care.

Kit abruptly dropped his hand. She opened her eyes fully again.

And they stood again quietly together for a moment, simply looking at each other. A peculiar peace stole over Susannah, a lovely, dreamy sort of fullness.

He cleared his throat. "Well, I think we can forego riding and drawing today, Miss Makepeace. *Again.* I'd like to watch these two"—he gestured with his chin at the horses—"for a time. I'm afraid your riding habit is quite ruined."

Susannah looked down; it most certainly was. "I've more of them at home."

For some reason this made him smile and shake his head slowly back and forth.

Susannah rubbed her sticky hands against her already ruined skirt and took another look back at the little filly, trapped and twisted only moments before in her mother's womb, now thirstily taking her first meal. She smiled, felt her heart squeeze sweetly. She would sketch the mother and baby, tomorrow perhaps.

"What will you name her?" she asked.

"I was thinking 'Susannah.'"

That had certainly been quick out of his mouth. His eyes glinted devilishly.

Susannah tipped her head to the side, pretending to mull this. "Perfect," she pronounced finally. "It's the perfect name for such a beautiful creature."

And then she spun prettily, casting a saucy look at him through her lashes over her shoulder, and headed up the path for home.

And as she walked, she cherished the last expression she'd seen on his face. It hadn't been amusement, for a change. Or indifference. Or impatience.

It had been something else entirely.

And a strange, sweet hope bucked inside her.

Chapter Eleven

Sleep that night was a deep, endless black well, and Susannah didn't so much fall as plummet into it. It felt natural to wake with the light now, to birdsong and the first sense of the day's weather filling the room. She felt rested to the depths of her soul, a different kind of rest than she'd ever before felt.

Warm again today. What a streak of weather they were having. Susannah lifted herself out of bed, startled to find her arms and back so stiff, and then remembered why: the little filly. *Susannah.* She smiled. She might not have much of a family, but there was now a new little filly named for her. She supposed it was something.

Today . . . today she'd wear the buttercup-colored muslin, the one that found the gold in her eyes, made them glow almost amber. She knew the viscount would notice. Oh, he'd never *say* anything quite so frivolous. But she knew . . . she knew he would notice.

He'd liked her hat. The green one. Goodness knows what other remarks were lurking in his full and enigmatic mind, if *that* was the one that slipped out when a horse fell upon him.

Her heart gave a sharp, sweet, peculiar leap.

She slipped the dress on; tightening the laces was a little more difficult this morning, with her stiff limbs, but she got it done. She put the miniature of her mother into an apron pocket; thinking she might show it to Kit. He'd asked, after all; for some reason she wanted him to see it.

She'd just begun her descent when her aunt's voice sang up the stairs.

"Susannah . . . I have a *surprise* for you . . ."

Oh, no. She wanted her tea and fried bread as well as something heartier this morning, and she knew they had sausages because the viscount's money had allowed them into the budget. She didn't think she'd ever be able to look at a picnic basket again without flinching. And after the revelation about her father a few nights ago . . .

No more surprises, please, Aunt Frances.

So she slowed her pace. As she rounded the bed of the stairs, she froze. Her heart clogged her throat.

"Douglas."

She was suddenly very glad she was wearing the buttercup-colored muslin.

"Hello, Susannah." His face was aglow with the sight of her. "You look . . ." His eyes took her in like a man starved.

". . . wonderful," he concluded softly.

At first, she couldn't speak at all. Her heart was kicking like a parade drum. "Thank you, Douglas," she said finally. "You look very . . . fine, as well."

Oh, and he did. She'd nearly forgotten how handsome Douglas was—could it really have been only a few weeks since she'd seen him?—with his dark hair and fine features, those clear gray eyes that she knew as well as her own.

There could only be one reason he was here. A frisson of anticipation made her breath catch.

Aunt Frances stood next to Douglas, her hands clasped in front of her, her delighted, curious gaze darting from Susannah to Douglas and back again.

They stared at each other for a moment longer before Susannah considered she should probably descend the remaining steps. It *was* lovely to see him, but a bit jarring, too, like . . . finding a teapot in the bathtub. He didn't seem to belong here, in this small house, in the country.

"He doesn't want *tea*," her aunt said meaningfully. "He wants to go for a *walk*."

Meaning: He wants to be alone with you. Rather urgently.

There was now little doubt in Susannah's mind what Douglas had come for.

For days now she'd felt as though she'd been stretching to reach something up on a high, high shelf, something she couldn't quite see, something she couldn't even identify, something she suspected might have great value, if only she could reach it.

But if Douglas took her away from Barnstable, she could stop stretching. And oddly, at that thought, relief and regret seemed of a piece.

"Leave your coat here, Douglas," she said softly. "My aunt won't mind, and it's already very warm. We'll go for a stroll."

Aunt Frances took Douglas's coat, and her eyes widened and rolled exaggeratedly at the fineness of it, which made Susannah bite back a smile. And then Aunt Frances winked, which thankfully Douglas either didn't notice, or graciously pretended not to notice.

Susannah took Douglas past the roses, and out the front gate, and through the path in the woods, and the silence between them was almost comical in its awkwardness. It had been quite some time since they'd walked together, and then, they'd usually done it arm in arm. They walked side by side, instead; the distance of inches between them felt like miles.

Douglas cleared his throat. "So this is where you live, now?"

"No, I live in a barn, Douglas."

"You live in a *barn*?" And then he saw her expression. "Oh! Ha-ha!" he laughed nervously. "Sorry. I suppose that question *did* sound a bit barmy."

"I'm sorry, too. I should not have made a joke."

How clumsy they were with each other. How nervous and polite. And here Susannah had almost begun to suspect she'd forgotten how to be polite in the way one was polite in the *ton*.

"And how do you find life in Barnstable, Susannah?" Douglas tried again. Very politely.

She considered this question. "Lively." Also very politely.

"Is it?" Douglas looked dubious. They were quiet a while longer, and Susannah heard around them the sounds that had become so familiar: the rush of leaves and rattle of twigs above her as squirrels and birds leaped from branch to branch.

And then suddenly Douglas stopped and whirled on her, and Susannah jumped.

"Oh, enough politeness. Susannah, I miss you terribly."

"Do you?" The words emerged a little breathily. His sudden stop and his words had her heart bumping hard.

"Oh, yes. Nothing is the same, you see." His voice was rushed and ardent. "I haven't laughed quite so much since you've gone. No one *dances* quite the way you do. And no one"—he gathered her hands in his and pulled her into his chest—"*looks* at me quite the way you do . . . with those . . . those eyes of yours . . ."

He trailed off into silence. And then Douglas dropped his gaze to her mouth; it hovered there.

Douglas was going to kiss her.

She was going to let him.

And when his mouth touched hers, it was that same, just-slightly-more-than-chaste kiss she remembered, the kiss that had so intrigued her before with its hint of *more*.

But then, well . . . it *became* a little more.

His tongue crept out to touch her bottom lip, and he pushed himself closer to her. Through his snug trousers, through her fine dress, she could feel part of him stirring against her in an unmistakable, very masculine way.

Hmmm. Douglas was most definitely taking a *liberty*.

She opened her lips a little, partly out of curiosity, partly because it seemed . . . well, the *polite* thing to do. But she couldn't seem to lose herself in the moment; perhaps his mind had been filled with her since he'd jilted her, but her life had become filled with other things. Viscounts and voles and foals. Art and talent and bravery. Things that imposed a distance Douglas would have to cross before she felt comfortable kissing him again, let alone being pressed up against his significant arousal.

Confused, she turned her head abruptly away from his with a shaky little laugh.

Douglas took a deep bracing breath, collecting himself. But he didn't apologize, and he refused to relinquish her hands, even when she gave a little tug.

"Susannah . . . you must know the reason I came."

"I think I have an inkling, but I'd like to hear it from you." She smiled up at him, teasing.

"Well, it's this," his tone was eager, "I thought perhaps I'd buy a home in London for you to live in—"

So it *was* happening. Again, relief and a peculiar regret mingled. How strange it would be to slip back into her old life once more. How odd to treat Barnstable like a dream.

"For *us* to live in, you mean?" she smiled up at him.

Douglas smiled indulgently and lifted her hands, one then the other, to his lips, and then at last released them. "Well, I suppose on occasion I will stay there with you. But I'll of course be expected to live with my wife most of the time."

She stared at him, puzzled.

And then suspicion seeped in and leeched all sensation from her limbs.

"*But* you'll be expected to live with your wife?" she repeated on a nervous laugh.

"Well, yes, of course," Douglas continued, sounding conciliatory. "Amelia. Amelia Henfrey. We're to be married in a month's time, and I'll be expected to live with *her,* naturally. But you do know, of course . . . Susannah, I would much rather be with you, and I *will* be with you as often as possible."

He smiled down at her winningly, bent to kiss her again.

Susannah jerked her head sideways.

And even over the roaring starting up in her ears, and

the hideous rush of pain that gathered around her heart, somehow she got the words out, all in the right order.

"Just to be very clear, Douglas: Are you asking me to be your mistress?"

His brows dipped in genuine confusion. "Well, yes, of course. You know I can't be expected to marry a penni—"

Susannah's hand sailed upward, hard.

And then they stood utterly still, while Susannah watched in awe as the angry red outline of her fingers rose on Douglas's cheek. She looked down at her own numb and stinging palm as though it belonged to someone else entirely.

An unbearable silence skulked by.

"Susannah," he said quietly. "Please lis—"

She couldn't stop the words; they bubbled out like lava. "Who do you think you *are*, Douglas? Do you have *any idea* what I've been through? My arm was up to here"— she thrust out her arm and pointed to her elbow—"*here*, inside a *mare* yesterday—"

"A m-mare?" Douglas flinched backward defensively.

"A *mare*, you *ninny*," she repeated ferociously. "I've dodged danger, I've had everything I've ever known taken from me . . . and do you have any idea what that's *like* Douglas? But I've a sense of myself now. I'm strong, I'm resourceful. I'm *talented*. It seems"—she took in a deep breath, and managed, with a little dignity—"I also have a temper. And I suspect that *I* am more *man* than you will *ever* be."

"Susannah—"

"I want you to go. Go *now*. I never want to see you again."

"But—"

And oh, despite herself—and later she would despise herself for it—she waited, for hope, bloody hope, clung more tenaciously to life than a cockroach. "But *what*, Douglas?" *Say something to make it better, Douglas. Change everything it back to the way it was.*

"But—my coat—"

And of all the things he could have possibly said then, perhaps this was the very best, for he had never sounded more hapless and contemptible, and contempt went a long way toward balming her pride, which was so swollen and throbbing it threatened to strangle her.

And yet, even as she stared contempt into his once-beloved gray eyes, now clouded with genuine hurt and bewilderment, she knew it would have been impossible to change things back to the way they were. And it was her fault: *She* had already changed irrevocably.

"Have your *wife* buy you a new coat, Douglas. Give my regards to Amelia."

She'd heard of blind rage before. Until today, she hadn't been convinced it existed. Her hands went up to her face in horror, reliving the last few minutes: Douglas's last memory of her would be of her shrieking like a fishwife, her face contorted with fury.

Susannah bent down, scooped up a small stone and hurled it as hard as she could at nothing in particular.

A moment later she heard a dull thud followed by an indignant: *"Ow!"* Oh, dear God.

She squeezed her eyes closed. *Please, no.*

When she opened them again, Kit Whitelaw was standing before her, rubbing his chest and frowning darkly.

What had she come to—*battering* men? She put her hands up to her cheeks. "I'm so sorry—are you—did I—"

She stopped abruptly when a grin slowly spread across his face. "Your arm is good, but your aim needs work, Miss Makepeace. You missed. Care to try again?" He hefted her missile in his hand, then held it out to her invitingly.

She spun on her heel and stormed roughly in the direction of her aunt's house. A moment later, she heard the hurried crunch of footsteps behind her.

"Before you do yourself or anyone else an injury, Miss Makepeace, perhaps you'd like to tell me what's troubling you."

She whirled on him. "If you *must* know, my fiancé—*Douglas*—"

Kit's expression went from teasing to opaque in a blinding instant. "Lovers' quarrel, Miss Makepeace?"

"We aren't *lovers,* it wasn't a *quarrel,* and it's been over for some time. That is, more accurately, he's no longer my fiancé. When my father died, Douglas promptly jilted me, because his *mama* told him to, as the heir to a marquis couldn't *possibly* marry a penniless girl. And today he returned to inform me that he intends to marry my best friend, and to ask me to be his mistress."

This recitation seemed to strike the usually glib viscount dumb. Susannah was strangely gratified: So it *was* every bit as bad as she'd thought it was.

Kit remained thoughtfully quiet for some time. "Do you plan to cry?" He sounded curious.

"*No,*" she said incredulously, as if the very idea was an insult.

He studied her carefully, the tiniest of furrows between

his eyes. Then he fished about in his pocket, came up with a handkerchief and held it out to her.

She promptly burst into tears.

"I'm not dis-dis-*traught*, mind you," she choked out. She lowered herself fumblingly to a tipped log.

"Of course not," he agreed equably, calmly. He settled down next to her, stretching his long legs out.

"I'm bloody *fur-fur-ious*."

"As anyone would be."

"It's j-j-ust . . . *everything* that has h-happened, you see . . ."

"There's been a good deal."

"He's a bloody *c-c-cad*."

"The very bloodiest." Kit reached down, selected a twig thoughtfully from the floor of the woods. "Shall I call him out for you?" He said it idly, twiddling the twig between his fingers.

The sobs stopped almost immediately. Susannah slowly turned eyes round with astonishment on him. "You'd d-do that for me?"

Kit rolled and rolled the twig, as though he intended to start a fire with it. "Perhaps I'd only make him bleed a little."

She gave a short laugh, half-bitter, half-startled, and dashed her knuckles roughly across her damp cheek. "You could do that? Not kill him, I mean . . . only wound him a bit? Wouldn't that be . . . well, difficult?"

He turned away from her for a moment. "Oh, yes," he said, finally. His smile was faint, a rueful, grim thing. "I could do that."

He turned back to find Susannah watching him speculatively, as if weighing her options. "He isn't worth the danger to you," she decided.

This made him smile. "Your concern for my safety is flattering, Miss Makepeace. But why you'd believe he'd pose any sort of danger to *me* . . ."

She turned away and unfurled the crumpled handkerchief in her fist; her thumbnail began worrying the embroidered initials on it, CMW, tracing them over and over. Only an occasional forlorn hiccup remained of her storm of tears.

"How do you know that *I'm* not dangerous?" she said suddenly, and slanted him a look from between her lashes.

A little burst of admiration warmed him; he felt like applauding. *Well done, Miss Makepeace. All is not lost if you can still flirt.* "Oh, I've no doubt you are," he assured her. "With stones, at least."

She smiled, a little. And then she sniffed, and dabbed with quiet dignity at her eyes. They said nothing for a time, simply sat together, fingers of sunlight piercing the trees and enclosing them in warmth and swirling dust.

A squirrel chittered irritably overhead, sounding for all the world as if it were shaking its tiny fist at them.

"I slapped his face," she confided suddenly, in almost a whisper. Sounding half-ashamed, half-thrilled.

"Hard?" Mildly said.

"I'm afraid so."

"Good. Then you left him in no doubt as to how you feel about his . . . proposal."

"No," she said sadly. "No doubt."

She fell silent again, and he honored it. Odd how peaceful the aftermath of a storm of tears could be.

Susannah smoothed the sodden handkerchief out in her lap, over and over, as though preparing to lay a table on it. "Have you ever been in love?" she asked softly.

He almost laughed. Oh, how like a woman to ask such a question. Flippant words poised to leap from his tongue.

But then he turned and took in her mottled, flushed cheeks, her eyes still brilliant with tears. She was trying to discover, he realized, how much he knew of broken hearts.

He inhaled deeply, exhaled. All right, then.

"Yes," he told her gently.

Her eyes widened; she was seeing him anew, perhaps. And then she looked swiftly away, as if it was difficult to see him this way.

"Do you love Douglas?" He was surprised to find himself asking it, but suddenly it seemed imperative to know. He'd been prodding at this young woman for days, teasing her, unfolding her, in part for his own entertainment. And discovering, to his surprise and discomfiture, there was much more to her than he'd suspected.

But he'd never really given any thought to the content of her heart.

"I do," she said softly. "I did. That is, I thought I did. Which, I suppose, amounts to the same thing, doesn't it?"

He was struck silent by the bravery of her words. "Perhaps it does," he agreed softly.

He thought about the poor young buffoon who'd just been slapped and sent packing, a young man who thought the solution to his own misery was to keep Susannah—who loved friends and gaiety, who was more passionate and brave and unique than even she knew—in a house in London and attend her only every now and then. Like a pet parrot.

He must have tensed, for the twig he'd been twiddling snapped between his fingers.

Kit released the pieces of it to the floor of the woods, and then searched for words, something of comfort and use to her. God only knows, he wasn't any good with diplomacy, or soft platitudes. He only knew how to offer his own truths.

"I know it's difficult now, Susannah. . . ," he began hesitantly, "but try . . . try not to think too badly of Douglas, if you can bear it. Young men are so often at the mercy of their parents and society. I expect he thought he was making things better for both of you. And . . . well, he may always regret the loss of you."

She lifted her head and gazed at him, studying him like a map. He submitted to it without blinking, lost momentarily in the lovely complexity of her eyes. All those colors. Like the pond dappled in morning light, those eyes were, the shifting play of green and gold; tears had made spikes of her chestnut lashes. It was all he could not to brush a thumb across them, taste the salt of them, to run the cool back of his hand against her flushed cheek, soothing it. He wondered why it had begun to seem more unnatural *not* to touch her . . . than to touch her.

At that thought, something kicked sharply inside him, once. And then it unfurled, slowly, slowly, filling him with an ache both unutterably sweet . . . and as old as time.

It occurred to him then: *She might very well be right. She might just be a little dangerous after all.*

"Who is Caro?" she asked suddenly.

Hell. He narrowed his eyes at her by way of reply, and she smiled, amused at him and pleased with herself for the ambush.

"Do you want to know the worst of it?" She paused, and took in a steadying breath, released it. "When Douglas appeared this morning, I thought . . . *at last*, I *have* someone. I'll have my old life back. I'll have a family. Did you know that all I have of my old life are my clothes? And those only because I threatened a man with a vase for them."

"They're excellent dresses," he assured her gently.

She smiled at that, and shook her head much the way he shook her head at her every time she showed up for a day's work exquisitely groomed. "They certainly are," she agreed with him, in the spirit of accuracy. "Anyhow, when Douglas came today, I thought . . . well, he'll propose, and then I suppose I'll finally have a family of my own. Because a few days ago my aunt told me that my father . . . wasn't even my real father."

"James wasn't your father?" The quick intensity in his voice made Susannah start a little.

"No. I asked about my . . . my talent, as you suggested. And my aunt . . . well, all Aunt Frances knows is that my father went away one day, and when he returned, he had a very little girl with him: *me*. He never explained it to anyone, he never married as far as anyone knows, so you see, I've no idea at all who I truly am. And now . . ." She made a sound; it was almost a laugh, except laughs were seldom so ironic and heartbreaking. "I have no one."

But Kit felt the hair on his arms lifting. He knew, somehow, the answer to his next question. "Susannah, the name of the town where your father found you . . . do you know it?"

"Gorringe. Named, apparently, by a duke who—"

"—was looking for a rhyme for 'orange.'"

She looked at him in surprise.

He wasn't surprised.

He shifted his gaze into the leaves overhead instead. It was like looking up at a collection of puzzle pieces, the sharp-edged oak leaves bunched thickly but still cut through with light, and he thought the metaphor apt: For all he had was a collection of facts and coincidences, and he couldn't quite make them join; there were gaps between all of them. There was a girl sitting next to him who had lost everything twice over now. James had not been her father, and he had been killed after mentioning Morley to Kit. And now it seemed as though someone was trying to either kill Susannah, or at the very least, thoroughly frighten her.

And Caroline had written him from Gorringe, shortly after she'd disappeared, no doubt with Thaddeus Morley.

"Here is my mother," Susannah said shyly. "You wanted to see her. I thought I'd show it to you today."

Very gently, she settled the miniature of her mother into his open palm.

A beautiful woman. It was Susannah's face, or very nearly.

Kit needed to look away from her to make his decision; up into the trees again.

It was maddening. The answer hovered on the periphery of his vision, but it dodged away every time he spun to face it. Excitement and an overwhelming frustration surged.

Perhaps he *was* going mad. Perhaps his suspicion of Morley *was* unreasonable. Perhaps his instincts weren't instincts at all, but the delusions of a man too long immersed in the necessary, disciplined paranoia required of a spy.

And perhaps pigs fly.

The threat of Egypt hung over his head like the sword of Damocles. But when he looked again at Susannah Makepeace, he knew he didn't have a choice.

"Let's forget about drawing today, Susannah. I'll take you to Gorringe instead."

Chapter Twelve

It was two hours to Gorringe over extravagantly rutted roads, which Kit suspected might be as effective as moats for keeping visitors away from the town. The journey might have gone more quickly on horseback, but he wasn't sure his ribs and arm could withstand the ride, and he preferred the relative shelter of a coach to making open targets of both himself and Susannah, since he was convinced someone was determined to hurt her. He was armed with a pistol tucked into his boot, another inside his coat alongside a sheathed knife, and the supreme confidence that he could best almost anyone—or two, or three—who attempted to accost them, despite the fact that his arm was freshly out of a sling.

At last, a short stone bridge arcing across a stream took them into the town, and Gorringe bloomed into sight before them.

Gorringe was a lovely surprise. Small, clean white-washed houses, huddled together like gossiping neighbors along a cobblestone road that clattered very agreeably beneath the carriage wheels. Flower boxes burst with bright summer blooms; a few shops—a bookshop, a tavern, a cheesemaker—appeared on the main road. Against all odds, Gorringe seemed a neat and thriving little town, very self-contained and peaceful in its way.

"Does anything look familiar to you?" he said to Susannah. She'd gone very still, tense. She gripped the edge of the seat.

"I wish I could say yes," she answered hesitantly. "It's lovely, isn't it? It looks as though one could be happy here."

The wistfulness in her voice cut him. He'd always had the luxury of knowing he was part of an ancient lineage, that he had cousins and uncles and aunts and spread all over England. Many of his ancestors were complete reprobates, but those were offset by numerous noble Whitelaw achievements and a sprinkling of genuine heroes. He had two sisters, who both loved and annoyed him and were loved and annoyed by him in turn, a father, and a whole treasury of memories of his mother.

A flash of jeweled colors winked on the edge of his vision, and this was how he found the church: It presided over the small homes from the center of town, solemnly medieval and yet surprisingly elegant, inset with stained-glass windows. The windows were a bit of a surprise, as so many had been destroyed years ago, when the church was eager to eradicate all traces of popery. Hence, images of the Virgin Mary and the saints were scarce. Perhaps these windows had been spared because their subject matter was more neutral.

"I thought we'd begin with the church. They may have records of your birth, Susannah, if you were born here."

She didn't answer him. He could see the anticipation in the set of her jaw, in her pale lips. Her fist was closed possessively over the miniature of her mother. He said nothing more; he knew she was too tightly wound to welcome reassurances right now.

They proceeded up a path that cut through a tidy churchyard featuring headstones both ancient and new. Susannah glanced at them and quickly glanced away: her mother, or her real father, could very well be beneath one of them.

Kit secretly loved churches. The pews of this one glowed darkly, seasoned by centuries of prayer and polished by centuries of shifting bums, and the stained-glass windows threw brilliant green and red and blue shapes down onto the floor. He'd been right: These *were* simple windows: three of them on either side of the room, roses and lilies twined around the borders of each. The words FAITH, HOPE, and CHARITY, were etched in extravagant Gothic lettering across each one.

"Hello." A politely cautious voice came from the apse. "May I help you?"

The vicar shuffled toward them. His head was tiny, his neck fleshy and boneless-looking, like a turtle's, and his vestments swamped him. When he was near them, his chin moved up and up and up, as though some internal machine was slowly levering it. His gaze finally arrived on Kit's face.

"Good afternoon, my lord," he said pleasantly. "You *are* a 'my lord,' aren't you, son? I'm the Vicar of Gorringe, Mr. Sumner."

The vicar had clearly reached that satisfying stage of life when he didn't particularly care what he said to anyone. Kit, personally, was looking forward to that particular stage.

"We are visitors to your fair town, Mr. Sumner. I was just noticing your windows—they're splendid."

"Aren't they? They aren't original, you know. A . . . generous benefactor donated them some years ago, along with our mausoleum behind the church. I suppose he believed he'd be buried there, but God had other plans for him, as He so often does. Is there something I can help you with today?"

Kit had noticed the special warmth given to the words "generous" and "benefactor."

"We rather hoped you might be able to assist us with a query. I've been known to be a generous benefactor, on occasion. I might even require a mausoleum some day."

"I'll certainly try to help, sir."

Susannah, in a mute form of blurting, thrust out her hand with the miniature in it. Kit supplied the question: "Do you know this woman?"

Hesitating a moment, the vicar gently took the miniature and gazed down at it for an inordinately long time, perhaps leafing through decades of memories.

"Time does get to blurring, you see, at my age." His eyes peered up at them serenely. "Things, and places, and people all run together . . ." He drifted off, gazing toward the windows.

There was a long silence. Acting on a suspicion, Kit leaned forward and gave a discreet little sniff. Wine had most definitely been part of the vicar's midday meal.

"All run together. . . ?" he prompted politely, before Susannah's head shot from her neck like a cannonball out of impatience.

"Er, yes. All run together. But I aver, you're the *spit* of your mama, young lady."

The expression on Susannah's face was glorious. The words lit her from within like one of the stained-glass windows. Kit felt again a tiny, sweet clutch in his chest.

"You knew my mama?" Hope made Susannah's voice weak.

"Pretty, pretty thing, she was," the vicar mused dreamily. "Had a daughter baptized here. We didn't see much of your mother in church, otherwise, I'm afraid, and I cannot quite recall her name. It's been some years, though sometimes it feels like only yesterday. But then, of course it wasn't yesterday, at all, was it, because look at you—all grown." He beamed at them.

Kit hoped for the parishioners' sake that the curate gave the sermons, not the vicar. He hoped there *was* a curate.

"Anna," Susannah said excitedly. "Her name was Anna!"

The vicar frowned. "No, that wasn't it."

"But—" Susannah glanced at Kit, who widened his eyes and gave a slight shake of his head, and she wisely decided not argue the point. "But you *do* remember her? What was she like?"

"A pretty, pretty thing." The vicar sounded surprised to have to say it again.

Kit intervened quickly. "One more question for you, sir: Do you by any chance recall a woman by the name of Caroline Allston?"

He felt Susannah's eyes on him, quite as intense as a pair of torches.

"Caroline Allston . . . Caroline Allston . . ." the vicar mused. "Can't say that I do. Was she pretty?" he asked hopefully.

"Very." Well, it was true, wasn't it? And "pretty" did seem to be the thing that branded someone into the vicar's memory. "Dark hair, dark eyes, fair skin. Very difficult to forget once you saw her. Was perhaps about eighteen years old when she first lived in Gorringe."

"Miss Allston does sound pretty, sir. But no, I cannot recall anyone specifically by that name. You're welcome to look at the records, as you don't look the sort to steal them."

Damned with faint praise. The vicar led them back to a room that housed the church records: shelves of books recording births, deaths, marriages, and baptisms—any occasion the church at Gorringe had marked.

"I'll leave you to it, then. I ask that you come to see me before you leave so that I may lock up after you."

"When were you born, Susannah, do you know? How old are you?" Kit was tracing a finger over the spines of the registries, looking for likely years.

Susannah didn't speak for a moment. Her mind was obsessively playing and replaying his words of five minutes ago. And finally she could contain them no longer.

"'Was she pretty?' she mimicked the vicar's creaky tones. "'*Very*,'" she answered, in a very good imitation of the viscount's own baritone.

Kit snorted a laugh.

But really, Kit had waxed almost lyrical about Caroline Allston—*Caro,* no doubt. Susannah wondered if Caro was carved on the viscount's heart the way it was on the oak, scarred and thick with age.

"I'm twenty—at least I thought I was," she said it

coolly, though why she thought she was entitled to coolness was beyond her understanding.

"And what day do you normally celebrate your birthday?" he said, as though her tone hadn't changed at all.

"The twelfth of August."

"Soon, then," he said cheerfully.

Ah, now he was trying to distract her. And she did love birthdays. Thought this pending birthday might be a trifle less climactic than her others, given that she'd held a grand party and received the gift of a horse for her last one.

Something occurred to her that swept petty jealousy right from her head.

"What if my name isn't really Susannah?" The thought horrified her. "What if my father—that is, James Makepeace—changed it? What if my name is Myrtle, or Agnes, or—"

"Something splendid or exotic, like Alexandra, or Katarina?"

Suddenly she felt strangely light-headed. "I could be anyone at all," she murmured, half to herself. "Anyone."

She felt oddly formless, unanchored, as though she could drift away or be absorbed into the air like vapor if she didn't soon find some bit of information, an actual name, or a mother, or a date of birth, to serve as ballast.

"Are you going to faint?"

Kit was watching her intently; he sounded more curious than concerned. As though she were a mystery to analyze, rather like voles. She had to admit, however, that she found this approach bracing. It made every surprise or upset or triumph seem merely part of an interesting puzzle, and it sobered her rather quickly.

"No."

He regarded her solemnly another moment, ascertaining the truth of this. Then he gave her the sort of smile she could make a crutch of forever: reassuring, warm as an arc of light.

Someday she might not blush when he smiled at her. Today would not be the day.

They returned to working in silence for a time, paging through the registries, running their fingers along the names. Fortunately Gorringe was a small town. Unfortunately, a good half of the women in the town seemed to have been named Anna, and they all seemed to have been abundantly fertile. None yet had given birth to a Susannah.

"There *are* other names in the world," Susannah groused. "Mary—perfectly acceptable name. Martha. There's another one."

"Myrtle," Kit suggested absently from over his book.

"Precisely," Susannah agreed. "You'd think these people would have heard of one or two of them."

The faded writing and poor light in the room taxed their eyes as they pored over the lists of names, whole lives, hundreds of them, summarized by three or four simple notations: birth, marriage, more births, death. Despite the business at hand, Susannah's thoughts were evenly divided along two tracks, when really they should have been focused on the one.

And then, because she couldn't help it:

"'*Difficult to forget,*'" she mimicked. It was a spot-on imitation of Kit's low, refined voice.

Kit looked up from his work and stared at her. "*Is* something troubling you, Miss Makepeace?" he asked mildly.

Oh, she hated that mild tone. "*Who* is Caro? And why did you ask about her?"

He returned his head to the book he was perusing. "You ask that almost as though you expect me to answer it." He sounded amused, distracted. Dismissive.

And this infuriated her. "You know everything about me—"

"Correction: We know nothing at all about you."

"You know what I mean! And *I* have a reason. You are simply secretive because . . . you are *afraid* to be otherwise. You hide from *everything*."

His head slowly, slowly lifted up.

I take it back! she wanted to say immediately, because his expression frightened her. His eyes fairly glittered, hot and blue; he was furious, this time at her. But something taut in his face made her think that she had somehow hurt him, too. Perhaps even . . . unnerved him. As though she had somehow unwittingly reached a place in him he didn't know how to defend, and so he could only offer up this silence.

She couldn't look away. He *wouldn't* look away.

When he finally spoke, she flinched. But his words weren't the kind she'd been expecting.

"'August of 1799,'" he said. "'Born to Anna Smith: Susannah Faith.'"

Her heart nearly stopped. "What? *Where?* I . . . I exist!"

She forgot she was frightened of him and scurried over to his side, and his posture eased as he moved aside to allow her to read the entry. "Who was my father?"

He paused a beat. "No father is listed, Susannah," he said gently.

She disliked the gentleness, and the implication. *Perhaps you were born on the wrong side of the blanket, Susannah.*

"Perhaps my father was killed in the war!" she said indignantly.

She doubted anyone had ever said that sentence quite as hopefully. Kit looked at her askance.

"Susannah Smith . . . Susannah Smith . . ." she tried out the name. "It's rather nice, don't you think? I wonder who my father was?"

"One hopes his last name *was* Smith," Kit said dryly. Clearly he was slightly less romantic and optimistic than Susannah. "It rather sounds like an alias. Now on to the deaths."

"But we've only just discovered I was actually born! Can I not savor it a moment?"

"And also have you home in time for your supper, Susannah? I think not. I won't have your aunt worrying about you. Deaths it is."

Twenty minutes later they'd discovered that no Smiths had expired in Gorringe, at least none that were recorded in the church registry.

Susannah was giddy with possibility; her name was a brush she could use to paint her whole life over. "What if . . . what if they're still alive? What if . . . James Makepeace kidnapped me, and my parents couldn't meet the ransom, and—"

"Then Makepeace decided to keep you, as, after all, he'd always wanted a daughter with very expensive tastes, and your parents gave up, because they couldn't afford to keep you in dresses?" Kit suggested. "One thing at a time, Miss Makepeace. We know that you were born here; it appears as though your parents neither married nor died here, though we can explore the cemetery if you wish. But we can move on to our next task: Trying to find someone in the town who may have known Anna Smith. I know just the place to start."

This tavern was thick-timbered, dark, scented with a few hundred years of wood and cigar and cooking smoke. Two men were leaning across the table over a rough-hewn chessboard and chess pieces smooth with use and age. It looked the sort of establishment that welcomed both men and women; it probably served a decent supper, Kit surmised. As it was the middle of the day, a few men were sprinkled about the tables enjoying a lunch of sausages and potatoes and ale. They looked up and continued looking, though not in any hostile sort of way, when Susannah and Kit walked in.

Kit steered Susannah directly to the bar. "Good afternoon, sir."

"Good afternoon, to you, sir," the barkeep, a wiry man with thinning hair, volunteered cheerily. "Name's Lester. What can I do for you today? Good meal? Ale's good. My brew is famous."

"Good afternoon, Mr. Lester. I am Mr. White. I was wondering whether you knew this woman, sir. She lived in Gorringe some years ago, 1802 or so. We think her name is Anna Smith."

He held out the miniature, and the barkeep perused it with the squinting frown specific to those who would soon need spectacles to read anything at all. "Anna Smith . . . Anna Smith . . . *Frank!*" Mr. Lester bellowed. Kit winced and Susannah jumped a little. "He's hard of hearing, ye see," he apologized to the two of them. One of the men playing chess turned slowly around.

"D'yer ever know an Anna Smith? 'Round about . . . 'oh-two, ye said?"

"Wasn't she the gel what 'ad a brother come to visit now and agin? Fine cattle—remember that 'orse, Bunton?"

The other man lifted his head from the chessboard. "Oh, that *was* one fine animal! Nivver saw the likes in these parts. And he come in that fancy contraption sometimes—"

"That open coach, like—a broosh?"

Ah, men, Kit thought, amused by his own gender. *Can't remember a man's name, or a woman's name, but they'll remember a man's horse and barouche for decades.*

"I recognize 'er face, guv—'ard to forget a face like that, ye see—but I saw 'er but a few times. Kept to 'erself, like. Dinna know who else might have known 'er. She lived 't the end of town. But you know who did know 'er?" He paused and glanced sideways at Susannah, then gave Kit a long meaningful look, which Kit interpreted correctly: He didn't want to repeat it in front of the lady. Intriguing. Kit nodded almost imperceptibly, giving permission to say it.

"'er name's Daisy Jones," he said sotto voce.

Good Lord. Kit was impressed. "*The* Daisy Jones?"

The man nodded vigorously. "Lived 'ere in Gorringe before she made a . . . a . . . name fer 'erself."

"Who on earth is Daisy Jones?" Susannah was impatient.

The men ignored her. "Last I 'eard she was in London."

"Oh, she's still in London, all right," Kit confirmed. The men exchanged wicked, manly grins and Frank turned back to his chessboard.

"*Who* is Daisy Jones?" Susannah tried again, the irritation amplified.

Kit pretended not to hear her. "And did you by any chance know of a woman named Caroline Allston? Was here about fifteen years ago? Dark hair, dark eyes, pretty—"

"Difficult to forget," Susannah interjected crossly. "Once you see her—don't forget to tell him that."

The barkeep gave Kit a commiserating look that said: *Women.* "Can't say that I did, guv. Sorry about that. *Frank!*" he bellowed again. Kit winced.

Frank turned around again at a leisurely pace.

"D'yer know of a woman name of Caroline Allston?"

"She was *very pretty,*" Susannah supplied, loudly, for Frank's benefit.

Frank ruminated on this for a time. "Can't say as I did, guv," he said. "'Nuther cove were in 'ere t'other day askin' the verra same question."

Kit was fairly certain he knew the answer to this question, but he thought he'd ask it, anyway. "This cove—do you remember his name?"

"Didna say, guv. Handsome, though. Fine figure of a man."

The men at the other tables broke into jeers of laughter at this. "'*Fine figure of a man!*'" they bellowed, slapping their tables.

"I'm only *sayin',*" Frank muttered defensively.

John Carr, Kit thought with resignation. He'd somehow followed Kit's leads about Lockwood to Gorringe.

"Thank you, sir. You've been most helpful." Kit proffered a few coins to the barkeep.

The man waved the coins away. "Oh, no need, no need. But I'll take yer money if I can give yer wife and yerself some lunch."

Wife! The word was so jarring that Kit pulled back his handful of coins in confusion.

Susannah was smiling, pleased at his discomfiture. "Give the man his money, dear."

Clunk. Clunk.

Two plates of sausages and potatoes and two tankards of foaming ale were deposited with some ceremony on the table in front of each of them. Susannah stared at her plate, then gave the sausages an experimental poke with her fork. She'd never before eaten in a pub; she'd never before been treated to a tankard of ale, for that matter. She peered into it. It was certainly pretty: dark golden, with a pale silky head.

Kit was watching her poke at her meal. "You put them in your *mouth*," he explained. "I recommend cutting them into pieces first." In direct contrast to his recommendation, he stabbed his sausage with his fork and bit off the end of it.

She gave the sausage another halfhearted poke.

"You're not hungry, Miss Makepeace?" he asked, when he'd swallowed.

"It's just . . ." She couldn't eat until she knew. "Confound it, who is Daisy Jones? You *must* tell me. If she knew my mother . . ." *And who is Caro?* But she hadn't the courage to ask that question yet again.

Kit took a long quaff of his ale, as if fortifying himself, and leaned back in his chair, studying her, his face lit with some secret amusement. She heard the click of chess pieces being knocked off the board behind them in the silence that followed.

"Daisy Jones . . ." She could almost hear Kit sorting

through a selection of words in his mind. ". . . Is an opera dancer." He was struggling not to smile.

Susannah narrowed her eyes at him. "No, she isn't. She's something much worse, isn't she? I can tell."

"Or much better. I suppose it all depends on whether you're a man . . . or a *clergy*man." He was laughing silently now.

"It's not funny! If my mother was the friend of an opera dancer . . ." She trailed off when a suspicion struck. "Are *you* friends with opera dancers?"

"It's difficult *not* to be friends with opera dancers. Opera dancers are very friendly."

She almost laughed. But then she thought of what he might *do* with opera dancers . . . and an astonishing pair of feelings reared:

Jealousy that someone else would be able to freely touch him.

And an extremely perverse wish that she might, for even a moment, be an opera dancer, so that she could freely touch him, too.

Oh God, she now knew it was almost certainly true: Her mother must have been an opera dancer. For no one but the daughter of an opera dancer would have those sorts of thoughts. She'd almost certainly inherited her "passion," such as it was, and all these wayward impulses, from her mother.

"What if my *mother* was . . . was an opera dancer?" she said it in a whisper.

Kit stopped chewing. "Well . . . would it matter to you? Would you still want to know about her?"

She thought about this. "Yes. It would matter to me— how could it not? But yes, I would still want to know."

"All right, then. Eat your lunch." He resumed devouring his own.

She watched him eat for a moment, fascinated. There was nothing fastidious about the way he ate; it was purposeful and practical and astonishingly fast, but not the least bit untidy. He ate as though it were his last meal.

"Would you be shocked?" she asked him.

"If you ate your lunch? I might be."

"If my mother was an opera dancer."

"On the contrary. I'd be *delighted*." He looked up and smiled at her expression. "Come now, Miss Makepeace. Very little shocks me."

"Except the word 'wife,'" she said tartly.

He stopped chewing; regarded her across the table with that vivid blue stare. His expression was difficult to read, but it was definitely not what she would have called warm. More . . . considering. Specifically, as though he were considering whether or not to spear her with a fork.

It's your fault! she wanted to blurt. He was forever coming at her with all his little challenges and feints, which worked to shake her more controversial thoughts loose, and then out they came.

She supposed, however, if he could do that so easily, she was engaged in far too many controversial thoughts.

No doubt because her mother *had* been an opera dancer.

"Are you going to drink your ale?" he said finally.

"Some of it," she said airily. She lifted it up, took a long sip, and then coughed until her eyes teared.

With dignity, she brushed her hand across her eyes, then pushed the ale across to the now smiling viscount. And then she cut the sausage in half, and deposited half on his plate. He looked as pleased as if Christmas had just arrived, which for some reason pleased her just as much.

It had been some time since Kit had done anything quite so ordinary as promenade on a beautiful day with a pretty girl.

"Give me your arm," he said to Susannah.

"Why, your *lordship*—" she teased.

He frowned darkly at her, which made her bite back a smile, and she tucked her gloved hand into his arm. He felt faintly ridiculous and smug all at once; it seemed right, oddly peaceful—a pub lunch with a lovely girl, a stroll after it. The crowds were thickening at this end of the street; a summer fair was in progress, and stalls offering ribbons and sweets and games were lined up on the cobblestones, cheerful attendees jockeying to get a look at them. He wished they had time to linger, to poke about. It had been ages since he'd lingered anywhere purposelessly, ages since he'd wanted to, really.

Their carriage was just coming into sight when Kit saw the man coming toward them, head lowered, moving at a casual clip like everyone else in the crowd, his head turning about aimlessly, admiring booths, deciding where to linger, perhaps.

As he drew closer to Kit and Susannah, he glanced up from underneath his hat, slipped his hand inside his coat.

And the world narrowed to a glint in the man's hand.

Kit twisted his body in front of Susannah before the knife struck. He flung his arm up to block the blade, felt the bite of it through his coat across his forearm and bicep, and kicked out, hard, catching the bastard in the knee. But the knife flashed up again as the man crashed to the ground, and Kit dropped and half-rolled to the side to duck it.

In the moment he'd looked away, the man had slipped off into the crowd, dodging, weaving neatly and quickly, never really breaking into a run, never causing more than a head or two to turn in his direction. In other words, he wasn't new to this sort of thing. He was a professional.

Kit sprang upright, reached out for Susannah, closed his hands over her arms and pulled her soft body into his chest so tightly he could feel the hammer of her heart against his ribs. She was white-faced, but not in shock; the color was even now returning to her cheeks.

"Are you all right?" he demanded quietly.

He wasn't, quite; his arm was already hurting like a bastard now. *Same damn arm.* He was fairly certain it wasn't a serious wound; his coat had taken the brunt of the strike. Still, he would need to see to it.

A couple strolling toward the festivities gazed at them with some concern. "He's had a bit too much ale," Susannah whispered to the woman, who looked amused and sympathetic, and turned her head discreetly away.

"I think you're bleeding," she said to Kit, sounding faintly accusing.

"It's only a—"

"You're *bleeding*." She sounded furious now, near tears. "We'll go to the tavern. We'll see to your arm there."

He half-smiled. "Yes, sir."

"Don't you *dare* make light of this. You make light of *everything*. You could have been *killed*. And it's because of me, wasn't it? I know that now. It's because of me."

Her voice trailed off. She jerked her head, not wanting

him to witness her tears yet again; she tried to pull away from him. He released her.

"Yes," he told her gently. "I think it may very well be."

"You could have been *killed*." She said it again, softly. Her hand rose up; for one astonishing moment, he thought she meant to touch his face. Perhaps he looked alarmed, because she dropped her hand to her side again, curled it into a fist instead, lowered her head, took in a long breath, steadying herself. He watched, admiring every bit of it.

"Thank you for saving my life again," Susannah said with some dignity.

He couldn't help it: He did smile then, though the burning pain in his damned arm made it a little more difficult than usual. "Not at all, Miss Makepeace. Or whoever you are. It's always a pleasure to save your life each and every time. You're having a very eventful day, aren't you?"

She smiled a little thinly. "You're not a naturalist."

"I am," he disagreed, startled.

"But that's not all you are."

"I was a soldier," he allowed.

"But that's not all you are."

He hadn't yet outright lied to her. And for some reason, though he could easily, colorfully lie in the name of an assignment, it seemed important not to ever directly lie to her.

"No," he admitted.

She gazed up at him and said nothing more, knowing, perhaps, his limits. She seemed entirely composed now.

Perhaps she was growing a little too accustomed to danger.

With this thought a sizzling fury jagged through his veins, hampering his breathing.

"All of it. The coach . . . the adder . . . the horse . . . Why does someone want to kill me?" She sounded a little awed.

He almost smiled again. Almost. Fury and pain weren't conducive to smiling.

"I was wondering the very same thing. You must be tremendously important, Susannah, if someone wants to kill you." He thought he'd try for a joke.

"I thought that went without saying." Almost breezily said.

And damned if she didn't actually look a little amused.

Kit looked down at her, and felt another sharp little poke in the vicinity of his heart, an uncomfortable reminder that he did indeed have one. And with a breathlessness that had nothing to do with the fact that he'd just been rolling on the ground with a knife-wielding attacker, he realized the fact that Susannah was still warm and breathing and smiling up at him made him light-headed with a quiet elation.

I'm probably just losing blood.

And again, the puzzle pieces were before him, but he couldn't quite make them fit. He suspected that it would now be more dangerous to stop searching than to leave it.

Damn his father and Egypt, anyway. Someone had just tried to thrust a knife into Susannah Makepeace. And it *wasn't* a coincidence, he was certain, that someone had done the very same thing to James Makepeace, not to mention Richard Lockwood fifteen years ago.

"I don't know who's trying to kill you, Susannah. But they'll certainly have cause to regret the attempt when I find out. And I will."

* * *

"Back so soon, Mr. White?"

Susannah spoke before Kit could. "We were wondering if we might trouble you for a basin of water and a room for just an hour or so?"

Somehow taking charge of this situation at least helped her feel a little less helpless, and not as though someone had been trying to kill her since she set foot in the county, and not as if this man had spent the past several days saving her life.

"Just an *'hour or so,'* eh?" he said to Kit, with a wink, who gave him a rakish smile and a return wink, as he held the slit edges of his sleeve discreetly closed. Susannah could feel heat in her cheeks, which probably did nothing but convince the barkeep of what they were about to get up to, but she held her head haughtily as he led them to a room. He left them with a basin of water and another wink.

Kit stripped off his coat and shirt with unself-conscious alacrity and twisted around to look at his arm.

She'd seen him completely undressed before, but that had been at a safe distance. From a few feet away, his beauty stunned. There wasn't a spare ounce of flesh on him; hard, distinct muscles were cut in his back and chest and arms, and of course he was covered all over in that smooth, pale gold skin. She saw scars on him now that she was closer, a long white line, puckered at the edges scored a shoulder blade; a roughly round patch of skin, thick and white, on his back, closer to the top of his trousers. War had done that to him, no doubt. A bruise turning greenish spread over his chest, where the horse had fallen on him; and a new angry red line slashed across his forearm and up over his bicep.

What a sharp knife it must have been to cut through his

coat and shirt and skin. How much more easily it would have sliced through her.

He might be a quicksilver man, maddeningly glib, unnervingly skilled, but that angry red line proved he was as vulnerable as any other human being, as temporary. He'd flung his body in front of hers, to take the knife meant for her, but in the end blood flowed in his veins the same as anyone's, and could be spilled just as easily.

Well, nearly as easily. She'd watched him spin and kick and duck, and she simply couldn't imagine Douglas, for instance, doing that. And if she'd been promenading with an actual naturalist, no doubt she'd be dead by now.

He looked up, startled, and then a little abashed, as though he'd just recalled she was there. "It's *blood*," he half-warned, half-apologized. "I'm sorry, I didn't think. I shouldn't have—"

"*Your* blood," she said. The words came out through a knot in her throat.

He regarded her levelly for a moment, a tiny crease between his brows, as though he was worried yet again that she might faint. And then he reached for the basin of water, and took the hem of his shirt in his teeth.

"Then again," he said, and tore a bandage from the hem, "you're *accustomed* to seeing me in the undress, aren't you, Miss Makepeace?"

Wicked man.

"One *time* does not make one accustomed." That was certainly an understatement.

He opened his mouth and for a moment it seemed as though he intended to say something typically Kit, but he stopped himself and looked back at her instead, his eyes suddenly guarded. And the fact that he had stopped himself made her profoundly aware that they were in a room together, alone, and one of them was without a shirt, and that he had realized the implications of precisely the same thing.

"Give the water to me," she tried, casually. "I'll do it. I can see the wound better than you can."

He looked almost as uncertain as she felt. "It's blood," he warned again, weakly.

"I had *this hand* inside a horse the other day." She lifted it up.

His eyes brightened at the comparison. "I hope I'm an improvement."

"Somewhat. At least it's your *arm* we're interested in."

He snorted a short pleased laugh and sat down on the bed. When she drew near the rich musk of him wrapped her again: shaving soap, ale, and that delicious, darker, something—*him*. It might as well have been opium for what it did to the run of her thoughts.

Focus. She took up one of the rags he'd made, and there was silence for a time, apart from the quiet dip of a rag into the water, and the trickle of water back into the basin, which was pinkening now with his blood. He held obediently still, like a little boy, his eyes calmly fixed on the white wall ahead of him, and he didn't flinch at all. Perhaps it hurt very little compared to whatever had put the other scars on his back.

She bathed him, but the rhythm of the rag dipping into the water slowed, as she wondered why everything he did—blinking, breathing in and out—seemed more significant when *he* did it than when any other human did.

A minute, perhaps more, passed before she became aware she'd stopped swabbing altogether, and had been standing very still instead, watching the fair, fernlike trail that traveled from his flat belly up between his ribs rise and fall, rise and fall, with his quickening breathing.

He turned his head, slowly, slowly lifted his eyes up to hers.

This . . . *this* was desire. Not the near-chaste kiss pressed upon her earlier today by another man, but this thing that made a tyrant of her senses, that made it seem absurd to stand this close to him and not taste the smooth curve of his shoulder, not trail a finger along the hair that began between his ribs and disappeared into his trousers. This thing that sealed the two of them in heated, fraught silence; that suddenly made thought seem pointless, even frivolous beyond words.

But in this moment it didn't matter at all to Susannah whether Kit had made love to one woman or a million, it didn't matter at all to her whether he saw her as just a body from whom to take pleasure. She didn't care whether he was here for her sake, or for the sake of Caroline Allston. She wanted him with an incinerating ferocity, because in a sense it was all she had to give to him.

His eyes read hers. His chest expanded, sank, with a long, unsteady breath.

I'm lost.

"Thank you," he said softly. And turned away from her. And stood.

"Use this piece to make a bandage"—he gestured to a shred of his shirt—"and wind it snugly, but not too snugly, or my circulation will be impaired, and my arm will fall off. And that would be inconvenient, to say the least."

A familiar glib lilt to his words. The moment was gone as if it had never been.

He *was* a bloody gentleman, then. The mad longing slowly released its grip on her, leaving behind a shamed empty fluttering in the pit of her stomach. Perhaps later she would feel grateful to him, but now she simply felt ashamed: not for having wanton thoughts, but because she'd so brazenly given him an opportunity, one that he clearly wanted, and he'd chosen not to take it.

She wound the bandage as instructed, her hands shaking a little. "That should keep your arm on," she told him, trying again for bravado.

"I'll apply a little salve of Saint-John's-wort when we return home," he told her. "Wards off fever."

What do you have for warding off another kind of fever?

"I'll remember that for the next time I'm accosted by a knife-wielding attacker."

"That's enough," he said coldly.

She froze as though he'd slapped her.

Kit thrust his arms almost angrily in the remains of his shirt, and then his coat. "We'd best hurry home."

It was late afternoon when the carriage took them home, more subdued, more edified, than when they'd originally set out. Kit assured her that his coachman and footmen were as bristling with weapons as he was, and they were as safe as they could hope to be at the moment.

"Should I tell Aunt Frances about . . . today?"

Kit turned to her, all solicitous politeness. "What would you like to do?"

Susannah thought about it. "I shouldn't like to worry her, or make her afraid for me. I shall continue in your employ."

He nodded, as though anything she might have said would have suited him.

And then the silence in the half-dark of the coach grew thick and uncomfortable, and then Susannah's thoughts began to blur and she began to drowse.

"I fought a duel over Caroline Allston when I was just seventeen."

She was fully awake now. She watched him quietly for a moment, assessing his emotional temperature.

"With my best friend," he added. His voice was strained, as though he'd been rehearsing the words in his head for some time. She heard the wry shame in them.

"Did you kill him?"

He smiled faintly. "No, he walks among us still. And he's still my best friend."

"And you don't know what became of Caroline?"

"No. She disappeared the very next day."

"And you've reason to believe she might have been in Gorringe?"

"Yes."

She'd noticed how succinct he became with issues that actually revealed him.

"Did you love her?" she asked, almost gingerly.

"Oh, I thought that I did, yes. But then again, I was just seventeen." He said it lightly, as though being seventeen precluded it being love.

She considered teasing him: *So that's your scandal?*—but something told her to refrain.

And then he gave her his usual cocky smile, and she thought she understood better the origin of that smile now. He was a very good discoverer of secrets, true. But he was also very good at keeping a smoke screen around what she now suspected was his own secret: his heart was as breakable as her own. Had in fact been broken before.

She smiled back at him, shook her head, didn't push for more. Somehow she knew it was the only way more would be forthcoming.

And she was asleep soon thereafter.

He watched her sleep with some complex emotion; it seemed to have tiers and facets, and the moment he managed to get one facet in focus, another one winked into prominence. He'd begun to suspect he was a romantic, despite everything, and the thought irritated him and amused him. It was a tremendously inconvenient thing to be, and not at all what one expected to find lurking in the heart of a spy.

Today . . . how easy it would have been to slide a hand over the small of her back, pull her forward into his bare chest, and touch his lips at last, at last, to that soft, soft mouth. He was, in fact, dangerously close to *needing* to know how her mouth would feel against his. He'd watched the pulse beating in her smooth throat, and for an extraordinary moment he'd had every intention of pressing his mouth against it . . . after he'd tasted her lips, of course. And from there . . .

This bloody folio assignment. His bloody, bloody father. A month away from a painstakingly wooed and won countess was simply too much to ask of a man in his prime.

Susannah was a beautiful woman, a soft and sensual woman just coming to understand the depth of her own passion and strength, and it was a breathtaking thing to witness. But he understood his own role in fomenting the heat he'd seen in her eyes today and rued it a little. He wondered if, in doing so, he'd done her a disservice, for who or what in a town like Barnstable could ever satisfy it? She would be a delightful interlude, at best, but truly he wanted nothing more than that. Indulging himself even a little would only hurt her, as she was so very nearly innocent. She'd already known too much of hurt.

Best to cast his lot in with the countess, who knew very well how to play the game. Best to impose a distance comprised of politeness and gallantry for the duration of his folio assignment. He would do his best to discover why someone intended to kill her, and then he would resume his life in London.

Still, there was something he'd wanted to know for some time now, and he found he couldn't deny himself this particular opportunity. Very gently, almost stealthily, he leaned forward and rested the backs of his fingers against Susannah's cheek.

He regretted it instantly. For her skin was every bit as soft as he'd dreamed.

Chapter Thirteen

Kit arrived home to a letter from his father, and in the mood he was in—the arm *did* hurt, Saint-John's-wort salve notwithstanding—every word of it seemed sarcastic.

> Dear Christopher,
>
> I do hope you're enjoying your stay in Barnstable. I'm eager to review your findings. Would you be so kind as to send a sampling of your notes and your sketches to me posthaste?
>
> Warmly,
> Your Father
> Earl of Westphall
>
> P.S. I've booked passage for you on the next ship to Egypt. It leaves at the beginning of next month.

Bloody, *bloody* hell. Thanks to the fact that someone was trying to kill Susannah Makepeace, all he had were some sketches of voles, a few ferns, and a tree or two. Oh, and of course, there was a wonderful sketch of him naked on a pier. They'd barely scratched the surface of Barnstable's flora and fauna. He didn't know whether to be amused at how well his father knew him; incensed that his father clearly didn't trust him; or ashamed that the mistrust was *warranted*, given that he'd spent the day in Gorringe with the daughter of a dead spy, for reasons both altruistic and selfish. And, coincidentally, related to Morley.

Another indication of how well his father knew him. And now when he knew something was genuinely amiss— as evidenced by someone lunging at Susannah with a knife—he couldn't tell his father about it.

He couldn't complete this assignment on his own; his pride simply wouldn't let him submit his own merely adequate drawings. And . . . well, he wanted to make a success of this, for if Susannah's drawings were to become known, perhaps she would have a life outside of Barnstable.

And a woman like Susannah deserved to have an interesting life.

Now all he needed to do was keep her alive long enough for her to *have* an interesting life.

She'd left her sketchbook behind in the coach again. He leafed through it, but he could never seem to do it casually. The near effortlessness, the grace and precision of the drawings still awed him a little, it was like watching someone he knew wave a wand to conjure something— and so little awed him anymore. Her drawings had been brave and passionate long before she knew that she was. The clues to her were there for anyone who'd known to look for them.

He stopped his leafing when he saw a drawing he hadn't seen before.

Me, he thought, surprised.

It wasn't an overly handsome drawing, as he wasn't an overly handsome man, and his pride did twinge a little. But somehow, she'd seen intensity in the set of his jaw, wit and steel shaded with vulnerability in the cast of his eyes; she'd made a downright poem of his mouth.

When had she drawn this? More importantly: How had she . . . *seen* this? It was almost more uncomfortable than being sketched in the nude. Somehow it revealed as much about Susannah as it did him.

He liked the way she saw him.

Sunset was streaking the sky in citrus shades now, and dark would fall hard in less than an hour. He thought of Susannah alone in the cottage with Frances Perriman, and of a twig and a sawed saddle girth, of a nondescript man artfully lunging from the crowd with a knife in his hand.

And he collected blankets, a bottle of brandy, a lantern, a box of matches, and loaded his pistols with fresh powder and shot. He loaded a musket, too, because one could never be too prepared. He was downstairs in minutes.

"But you've just arrived home, sir." Bullton looked confused. "And you're going out again? Is there an assem . . ." He trailed off when he noticed Kit's bundle and his clothing. "Will you at least take some dinner?" he asked in resignation.

"I'll stop in the kitchen, Bullton, and take some food out with me. But I've . . . work to do outside tonight."

Bullton stepped aside, and Kit stepped into the kitchen for some bread and cheese and cold chicken. He pumped a flask of water for himself.

And then he was out of the door and down the pathway. He knew just where to set up a little camp that couldn't possibly be seen by anyone in the cottage, but which would afford him the ideal view of it. The pain in his arm would ensure he stayed awake; the brandy would keep the arm manageable.

But no one else would be able to get near her.

And if anyone tried, by God they'd rue it.

He'd waited, listening to crickets, to deer picking through the underbrush, to the first birdsong. When dawn began to light the sky, he took himself wearily to the pond for a quick swim, rinsed his mouth with water from his flask. His eyes felt as though they'd been plucked and replaced with two musket balls. He swiped a hand over his bristly face; the shave would have to wait.

He was standing at Mrs. Perriman's gate, rumpled, weary, but strangely satisfied when Susannah ventured out the door, basket on her arm, looking posy-fresh in pale, striped muslin. The sight of her was bracing. He was suddenly glad she'd threatened a cockney workman with a vase for her dresses.

She saw him and stopped. "You look as though you engaged in a debauch last night," she said lightly. "You've rings beneath your eyes, and . . ." She trailed off, and her gaze became something uncomfortably like concern.

"You're familiar with the look of debauchers, are you, Miss Makepeace?" Which effectively disconcerted her, displacing her concern, as he'd intended. "The arm is still attached. We'll see what today brings, however, as fate seems determined to separate me from it. Are you ready to put in a day's work?"

"Are *you*?"

"I've no choice," he said grimly. "Duty calls. And I've your sketchbook."

"Oh." She looked uncomfortable. "I didn't mean to leave it."

He would have teased her about the drawing, but he couldn't bring himself to do it. It seemed somehow as intimate to her as his revelation about Caroline was to him, and suddenly, he felt a little shy.

So he shrugged, and handed the sketchbook to her.

"Are we riding or walking today?" she wanted to know.

"Walking. Today I thought we'd finally sketch the Hellebore."

"And do you have your pistol?" She'd asked it almost matter-of-factly.

"Wouldn't dream of going anywhere without it." And he wasn't the least bit wry about it.

"Well, then. Shall we?" She squared her shoulders. A soldier in striped muslin.

He wasn't in the mood for conversation—he wasn't certain he could string words together at all, weary as he was, though his thoughts were certainly active enough—and Miss Makepeace was quiet, too.

She was working up to something, however, he could almost feel it.

"Will you take me to London?"

Ah. And there it was.

"You're not one for circumspection, are you, Miss Makepeace?"

"No, but *you* are."

"You wish to get a late start on the season, is that it?" He said it over his shoulder, and he saw a little shadow pass over her features. He silently cursed himself. He doubted voles and adders made up for Almacks.

"I wish to see Miss Daisy Jones," she said.

So did he, for that matter. He *wanted* to take her to London. He wanted to talk to Daisy Jones, both to attempt to unravel the mystery behind Susannah Makepeace's life . . . and behind the reason someone wanted her dead.

But of course, if his father knew of his presence in London, Kit wouldn't be in London for very long. He'd be waving good-bye to London from the deck of a ship bound for Egypt or some other godforsaken place that lacked countesses and gentlemen's clubs.

"I'll think about it," he told her gruffly, and kept walking. On past the white oak, beyond the pond, deeper into the wood, where trees prevented the worst of the heat from beating down on them. He could scarcely think now. There was a clearing, mossy, where hellebore grew, and by God, despite everything, he still wanted to document the hellebore.

Then he heard a little shriek, and spun. He watched Susannah stumble, her arms windmilling slightly; she fell hard on her rump hard before he could catch her.

Kit dropped to his knees next to her, his heart in his throat. "Good God. Are you hurt?"

She laughed up at him. "It's all right . . . I merely stumbled over a stone. And I'm not made of glass. Just clumsy."

He wasn't amused. "Forgive me, but I'm a little sensitive to *shrieking*, Miss Makepeace, given the events of the past few days." He thrust out his hand.

She ignored his outstretched hand in favor of propping herself up on her elbows and throwing her head back to study the sky, as if surprised to find such a thing above her. Her hair was coming a little loose of its pins; her dress had hiked up a little, too, revealing a hint of long, calves, lyrically curved, tapering into slim ankles. All of it covered in pale stocking. Susannah the siren.

"That cloud?" she said suddenly, gesturing skyward with her chin.

"Yes?" He crouched next to her, ready to help her up when she was ready to be helped up, and tilted his head back to see what she saw.

"Looks like a unicorn."

He studied it: That white, spiraling, vertical puff was the horn, he supposed; the wisp behind *could* be a tail.

"So it does."

She lowered her head and gave him a wry look. She knew he was humoring her.

The next thing he did was absently, and truly almost innocently done, born of the playfulness of the moment, perhaps, or simply because the purity of the line begged for it. He reached out and drew his finger lightly from her ankle right up the curve of her calf.

When his finger reached the crook of her knee he stopped. Astonished to see it there.

Silently, a little frantically, he considered excuses: *An insect was crawling up your stocking, Susannah. I was checking to see if you were injured, Susannah. I was—*

"Don't stop." It was her voice. Husky, abstracted.

And the words roared like a brushfire over his senses. He briefly closed his eyes. When he opened them again, the very quality of the day had changed: thickened, slowed, enclosed the two of them.

He slowly lifted his head. He found a dare in Susannah's eyes, and a heat easily the equal of his own, and the sweetest sort of anxiety. She wanted this, or thought she did, and was afraid she'd be rebuffed again.

And yet he wasn't sure she truly understood what it was she wanted.

He was all too sure what *he* wanted.

A breeze, mindless of the significance of the moment, gaily tossed a streamer of her hair across her forehead.

Just a little, a voice in his head urged him. He could show her just a little of passion, he reasoned; he could show her gently, skillfully, give her just a taste. Because lord knew what would become of her, and what sort of man would ultimately have the taking of her. He was certain he could give her pleasure, and she deserved that.

He was distantly amused, even a little alarmed, at how reason and lust had conspired to make his desire to crawl beneath Susannah's Makepeace's skirts seem noble.

And so he did it: He drew his finger as slowly as he could bear along the length of her practical stocking, up over the curve of her calf, and he could feel the warmth of her skin beneath it, hear the stuttering catch in her breath, and her mounting excitement flowed into him. He reached her garter, a surprisingly plain one, given that this was Susannah Makepeace: a pink ribbon, no satin rosettes, just a bow. And with his finger he leisurely traced, once, twice, again, the satin of it, deliberately postponing for both of them the moment when he would touch the skin above it.

Her eyes fluttered closed.

"No," he commanded softly. "Open them."

She did, but her lips parted slightly with breathing that was growing ragged with anticipation. Slowly, slowly he uncurled his fingers and laid his open hand against the top of her thigh, over her stocking, just below her garter. He left it there, resting at that threshold between stocking and skin, for as long as he thought they both could withstand it, and smiled down, a crooked, slow smile. A silent declaration to her that he would be leading every moment of this interlude, that he would determine the start and finish of it.

At last, he slid his hand smoothly upward to touch the skin of her thigh. His smile vanished.

The vulnerable, silken heat of her skin . . . quite simply, it undid him.

Kit understood then that he'd been fooling himself, had been fooling himself for days. It was she who owned both this moment . . . and him.

And when he eased his body down alongside her, her hand rose up as though the air had become as viscous as honey, and she cradled his lowering face as though they'd been lovers forever.

Forever. He found himself wanting to stretch each second, to heighten each moment, to make distinct memories of them all: *Now I'm touching her skin . . . now I'm kissing her lips . . .* His lips touched hers, just a brush, once, twice, over the full softness of her lovely mouth, discovering what she knew of kissing. With devastating instinct, she echoed him, dragging her lips softly across his, with his, until the desire in him was coiled so tightly his limbs trembled from it.

"*Susannah.*" A ragged whisper. She sighed a warm breath out against his lips and brought her other hand up to hold his face; in her hands he could feel her tension and urgency. And he'd meant to linger over this kiss, to take it deeper with delicacy and finesse, and then to end it, but he found he could not. His desire was suddenly untenable;

he was convinced only the taste of her could ease it. He touched an impatient tongue to her lips and coaxed them open. When she parted her mouth he sought her tongue, and discovered, with a low sound in the back of his throat, the hot, silken sweetness inside her mouth. Her tongue tentatively moved, tangled with his. *Oh, God.*

"Like this?" she whispered.

"*God,* yes," he breathed.

She smiled against his mouth.

"No smiling," he murmured. "Only kissing."

Their mouths moved languidly over each other at first, nipping, delving deeply, retreating. And gradually it built to urgency. He rose up over her to take his kisses deeper still, to taste the contours of her mouth, teeth clashing against her teeth, and still it never seemed enough. The sensation was like soaring in place; Kit couldn't feel the ground beneath him, or the air above him; he was aware only of the sweetness of the woman joined with him, and distantly he marveled, he'd never felt quite so lost. He tucked his hip in firmly against hers, astounded at how painfully aroused he was.

"Sweet," he murmured, moving his lips from hers to kiss to nip beneath her chin, to draw his tongue down the cord of her throat. Her breathing was rushed, and with the rise and fall of her chest he could see the tight darkness of her nipples beneath the fine fabric of her dress. "Sweet," he sighed again, moving his mouth to breathe against her breast; he touched his tongue to her nipple through the fabric. She caught her breath at the sensation, arced up a little to meet him. And as she did, his fingers, five feathers, began to stroke the tender skin inside her thigh.

At first she tensed; the muscles of her thigh quivering, uncertain. But then her legs parted a little more for him.

"Stockings, but no drawers?" he teased, breathlessly. He nudged the neckline of her gown lower with his teeth, exposing her breast, distracting her as his hand glided farther up her thigh, to come gently to rest against the damp, silken curls at the crook of them.

"Too warm for ... drawers ... but I liked the ... garters ..." She gasped out the words, and he gave a short laugh before he took her nipple into his mouth. Puckered velvet, it was, the palest, most delicate pink, like her lips; her breast could fill the palm of his hand. He knew because he skimmed his palm over the other one.

"*Kit,*" she rasped. "*God.*"

"One and the same," he murmured. He heard her gasp something, either a tortured laugh or a word, which may have been "beast," but she stopped abruptly when he took her nipple into his mouth again and drew slow circles around it with his tongue. Her softly sighed "*oh,*" her back arching up to meet him, her fingers combing over his head, made him wilder than he thought he could bear.

But he would bear it. Today was for her, and today was all there would be.

He settled for tucking his hips closer to her, his aching erection brushing against her. His fingers stroked lightly over the curls between her legs, twining in them. And then he returned his lips to hers, gently, because he wanted to watch her eyes when he slid a finger lightly along her cleft.

He felt her body go taut when he did; she drew in a sharp breath.

His hand stilled. "No?" he said softly.

"Yes," she disagreed on a whisper, touching his face.

He kissed her softly, as his finger slid lightly again, and then again, and at last her legs slipped open wider still, inviting him in. Desire clawed him, a great bird of prey clinging to his back, he could scarcely breathe. With his fingers, he circled her gently, slowly at first, and then insistently, listening to the pulse of her breath, to her soft murmurs, to learn the rhythm she wanted, until her desire drenched his fingers. He touched nearly chaste kisses to her mouth as his fingers played over her, and watched, triumphant, as her pupils grew large, her beautiful, complicated eyes opaque, her breathing become a quiet storm.

"Kit?" she whispered urgently. "I—it's—"

"I know," he sympathized hoarsely. "Move with me now."

And she began to move her hips in time with his knowing fingers, colluding with him in her own pleasure, and he moved his own hips against her, craving his own release even as he knew he must deny it. He covered her mouth with a kiss, a deep kiss, tangling his tongue with hers, and oh the taste of her: honey and velvet, rich as plums. He moved his fingers in time with his tongue, knew by her escalating breathing, the rhythm of her hips, that it would be soon.

She took her lips from his, her head thrashed to one side. *"Please . . ."*

"Hold on to me, Susannah." She was utterly focused on her own journey now, and God, how he wanted to go there with her.

At last, her fingers dug into his arms and she bowed up with a soft cry, pulsing against his hand.

And somehow, this seemed nearly as precious as the

beat of her heart, and the pleasure he took in her release was so acute it might well have been his own.

Kit gently took his hand from her, breathed in deeply, breathed out again, steadying himself, willing his own need to ebb, and tried desperately to knit back together the frayed ends of his senses.

For so long now, part of the pleasure in making love to a woman had been the mechanics of seduction. He'd always been the master of each step of it, and this, too had been part of the pleasure for him.

But . . . this pleasure was different. It was in Susannah's breath, warm against his neck in the aftermath of her release. The flush in her cheeks and creamy throat. In the scent of her hair. In her lovely eyes going opaque from desire, her hands in his hair. In—

"Did we just make love?" Susannah wanted to know.

In questions like that.

He smiled faintly. "Very nearly."

"There's . . . more . . . for you, I know." She said it shyly, and reached out and tentatively covered his subsiding arousal with her hand. He sucked in a breath and clutched her wrist to stop her. And then he rolled over on his back to look at the sky, a distance away from her.

The sky looked different, somehow. Probably the whole world looked different now.

"It's just . . ." He faltered, after a moment of silence, for he was afraid he'd hurt her with his words. "There will be no going back for you, then, Susannah."

But was that what bothered him precisely? Now that the fever of the moment had passed, a strange panic was welling inside him, and he didn't know how to identify it.

He had a tremendously ungentlemanly impulse to run like the devil.

She was quiet next to him for a moment; a bird trilled its song into the silence and the trees shook their leaves into a welcome breeze.

"Perhaps . . . perhaps I don't want to go back," she said. Oh, and already he heard the hurt in her words.

He rolled over on his side to look down at her for a long moment. "Susannah," he murmured. He traced her lips, swollen from kisses, with his finger, and then kissed them gently. He stroked her hair away from her face, avoiding looking into her questioning eyes. He brushed his lips over her cheek, her brow, then plucked a leaf from her hair, and tenderly straightened her bodice, all while she silently watched him, studying his face, well aware he was refusing to look directly at her.

Finally, he levered his tall frame to his feet, and his arm, which for the past half hour he hadn't felt at all, was throbbing.

"Come. I'll walk you home. I find . . . I find my arm is aching." He reached his hand down; after a moment's hesitation, she took it, and he helped her to her feet. She brushed the leaves from her dress. They set out for home, not touching.

The walk was silent; he left her at her aunt's gate with a bow. It was a strangely formal thing to do, and he saw Susannah flinch a little. But for some reason he needed to impose a distance.

"Hellebore tomorrow then?" she said it brightly. Tinsel bright. It rang falsely in the still of the day.

He'd done this to her, he'd put that falseness in her voice. Still, there was nothing he could do to make her feel any more certain, because it was possible no one had ever felt as uncertain than he did at the moment.

"My arm." He shrugged apologetically. "Perhaps a day of rest. . . ?"

Coward.

He'd never before been one for lying. But then again, he'd never before been afraid of the truth before.

Susannah's brightness faltered. "All right. I do hope it feels better soon."

"So do I." He tossed the words out lightly, but they sounded awful, jarring, instead. He could have kicked himself.

I never should have touched her.

Funny, but a mere half hour ago it didn't seem that he'd had any choice at all.

He gave another short bow, and left her staring after him at her aunt's gate, and noticed as he backed away there was one last tiny leaf still clinging to her hair.

Susannah stood at the gate flanked by her aunt's roses, and watched Kit disappear down the path. A leaf clung to his bright, close-cropped hair. It added a little whimsy to what was otherwise an almost cruelly dignified departure.

She remembered traveling down that very same path on her very first day in Barnstable, lured by recklessness, a little bit of despair, a need to test the boundaries of her new life. She'd discovered him on the other end of it, stark naked, arms up in the air, roaring a satisfied *"Ahhhh!"* to the elements. He wasn't precisely a pot of gold at the end of a rainbow. Perhaps a treasure chest instead. The kind one finds at the bottom of the ocean, filled with rubies and doubloons, guarded by snapping crustaceans and darker things that perhaps no one had yet discovered or named.

She considered whether to regret taking that path that morning. She couldn't quite decide yet.

But she'd certainly got what she'd thought she wanted, hadn't she?

The taste of him lingered on her lips; she could smell him on her clothes. It was almost as though he stood there with her still. She put her fingers up to her lips; they felt chafed and tender and thoroughly, properly, used for perhaps the first time ever. A white heat of desire threaded through her veins again; it stole her breath. She closed her eyes.

She knew now what his beautiful mouth could do. It could prod her with sarcasm and truth and wit. It could devastate her with tenderness; it could relentlessly build a storm of pleasure in her. It could own her until that storm broke over her.

Oh, and after that, too. Because she couldn't imagine now ever drinking her fill of him.

She wondered, however, if Kit had taken his fill of *her.* He'd rolled over, been distracted and silent and pensive. Bloody *polite,* in fact—which is how she'd known something was terribly wrong. Perhaps she'd been too innocent, or too eager, or too dull for a man like him, a man who'd fought a duel over a woman when he was scarcely yet grown, who'd seen war. Who'd befriended opera dancers. And she—well, before Kit, she'd been kissed by Douglas, twice, and pressed up against his erection once. It hardly counted as worldliness.

No, she'd seen it—Kit's narrow face, homely and beautiful all at once, had been brilliantly open to her in that moment when his mouth had touched hers. He'd been trembling, too. They'd been equal in that moment. Both in want . . . and wonder.

She'd almost be willing to wager the remainder of her wardrobe upon it.

She'd hoped to give herself to him, but that would have been more of a gift to herself, she understood now. She knew now what she really needed to give him: time.

To decide what it was he wanted from her, if anything at all.

And for some reason this seemed riskier, more terrifying, than giving him her body.

Kit stopped in to see to the horses. Since he'd sacked the stable boys, it was his job now until he could find someone else to do it. Susannah the new little filly gamboled over to see him, and he had a thought: *I'll give Susannah to Susannah when she's grown.*

Moving slowly with the horses, breathing in their animal scent, spending time in the simplicity of their presence, soothed his thoughts, calmed his body; he returned to the house in a slightly easier frame of mind.

He nodded to Bullton as he made his way up the stairs.

"If you'll pardon my saying so, sir, you've a leaf clinging to the back of your head."

Kit halted and swiped an alarmed hand over his hair; a tiny maple leaf fluttered to the ground. He gave Bullton a sharp look, but when Bullton wasn't full of whiskey, he was a butler to his toes, which meant he wasn't about to let judgment or amusement or anything of the sort show on his face.

Kit collected his dignity quickly, began again to head up the stairs, and Bullton bent to pick up the leaf.

"It's a *green* leaf, sir. A very fine color. Green."

Kit stopped and turned swiftly. Bullton's face was entirely enigmatic.

Bullton might just make a wonderful spy, Kit thought admiringly.

"And you've a letter, sir."

"Oh. Thank you, Bullton." Kit accepted the letter and took the stairs slowly, splitting the seal on his way.

Dear sir:

In response to your inquiry regarding the accident in the coaching inn of May the twenty-third.

The conveyance in question was determined to have been in excellent repair. The cause of the accident has been traced to the linchpin on a forward wheel, which was of a size and width inconsistent with the other linchpins, which subsequently unbalanced the wheel and caused it to loosen. This in turn led to the unfortunate incident in the inn yard. A comparison with other coaches in our fleet reveals that this is a singular incident, as no other linchpins of this sort occur anywhere on any other coach.

We regret to inform you that we have been unable to trace the offending linchpin's origin, but we will redouble our efforts to ensure that such an accident does not happen again. In the meantime, we will be happy to sack the employee of your choice, should you feel it necessary, and reimburse you for the cost of the irreparably damaged hat. Do buy another green one.

Yours sincerely,
M. Rutherford

Kit couldn't help but laugh, pleased with M. Rutherford, whoever he might be. Some harried bureaucrat placating a spoiled aristocrat with thinly disguised irony and steeled patience. Kit didn't blame him in the least for the tone, nor was he the least bit embarrassed by it. His petulant, whiskey-inspired letter had accomplished precisely what he'd wanted to accomplish, and he knew he wouldn't have received such a timely response without acting the part of the put-upon viscount.

He had his answer now, but he'd already known it, really: The shortened linchpin meant the coach Susannah Makepeace had taken to Barnstable had been cleverly, subtly, deliberately sabotaged.

He was seized by a sense of helplessness that infuriated him. Susannah was wrong: Her luck wasn't bad, it was extraordinary, considering someone was methodically attempting to kill her, and with yesterday's knife, had at last abandoned any pretense of subtlety.

He'd been lucky, too: He'd been able to keep her alive. But he didn't know how long his own luck would hold.

Oh, he'd been right, he was so seldom wrong, after all. She most definitely had an instinct for passion, an instinct that matched his own, that had nearly caused him to lose his head. Well, now he knew her skin was petal smooth; he knew the rich wine of her mouth; he knew the feel of that delicate, puckered nipple rubbed against his cheek—

Kit swiped two frustrated hands down over his face, rubbed his eyes. God, he needed a shave; it was a wonder his whiskers hadn't cut Susannah's tender skin.

There was a reason, after all, that he'd cultivated the countess so carefully, and it wasn't as though she wasn't skilled at what he'd . . . well, cultivated her for. Mistresses most definitely had a purpose. Perhaps he could sneak in a visit to the countess, to remind her of his existence and to take the edge off this foolish, misguided—boundless—want for Miss Makepeace.

His father would see him in Egypt if he saw him in London, that much was clear. But even if he wound up in Egypt, maybe he could make a gift to Susannah of the truth about her past. Maybe, maybe he could save her from whatever forces wanted to prevent her from having a future. Maybe he could make sure she *had* a future.

For Susannah, then. For Susannah he would risk Egypt. He would take her to London.

Chapter Fourteen

"*Susannah!*" her aunt sang. "I have a *surprise* for you."

Dear God, please *no,* she thought. And to think, she used to like surprises.

She hadn't slept much the previous night, having spent the evening reliving her interlude with the viscount until sleep dragged her under for a few inadequate hours. Feeling decidedly surly, Susannah hurled herself out of bed, padded to the top of the stairs, and peered down. Then reared back, alarmed.

The viscount stood in the parlor, hat in hand, dressed for traveling. He looked like a gentleman caller. Except, of course, he was not: He was her employer.

Her employer, who'd had his hand between her thighs only yesterday.

A rush of heat nearly buckled her knees as her body remembered precisely how that felt.

As deuced luck would have it, Kit had been looking up at the stairs just as she was peering down. His face split into a grin.

She flew back into her room, her heart thumping. She'd been certain she wouldn't see him today, or perhaps even the following day. Perhaps not ever again, given the nature of their leave-taking yesterday. She heard her aunt make a scandalized noise, which Susannah suspected was all pretense, because it was difficult to maintain a true sense of scandal in the face of the viscount's cheery insouciance.

"Come down when you are able, Susannah," her aunt called up. "Viscount Grantham would like a word."

Her aunt sounded quietly thrilled. *This isn't a Jane Austen story, Aunt Frances,* she thought. *He isn't here to confess our indiscretion yesterday and make an honorable woman of me.*

Then again, perhaps he was. This was, after all, a man who loved surprises.

She dressed, as quickly as her shaking fingers could manage, and presented herself in the parlor after a few minutes. Her aunt had pressed some tea on the viscount. He stood and bowed when she entered, as proper a gentleman as she'd ever encountered.

"I need to present my folio findings in London, Miss Makepeace, and I am here to request permission from your aunt for your company. You will, of course, be well-compensated for your time. And we shall, of course, be accompanied by the appropriate number of servants."

This was to reassure Aunt Frances of the propriety of their excursion, doubtless.

But there was nothing at all proper about Susannah's thoughts at the moment. In fact, Susannah could not help but translate "well-compensated" in a distinctly *improper* way.

She imagined Aunt Frances interpreted "well-compensated" as more beef and sausages.

"Well, if you have need of her, my lord," Aunt Frances finally conceded, "by all means, you must take her. I shall get on without her for a day or so."

Poor Aunt Frances. Susannah's arrival had meant one awkward moment after another for her.

Kit thanked her somberly. "I shall wait while you pack the appropriate number of dresses, Miss Makepeace. The coach will be brought round to the road below."

He'd kept conversation minimal and bland during the hours of their trip to London. Susannah had attempted, with strained lightness, with idle questions, with looks between her lashes to scale the slippery walls of his breathtaking politeness, but she was no match for him. At last, she fell silent. Kit spent the remainder of the trip poring over books, for all the world as though he fully did intend to report to his father.

The carriage they rode in was older—the Whitelaw family didn't keep their finer equipages at The Roses, after all, and the four geldings seemed surprised to find themselves actually pulling a coach again—but he'd been able to obscure the coat of arms on it with a clever piece of painted board. The full complement of servants he'd promised Susannah's aunt was comprised of a driver and two footmen.

He was entirely alone with her niece, whom he intended to surprise with the purpose of their visit to London, and who, he trusted, would not convey the particular lack of appropriate servants to her aunt.

It was late afternoon by the time they reached London's

East End. The White Lily Theater wasn't shy about announcing itself: An enormous sign painted with a lush, almost lurid flower—no actual lily had ever looked like this—hung over the entrance, which was flanked by two Grecian columns. Shiny *new* Grecian columns.

"You couldn't have drawn it better yourself, Susannah," Kit told her, gesturing to the sign with his chin.

She was enough of an artist to look insulted by that.

And then, as she began to understand why they were at the White Lily, he found himself turning away from the soft, glowing gratitude dawning on her face.

He pushed open the door to the theater and jaunty, nearly frenetic pianoforte music—played with much enthusiasm and a heavy hand—burst out, as if frantic for escape. A stage hugged the north end of the theater, and tiers of seats climbed up to the balconies and then to the ceiling. All of the seats were empty. From the looks of things, the establishment could comfortably accommodate several hundred people. The architecture roughly approximated classical, a florid sort of classical, with pillars propping up the corners, urns tucked into niches, and great heavy velvet curtains roped in golden cords lining the stage. Maidens in togas with breasts exposed and lasciviously grinning cherubs gamboled across the ceiling.

A tall, fair-haired man stood in the center of the aisle facing the stage, on which a row of heavily-painted girls, clad in what appeared to be modified shifts, appeared to be stumbling about. The man was marking time with his walking stick.

"All *right* girls! And one, and two, and *kick* and *slide*, and four, and turn, and—no, *no, NO!*"

These last three syllables were punctuated by the vehement thump of walking stick against floor. "Josephine!" the man barked, and the pianoforte music crashed to a discordant halt. And then he heaved a gusty, long-suffering sigh. "We open tomorrow *night,* ladies."

The girls stood in a dejected row, toeing the stage sheepishly with their bare feet.

"General," drawled the man who stood with his hands folded over the top of his walking stick, "would you please show the ladies—once *again*—how it's done?"

Hmmm. There *was* someone sitting in one of the chairs, but when he rose up, his head reached only a little higher than Kit's hip. The General, it seemed, was a dwarf. His face was darkly handsome, slashes of brows, a stern chin, dark eyes, and like his friend, he was clearly a bit of a dandy: His waistcoat was an unsubtle purple and metallic gold brocade, and a ruby stickpin gleamed dully from the complicated folds of his cravat. He strode down the aisle to the stage and hefted himself up.

"Josephine, if you would?" His roundly elegant voice filled the theater.

The music started up again, and the general, with a complete absence of irony, perched a hand on his hip, tilted his head coyly, and began to dance.

"And a one, and a two and *kick* and *slide,* and four, and turn, and *kick,* kick, back and *dip* . . ."

With accomplished precision the General danced for several bars, then stopped abruptly, waved a hand at Josephine for silence, and turned to the row of dancers.

"*Do* you ladies have it now?" He sounded as exasperated as the fair-headed fellow.

"Yes, General. Sorry, General." Sheepish feminine apologies. The General hopped down from the stage and rolled his eyes in exasperation at the other man as he came back up the aisle, which is when he noticed Kit and a gaping Susannah standing in the entry.

"Tom," the General nudged his taller friend. "We've visitors."

The man with the walking stick turned, and Susannah drew in a sharp breath. Kit could hardly blame her—the bastard was devilishly handsome. No, not *devilishly* . . . he was more like Pan, broad across the cheekbone, narrow at the chin, his nose and lips finely etched but unmistakably masculine, damn him. A fashionably unruly mop of red-gold hair dropped rakishly over one eye, and his eyes were pale, almost silver, in the theater's dim light. He was dressed as festively as the General, his waistcoat striped in silver. He radiated impish well-being.

"Good afternoon!" He swept a low bow to them. "Mr. Tom Shaughnessy here. I'm the owner of this fine establishment. The General here—" the General bowed, too— "is my partner and choreographer. And you would be . . . Mister? Sir? Lord? . . ."

"White. Mr. White." Kit bowed low in return. Mr. Shaugnessy stood back, rubbing his chin. "You look familiar, Mr. White."

"No, I don't," Kit said meaningfully.

Mr. Shaugnessy's brows rose. "Oh, of *course* not." He grinned, pleased. "My mistake. And what have you brought to me today, Mr. . . . . White?" He swept Susannah with a thorough, appreciative, professionally speculative gaze. "Let me assure you, our girls are well-cared for and *completely* free of disease—except for poor Rose, of course, and we'll have you right as rain in no time, won't we Rose?" He called up to a girl on the stage and smiled encouragingly, sympathetically. "You'll choose the right fellow, next time, yes?"

He turned back to Kit and Susannah, cheerfully oblivious to the fact that one of the girls on stage was now a brilliant scarlet. The other girls were watching her curiously.

"Crikey, wotcha 'ave, Rosie?" one of them murmured.

"That's very, er . . . reassuring, Mr. Shaugnessy," Kit replied, "and I've heard . . . impressive . . . things about your establishment. But I didn't bring my"—he cleared his throat—"wife . . . to you. We are here on a personal matter. We were hoping to have a word with Miss Daisy Jones."

"Ah, my Miss Daisy Jones. Daize!" Mr. Shaughessy turned and bellowed in the general direction of the back of the theater. "Visitors!"

He turned to face them again. "Good heavens, my apologies, Mrs. White, Mr. White. No offense meant. But my deepest congratulations on your wife, sir." He mimed tipping his hat to Kit, raised his brows again in appreciation. "She'd do quite well, here."

"No offense taken, sir," Susannah assured him, with coyly lowered lashes, which earned an appreciative grin from Mr. Shaughnessy. Kit fought a scowl, but still. The man was so bloody ingenuous he found it difficult to be genuinely annoyed with him.

A brassy woman's voice boomed from the back of the hall. "Do you 'ave to bellow now, Tom, I was in the middle of me—"

The woman froze when she saw Susannah, and clapped one hand theatrically over her heart.

Kit suspected the gesture was genuine enough. Her handsome, round face had gone pale, turning the two perfectly circular spots of rouge on her cheeks into beacons.

She was draped in some sort of toga made of purple satin and feathers, and bits of sparkly paste jewels clung and twinkled everywhere on her, including her hair. She was a flaming, buxom, constellation. Apparently she was preparing for, or just recovering from, a performance.

"Ye look jus' *like* 'er, dear, ye do," she breathed.

She stared at Susannah another moment. Then she became brisk, speculative. "We best talk in me room." She transferred her gaze to Kit, and it widened, became sultry. "'Aven't seen you in—"

"Ever. You haven't ever seen me, Miss Jones," Kit amended quickly, earning him a lifted eyebrow and a smirk from Miss Jones. "Allow me to introduce myself: I am Mr. *White*, and this is my . . . this is my . . . friend."

"Pleased to meet ye, Mr. . . . *White*." Daisy Jones extended a hand theatrically, and Kit bowed over it. Miss Jones was a pioneer of sorts, and though he'd never personally partaken of her particular charms, he'd been an enthusiastic audience member on more than one occasion, and had once even sent flowers to her. For one did want to encourage pioneering in the arts.

They followed Miss Jones, who, though past her prime, still had a marvelous derriere. It swung like the deck of a ship in a storm, and Kit was nearly hypnotized by it as he followed her. At the end of a warren of halls they came to a closed door, and Miss Jones flung it open and gestured for them to precede her.

It was like entering a giant . . . *mouth*. The walls were papered in vivid pink, in a pattern that Susannah was certain had never seen the inside of a London town house. Two settees upholstered in matching pink velvet lolled across the room like enormous tongues. A number of chairs also covered in velvet and plump enough to accommodate Miss Jones's majestic derriere were scattered about, as though she received hordes of visitors nightly. Mirrors took up almost an entire wall, and a variety of strategically placed lanterns set the place aglow.

"I've me own room to dress in now, ye see." She waved her arm about proudly. Then she stopped and stared at Susannah fondly, then clapped her hands on Susannah's cheeks. "I simply canna believe it. Now—forgive me, but I jus' 'ave to—"

She seized Susannah and pressed her into her enormous, muskily perfumed bosom, and Susannah felt a feather climb into her nostril. When she was finally able to squirm out of Daisy's grasp, she sneezed discreetly into her hand.

"Yer the spit of Anna, ye know. She was just *beautiful,* and of course she didna last long 'ere at the White Lily. She was snapped right up. She talked me into retirin' a bit wi' 'er out in that little godforsaken town named by a duke who—"

"Gorringe," Kit and Susannah said simultaneously.

"Gorringe. And I thought I'd get me a respectable life of sorts, too. But I was so bored I thought I'd *die.* Spent most of me time at the pub. So bored I dreamed up me *act* there, ye see, so I suppose it wasna complete loss. It's a popular act, ye see."

She smiled meaningfully up at Kit, who smiled back at her, while Susannah tried with difficulty not to mind. Daisy leaned toward Susannah. "You see, dearie," she confided, "I was the first one to get up on stage and give the audience a real close look at my—"

"Was her name really Anna Smith?" Kit interjected hurriedly, leaving Susannah in suspense.

"Smith?" Daisy looked bemused. "Why d'yer think 'er name was Smith?"

"The church records in Gorringe," Susannah told her. "Her name was recorded as Anna Smith."

"Well, I suppose she wanted to live quiet like, an' a name like Smith. I knew 'er as Anna 'Olt. Now which one are ye?"

Susannah noticed that Kit had gone completely still, for some reason, at Daisy's words. She frowned. "I beg your pardon, Miss Jones?"

"Are ye Sylvie, Sabrina, or Susannah?"

"But I don't under . . ." Susannah stammered. And then suddenly she did, and tiny little moth wings of excitement fluttered inside her.

"Anna had *three* daughters," Daisy Jones leaned forward again and explained slowly, as though reciting the beginning of an arithmetic problem. "Which *one* are ye?"

Susannah's mouth dropped open, and then her hands went up to her face. She spun to Kit. "Sisters! I have *sisters*! I have sisters?" She whirled back to Daisy to confirm it.

And when Daisy nodded, Susannah impulsively seized the laughing Miss Jones in a hug.

Where a day or so earlier she was a cipher on the tablet of time, she was now Susannah, last name of Holt, possibly, and—very likely—had two sisters.

"Oh, ye poor thing, ye didna know? I suppose that's possible, ye were all so very small when Anna left, and the three of ye were split up."

"But . . . what was my mama like? What became of

her? My sisters? My father? I'm Susannah. That's which *one* I am."

Daisy laughed at Susannah's enthusiasm. "Well, me dear, ye'd be the baby, then. Ye mama was in the chorus 'ere at the White Lily until yer papa clapped eyes on 'er, and then it was *all* over for 'er: a little 'ouse in the country, tha's what she wanted, and babies, and yer papa. And Anna—oh, she was the sweetest, funniest, lass, and *oh*, she'd a temper—a fiery one, my *goodness*. She was honest as the day is long. Spoke the truth as she saw it."

Susannah was silent, astounded to hear her mother described after so many years, to feel her come into view. She *must* be alive. She . . . *felt* alive.

"Yes, she was me dear friend," Daisy sighed. "And she never done it, ye know. I'm certain of it."

"Done it?" Susannah immediately regretted the question, because the answer was bound to be something frankly prurient, which would have been both fascinating and appalling.

"Why, murdered yer papa, lass."

Chapter Fifteen

Daisy Jones looked horrified when she saw the look on Susannah's face. She turned to Kit beseechingly. "She didna know?"

He shook his head once, curtly. Kit was still oddly tense; Susannah had the sensation his every muscle was knotted in preparation to bolt from the room.

Daisy took a deep breath, and began in a gentle voice. "'Is name was Richard Lockwood, Susannah. Beautiful man, devoted, loved yer mama, loved ye and yer sisters very much. 'E was a politician, very important, very rich. As I said, clapped eyes on Anna one night 'ere at the White Lily and, well . . . 'E never married anyone else—nor did 'e marry 'er. But 'e set 'er up in 'er own lodgings 'ere in London. And after yer two sisters were born, 'e moved 'is family to Gorringe, because Anna fancied a country life, and because 'e got it in 'is 'ead that Gorringe was a funny place, what being named by a rhyming duke, and all. 'Ad a sense of 'umor, did yer papa.

"But then yer dear papa—" Daisy gentled her voice,

remembering. "'E was murdered, Susannah, and it was spread about in all the papers that Anna killed 'im. Crime of passion, they said. There were witnesses, they said. As fer me, I never believed a word of it, an' still don't. 'E was in London, and Anna was in Gorringe with ye girls at the time, I'm certain of it. And she never would 'ave . . ." Daisy paused, and her face went rueful and dreamy. "If ye'd seen how they loved each other, Susannah . . . real love, Susannah. Not just . . . passion."

She paused and peered into Susannah's face with concern. "Ye've gone a bit peaky, luv. Do you need to lie down?" She patted the big tongue of a settee invitingly, sympathetically.

"Why does everyone think I'm bound to faint?" Susannah protested, though, admittedly her voice *was* thin. Her mother was an opera dancer, a mistress, and an accused murderess. And it seemed tragic love affairs ran in the family. If ever she were entitled to faint, now would be the time.

She wondered why Kit had gone so still, so silent. Perhaps he regretted ever associating with her. Perhaps he was cursing his folio assignment, thinking to himself: *Bloody voles got me involved with the daughter of a murderess.* Perhaps he was regretting he'd ever touched her, tainted as she was with the scandal of murder, and wanted to wash his hands of her as soon as he could safely deposit her at home.

Which made a different kind of fear arrest her breath.

And then Kit moved, and such was his stillness the moment before that Susannah jumped. He lifted the pitcher on Daisy Jones's vanity, sniffed it, splashed a little into a glass. He handed it to her.

"Drink." A soft command.

It was brandy. It went down hot and smooth, and quickly buffered the jagged ends of her emotions.

Susannah realized then that Kit had quietly seen to her needs in just this way from the moment she'd arrived in Barnstable, from tempting her to waltz at the assembly to risking his own life to keep her alive. He might never touch her again, but he would never let anything harm her.

And then he was still again, as still as a sentry; his entire being seemed both utterly absorbed and utterly remote at the same time, preternaturally alert, leaving Susannah to ask questions.

"What became of my mother, Miss Jones? Do you know?" she asked when the brandy had worked its magic.

"That's just it, ye see. *No* one knows. She disappeared right after yer father's death."

"But . . . my father . . . that is, James Makepeace, I mean . . . do you know how I came to be with him?"

"Well, I was in London when the uproar over the murder happened—yer real papa, Richard, was a popular man with the people, young lady, and *'andsome*! I don't mind saying. And then a few days after 'e was killed I was 'ere at the White Lily when Makepeace came to me, all in a tizzy like. 'E was a theater buff, Makepeace was, and a friend of Richard's. 'E told me 'e had ye three girls. 'E swore me to secrecy. And keeping a secret for Anna's sake—well, that was no burden to me. So James kept ye, and I found a home for Sylvie—"

"Like a puppy?" Susannah tried not to sound bitter. Kit's hand dropped onto her shoulder, just the barest hint of a touch.

"What did I know of babies, my dear?" Daisy said

gently. "I'd have taken the lot of ye, luv, for Anna's sake, but I was poor as dirt, then. It seemed safer for Anna, and all of ye, somehow, to split you girls up; for the papers had it that Anna had disappeared along with her girls. And if I'd been discovered with three little girls . . . if *James* 'ad been discovered with three little girls . . ."

Susannah could imagine the fear of the time. The loyalty and love that had kept her mother's secret.

"I'm sorry, Daisy," Susannah said softly. "You lost her, too."

Daisy's eyes were a little moist now and she touched a finger to the corner of one, to keep a tear from racing down to smear the rouge.

"And so . . . well, I was discreet. A French dancer name of Claude took a shine to Sylvie and offered to care for 'er, and so . . . off she went. No doubt raised French, more's the pity," Daisy added sadly.

"What about Sabrina?"

"I don't know, luv. I'm sorry, I just don't know. James knew of a vicar's family who may 'ave taken her on, but I never knew for certain."

"I was very fortunate, given the circumstances." Susannah took refuge in formality, as she didn't know quite what to believe yet, or how to feel. It was a little like falling off a cliff, and being thrown a rope . . . only to discover the rope was actually a snake.

"Did you ever hear from Anna Holt again?" Kit finally spoke. His voice was taut and strange, abstracted. As though he were working a problem out in his mind.

"Never heard from 'er, I swear to ye. No one knew where she went, she was never found, and the 'ubbub eventually died. But Anna would *never* willingly leave her babies—

never. And I would swear on all that I 'old dear—my gorgeous bosom"— Daisy swelled up to display her assets matter-of-factly—"and my new town house, which my gorgeous bosom bought for me—that Anna didna kill yer father."

"I don't think she did it, either." This came from Kit, low and emphatic, and so quietly, surprisingly cold and furious the hair stood up on the back of Susannah's neck. She turned to stare at him. But her mind and heart were too crowded, too confused for her to speak; she needed to let all she'd heard settle in.

"You said James was a theatergoer, which was how he knew you," Kit prompted Daisy Jones.

"Yes. James was a lover of . . ." Daisy paused delicately. "Costume. And spectacle. But particularly . . . costume."

She exchanged a meaningful look with Kit, which bewildered Susannah.

"And you have no idea how James came to have the children?"

"No, but ye might talk to—" Daisy stopped abruptly.

"To whom, Miss Jones?"

"Well, ye do know James was a good man, Mr. White . . ." she began hesitantly.

"I knew him," Kit said softly. "I agree." It sounded like permission for Daisy to continue.

"Ye should have a word with Edwin, then," Daisy said. "Edwin Avery-Finch. 'E's a gentle sort, Edwin is. 'E was James's . . ." She paused again, selecting a word, it seemed, to Susannah. Since delicacy didn't seem to come naturally to Daisy Jones, Susannah found these pauses to choose words intriguing. ". . . Very good friend," Daisy finally completed. "'E sells antiquities. West of Bond Street, 'is shop is. 'Asn't been in the theater since James . . . well, since James was done in."

"Thank you, Miss Jones," Kit said.

"Oh, by *all* means, Mr. White." Now that the interview was over, Daisy was all winsome prurience again. "It would be my *pleasure*." She winked at Kit, then folded Susannah into her fragrant bosom.

"I hope ye find Anna, my dear," she said into Susannah's hair.

"So do I, Miss Jones." Her voice was somewhat muffled against Daisy's chest. "I want to clear her name." Daisy finally relinquished her, and Susannah gulped in a breath.

"May we speak to you again about this, Miss Jones, if the need arises?" Kit asked. "We need to be somewhere else at the moment."

"It would be me *pleasure*, Mr. White."

He'd all but dragged her out of the White Lily by the elbow, such was his speed. Past the handsome Mr. Shaughnessy and the General and all the rehearsing girls, into the waiting unmarked coach. He thumped the roof to get it moving, and hauled her so quickly up to a room at an inn not more than ten minutes from the theater that her feet nearly left the ground, all the while ignoring her protests, her requests for explanation, until Susannah at last gave up. He closed the door, locked it, all but flung her into a chair, and spoke before she could take a good look around.

"I have something to tell you, Susannah. And you need to be sitting for it."

"I never would have guessed it."

He didn't respond to her sarcasm. In fact, he still wasn't

entirely here with her, she could tell; his eyes still had that remote, abstracted light to them, as if he were reading something written inside his own head.

"I think James Makepeace was murdered. And I think the same people who murdered him killed your real father, Richard Lockwood, and are now trying to kill you."

And to think, this time last year she was choosing her new dress patterns and swooning over Douglas.

She doubted anything would ever again make her swoon.

"And why do you think this?" she asked. The very steadiness of her voice seemed almost absurd, given that they were discussing her own possible murder.

She looked about the room while Kit took a deep breath, organizing his thoughts, no doubt. One large bed, a little elderly, judging from the person-length dent in the center of it. A bureau, against which Kit now propped his long frame. A pair of lamps. It all looked clean enough. It was suspiciously close to the White Lily Theater, too, and Kit had seemed to know precisely where he was going. She didn't want to think of the opera dancers he might have pressed into the dent in that particular mattress. "Friends," he'd called them. Opera dancers. *Friendly.*

"Let me tell you what I know now," he began. "Richard Lockwood was murdered fifteen years ago. Officials intended to arrest his mistress for it. But she disappeared, and no one knew what became of her, and no thought was given to what became of her three little daughters—it was assumed she'd managed to escape with them, I suppose. But today we learned from Miss Daisy Jones that your mother was not Anna *Smith*—she was in fact Anna Holt, Richard Lockwood's mistress. Lockwood was your father. *And* you have two sisters. You, for some reason, wound up in James Makepeace's safekeeping. And now James is dead, too."

"But . . . why do these murders have anything to do with *me*?"

"Well . . . Richard Lockwood was investigating a politician named Thaddeus Morley—"

"Oh! You've mentioned Mr. Morley. People think very highly of him, do they not?"

Kit's face darkened subtly. His mouth parted as though he intended to comment, but then he shook his head roughly and continued. "Richard Lockwood was gathering evidence to prove that Morley had acquired his fortune in part by selling information to the French, but he was killed before he could present his proof to anyone. And I believe he was killed because Morley was somehow warned."

Susannah pictured this . . . her father, a politician, attempting to prove the guilt of an alleged traitor.

And then . . . *Wait.*

"How . . . how on earth do *you* know all of this?"

Kit studied her, as though gauging the current state of her internal fortitude. And then exhaled resignedly. "I'm a spy."

Blue eyes unblinking, face unreadable, he awaited her response. She stared at him, and suddenly:

"I *knew* it!" she said triumphantly.

This made him smile at last. "You didn't *know* it."

"When you're always so prepared for disaster, and so good at warding it off, and armed to the teeth, and unnervingly observant, you had better either be a spy or a criminal. I knew you couldn't simply be a soldier. I've danced with a soldier or two. They hadn't your . . ."

She wanted to say "confidence." Or "presence." Or "air

of danger." But that would probably amuse him and embarrass *her,* so she stopped speaking.

He was trying not to look impressed, anyway. "You know so much about spies then, do you? You are simply very perceptive, which I believe is part of being an artist. I disguise it very well."

"*Am* I an artist?" she was momentarily diverted. She was growing accustomed to considering herself talented, but "artist" was a new and very distinct definition of herself: Susannah Makepeace/Lockwood/Holt, artist. A wanton, brave artist with a temper. She was coming into focus as a person, a bit at a time.

"A gifted one," he confirmed, and she knew it wasn't flattery, because he'd probably never said a deliberately flattering thing in his life. "You don't seem terribly shocked to hear that I'm a spy." He sounded almost affronted.

"What could shock me anymore?" she said with a faked insouciance that made him snort. It seemed the lesser of revelations at the moment, truthfully. "But how did I come to be with James Makepeace? And how would James know about Richard Lockwood, and Morley, and the French, and the documents, and all of that?"

"I don't know how you came to be with James, Susannah. But James must have been the one to warn your mother to flee. He was a spy, too."

Susannah gaped. "He *can't* have been."

Kit's mouth quirked wryly. "Not every spy is required to defend maidens. In fact, we *seldom* are. James was a . . . courier, not a warrior. I worked with him a few times. He was a liaison of sorts in any number of important situations, worked through the Alien Office, which is related to Bow Street, which is probably how he learned both of

Richard's murder and the intent to arrest your mother for it in enough time to warn her. But the night he told me of his suspicions about Morley, he never mentioned you at all, Susannah. I imagine it was force of habit: He would never have wanted to compromise your future by exposing you to the truth. You *were* engaged to an heir, were you not? James Makepeace had protected you from the truth his entire life."

But how different her life would have been if not for James Makepeace.

"He risked so much for me," she mused softly. "And for my mother and father. If anyone had discovered he was harboring the daughter of an accused murderess . . ."

Kit nodded once, as though completing the sentence in his head. "As I told you before, I considered James my friend, though I confess I don't believe I truly knew him. James was a kind man, a gentle man, Susannah, and a brave one. And I don't think it's a coincidence that both James and Richard Lockwood were murdered while they were allegedly investigating Mr. Morley."

"But why would they"—it was so strange to say 'they,' such a nebulous word; who were 'they,' anyway?—"or he, want to kill me, too?"

Kit pushed himself away from the bureau and stood tensely in the middle of the room. "*Think,* Susannah. Could you possibly *know* something significant?"

He rubbed the back of his head impatiently, and Susannah was briefly distracted. Anyone would have thought his hair crisp to the touch, because it was so short and so fair it shone nearly metallic in the light, but it wasn't: it was silky. She remembered the surprise of it beneath her fingers in a moment that had already teemed with new sensations: the breeze on her bare skin, then his breath, then his lips, then the scrape of whiskers, and then . . . oh God, the velvet heat of his tongue curling around her nipple. She'd combed her fingers through his hair then, finding it unexpectedly soft.

Everything about Kit Whitelaw was unexpected.

Blood instantly stormed the surface of Susannah's skin, and what could only be described as lust gave a great demanding thump inside her.

All because he'd rubbed the back of his head.

Kit must have seen something in her expression then, for he went utterly still for an infinitesimal moment, his pupils flaring hot. As though he could read the precise memory in her eyes.

And then, damn him, a mere instant later, he turned his head casually and continued talking, as though nothing about her had ever affected him at all.

"Susannah, did you see or hear something, anything that might incriminate Morley? Do you *have* something that might make Morley think you're a danger to him?"

"I don't think I've ever seen Mr. Morley before in my life. I rarely ever saw my father . . . that is, James Makepeace. The only thing I came away from my old home with was all of my dresses and a miniature of my mother. It was the only thing I have of her. The only image of her anywhere in the house."

"May I see the miniature again?"

Susannah had examined the image so closely so many times it was a miracle she hadn't worn away the image with the sheer force of her longing and wondering. Before she handed it to Kit, she looked down at it one more time, at that sweet face, the humor lighting her pale eyes, and thought: *No. This is no killer.*

Kit took it from her.

"For Susannah Faith, from her mother, Anna," Kit read aloud from the back of it. "Could it be code, or . . . does it open?" He began to peer more closely at it, rub his thumbs at its edges.

Susannah squeaked, and he looked up at her inquiringly.

"Please don't hurt it."

Kit restrained his eagerness with some effort, and returned the miniature to Susannah, who received it in cupped hands like a tiny baby, and looked down at it again.

"Kit . . . even so . . . even if the miniature was somehow a clue, how would Mr. Morley know I have it?"

"I don't know, Susannah." He fell silent. "Did your father—James, that is—know you owned this?"

"Yes. In fact, shortly before he died I saw him looking at it and . . ." She trailed off, as something occurred to her. "He said, *'Of course,'* Kit."

Kit frowned. "I beg your pardon?"

"I found him in my rooms a few weeks ago . . . he was looking at the miniature." She flushed, feeling a little foolish. "But he was looking at the back of it, not at her face, which seemed wrong to me. And then he said, *'Of course.'* He sounded . . . pleased. Rather excited, in fact."

"He'd realized something, perhaps." Kit fell silent, thinking. He dropped his body into the chair, stretched out his long legs. "Why did you come away from your house with only your dresses and the miniature, Susannah?"

"Because the men stripped the house of everything else. Apparently nothing else was paid for."

"What were they like, these men?"

"They were all almost offensively cheerful. They rather looked alike, too. The one I threatened with a vase was stocky, had only one eyebrow, blue eyes . . . Oh! I just realized. I . . . I must have my *mother's* temper! Miss Jones said my mother had a temper." The thought cheered Susannah, perversely. It was nice to know she had somebody's *something*.

But Kit's face was grimly speculative. "My guess is those men searched your home on Morley's behalf. But again . . . I'm not certain I can prove it."

"But my father *was* penniless when he died . . . the solicitor told me so. And how would Mr. Morley know if my father . . . *knew* something?"

"I don't know." Kit slumped in his chair, rubbed his hands over his face in weary impatience, then flattened them on his thighs, as if to deliberately stop them from moving.

Susannah watched him. She'd never seen him quite like this: edgy, weary, stripped of dazzle.

Kit thought for a moment, and then brightened. "*But* . . . if they searched everything they wouldn't be trying to kill you if they'd found what they were looking for. So we still have a chance."

"Ah. So it cheers you that they're still trying to kill me?"

"Yes. Because I so enjoy endangering my own life on your behalf, Miss Makepeace."

"I think you *must*."

The corner of his mouth twitched upward. "I wouldn't do it otherwise."

"Because it would be more inconvenient to dispose of my corpse than to prevent my becoming one?" she quipped.

"That's enough." And again, he said it so coldly, so sharply, that warmth started up in her cheeks. She would have apologized, but she simply didn't know what line she had crossed.

Kit stood and began to pace. Pacing seemed unlike him, too. He'd never seemed one to waste motion. She watched him for a moment, back and forth, back and forth . . . until he paused, and quite sensibly, lit a lamp, and then another. The room filled with light.

"Kit . . ." she faltered. "Why are you so certain Mr. Morley is guilty of these crimes?"

"I'm *not* certain."

"Please don't be oblique. You seem convinced of it."

He hesitated. "Instinct." He said it lightly, offhandedly.

But the hesitation told Susannah that her own instincts were correct: there *was* something more here. Something deeper, something older. Something she preferred not to hear, but needed to know. "It has to do with Caroline Allston, doesn't it?"

She made the words sound as casual as she could, so he wouldn't feel cornered, and wouldn't be stubborn, and wouldn't be glib.

What a delicate thing it was to manage a man.

Well, *this* man.

Kit abruptly stopped pacing, and turned and leaned up against the bureau again, folding his arms over his chest, staring back at her, his expression studiedly neutral. She met his eyes bravely. She was learning there were many types of bravery in the world. Patience—particularly patience with Kit Whitelaw—was another form of bravery, too.

And then, at last, a faint, appreciative smile curled his mouth.

He was funny that way—he loved to be challenged. He loved to be caught out. She suspected he was rarely *truly* challenged.

"I couldn't help her." His voice was soft, as though the words had traveled a distance of years. "Caroline."

"Why did she need help?" Her voice was conversational. To make it easier for him.

It was another moment before he spoke again. When he did, he looked away from her and spoke . . . well, to the lamp, it seemed. "Caroline was the daughter of a Barnstable squire. And the man was . . . well, he drank too much, he gambled away their money . . . Caroline used to try to keep him in liquor so that he would drink himself into a stupor, because that way he wouldn't be able to hit her." Kit gave a humorless laugh. "He had hands like mallets—put bruises on her. I used to steal my father's liquor, so she could give it to her father. Until my father caught me and thrashed me. Thought I was stealing it for myself. Not that I *never* stole it for myself . . ." he added, with a swift glance at her. In the spirit of accuracy, no doubt.

"I'd expect nothing less of you," Susannah teased gently. But her stomach contracted, hurting for him.

A little of the tension left his posture; his arms unfolded. He was more comfortable now that he'd committed to wading deeper into his story.

"Caroline was . . . well, she was beautiful. There's no other word for it."

"So I've heard." She couldn't resist saying it.

Kit's brow arched upward, appreciating her sarcasm, as usual. "And . . . she was manipulative. That, I can see now. But back then . . . well, John and I—John Carr, my best friend—we were mad about her, and she knew it, too.

She played us against each other. Still, there was something about Caroline that made you . . . want to protect her, no matter what." He looked directly, almost defiantly, at Susannah. "I wanted to marry her."

It sounded almost like an accusation, or a defense.

And she wondered at the tone: Did he think she would judge him for not marrying Caroline? Or did he think that perhaps she, Susannah Makepeace, aspired above her own social station, as Caroline had?

"If I'd the courage, I would have married her. But my father would have killed me, and so . . ."

"You were only seventeen," she said gently.

"One can breed at seventeen, Susannah," he said bluntly. "It's been done. People marry at seventeen all the time. My parents married at seventeen."

She flushed a little. "But you also were the son of an earl."

"Still am," he said half-whimsically, half-bitterly. "So, in short, I could have saved her, but I didn't. Because I was seventeen and the son of an earl and afraid of my father."

"What of John Carr?"

He paused. "Oh, he would have married her, too. He wanted to, just as desperately. His father didn't like the idea any more than mine. And she preferred me. We both knew it."

He looked directly at Susannah then again. Assessing her reaction to these words.

"I am the son of an earl," he repeated, by way of explanation. "And John is the son of a baron."

"No," Susannah said almost without thinking. He looked at her, puzzled, and she felt compelled to finish her sentence, even as her face grew warm. "It's because you are"—she faltered—"you."

He looked startled. And as she'd said a very good deal more than she'd intended to with that one little sentence, she spoke hurriedly. "Go on."

"Well, when my mother was alive, my father used to hold yearly parties at The Roses, and all the local villagers were invited. This particular year, Mr. Morley attended, too—I believe he was trying to get elected, and wanted my father's support. I remember when Morley first laid eyes on Caroline . . ." Kit stopped, gave a short humorless laugh. "I was so envious he could appear . . . unmoved."

This, Susannah thought, wasn't easy to hear, either.

"Caroline spent most of the evening speaking to him. It was very nearly unseemly, and she knew precisely how it affected me. And John. Morley looked up at me . . . And he . . . *smiled*. And Susannah . . . everything the man is was in that smile. It was like he . . ." Kit paused. "He hated me. He didn't know me, but he hated me."

"And then I turned my back . . . and they were gone. Caroline and Morley. And John turned to me and said . . ." Kit turned away from Susannah, as if to spare her the sight of him saying the words. "He said, 'She's just a whore, Grantham.'"

He let the ugly words ring in the room for a moment. Susannah heard them as he must have heard them, a proud young man in love, about to lose everything he wanted to a man he couldn't hope to compete with: Morley.

"And so naturally, I had to call John out." Kit's tone was mocking, but she still heard the twinge of shame in it. "Despite the fact that he was my best friend. And John and I dueled, and I shot him, and our fathers sent us into the army. But the night of the party was the last time I ever saw Caroline. And Morley was gone the next morning, too. And I do I believe that's the end of the story. He took her away."

"And that's why . . . that's why you dislike Mr. Morley." She said it slowly, as the understanding dawned.

Kit frowned. "What do you mean?"

"Because he took Caroline away, when you could not. Because he saved her . . . when you could not."

Kit stared at her, the sort of stare that should have frightened her but didn't now, because she was growing accustomed to it. And then his expression went . . .

Well, oddly, he looked *bored*.

And suddenly he was all swift, abrupt motion. "I'll step into the corridor while you get into your night rail and beneath the blankets, Miss Makepeace. We've a Mr. Avery-Finch to visit in the morning. I'll sleep in the chair."

He'd waited a suitable amount of time in the corridor while she fumbled her way out of her clothes and into her night rail. Then he entered the room again, doused the lamps, and stretched out in the chair without saying a word.

Susannah could not have said how much time passed in the dark, but neither of them slept. The events of the day, of the past few weeks, the danger and the sweetness and the discoveries, milled about in her head, colliding and creating more questions. And she dared one.

Her heart began to pound a little harder with the boldness of what she was about to say. "You'll sleep badly in the chair, Kit. Would you like to sleep next to me? I promise not to thrash about."

She tried to make her words light. Tried to make them

sound like a practical suggestion, and less like the wanton invitation they disguised.

There was a long quiet so thick Susannah could have grabbed fistfuls of it.

"No, Susannah. I will sleep even more badly next to you."

His voice was night itself: ironic, dense with meaning, a little dangerous. He might as well have slipped a hand beneath her nightdress for how it made her feel.

"Good night, then," she said. Her voice trembling. Doubting she would sleep at all. Wondering why, for heaven's sake, he refused to touch her now, as surely they had gone beyond honor and propriety. Wondering if it was all for the best. Wondering that her body seemed to have a reason all its own, that had nothing at all to do with her rational mind.

And knowing he was very likely right not to touch her, which didn't make it any easier. And trying to be grateful for what he was offering her: safety and the truth about her past.

And not to want anything beyond that.

"Good night, Susannah. We'll visit Mr. Avery-Finch in the morning. I shan't let anyone murder you this evening."

"Thoughtful of you," she murmured.

His eyes had finally adjusted to the dark. He could see her breasts lift and fall gently with her breathing. She'd thrown off her blanket. He watched now. Feeling like an adolescent. Just as ridiculous, just as enthralled.

He imagined going to her, lying next to her on the bed, pulling her into his arms, waiting for her to stir awake. He imagined the feel of the fine, fragile fabric of the night rail against his hands—it would be warm, fragrant from her—and the whisper of sound it would make as it slid over her body when he lifted it from her. He imagined his hands gliding over the curve of her shoulders and hips; over the petal skin of her breasts, and her softer-still nipples. He imagined her lithe body rippling beneath his touch as he discovered her again, and thoroughly this time, he imagined his mouth finding, tasting every bit of her, the hollow of her belly, the musk between her legs, her soft cries of pleasure as he did. He imagined the slow final taking of her, moving inside her as she clung to him—

Oh, God.

He wanted. He wanted. He wanted.

Breathe through it, he told himself mordantly. *As you would any pain.*

And over the years, he'd become a walking weapon; he knew just what to do with his hands and feet, with sword and pistol, to preserve his own life or save another, and he'd done it again and again in service to his country. He knew he was remarkable; he had enough clarity to see it and was arrogant enough to be proud of it. Still, no matter how he hated to admit it, he knew he was far from infallible. Ah, but fate, with characteristic ironic humor, had thrown yet another endangered female into his all too fallible hands. And this one—

He half-smiled in the dark. *Mr. Morley saved her when you could not.*

She'd said it so casually. When, in fact, it rather unlocked more than a decade of his life.

This one . . . *saw* him. Clearly and fully, in a way he'd never before felt seen. He found himself offering up his secrets to her; she seemed to know them anyway. He knew she surprised herself even as she surprised him, with the depth of her passion, her strength and resilience. Her wit. And oh God, her beauty burned in him.

Yes, he knew he was remarkable. He knew he was fallible. And he knew, sitting there in the dark, that he was afraid now in a way he didn't fully understand, perhaps more afraid than he'd ever been before.

Bob arrived with a limp.

"That great geezer she's always with nearly killed me. Fought like the bloody devil. Knew what he was about, he did. A *real* fighter."

Bob sounded irritated; he wasn't paid enough to deal with someone who actually *fought back*. Let alone competently.

"So she's alive," Morley said flatly. It had been a little more than a week since he'd had the pleasure of Bob's company. He supposed good news was too much to hope for.

"Yes," Bob said. He didn't sound the least bit apologetic. "And I know his name now, too," he added. "Heard it in the pub there in Barnstable. Getting mighty sick of Barnstable, Mr. Morley. There's a chap what's always at the pub. Mr. Evers. Right boring chap. You said to come if I had news."

"Well?" Morley was impatient. "The name?"

"It's Grantham. And he's a *viscount*."

Morley's heart balled into such a tight fist that he coughed.

"Merowr?" Fluff questioned from his feet.

"A *viscount*." Bob repeated, marveling. One didn't expect a viscount, after all, to be able to fight like the devil.

Oh, Morley thought, *I really could do without nasty surprises for a day or two.*

He suspected his heart was not at all what it used to be. He could have sworn it had taken more than a second there to continue ticking. But it was ticking now, and so was his mind.

"Heard it in the pub," Bob said again, when Morley didn't say anything. "Local lord."

Dear God, what on earth was *Grantham* doing with Makepeace's daughter?

"Sir?"

Morley supposed he had been silent overlong. "Interesting," he said, sounding offhand. Just to interrupt the silence with a word. Just to make sure Bob noticed nothing amiss.

Maybe, Morley thought, it was a harmless courtship. Grantham hailed from Barnstable, too, and it was entirely possible their paths had innocently crossed. She was pretty, Susannah Makepeace, if she looked at all like Anna Holt. Grantham was a womanizer; that was well known. Perhaps he was merely passing his time in a way any young rake would find agreeable.

But it was another bloody coincidence in a series of bloody coincidences.

Then again . . . well, he really didn't believe in coincidences, so why bother with the word at all?

He had to admit, however, it was looking worse and worse.

That night, years ago, at the Earl of Westphall's with a single smile, he'd made certain Grantham had known what he was about to do. Perhaps that had been a mistake:

allowing his triumph to show, his contempt, his hatred for all the things the lordling had represented, the things that had been denied Morley. He'd forgotten that boys became men, often with long memories.

Morley considered the pieces before him on the chessboard, the people in play.

And with a little thrill, a daring strategy occurred to him.

He couldn't kill Grantham—he could simply imagine the magnitude of the investigation that would ensue, and the difficulty involved in killing him, regardless—but he could play upon the things he knew about him: a taste for heroics, for honor . . . and for women. One woman in particular, in fact. He might be able to trap him neatly. Possibly discredit him; at the very least, he might be able to distract him from Susannah Makepeace long enough for Bob to do his job, or extract a little information.

"Find Caroline," he said to Bob, "and bring her here."

"*Bring* her here? She's right dodgy now, sir. Can't get close to her. Can't say as I blame her, either, sir."

"Tell her . . . it's all been a mistake. All is forgiven."

"Beggin' your pardon, sir: She might not be clever, but she isn't *stupid*. You may have to tell her yourself. After all, she knows *you* won't . . ." Bob drew a finger eloquently across his own throat.

Bob was right. Their only chance of corralling Caroline involved Morley himself.

He would have to meet her.

And then his heart moved again, and it wasn't a dangerous clench this time, but something unexpected.

"Where did you last see her, Bob?"

"A coaching inn outside of Headley Meade. A few days ago."

Headley Meade. Only an hour or so away from London.

"Think you can find her again?"

"Of course, sir. I'm a prof—"

Morley sighed heavily. "Then arrange a meeting as soon as you can."

Chapter Sixteen

Mr. Avery-Finch's shop was ripe with the must of age, and stuffed and stacked full of dully gleaming, hopelessly breakable objects: vases and tea sets, plates and pillars, statues and paintings, trunks and chandeliers and plump stools, arranged, it seemed, for maximum precariousness. Some shopkeepers hang a bell upon their door, Kit thought, to alert them of entering customers; Mr. Avery-Finch probably just waited for a potential customer to send something crashing to smithereens.

It wasn't all fine stuff; the fine mingled with the much less fine, but only an educated eye would be able to discern it. He wondered whether this arrangement was carelessness or a device to discover just how much a customer really knew about antiquities, and how much money could then be extracted from them.

Susannah looked afraid to move, burdened as she was with skirts. Kit picked a path between a reproduction of Venus de Milo and a gilded chest, and thought perhaps he would need a compass to find his way back to the door.

"Good afternoon! And what can I do for you, sir?" A man who could only be Mr. Edwin Avery-Finch stood before him, and bowed.

When he was upright, Kit was struck silent.

It was his eyes. Mr. Avery-Finch looked like many Englishmen in their middle years: a palm-sized scrap of hair remained on his scalp; his chin had gone soft; he was dressed well but not ostentatiously.

But his eyes were astonishing. Dark, bleak, and set into hollows carved brutally out by grief.

"Mr. Avery-Finch, I presume? I am Mr. White."

Bows were exchanged. Precise, careful bows, so as not to upset the stacks of things. "Good afternoon, Mr. White. Something for the lady today? I have a very fine Louis the sixteenth settee in the back. Perfect for one of your country homes."

Kit almost smiled. Mr. Avery-Finch had sized them up very neatly and quickly: wealthy, profligate. But the man's cheerful voice was almost in macabre contrast to that grieving face.

"Mr. Avery-Finch," Kit said gently, "Miss Daisy Jones sent us to you. We understand you were close to Mr. James Makepeace."

Mr. Avery-Finch went very still. Before their eyes, the false cheer drained from his face, leaving it gray and empty.

"Yes." His voice was graveled with emotion. "I was."

Kit knew then that "friend" did not begin to encompass what James Makepeace was to Mr. Avery-Finch. And suddenly, in the form of this plain little dealer in antiquities, James Makepeace was no longer a cipher, but a person who had been loved.

"We're investigating his death." *And his life, apparently.*

Mr. Avery-Finch said nothing. Stood motionless, as though the mere mention of James had clubbed him senseless.

"I'm sorry for your loss," Kit said quietly. "He was my friend."

"Were you . . . perhaps in the same line of work as James, Mr. White?" Mr. Avery-Finch ventured gingerly.

"Would that be . . . importing antiquities?" Kit said just as gingerly, making it sound like a question.

Mr. Avery-Finch smiled faintly. "You are, aren't you?" He had guessed correctly that this was a sort of code for "spy."

"And you are. . . ?" Mr. Avery-Finch directed this question to Susannah.

"I was his daughter, Mr. Avery-Finch. My name is Susannah."

Mr. Avery-Finch's eyes widened, and he stared at Susannah, but not in surprise. More in . . . speculation. Studied her, as though taking inventory of her features. His mouth parted, as if he intended to say something. He stopped himself.

"Perhaps we should have a seat and a chat in my back parlor. I'll just hang the sign on the door, now . . ."

Mr. Avery-Finch expertly picked through his delicate stock and turned the door. "I can make tea," he offered over his shoulder. "Goodness knows I've no shortage of teapots." He gestured, albeit carefully, about the crowded room.

Susannah laughed and Mr. Avery-Finch smiled a little, pleased that his small joke could lighten things.

"Miss Makepeace knows that James is not her father," Kit said once they were all arranged on settees and clutching cups of steaming tea. He thought he might as well begin that way.

Mr. Avery-Finch stared back at Kit, cautiously, consideringly.

"It's all right, Mr. Avery-Finch. Your confidences could not be safer with me. I do not think James's death was an accident, which is why we are here."

"I just wish he'd come to me before he . . ." Mr. Avery-Finch's voice broke. "James was in debt, you see. He had such a weakness for fine things, and a better eye for them than anyone. It was how we met—he came into the shop nearly twenty years ago." He offered a weak smile. "He was practical in so many ways, James was—he actually had quite a head for figures—but he couldn't seem to stop acquiring things he could not afford. He adopted them, like children. Seemed to need them. And . . . well, I had no idea how desperate he'd become for money."

"How desperate *had* he become?" Kit asked. He sniffed the tea. It wanted sugaring, he suspected, but Mr. Avery-Finch hadn't thought to supply any. He took an experimental sip, anyway.

"He told me over claret—James loved his claret . . ." He smiled a little, looking into Kit's and Susannah's faces, hoping they shared this memory, too. Susannah could only give him a weak smile of encouragement. "He told me he'd sent a letter to Thaddeus Morley."

"A blackmail letter?" Kit guessed bluntly.

"Well, what other sort will get you killed?" Mr. Avery-Finch said with startling tartness. "Yes, the bloody fool, that's what he did. He should have asked me for help. I'm not a rich man, but I could have found a way . . . together we could have found . . . have found a way . . ."

Kit waited quietly for Mr. Avery-Finch's grieving rage to ebb before he asked another question. "Why did he send the blackmail letter to Mr. Morley in particular?"

With this question, Mr. Avery-Finch suddenly seemed to find the teapot fascinating. He stared at it as if he were counting the painted flowers that sprawled over it.

Susannah spoke softly. "If there's anything at all you can tell us, sir . . . I would be so grateful. For you see, I have no family at all now . . . and if you perhaps know anything about them . . ."

Mr. Avery-Finch's face spasmed in sympathy then. And after a moment, he nodded, as if giving himself permission to speak.

"It was for Richard, you see, that James did it. Took on you girls."

"Richard Lockwood?" Kit said quickly.

Mr. Avery-Finch looked up at Kit, his expression wry now. "Mr. White, why don't you tell me what you *already* know about Richard and James, and I shall endeavor to supply you with new information."

This was a reasonable request, Kit decided. "We know Richard Lockwood and Anna Holt had three daughters, of whom Susannah is the youngest. We know that Lockwood was murdered, and that Anna Holt was accused of the murder, but disappeared before she could be arrested for it. No one seemed to give any thought to what became of the girls; I suppose it was assumed they were with their mother. And shortly before his death a few weeks ago, James told me he suspected Thaddeus Morley was involved in Richard Lockwood's murder. We learned yesterday from Miss Daisy Jones that it was James who took on Anna's three daughters."

"You know rather a good deal, Mr. White." Mr. Avery-Finch's mouth twitched, and he sat for a moment, thinking. "I will tell you this: James and Richard were dear friends. Met at the theater. Shared a love of spectacle, a similar sense of the absurd. They shared a love of antiquities, too, Richard and James. Yes, they became good friends." There was a touch of wistful envy in Mr. Avery-Finch's voice. "Richard confided in James . . . knew James was very good at"—he looked Kit directly, almost challengingly, in the eye—"keeping secrets."

He would have to be, Kit thought. "James shared secrets with you, however," Kit guessed.

"Of course," he said. We were—" He stopped himself, glanced at Susannah, then back at Kit. "Very close." A faint smile touched his lips.

"What about Mr. Morley? Was he acquainted with Richard, too?"

"Well, Richard was Mr. Morley's political rival. Richard never liked or trusted the man—I thought it was snobbery, at first. Richard was from a fine family, and Morley was not, and as my family origins are hardly lofty, I was inclined to sympathize with Morley. But then I had an occasion to meet Mr. Morley and . . . well, I didn't care for him, either. It's difficult to say quite why." He looked at Kit to see whether he understood.

"Sometimes these things are instinctive."

"Yes," Mr. Avery-Finch agreed, sounding relieved. "And James told me all about how Richard had undertaken his own investigation into Morley, and had apparently actually found something desperately incriminating. When Richard was murdered, I was inclined to believe him.

That's when James rushed to take you girls, Susannah—so the authorities couldn't take you away."

"Did James tell anyone else besides yourself, Mr. Avery-Finch?"

"James was close to two people, Mr. White. You're looking at one of them. Richard was the other. He did not share confidences lightly."

"And James was close enough to Richard to risk his life by warning Anna and taking on three little girls?"

Mr. Avery-Finch looked up, surprised. "Close? James was in love with Richard."

In the silence that followed, one could almost hear the dust settle on the stacks of china and tea trays.

"More tea?" Mr. Avery-Finch took a delicately ironic sip of his own.

"I'm sorry, my dear," Mr. Avery-Finch turned to Susannah, though he looked a trifle more mischievous than sorry. "Do I shock you?"

"No," Susannah said quickly. Her eyes seemed to have frozen into a wide position, however.

Liar, Kit thought.

"Your father, Susannah, was a very handsome man," Mr. Avery-Finch explained. "I liked him, too, you know, but I was never invited into a friendship with him the way James was. And yes, I will confess that I was somewhat jealous of their friendship, but . . . well, James did spend most of his time with me, so I didn't fuss, and Richard was passionately in love with your mother, Miss Makepeace, you should know that. What he felt for James was . . . was friendship only. Truly. But James loved him very much."

Mr. Avery-Finch's voice trailed away, as though the

magnitude of this revelation had tired him. And then for a disconcerting moment he peered at Susannah as though she were somehow a window through which he could see the past. "You're the spit of your mother you know, my dear," he said finally. "Except for this." Startling her, he reached out and pinched Susannah's chin gently between two fingers. "This square little chin. That was Richard's."

Susannah's eyes flared with poignant astonishment and then a soft pleasure. And when Mr. Avery-Finch took his fingers from her chin, she surreptitiously replaced them with her own, wonderingly. Kit felt again that strange kick in his breastbone again. As though his heart beat in tandem with her own.

Mr. Avery-Finch cleared his throat. "Forgive me, as I am rambling now. So yes, James kept *you,* Susannah, for Richard's sake. And he found homes for your sisters, for Richard's sake. And he was silent all of these years, for Richard's sake. And he warned Anna to flee . . . for Richard's sake. He kept quiet, too . . . for the sake of you girls, thinking perhaps he'd find Anna, or Anna would return. She never did."

"And you haven't any idea where Anna might have gone?" Kit asked. "Or the other girls?"

"Nary a clue, and I *am* sorry. I can imagine what it must have been like for her . . . to lose everything she loved . . . all at once."

His voice didn't quite break. Englishmen, on the whole, Kit reflected, were made of stern stuff, regardless of whether they fought on battlefields or sold teapots. Mr. Avery-Finch took a deep breath, and another sip of tea. "Louis the sixteenth," he said, gesturing to the teapot. "I'll give it to you for a very good price, if you'd like it."

"Thank you, Mr. Avery-Finch. I shall take it under consideration," Kit told him solemnly.

"I knew . . ." Mr. Avery-Finch continued once the tea had restored his composure. "I knew if ever a chance came to get justice for Richard, James would take it. But his debt rather interfered with his plans, and addled his thoughts, I believe. Though his profession called for a unique sort of . . . discretion, shall we say, dishonesty didn't come naturally to James, and when he tried to kill two birds with one stone—that is, get justice for Richard and pay his debt—well . . . the bird killed him instead, didn't it?" His mouth twitched at his own morbid joke. "He rather went about things backward, didn't he? He blackmailed first, and then set out to find proof."

"Pity they don't teach the proper way to blackmail at Oxford."

"Isn't it?" Mr. Avery-Finch concurred on a murmur, and took another sip of tea.

"Mr. Avery-Finch, did James ever mention anything to you about the nature of this proof Richard Lockwood had collected . . . anything at all about 'Christian virtues'?"

"'Christian virtues,' Mr. White?" Mr. Avery-Finch's eyebrows lifted ironically. "No, I'm afraid the two of us did not spend much time reviewing Christian virtues. Are they important to our discussion?"

"James told me that Richard had been clever about hiding his proof of Mr. Morley's guilt. Apparently the hiding place had something to do with 'Christian virtues.'"

"Well, that *does* sound like Richard. He was fond of being clever. I wish I could provide some enlightenment with regard to that, sir, but I cannot. Perhaps James was protecting me from what he knew. Perhaps I should even now fear for my life, given what I *do* know. But I rather find I don't care much what becomes of me, these days, so it's all the same."

Kit didn't know what to say; he couldn't very well pat the man's hand, and he knew words were all but useless when it came to easing grief.

"We shall get justice for James, Mr. Avery-Finch, and for Richard and Anna. And I will do everything I can to see to your safety."

Mr. Avery-Finch's shoulder merely went up in a slight shrug.

It was certainly an extraordinary amount of information to take in all at once, for anyone. "Are you all right?" Kit asked Susannah.

For a time, she didn't answer. "It's very sad, isn't it?" she said finally. "I suppose I'm glad to know that even if James Makepeace didn't love me, he did love my father. They were lovers, weren't they? James Makepeace and Mr. Avery-Finch?"

He could only answer honestly. "Yes. I believe they were."

More silence. "I suppose I'm . . . I suppose I'm glad that someone loved him. My father. James Makepeace, that is. And that someone truly knew him. And misses him with his . . . his whole heart."

With his whole heart. Every day he was discovering ways in which she was remarkable.

"So am I," Kit told her softly.

He held out his arm and she took it. He scanned the street with his grimly talented eyes, ready to duck, or dodge, as necessary. Their unmarked carriage was only a few feet away, but a few *fraught* feet, given that someone was trying to kill Susannah and his father would love to send him to Egypt should anyone sight him in London.

"Your mother and father loved you, Susannah." His voice was a little rough with the sentiment; he certainly didn't say such things easily. But he wanted her to believe that someone had once loved her with a whole heart, too.

She simply smiled a little, and her fingers went up to touch her chin again.

Which is when Kit saw a handsome, tall, very familiar figure approaching them.

"Mr. White," John Carr tipped his hat as he passed Kit on his way into Mr. Avery-Finch's shop.

"Mr. Carson," Kit said politely.

"Heard Egypt is quite fine this time of year," John said over his shoulder.

"You wouldn't *dare*."

John Carr merely laughed and continued past them.

"Mr. Carson?" Kit said sharply, suddenly.

John Carr stopped, turned an expectant face toward Kit, flicked a glance at Susannah that widened into deep appreciation, and then looked back at Kit, his eyes glinting a merry question.

Which Kit didn't answer. Instead he gestured with his chin to Mr. Avery-Finch's shop. "See to his safety, will you? Hire a runner?"

John Carr's face became somber, and he nodded shortly, then turned with soldier precision and continued toward the shop.

Susannah was gawking. "Who on earth—"

"Someone I shot once, long ago."

"Someone he *missed* once, long ago," came John's voice

over his shoulder, as he vanished into Mr. Avery-Finch's shop, to pursue his own line of questioning.

Kit watched him with an inevitable and utterly unworthy sense of competition rising. "On to Miss Daisy Jones to inquire about the miniatures, then back to Barnstable," Kit said.

Susannah was still staring back at the shop doorway. "Was that John Carr? Your best friend?"

"Yes. Handsome, isn't he? Fine figure of a man."

"Was he? I hadn't noticed."

"You're a poor liar, Miss Makepeace."

She laughed, a sound that delighted him beyond reason.

When Kit and Susannah entered the White Lily Theater, Daisy Jones, Tom Shaughnessy, and the General were on stage arguing fiercely, three sets of hands gesticulating wildly. Daisy was perched on a swing dressed as a mermaid, and every time she made a point she flapped her tail vehemently. It was a magnificent tail, purple, and covered all over in some sort of sparkling net that was meant to look like scales, perhaps. A billowing red wig flowed from her head down over her . . . primary assets . . . and Kit saw the brilliance of the act: when she swung backward and forward, that red wig might just fly up and—

Good heavens. Kit rather hoped he'd be in London to see it.

The General finally flung both hands up in disgust, flounced off the stage, and stalked, muttering to himself, up the aisle. "*Mumble mumble* not bloody *Shakespeare,* for God's sake. Bloody *mumble mumble* thinks she's bloody Nell *Gwynn.*"

He stopped abruptly when he saw Kit and Susannah. He

bowed low, and pivoted back toward the stage. "*Madame* Jones," he drawled with exaggerated politeness. "Visitors."

Announcement made, he continued stalking and muttering toward the back of the theater. "Bloody fat spoiled *mermaid*," was the last thing Kit heard as he disappeared.

Tom Shaughnessy looked up from Daisy, whom he now appeared to be placating. "Ah, if it isn't Mr. White, and the charming and beautiful Mrs. White," he boomed. He swung gracefully off the stage. Today he was wearing fawn trousers and a bottle-green waistcoat, and his red-gold hair was a masterpiece of calculated messiness.

"Mr. White, if you'll give me a hand with our fair mermaid?"

Daisy hopped up off the swing and shimmied in her tail toward the edge of the stage, and Tom Shaughnessy and Kit each took an arm and swung her down. Her long red wig remained in place due, perhaps, to some cleverness of glue.

"We've just a quick question for you, Miss Jones, if you've a moment. We're terribly sorry to interrupt," Kit said.

"An interruption is what we needed, Mr. White," Tom Shaughnessy said smoothly. "I'll just gracefully retreat, shall I? To allow you to speak in private?" Mr. Shaughnessy bowed low, managing to make the simple gesture downright sultry, for Susannah's benefit, Kit was certain, and backed away. She dimpled, watching him go.

Kit cleared his throat, and she twitched her eyes away from Mr. Shaughnessy almost guiltily.

He turned toward the sparkly mermaid in front of him. "We've just one question, Miss Jones, and then we'll leave you to your rehearsal. Do you happen to know whether

Anna Holt's other daughters—Susannah's sisters—had miniatures with them when James brought them to you?"

"Miniatures?" Miss Jones's red eyebrows met in a "V" of thought. "Yes, of Anna, now that ye mention it. The girls each 'ad miniatures of Anna, and little bundles of clothes. I remember thinking 'ow lovely it was for them to 'ave miniatures of their mama . . . and 'ow dangerous it would be if anyone discovered them."

"Do you recall whether anything had been written on the back of the miniatures?"

"I only saw Sylvie's miniature, Mr. White, but I do believe it said . . . it said . . . 'To Sylvie 'Ope, of 'er mother, Anna.'"

"Sylvie Hope?" Kit wasn't sure whether this was significant, couldn't have said whether it was a clue yet, but he added it to his collection of information, to revisit later.

"Thank you, Miss Jones."

"Any time, as I said." Daisy swept Susannah into a mermaid hug, and then thrust out her hand for Kit to bow over, and swiveled in a very determined fashion back toward the stage.

"Tom! General!" she bellowed. "We are *not* finished 'ere. I need 'elp into me swing."

"Alert the bloody *navy*!" the General bellowed from somewhere in the back of the theater. "Tell them to bring a bloody *whale* net!"

It was the kind of establishment he hadn't visited in years, but astonishingly he wasn't entirely uncomfortable in it.

That realization, however, succeeded in making him feel a little uncomfortable.

Dark, the sort of dark that simply defeats lamplight,

Morley thought. The darkness came from the floors, stained with a century or so of spilled spirits, food, blood. From the ceilings, low and permeated with smoke. The air itself was thick and fetid with food and smoke and customers, none of whom appeared to have washed any time recently, and none of whom appeared to have all of their teeth. Morley was certain he knew a few of them personally. Had perhaps even run through the streets of St. Giles with a few of them.

Bob had chosen the meeting place. Had gotten a note to Caroline, somehow.

It was a dangerous place for a woman, but then, Caroline wasn't an ordinary woman. She had an instinct both for getting into trouble and getting out of it, like a cat. Had about the same quotient of defenses as a cat, too. He wasn't concerned, but again, he felt it: a tiny, not unpleasant clutch of anticipation in his chest.

She appeared from the shadows. "Hello, Thaddeus. You've been trying to kill me." She extended her hand.

"Hello, Caroline." He kissed the hand. "You've been trying to blackmail me. I'd rise, but the leg, you know."

She clucked in sympathy.

"Why don't you have a seat?" He pulled out a chair. She gazed down at it fastidiously, and then resignedly settled into it.

"I needed the money, Thaddeus."

It wasn't an apology. He almost smiled. "You could have simply *asked* me for the money."

"Really, Thaddeus? For some reason I didn't think I'd find you in a charitable mood." She said it ironically. "And I *really* needed the money."

She was right, of course. One didn't reward the sudden

defection of a mistress by giving her money, unless one was stupidly sentimental or desperate. And he was neither.

"What became of the American merchant?" he asked her.

"Is this a trap?" she asked lightly instead of answering. "With your desirable self as the bait? Will your little man sneak up and stab me between the shoulder blades?"

He didn't respond to that. "Would you like something to drink, Caroline?"

"Here? I think not. Liable to catch all manner of diseases. Not up to your usual standards, Thaddeus."

"But private."

Dressed all in black, Caroline was nearly invisible, but for the striking luminosity of her skin. Her eyes had it, too, that luminosity; like water at midnight, mysterious, fathomless. Making love to her had been maddening: delicious, always elusive. Like making love to the moon.

If the moon had adventurous sexual tastes, that was.

He couldn't help himself, he needed to ask. "Why did you leave me?"

She shrugged.

And he supposed that was as accurate an answer as he could expect from her. He almost understood: her life had begun in turmoil and upheaval, it was her native state, the only state in which she felt comfortable.

Whereas Thaddeus, as he aged, was discovering a taste for consistency and peace. He resented the events of the past few weeks; this need to kill people made him weary.

"I simply cannot allow you to threaten me, Caroline."

"Well, I *know* that now," she said whimsically. "Your little man with the knife rather drove the message home. Why did you want to see me tonight, Thaddeus? To tell

me simply that you 'cannot allow me to threaten you'?"
She imitated his grand tones.

He couldn't help but smile a little. "I need your help,
Caroline."

She laughed. "Well, *that* sounds rather more like you,
now. I should have known you wouldn't beg to have me
back." The tone was ironic.

But would you come back? No, he would never beg. He
wasn't even certain whether he wanted her back. Despite
the fact that of all the people who had entered his life . . .
perhaps she had understood him the best. There was both
profound safety and profound danger in that.

"It's simple, really," he told her. "I need you to seduce
Grantham and find out what he's doing with Makepeace's
daughter. Find out whether it has anything at all to do with
me. Then come back here and tell me all about it, so that I
may decide what to do next."

"Grantham? Kit Whitelaw, you mean?" she was startled.
He nodded.

Her face was expressionless for a moment, frozen in
pure surprise. "Kit," she repeated softly. Her eyes distant,
face unreadable.

"What makes you think I can do it, Thaddeus?"

"He still hates me after all of these years, Caroline.
And it's because of you."

This pleased her. She smiled, small white teeth shining
in that dark pub. "Do you think so, truly? But he's a
grown man now."

"Yes. A grown man with a weakness for women and
who, no doubt, will find it difficult to keep away from you."

She simply nodded; this was true of most grown men,
anyway. "He isn't married? Kit?"

"No."

"And who is Susannah Makepeace?"

"I think she's one of the daughters of Richard Lock-wood and Anna Holt."

Caroline jerked back at those words. "With Kit?" she said softly. "She's with Kit? But why?"

"I don't *know*, Caroline," Morley explained, impatiently. "It's what I need you to discover. But he's a spy now. He's not a . . ." He searched for adequate words. ". . . Soft man. Or an easy man. He is, in fact, a clever and dangerous man."

And all at once he could see that Caroline understood the assignment wouldn't be as simple or pleasant as it sounded. He could see her mulling it. She fussed with her gloves in silence. Looked about the pub, made a face at the quality of the clientele, returned her eyes to him.

"How would I do it? Gain the information you need?"

"Tell him you're frightened of me. You need his help. He won't be able to deny that sort of plea."

"Will you stop attempting to kill me if I agree to help you?" she asked.

"Will you stop giving me reasons to attempt to kill you?" he asked, almost whimsically.

She half-smiled, but didn't answer. He took it as an agreement.

"How . . . how is your leg these days?" she asked after a moment.

"Hurts. Talks to me during Commons sessions. Swears at me, more accurately. Drowns out the more boring speakers."

She laughed. "It's damp in those chambers. Perhaps the baths . . ."

"I may go when the Commons adjourns."

She nodded. "You really should. It helped before, did it not?"

She knew him so well. And suddenly it was strangely difficult to speak, so he simply nodded.

"All right, Thaddeus. I'll do it."

He cleared his throat. "Where are you staying this evening, Caroline?"

"With you?" she suggested lightly.

He took her hand, held it in the dark of the pub. Her fingers curled into his, and it was familiar, painfully sweet. "I'm old, Caroline."

"We shall see," she murmured.

Chapter Seventeen

"Susannah?"

Susannah stared out the window at her aunt's roses, many of which were beginning to wilt, at last defeated by the heat. Rather like her spirits.

He'd kept his conversation neutral and bland the entire long, *long* ride home from London. And when they'd arrived home, he'd helped her down from the carriage, a proper gentleman. And helped her with her trunk, a proper gentleman. And then he'd bowed, and touched his hat, and smiled pleasantly, and left her. Proper, proper, proper.

It was like being *assaulted* with manners. What was the *matter* with him?

"Susannah?"

They were brilliant manners, too, shiny and impeccable and as inviting as a suit of armor. He'd scrambled into them in order to keep her at arm's length from the moment they'd arrived in London. It was only in the dark she could get him to speak about himself. As though things said into the dark counted for nothing. He was like a child covering his face with his hands and thinking he could not be seen.

And he wouldn't touch her. No, he'd slept in a chair.

And she needed to know: *Why* wouldn't he touch her? Was it her questionable birth and decidedly unusual history? The fact that he was a viscount, and would never dream of marrying a woman of her status—or rather, lack of status? That she no longer held any appeal, now that he'd touched her once?

No appeal? Well, *that* much, she was certain, wasn't true.

He cared for her; she knew he cared for her. He desired her; she knew he desired her. She knew it as surely as she knew that female adders were shy, and that long-tailed voles were rare in this region, and that the insides of a horse were warm and wet.

But he wasn't being forthright, which was entirely unlike him. Which could only mean . . . he either didn't know what he intended to do about her, or he felt that telling her the truth of how he felt would be much too devastating for her, and he wanted to spare her feelings.

Odd, but her feelings at the moment did not feel *spared*. More raw, jangled, crowded, frustrated . . .

Perhaps he was simply afraid.

Kit Whitelaw? *Afraid?* Afraid of what?

"Susannah?"

She slowly turned her head to look at her aunt. "Mmmm?"

"Did you know that was the third time I'd said your name, my dear?" Her aunt's voice was gentle.

"Was it? I'm terribly sorry."

"Is aught amiss? You seem distracted. Was London unpleasant? Do you miss your friends?"

Startling to realize that she hadn't even given a thought to her "friends" while she was in London.

What would Aunt Frances say if she said, *Oh, Aunt Frances, something is amiss. I'm in love with the viscount, and he won't touch me, whereas the other day he touched me at length, with his hands and mouth, and I thoroughly enjoyed it.*

"No," she said softly. "Nothing is wrong."

Her aunt frowned a little then, and came to her, sat down next to her in the window.

"The viscount . . . he didn't . . ." She delicately trailed off, to give Susannah an opportunity to complete the sentence in any way she chose. Her aunt's face was taut with concern.

"No." Even she could hear the leaden disappointment in her voice.

Aunt Frances burst into merry laughter. "Oh, all right. As long as nothing is *wrong* then, my dear." The words were ironic. "What is this clinging to your skirt?" She plucked something from it. "It sparkles."

Susannah looked at it. "Must be a mermaid scale," she murmured. Then frowned faintly and returned to gazing out of the window, her thoughts pulling her there like a magnet, her mind so powerfully full of other things that she forgot her aunt again.

"I *do* know a thing or two about the . . . difficult sex, Susannah," her aunt coaxed. "If you've a question or two. And by that, I do mean men, my dear."

Her aunt's voice registered as a low murmur beneath the insistent clamor of her thoughts, and the sudden clang of her decision.

He was afraid that someone was trying to kill her; he'd

probably kill her for leaving the house alone, because "don't leave the house" were the last words he'd said to her as he left.

But finally she knew what she had to do. She stood up and seized her sketchbook.

"*Susannah.*"

Her aunt said the word almost sharply, which made Susannah stop and turn around suddenly. Her aunt studied her quizzically, taking a moment before she spoke.

"My dear, I know I am not your aunt by blood . . . but I truly have no wish to see you . . . hurt."

Susannah paused, abashed.

"Oh, Aunt Frances. . . ," she said impulsively. "Thank you for caring. I'm so sorry. I promise . . . well, you have my solemn vow that I will not . . . I will do my best not to ever disappoint or shame you."

"That wasn't my concern, dear," her aunt said gently. "I'm certain you won't. But I do thank you for the solemn vow."

Her aunt *was* a wry one.

Susannah smiled a little. "Well, it's my concern," she said simply. "And I do mean it."

Her aunt studied her for a moment, her brown eyes thoughtful. She was clearly searching for words.

"When I said I had no wish to see you hurt, Susannah," she ventured, "I didn't mean you should never . . . take a risk. And risks would not be called *risks* if there were not some chance of hurt. Nothing in life worth having is easy, Susannah. And—oh, never mind, my dear. You're young yet, but I know you are sensible, so I've no need to issue warnings and spout platitudes and the like. And, as you say, I have your solemn vow. Go enjoy . . . 'sketching.' But be home for dinner, if you would."

"*Do* you think I'm sensible?" For some reason this surprised Susannah.

"Yes." Her aunt sounded surprised that Susannah was surprised. "I do."

How about that? Among all of the other things she now knew she was . . . she was sensible, too.

Susannah smiled brilliantly at her aunt and pushed the door open, and all but raced down the path, despite the heat.

She was almost certain she knew where she'd find him.

He was on the pier, roughly whisking a towel over his bare chest. He'd already slipped into his trousers, but his feet were bare and the lowering late-afternoon sun gilded half of him, leaving the rest of him in shadow.

All the way there she'd rehearsed in her head what she might say to him, how she would ask it, what she might do if his answers broke her heart. But then he turned suddenly and saw her. And his face, unguarded, told her everything she needed to know, and questions were no longer necessary.

"Oh, Kit. It's all right," she said softly. "I love you, too."

He stared at her, caught. And then he laughed a short laugh, which was no doubt meant to sound incredulous or devil-may-care, but which failed miserably.

Susannah approached him as carefully as one would a deer or squirrel, and his eyes tracked her, never leaving her face. She stopped when she was close enough to feel the heat of his body, stopped just short of touching him.

And then she did touch him: slowly, very lightly, she placed one hand against his ribcage.

"Truly," she said gently. "And I'm not going anywhere. I do promise."

She could feel his heart jumping beneath her palm, in time with her own, feel the lift and rise of his ribs as his breathing quickened. Awe, and then a fierce longing, tightened his features. He slowly lifted his hand and dragged the back of it softly against her cheek, across her lips. She kissed his fingers. She saw his eyes go nearly black.

"You have me at a disadvantage once again, Miss Makepeace," he murmured. "I am only half-clothed."

"Well, then . . ." Her eyes never leaving his face, and with a bravado she didn't entirely feel, Susannah fumbled behind her neck for the laces of her gown.

"No," he said sharply.

The word seemed to stop her heart.

"That is," he said swiftly, "*I* want the pleasure of it, Susannah. That way, you can always blame me later, rather than yourself."

Her heart sputtered into life, into hope, again. And she lifted her eyes.

Kit was smiling down at her, but his smile was tense and rueful, his face more intent than she'd ever seen it.

More deftly and quickly than she preferred to think about, he reached behind her neck and loosened her laces. She nearly smiled. She felt the dying breeze of the day wash over her bare back.

He slipped his fingers inside her dress, touched her skin very gently and exhaled a soft shaky sigh, almost of relief. He combed his fingers over her shoulder blades, down either side of her spine, the rough pads of his fingertips and the exquisite lightness of his touch turning every cell of her skin to glowing cinders, her legs to liquid. Susannah closed her eyes, wanting only to feel, wanting to heighten the pure exquisite pleasure of his hands on her skin.

And then his mouth was warm against her ear. *"Susannah,"* he breathed there, her own name as sensual as his fingers. It traveled along the fuse of her nerve endings and lit a furnace inside her. Her lungs labored to breathe. She flattened her hands against his chest, savoring, at last, at last, the warm strong beauty of it. His skin was satiny over the rigid planes of his muscle, and again, this softness juxtaposed with strength . . . this was Kit.

"I like that," he murmured against her throat, where his mouth had traveled from her ear. He opened his lips against the soft skin there, put a hot kiss there. "Touch me anywhere you please."

"If you insist," she said. She was trying for insouciance, but the words were a squeak.

And he laughed, bloody man.

She indulged all of her weeks of stored longings and dragged one finger around the contours of his muscled chest, tracing a broad figure eight, then drew it down between his ribs, down the pale line of hair that led to the bulge in his trousers, stopping short of it, and was rewarded when he sucked in his breath. She opened her hands then and clasped them around his slim waist, let them wander down to cup his firm buttocks through his trousers. He mumbled some unintelligibly pleasured sound.

"Do you think it's *fair,*" Susannah managed to breathe, arching her neck so he could place another kiss at the base of her throat, "that I have seen all of *you,* and yet you have seen none of—"

"Oh, I'm *keenly* interested in justice, Miss Makepeace."

His hands left her back and found the sleeves of her gown, began to ease them down.

"No." She said it suddenly.

He stopped. The look in his eyes made her almost regret saying the word.

"*I* want to do it. That way I have only myself to blame."

He paused, and what he saw in her face made him slide his hands to her waist and rest them there. Honoring her need to make this decision for herself.

And before his eyes, with hands that trembled, Susannah tugged her bodice lower, slowly, slowly, until more breeze than muslin covered her skin, until at last the tops of her breasts were bare. Kit's eyes never left her face; they dared her, gave her strength. She took in a long unsteady breath and pushed the bodice of her dress with her hands until it drooped to her waist.

She watched his eyes slowly drop from her eyes to her lips . . . to her . . .

"*God,*" he murmured with reverent enthusiasm.

She almost laughed, but he found her mouth again with his, and then his warm hands were on her bare waist, on her ribs, gliding up, up, up with torturous leisure, until his hands filled with her breasts, and his touch, his lips, became tender beyond words. She nearly sank to her knees. His thumbs traced her nipples into peaks, until at last she needed to take her lips from his and lean her head forward to touch his chest, shivering with helpless pleasure.

His hand moved to cup the back of her head then, so he could once more take a kiss as deeply as he could; his other hand pressed against the small of her back, bringing her into the heat of his chest. The sensation of his skin against the hard tips of her breasts was unlike anything she was sure heaven had to offer. She moved her hands down, felt the hard, thick length of his arousal beneath his trousers, dragged her hands over it. He muttered something like *"mmm,"* which she took to mean to do it again. So she did it again, and again, until his hands went down to cup her buttocks and roughly pushed her up against him. She looped her arms around his neck and pushed herself closer still.

She wanted desperately to crawl inside him.

"Making love to you, Susannah," Kit murmured against her lips, as his hips moved against hers, "would be a rare honor and pleasure."

"I want you to make love to me." Her voice was shaking now.

"Do you know what that truly means?" His hands had slipped lower now inside her dress, and his finger had found the crease of her buttocks to delicately trace. He looked intently down into her eyes.

"Yes."

"You *do* know? You know that I will be inside you . . ." He kissed her, this one languid, thorough, incinerating. "And that I will move inside you . . ." He kissed her again, the same way, until her thoughts were glittering fragments. ". . . Until we are both mad from pleasure?"

"I want you inside me." She was nearly weeping with the truth of that.

He abruptly swept her up in his arms, carried her from the pier to where the small wood shelter sat. He pushed the door open, lowered her to the ground. And then, with his usual unself-conscious speed, he stepped back and quickly stripped off his trousers. She saw the thick curve of his arousal arching toward his belly, the hard contours of his thighs, the uncompromisingly masculinity of his whole bare body only a foot away from her, and was jarred suddenly: *This is real. This is happening.*

She pulled her gown from over her head, mimicking his quick boldness, hoping it would be contagious. Still she stood, shivering and a little shy, a little uncertain suddenly, in her bareness. He bundled their clothes together on the ground, making a soft place for them, and this too, made it seem shockingly real.

"Come here," he demanded in a whisper. She stepped forward, and he gathered her into his arms, pressing her against the warmth of his body, and his strong hands moved down her back, clothing her in a soft trail of heat, dissolving her shyness.

His lips against her skin were tender and reverent. They knew her secrets, made her feel vulnerable when she wanted strength, wanted to believe she had a choice in this surrender, when there never had been any, really. His mouth traveled, tasted with lips and tongue, her throat, her temple, the bones at the base of her neck. And when they returned home to her lips she gratefully, greedily drank him in, meeting the searching heat of his tongue with her own.

His hands, deliberate now, on a mission not to reassure but to arouse, roamed her body with shocking skill; his fingers knew where to stroke and linger, how to tease soft moans from her, to make her beg. He found and savored the curves of her breasts, the peaks of her nipples, cupped and explored the warmth between her legs, until she was supple and boneless, clinging to him. And then wantonly nearly climbing him.

Time dropped away. They sank together to their knees, mouths joined, his fingers twisting in her hair and plucking out pins as it loosened; he pulled her head back to take his kisses deeper, his fingers roving her hair. Her hands on him were careful, tender, over his bruises of his chest, over his arm where the knife had slashed him. Kit closed his eyes when she touched him, as though he could hardly believe the wonder of it, and then folded his arms around her and pulled her down over him, lowering himself to his back.

"Now," he urged on a soft rasp against her mouth. "I need you, Susannah. Please let it be now."

"Yes." A breath of a word.

He rolled over with her in his arms, covering her. She cradled him with her thighs, pulling him closer, and he lifted his torso up, fitted himself to her, slid into her waiting heat. There was a quick bite of pain; Susannah took her lower lip in her teeth to stifle a gasp. But then came the extraordinary feel of him filling her, and in so doing somehow touching her body everywhere. She watched Kit's eyes close when he was deeply seated; the intensity of his pleasure seemed akin to pain.

He was still, hovering over her; for a moment they savored together the miracle of being joined at last. He opened his eyes. So blue. Smiled down at her, crookedly, with quiet, rueful amazement. Pulled back, and thrust forward again, dipped to touch his lips to hers. He was shaking; she could feel his lean body quivering, saw the sweat gathering, gleaming over the lean muscles of his arms and chest.

"I want to go slowly for you," he whispered raggedly. "God, I want to. I'm just not sure I—"

"Hush. It's all right." She covered his lips with a finger. "It's all right."

He sighed then, and began to move in her, his cadence even, purposeful. She arched to meet each stroke, taking him as deeply into her body as she could; reveling in the pleasure she was giving, in the dark desire she saw in his eyes. And she reveled, too, when control was lost to him. He turned his head away from her when the rhythm of his need took him over, escalated, drummed through her body, his hips quick and fierce. When he turned toward her again, she saw the singular mission in his eyes, the unconscious total pleasure, and from the rush of his breathing knew instinctively it would be soon for him. She dug her fingers into his shoulders, holding him fast.

"Oh, God, Susannah. Oh, God."

His long body went still; she felt his release shudder through him. Felt the almost tangible peace it instantly brought. A gratitude, a tenderness she could scarcely bear, filled her; she touched his lips. He kissed her fingers gently.

"Thank you," he whispered. His chest moved with ragged breathing still; Susannah touched her finger to a bead of perspiration traveling the seam between his ribs. Then touched her finger to her tongue, tasting the salt of him.

"Think nothing of it," she murmured.

He gave a short laugh. Pulled away from her. Eased down next to her, and wrapped her loosely with one arm, flung the other arm out above him. He sighed the long sigh of the replete.

And they were quiet for a time, the sweat cooling on their bodies.

"In case you were wondering," he volunteered lazily after a moment, "we just made love."

"Is that what you call it?" She rolled her eyes upward,

studying her view, saw his half-smile and closed eyes. "Your armpit is very handsome."

This made him laugh. "Only an artist would think an armpit is handsome."

"But it *is* . . . the line of it is, anyhow. The muscles and shadows and hair . . ." She traced the muscles and shadows and hair with her finger as she said the words, and her voice drifted.

She sat up suddenly and reached for her sketchbook and quickly rendered him, that arm stretched over his head, his bare chest, and long legs, his lolling, spent manhood resting in curling hair, his wonderful face reflecting smug satisfaction, easy intimacy.

"You're a very good model," she told him approvingly. "You hold cooperatively still."

"I don't think I could move if you pointed a gun at me," he murmured.

She kissed the birthmark in the shape of a gull on his outstretched wrist, then leaned down and kissed his nipple, tracing it with her tongue, tasting it the way he'd tasted hers. His hand trailed down her back as she did; she saw unmistakable signs of stirring below.

"You're moving *now*," she teased.

He gave a short, very distracted laugh. "Siren," he said absently. Clearly enjoying the run of her tongue over his chest.

"I think I shall torture you," she whispered. She dragged her tongue down the seam between his ribs, then her lips skimmed his stirring shaft, which all but leaped to attention.

"Or I you," he whispered. He sat up suddenly swept her into his lap so that she sat across his thighs, and breathed into her ear, touched his tongue there, traced the whorls of it. A silver-hot shiver of sensation coursed through her body.

"Do you like that?" he murmured.

"I don't know," she half-gasped. "It rather takes . . . everything over."

He dragged a single finger down her throat, over the fine bones of her chest, touched it to the stiff peak of her nipple. "Proof that you most definitely like it," he confirmed in a sultry whisper. She laughed a little, then stopped abruptly, because she needed all of her faculties to enjoy what he'd begun doing to her breasts with his hands.

And then they were quiet, and with a tacit sort of agreement, everything was soft as breath, delicate. With lips, and fingertips light as air, with breath itself, she caressed him, and he caressed her. She breathed into his ear, tasted the cord of his neck while his fingers gently, maddeningly, softly, played along her spine, her waist, her belly, the nest of curls between her legs, her throat, her breasts, as though he was bringing music from the most delicate of harps. Until every cell of her vibrated with desperate need. His breath was hot, then cool, in her ear. She finally gave up exploring him and submitted, hooking her arms loosely around his neck, selfishly wanting just to take the pleasure he could give.

He knew so much more than she did. But she would learn. She would learn.

"*Kit,*" she finally gasped urgently against his neck, when it became untenable. She needed him to ease her need. She would beg him, if necessary.

It wasn't necessary.

"It's all right," he murmured to her. "It's all right." He

cupped her buttocks in his hands, lifted her up, and guided her down over his shaft with a long sigh. When he was deeply inside her, their eyes locked.

Susannah's breasts slid against his chest, both of their bodies sweat-sheened, as she rose up again, knowing instinctively what to do. He smiled faintly, guided her down again. Which is when she saw his eyes go black again with desire and she exulted. She loved this power to give and take, this humbling exchange of strength and vulnerability.

"There's a place inside you, Susannah. . . ," he said hoarsely. "Guide me. You'll know it when you feel it. I'll hold on to you."

So she lifted up again . . . and slid down again . . . and oh, he was right. There *was* a place.

She moved up over him again, with a sultry smile, enjoying this new knowledge, feeling that mysterious need escalating . . . she held it at bay for as long as she could. Which, as it turned out, wasn't very long at all. For her body took over, found the cadence it craved, and she began to ride him in an instinctive rhythm that grew ever swifter, and he held her, his hips thrusting up to meet hers.

The world became the harsh roar of their breathing, incoherent sounds of pleasure, softly groaned words of urging. Susannah could feel her release pushing, pushing at the seams of her, roaring through her veins like a river of stars, until it flooded its banks and burst from her in an exultant cry. The unthinkable pleasure of it rocked her, shook her like a rag; she trembled and trembled from it.

Kit held on to her, his own hoarse cry following, and she could feel his seed filling her as she breathed her exhaustion against his neck. Felt his chest heaving against hers as they clung together.

And then sank down to his back, bringing her down with him, holding her loosely. His chest rose and fell rapidly, as did her own. He shifted her to make himself more comfortable. They didn't speak until their breathing settled, became more even.

"You will be my wife," he ordered quietly, finally. As though issuing an answer to a problem.

"All right," she murmured with sated equanimity.

A silence. *We're in a shack on a pile of clothes,* Susannah thought, sleepily marveling.

"My father will like you," he said musingly.

"I intend to like him, too."

"He won't like that you have no *money*—"

"Nobody seems to," she said happily.

"But he will like *you*."

"Naturally."

He laughed at that. "Because 'it's *easy,*'" he said, quoting her words to him the night of the Barnstable assembly. He did a passing good imitation of her voice, too, high and fluty, and she gave him a little swat.

"It *is* easy, usually. *You* seem to like me well enough."

He grunted a laugh.

"May we live in London?" she asked

"Most definitely. Unless you'd like to stay here among the voles and adders."

She tensed.

He was laughing now, shaking beneath her. "There are no adders here at the moment, sweet." She batted him a little again, settled back down, and when he grunted, shifted her head to the shoulder that wasn't bruised.

"And Aunt Frances?"

"Can come to live with us, if she'd like."

"And we can have friends?" Susannah pressed. "In London?"

"I'm a viscount. I can buy you all the friends you want. How many would you like?"

She laughed again. He pulled her close, squeezed her a little with one arm as she lay across his chest. His eyelids were sleepily at half-mast. His body, however, was tense, at odds, with the soft satiety of his face.

She lifted her head up and studied him, her hair trailing down over him. She traced his lips, his cheekbones, his chin with a single finger. Hers to touch from now on.

"Nothing will happen to me," she said softly.

For she knew this was what was bothering him. What made him snap at her when she jested about her death. This astonishing man with the breakable heart.

He opened his eyes wider, surprised at her insight. Drank her in with that vivid blue. But said nothing.

"Nothing will," she insisted. "You are Christopher Whitelaw, spy extraordinaire."

Then again, it was easy to be certain of the world when one had just been thoroughly made love to.

He smiled a little, and still he said nothing. But his hand began slowly roaming over her body softly, possessively, over the curve of her buttocks, her shoulder blades, up through her hair. More of a claiming than a caress. Making sure of her. Memorizing her.

I love him.

He hadn't yet said he loved her, but surely he must. Everything he did, the way he felt, spoke of a love so large it almost seemed wrong to confine it to a single word.

And oh, she did love him. It was beautiful and terrible, enormously comforting and terrifying, battle and peace all at once. What she'd felt for Douglas was a mere cinder of affection in comparison.

His hand ceased its roaming and he lifted his head up suddenly to look at her, as if he had an urgent question. She prepared herself for it.

"Do you think I'm handsome?" He sounded a little worried.

She almost laughed. Because, no, she didn't think he was handsome.

"I think you are beautiful," she told him emphatically, and quite truthfully.

He looked smugly satisfied with that answer, dropped his head again.

She could hear the sounds of the woods now as they lay quietly, and it was almost as natural now as his breathing. The pungent smell of crushed leaves, the soft sounds of wind shaking branches, the rustle of unseen creatures who made their homes in the woods . . . for her they would always be inseparable from the scent and feel of Kit.

"But we can stay in Barnstable, too, can we not?" she said suddenly. "Quite often?"

"Would you like that?"

She was surprised that what she was about to say was true. "I think I would."

"So would I." He sounded surprised, too.

Kit managed to escort Susannah home in time for dinner, and Kit insisted upon formally asking for her hand from her aunt, who did a marvelous job of feigning astonishment while Susannah rolled her eyes from behind Kit's back. Aunt Frances's delight, however, wasn't feigned, nor was her relief, which she gave vent to when Kit was once again on his way.

"A countess!" Aunt Frances said, when Kit departed. "You'll be a countess, my girl. Someday, anyhow."

"And a wife!" Susannah was beside herself. "Of Kit!" This was the best part, as far as she was concerned.

"Kit, is it?" her aunt teased. "He's a good boy. I knew he would make an honest woman of you, Susannah."

Susannah was amused at the idea of Kit being a "good boy," but then she heard the rest of the sentence, and wondered if her aunt knew just how wanton she had been.

Her aunt read the abashed question in her face. "You've leaves in your hair, dear."

Susannah felt the scarlet flood her cheeks. "Aunt Frances! What you must think . . ."

"I think it's been some time since I've had leaves in my hair, but rest assured, I've had them. I'd worry a good deal more if you came home with leaves in your hair and no viscount in tow to ask for your hand."

"Perhaps the neighbors will return to visit you, Aunt Frances."

"Oh, I don't intend to wait for them, Susannah. I'll pay visits and spread the news myself, my dear. Would you like to come along when I do?"

"I believe I might."

She did wonder how she would be received when she didn't try so very hard. And she rather relished the opportunity to begin again.

Kit actually whistled on his way back home. He was off to fetch his lantern, brandy, water, tea, a blanket, and something to gnaw on. And then he'd return to guard her.

He wanted her in his bed tonight and always, but he supposed he would need to at least *pretend* to care about the proprieties. He would marry her with unseemly haste, anyway, as soon as a special license could be obtained; until then he'd keep her close.

He was happy. It wasn't an easy happiness, surrounded as it was by the fringed ends of their pasts, a countess who would pout when he abandoned her in favor of his *wife* (he loved that word), a disgruntled father, and all the violence and mystery that had characterized their time together. But in a way, that's precisely what made the happiness more precious, more complete. If not for those things, he might not have allowed Susannah to know him. If not for these things, Susannah would not be who she now was. She might be married to that poor young buffoon Douglas, forever ignorant of her own passion and strength, and he might still be bedding a married countess and drinking too much and never allowing anyone to touch him deeply again.

There were different kinds of fear, he knew. Battle was only frightening before and after, never during, because during battle one only did one's job. It was after when the pain set in; it was before when anticipation did things to one's mind.

And that was love, too.

He glanced about, and it occurred to him then: everything that made him what he was had begun here in these woods, tracking adders and voles and the like: his ability to draw connections and conclusions. His patience and agility and precision. A vision that allowed him to see the layers of complexity in the most deceptively simple things.

His first taste of passion. His ability to love.

He glanced up at the trees overhead, and the late afternoon light pouring through them reminded him of the stained-glass windows in Gorringe. *Faith, Hope and Charity, he thought.* "The greatest of these is love," the verse sometimes read. "Love" and "charity" were interchangeable words, some thought.

But they were all . . .

Bloody hell. They were all Christian virtues.

Kit stopped in his tracks. He gave a short laugh, wondering whether anyone had ever before used the words "bloody hell" and "Christian virtues" before in the same sentence.

The windows and the mausoleum at the Gorringe church had been donated by a generous benefactor. He would bet his left arm—the battered one, anyway—that Richard Lockwood had been that generous benefactor.

And finally, all the pieces slid into place.

"Of course," James had said, looking down at the back of the miniature.

And what did the back of the miniature say? "To Susannah Faith." *Faith,* a Christian virtue. Sylvie's second name had been "Hope."

He was willing to wager that Sabrina's middle name was "Charity."

Each of those miniatures had been a tiny clue. The whimsical Richard Lockwood had used his daughters as signposts to the location of the documents.

Tomorrow. He would go then tomorrow. He *must* go tomorrow. For Susannah's sake.

And . . . well . . .

Honestly, he wanted to beat John Carr to it.

Chapter Eighteen

Susannah spent a quiet evening beneath Aunt Frances's roof. They'd begun another book, this one a horrid novel, and she'd had a little trouble sleeping due to the ghost, as well as heated thoughts of Kit. But she woke at the usual time, and when she wandered out with her sketchbook at the usual time, she found the viscount waiting at the gate for her.

My fiancé, she revised, in her thoughts.

She stopped for a moment and just looked and looked at him. Delighted that he simply existed. Savoring the joy that flared hot and bright in her chest all over again, that made the ground beneath her feet and the sky above her feel one and the same.

She walked to meet him, and when she reached him, he stretched out an arm and pulled her against him, and she put her face up. He kissed her, sweetly and simply, because they could share any manner and any number of kisses from now on, from sweet to incendiary.

His face was chilled against hers, as though he'd been

out of doors already for a good length of time. He tasted a bit of tea, but his mouth was cold, too. Again, the skin beneath his eyes looked faintly bruised. He wanted a shave.

She studied him critically.

And then a realization struck.

"You've been guarding me," she said, breathlessly. "At night. Watching the house. It's why you look so . . ." She trailed off.

"Very handsome?" he completed winsomely.

Susannah's heart almost couldn't expand enough to accommodate the awe that filled it then. She wouldn't gush, however, and make this tender, gallant man uncomfortable.

"Tonight," she said firmly, "I will let you in after Aunt Frances has gone to bed, and you will sleep on the settee, if you really must guard me. And you can be gone before Aunt Frances comes down. I will not have you going without sleep."

He thought about this, and then nodded once, agreeing, looking half-pleased to be ordered about. He extended his arm, and she took it.

He led her up the tree-lined path, this time not into the woods, but to the modest grounds of The Roses. Susannah looked about at the fountains and shrubbery. "I had no idea you had anything so ordinary as *roses* growing here," she teased.

He didn't laugh. He turned to her, and she saw the change in his posture, the look on his face, the intent, and was already lifting her face up to his as he reached for her. She met his lowering mouth with her own, and he groaned low in his throat and pulled her closer, closer to him, as though he could press her into his body and protect her from harm forever. Her body softened against his, and her hands slid up his chest to clasp around his neck. The kiss was deep and hungry, the one he'd wanted to give her this morning, but thought would perhaps be improper to do right outside of Aunt Frances's cottage.

He lifted his face from her to breathe. "There's something I need to tell you, Susannah. Today—"

He stopped and looked. There was a speck hurrying toward them from a distance, which turned out to be Bullton, who, as he drew closer, proved to already be reddening in the heat. Butlers spent most of their time indoors, after all.

"Is something amiss, Bullton?"

"Sir. You've . . . Well, you've a . . . visitor, sir."

Who could fluster Bullton so completely?

Bloody hell, it must be my father.

He'd forgotten to send any notes at all to the Earl. Kit braced himself, began to mentally compile excuses for his woefully thin folio, began to compile explanations for a mad dash to Gorringe, and looked up.

A slim, petite woman, dressed head to toe in mourning, stood diffidently in the garden. Her hair was gathered into a knot beneath a big black hat, from which hung a veil. And then, her gloved hands rose slowly, and she lifted her veil, turned her face up to him.

Kit froze, because that's what one did when one saw a ghost.

Unthinkingly, he dropped Susannah's arm. And with every step the ghost took toward him, the years dropped away.

She held out her dark-gloved hand to be bowed over and Kit, almost reflexively, lightly took her fingers. But she gripped his hand when he did that, and turned it over. Looked down at it closely instead. And smiled softly.

"Oh, Kit," she murmured. "It really is you."

And Caroline Allston kissed the gull-shaped birthmark beneath his wrist.

He didn't exactly *snatch* his hand away, but he did take it from her quickly. Caroline always did have a way with dramatic gestures, and it was easy to be caught up in them.

Recovering, he glanced at Susannah, the woman he'd just kissed within an inch of her life. She stared at Caroline with the same affection and admiration she reserved for adders.

Caroline wasn't any less beautiful for her years; she still had a remarkable face, dominated by those dark eyes, soft and deep, those feathery brows, the brows of a baby, almost. Those naturally red lips that had so fascinated a seventeen-year-old boy. It was still a delicate, passionate, wanton face. And yes, for all of that . . . still a vulnerable face. It made one instantly want to protect her, when really, one probably need protecting *from* her.

"Caroline . . ."

"Allston," she completed. "It's Allston." With no explanation of the mourning dress.

"Hello, Caroline. Allow me to introduce my fiancée, Miss Susannah Makepeace."

He reached for Susannah's hand proprietarily, tucked it into his arm. Susannah seemed to have gone into rigor mortis, however; her arm was decidedly stiff. He glanced down at her, meaning to reassure her, but she was studiously avoiding his eyes. Her eyes were instead still fixed on Caroline, as if she stared at Caroline just hard enough, she'd evaporate like a mirage.

Caroline was staring at Susannah, too.

"Congratulations on your engagement." Caroline managed to make the words sound ironic.

"We thank you. How many years has it been?" Kit strived for joviality. He wasn't entirely certain how to address a former lover, current alleged traitor.

"Seventeen," Caroline said. "Seems like only . . . yesterday."

The word "yesterday" was fertile with innuendo. It made it sound like it had indeed been only yesterday, and *goodness*, what they had gotten up to then!

How very, very like her. It was the sort of thing she'd done so many years ago, lobbing innuendo between John Carr and himself just to watch how they would volley it, just to see them bristle like fighting cocks. Could it be that she had remained entirely unchanged for seventeen years? Or perhaps it was something about *him* that launched Caroline into her games.

"To what do I owe the pleasure of your visit, Caroline?" His voice was decidedly cooler now that he'd recovered his composure.

Her face crumpled a little, and he saw in her face that girl who had tried so hard to be brave years ago, and whose only defense was lashing out in the only way she knew how. And his immediate impulse was to go to her, to make it better in the way he'd never been able to do for her before.

"I'm . . . I'm in trouble, Kit. Really in trouble. I didn't know whom else to turn to, I swear it. And you always . . . you always tried to help."

It was the word "tried" that embedded itself in him. *Tried.* He'd always *tried* to help. Tried and failed.

She must have seen the change, the softening in his face; her voice steadied, found dignity. "I beg a word, Kit. And forgive me, Miss Makepeace," she added gently. "For intruding on what must be a very happy time, indeed. I am more sorry than I can say."

Kit glanced down at Susannah, who had her teeth bared in a facsimile of a smile. She tried again to tug her hand away from him. Kit clamped it tightly with arm. *You're not going anywhere, Susannah.* In a way, she was his talisman.

Kit didn't know whether he could or should trust Caroline. The anguish on her face seemed real enough and, as it had so many years ago, the need in her spoke to something in him that wanted to make everything right for her.

But beneath it was a very unsentimental curiosity: He wanted to hear what she had to say. She was integral to this mystery now, and he wanted very much to unravel it. And for some reason, it seemed inevitable that she should appear.

He softened his tone a little; it was still, however, implacably polite. "Anything you need to say to me you can say before my fiancée as well."

"Kit . . ." Caroline sounded desperate now. "You . . . might not wish Miss Makepeace to hear what I have to say. I think only of . . . protecting her."

Worse and worse. But Caroline was very likely right about that. He didn't want Susannah at all tainted or implicated by the presence of a suspected traitor. He wondered if John Carr was still in the vicinity somewhere, watching him; whether Caroline managed to arrive undetected. The whole mourning kit . . . veil, the black gown . . . he supposed it was a disguise.

For a wild moment he considered whether John Carr had found Caroline and sent her to him. Whether even now the king's men were descending upon Barnstable to arrest Kit for consorting with a traitor.

It might just be the one way that John Carr would finally, at last, win.

The thought made Kit furious with Caroline. It couldn't be true, he didn't believe it, but he knew, in that wild moment, that Caroline's legacy was deep indeed. That years ago she had seen something simple and good—the friendship he shared with John—and set out to ruin it, simply because she could. Simply because the ability to do so was one of the powers her beauty conferred. Perhaps the only power she could lay claim to.

"Kit . . . he's trying to kill me," she said softly. "Morley."

Ah. The magic word: *Morley*.

Kit simply waited.

"I know I've . . . made some rather . . . unwise decisions," she continued, smiling nervously at her own expense, "but I swear I never meant to hurt anyone, least of all you. And I'm tired, tired of running, Kit. I'm so frightened."

He said nothing. There was a part of him that couldn't believe that Caroline Allston was standing in his garden. Another part of him, a primitive childish part that he wasn't proud of, that was glad, *glad* she'd come to him.

"Did you receive my letter?" she asked, when still he said nothing.

He felt Susannah tense next to him.

Which letter was Caroline referring to? The one that

John Carr had intercepted, or the letter sent so many years ago: *"I'm sorry."*

He nodded slowly, regardless.

"Kit . . . for the sake of long ago . . . will you help me?"

Susannah was stiff with uncertainty, stunned, radiating hurt. He wanted to tuck her away some place where nothing of his past or of hers could touch her. But that would solve nothing; it seemed his past was somehow entwined with Susannah's, and before they moved forward into a future together, he would need to methodically unravel the knots.

"Susannah. . . ," he said, regret and decision heavy in his voice.

"I'll go home right now," Susannah said quickly, too brightly. "To Aunt Frances. I'll leave the two of you to become reacquainted."

"No, you won't."

"I'll go to Aunt Frances and—"

"No," he said firmly. "You won't. You'll stay here in this house. It is *your house* now, too. We'll go inside. And I shall speak to Miss Allston privately while you wait for me."

"I would like to go to Aunt Frances." The words were cool; the two spots of color in her cheeks were not.

Kit turned looked down at Susannah. She steadfastly refused to meet his eyes, focusing on the roses beyond his shoulder. He took her stiff hand and lifted it to his lips, while Caroline's eyes followed it there, her expression enigmatic.

"It will be all right, Susannah," he said softly.

Susannah's expression told him that she didn't believe him. And she didn't precisely jerk her hand away from him, but she didn't want to be touched by him at the moment, either, that much was very clear. He might as well have been gripping a leather-bound copy of Marcus Aurelius instead of a hand, for how yielding it felt.

"Of course it will," she said. "Of course it will. Because you're always *accurate,* aren't you?"

Her irony landed with the grace of a crowbar, but he hadn't the time or patience to placate her now. Potential disaster, in the form of Caroline, stood before both of them. Potential answers. Potential truth.

"Thank you for understanding," he said to Susannah, which would have to suffice for now. "Shall we go inside?"

And so sandwiched between his past and his future, Kit led two beautiful women into the house.

He'd taken one look at that woman . . . and he'd gone as white as a blank page of her sketchbook. As white as the day a horse had fallen on him. And then he'd dropped her arm, as if he couldn't possibly touch *her* and look at Caroline Allston at the very same time.

And oh, but that woman was beautiful. An intimidating, thorough, *fascinating* sort of beautiful. A *complicated* beautiful. Complicated, she knew, appealed to Kit. "Difficult to forget"? Susannah gave a short bitter laugh, as she waited in the parlor. "Difficult to forget" didn't by half do Caroline Allston justice.

And Kit—the man who was her very heart—was shut in the library with Caroline Allston right now. And it did feel that way: As though her heart had been scooped out, and a high cold wind was whistling through the place where it had once been.

Here she was in a parlor filled with shining, stiff, glamorous furniture; alone with a giant painting featuring the Whitelaw family. Kit's pretty mother, his handsome father, a pair of little girls who fortunately looked more like their mother than their father, slightly demure, slightly mischievous. Kit's little face was sullen, poking up out of some sort of ruffled suit. It made her smile faintly.

Susannah reached up to touch that image of him, wishing she could have known him then. Wishing she could have known him always. Wishing she could have been the one over whom he'd shot his best friend, the one whose name he'd carved into a tree. Known him when he was just learning how to love, so she could be absolutely sure that he loved her.

He does love me, she'd thought confidently only yesterday. *He must.* She'd thought it again, only an hour ago, as they'd kissed shamelessly in the rose garden. *He must love me.*

But what did she really know of the shades of love? That extraordinary-looking woman in the other room had been his first love. And she needed him now. Perhaps Kit would see an opportunity to redeem himself.

Well, I love him. And that would have to do for now, she thought. Her love for him would have to suffice in place of certainty. Until he was ready to say it to her. If he ever did.

And she stared up at that big painting, and ordered her heart not to break.

He directed Caroline into a library chair and waited while Mrs. Davies, she of the spaniel-brown eyes, settled the tray of tea down with a rattle between them. Mrs. Davies wasn't nearly as gifted at inscrutability as Bullton was.

She slid her speaking eyes toward Kit as she left the room, and her disapproval was very nearly palpable.

He watched Caroline remove her gloves, finger by finger, and ball them into one fist. And then she unpinned her hat, a great black thing heavy with feathers and a veil, and sat it next to her on the settee, where it crouched like a familiar. Her hair was still black and glossy, she wore it coiled loosely against her long white neck. Soft hair, he remembered. It had been like smoke and silk in his fingers when he was seventeen.

"I *am* sorry, you know," Caroline said quietly.

And for a moment, the two of them were seventeen and eighteen years old, and Kit had just had his heart broken.

Had her heart broken even a little? Had she run off to punish him, or to save herself? He'd been so sick with misery then, with outrage, that it was a marvel now that he could regard her . . . aesthetically. Nothing at all moved in the vicinity of his heart.

"That night . . . you did leave with Morley?" How odd it would be to know for certain after all of these years.

Caroline hesitated. Then nodded slowly.

"Did he touch you or force you, or—" The old rage began swinging up.

"*I* suggested it to him, Kit."

Kit took this in. He remembered Morley's inscrutable face, the contempt floating just below the surface of it. That smile he'd sent toward Kit. Why *wouldn't* Morley have accepted Caroline's suggestion? Any sane man would have had difficulty denying it. Caroline at eighteen had been glorious.

"Perhaps you had no choice," he said gruffly. It was his pride speaking. His guilt.

"That *was* my choice." Caroline gazed back at him levelly.

Unspoken: It was her choice, because Kit couldn't, or wouldn't, marry her. Though he most certainly had been willing to touch her.

"And yes . . . yes, he did . . . touch me, Kit. That night. And many, *many* others, too. In many . . . *many* ways."

She drew the words out, drawling them, so that he could feel and picture each one thoroughly. And she smiled a little as she did it, enjoying his discomfiture. How very like her. Always wanting men to froth with jealousy over her. Never happy when the waters were calm, the skies blue. She had a talent for it, Caroline did, stirring those darker feelings.

He said nothing.

"I was very young then, Kit. And . . . I left Thaddeus two years ago."

"Thaddeus," Kit repeated flatly. It sounded downright wifely when she said it that way.

"Yes, that *is* his given name, Kit," she said ironically. "But . . . after I left him—"

"Why did you leave him?"

She shrugged lightly.

And somehow, that shrug seemed unspeakably cruel. He wondered if Morley had loved her, too. And whether that had anything to do with why he wanted to kill her. Kit could almost sympathize.

"You left because of a whim, Caroline?"

She looked up at him, puzzled. A look that said, *Well,*

you have *met me, haven't you?* Caroline was all but comprised of whim. And devoted to self-preservation.

"After I left him, times became hard, Kit, for me. So . . . I wrote to Thaddeus asking for money, thinking perhaps he might help me. And now he wants to kill me."

"Really." It was Kit's turn to drawl ironically. "Just like that, Caroline? A simple request for money and a well-known politician becomes murder-bent? Odd, but Morley doesn't strike me as an irrational man. Quite the opposite, in fact. He has managed to remain a politician for many years, and has likely only methodically killed a few people in the process. Only a few that I'm *aware* of, that is. Perhaps you know of more?"

Caroline flinched at this; he saw her skin draw tight around her eyes, suppressing some emotion. Shock, perhaps, that he would respond so coolly. Then she looked down at her folded hands in her lap, like a chastened child.

"Perhaps you threatened him for money, Caroline?" Kit suggested with gentle irony. "Now would be the time to tell me."

She lifted her head up and smiled impishly. "Well, it seemed a good idea at the time. My judgment never *was* the soundest, and well you know."

He sighed. "What, precisely, did you threaten him *with*, Caroline? Do you know something incriminating?"

She was silent. "He forced me to help him, Kit."

For some reason, Kit couldn't imagine anyone forcing Caroline to do anything she didn't want to do. Not even Morley. No doubt she'd gone into whatever it was thinking it would be a grand adventure. "Help him with what?"

She shook her head roughly.

"Help him with *what*, Caroline?" he repeated relentlessly. "And *how*, precisely, did he force you?"

He could almost see her mind working behind those mirrorlike dark eyes.

"Please don't make me tell you," she said finally, softly. "Kit . . . I'm just . . . I'm just so tired of running. I'm frightened. Please . . ." She leaned forward and placed her hand on his knee. "*Please* help me."

He looked down at the hand, and then into her face. The look he saw there promised things, and it would have buckled his knees if he'd been seventeen. At seventeen, he would have, in fact, had his trousers unfastened by now. He wasn't entirely immune to that look now; he *was* male, after all, and she'd had three decades to perfect it. But beyond a fluttering of flattered masculinity, he didn't feel much beyond curiosity. He stared at her the way he might a puzzle made for children. The sort of complication she presented had lost all appeal, regardless of its package.

He lifted her hand from his knee, very gently. He handed it back to her as though handing back his entire past, everything he'd once felt for her.

And the look on her face then was pure shock: shock that anyone would refuse her. Then confusion and panic; she hadn't anything left to her besides her looks and wiles.

"I can't help you," he said gently. "If you don't tell me why you think he's trying to kill you, Caroline. And Caroline . . . even if he *made* you help him, you'll be implicated, too, in whatever he's done. Unless you tell me. And maybe then . . . maybe then there will be something I can do to protect you."

She tried again: lips parted, she fixed him with a gaze that would have had a priest rending his vestments and leaping upon her. She clearly knew that men were simpletons, for the most part, and that her powers were potent.

Kit waited it out. He was excellent at waiting, when strategy called for it.

Caroline frowned a little, and the gaze went away, like a curtain being drawn, and she looked uneasy. Ah, at last. She was beginning to realize, he thought, exactly how much trouble she was in, and beginning to understand that Kit wasn't a seventeen-year-old hothead ruled by what swung between his legs. He sighed. He tried for the element of surprise.

"Caroline, there's a rumor that Morley sold information to the French. Do you know anything of this?"

"Is he being investigated then?" she asked almost eagerly. "Have you any proof?"

Interesting eagerness. Interesting question.

And then, with a mental *click,* he felt another piece of the puzzle slide into place, and he had an interesting realization.

He took great pains to disguise this realization with a carefully concerned countenance.

"What were you doing in Gorringe, Caroline?" He asked it casually.

"Gorringe?" she looked startled.

"The letter. The *'I'm sorry'* letter. You sent it from Gorringe. Many years ago. A year or so after you left with Morley."

"Oh," she said faintly. "I'd forgotten."

To him, it was the verbal equivalent of her earlier shrug. She'd *forgotten.*

But Kit was now certain he knew precisely what she'd been doing in Gorringe all those years ago. *He forced me to help,* she'd said. He doubted much forcing of any kind had been involved. Caroline had always had a taste for mischief; no doubt she'd thought the whole business exciting.

Ironic to think that Caroline had been a spy, too, long before Kit ever was.

He stared at her, his face revealing nothing, because he was trained to reveal nothing. He watched Caroline desperately, silently trying to gain a purchase on his inscrutable mood, to know what he was thinking, or how he felt.

This was what he was thinking and feeling: Caroline had helped shatter the lives of happy people, and deprived Susannah of a family, and assisted a traitor. And pity, the strongest emotion he'd felt for Caroline since she'd arrived today, was beginning to give way to the conviction that she was, in a way, an accessory to murder. A murder almost two decades old.

Caroline's life had begun difficult, but her own decisions had ensured it remained so. And very likely, finally, he realized there had never been anything he could do to help her, no matter how desperately he'd wanted to.

She cleared her throat. "Perhaps I should leave now, Kit," she said, briskly. "I'm sorry to have troubled you."

"No," he said softly. Placed a gentle but restraining hand on her arm. "I should like you to stay. I shall do everything I can to help you, Caroline."

It was a lie. But he didn't intend to let her get away now.

Susannah didn't turn around when Kit came into the room almost an hour later, but he was certain she'd heard him; he could tell by how her spine stiffened.

He sat down quietly next to her on the settee, didn't speak for a moment. He followed her eyes to the painting.

"How do you like my portrait?" he asked conversationally.

She thought about that. "You don't look happy in it."

"The painting was my father's idea. I remember those sittings well . . ." His voice drifted, he smiled ruefully. "My father is forever making me do something I don't want to do. Something I don't want to do . . . and then later I'm glad of." *Like the damned folio.*

Kit realized, irritated and amused, that his father was probably smarter than he was.

Well, if somebody *had* to be smarter than he was, he supposed he was glad it was his father.

"You have two sisters, too," she said softly. "Are they alive?"

"Yes." He wasn't about to regale Susannah about the mixed blessings sisters presented. Hopefully they would find her sisters, and she would discover those blessings for herself.

"Perhaps we can write to find my sisters. Daisy Jones said Sylvie had gone to France. Sabrina might very well still be in England. And maybe my mother . . ." She trailed off.

"We'll do that right away," he promised her.

She smiled a little.

He reached for her hand, which was cold, but soft, unresisting now. He brought it to his lips and held it there for a long time, turned her palm up and placed a kiss in it, folded her hand over the kiss.

"I need to go somewhere, Susannah, and I meant to tell you earlier."

"With her?"

"No."

He saw the relief on her face; had she really thought he would leave her?

"Where will *she* be when you go?" she wanted to know.

"The two of you will come along with me." He'd decided this was the only way it could be.

"*Wonderful.* Just the three of us. How very cozy."

Kit smiled crookedly. But he didn't want to leave Susannah alone at all. And he wasn't about to allow Caroline to leave The Roses now that she was here. And he wasn't going to arm Bullton with a rifle and tell him to watch Caroline, nor did he think it fair to leave Bullton in charge of guarding Susannah.

His only option, unattractive though it might be, was to bring both women along to Gorringe. And quickly.

Where was bloody John Carr when he actually needed him?

"Susannah, listen to me: Do you want this to be over? Do you want to be safe?"

"No, I rather enjoy dodging for my life, and wondering when you'll next be stabbed or crushed on my behalf."

He smiled again, pleased with her the way he always was when she was sarcastic.

"How can you *smile*?" she wanted to know, irritated.

"You forget, my dear, that danger has been a way of life for me."

She pondered this. "Wouldn't you rather just be a naturalist?" she said weakly.

He didn't answer; he just looked at her for a long moment. And then he leaned forward and touched his mouth to hers.

Her lips were obstinate at first, but then they softened beneath his, and her hand went up to cup his face—he loved it when she did that—and she parted her lips. For a short, dizzying moment, they feasted tenderly on each other. It was incomparably sweet.

And when he was finished kissing her, she looked down and ran her tongue over lips, tasting them, took in a long breath. He knew her head was spinning like his own.

"Where do we have to go?" she asked finally, composure regained.

"Do you remember when I said there were some papers incriminating Morley? I think I know where they are."

"Where?"

"Do you recall the stained-glass windows in the church in Gorringe? The vicar said they weren't original—he said they were donated by a 'generous benefactor,' along with the mausoleum behind."

"'Faith, Hope, and Charity,'" Susannah mused, and then her eyes flew wide. "Oh! I see it now! The *windows* were 'Christian virtues'! It's something to do with the windows!"

"Yes. And I think that generous benefactor was your father. Richard Lockwood."

"Good heavens," Susannah was impressed. "He *was* clever, then."

"Too clever by half. Too whimsical by half, perhaps. He might have been a little more direct—no doubt we all would have appreciated it—but where would the fun have been in that?" Kit said wryly. "I believe the documents he collected—if they exist—might be hidden in the mausoleum in Gorringe."

"But if he'd been more direct," Susannah said, defending the father she'd never known, "perhaps Mr. Morley would have found and destroyed the papers by now."

"Clever, aren't you." Kit's mouth twitched.

"I get it from my father, I believe."

"Perhaps," he indulged. "But you're right, of course, about Morley. The fact that he seems to be trying to kill you . . . I think it means he hasn't yet found the documents. I believe James threatened him with their existence, *then* set out to actually find them, which, as Mr. Avery-Finch told us, is a rather backward way to conduct blackmail."

"And then Mr. Morley searched my home for them, but didn't find them."

Kit nodded. "He probably thought it would be easy enough to eliminate you, just in case you had the documents and intended to use them, since he believed you hadn't any other means of income. He clearly hadn't reckoned upon *me*."

"I imagine you come as a bit of a surprise to most people."

He shrugged modestly. "Then again, the papers may *not* exist, Susannah . . . but it's the best hope we have for bringing Morley to justice."

"What if you're wrong? About the mausoleum, that is? And the rest of this?"

"I so seldom am." He gave her confident smile.

Which caused her to roll her eyes.

"But we do need to look for those documents *now*. Today. Because if they are what they seem to be . . . then we might be able to arrest Morley. And stop the, shall we say, inconvenience of frequent attempts on your life."

"And clear my mother's name perhaps?"

"And clear your mother's name. I hope."

"And save Caroline, somehow, as well." Susannah said the words flatly. "Because you must by all means save Caroline."

Kit hesitated. He didn't know how to tell Susannah what he suspected; he thought perhaps he wouldn't tell her just yet. For the moment, he needed her relatively calm and enthusiastic. "Perhaps," he said.

Susannah was quiet for a moment. "She's very beautiful."

"Yes," Kit agreed simply.

Susannah turned her head away from him, studying the portrait again. She seemed to be struggling with something; he saw the passage of thought over her features.

"How would you describe me, Kit?" she asked finally.

"I'm sorry?" It wasn't the last thing he expected her to say just then, but it was very near it.

"How would you *describe* me? It's just . . . I've never heard you do it. I've heard you call Caroline 'difficult to forget.' Dark hair, dark eyes. But . . . what do you see when you see *me*? How would you describe me?"

She said it urgently, as if she couldn't possibly exist until he'd delineated her in words.

Kit was startled by the request. He would describe a vole, an adder, a fern, a horse. He knew the facts of them, their colors, their habits, the connections between them.

But how would he describe Susannah? He tried to think, but images and feelings tumbled together, defying single words: wit and complicated eyes and a green hat and exquisite breasts and—

For some reason the only image that lingered was Susannah with her arm buried up to the shoulder inside a horse. It seemed important, that image.

He realized he couldn't describe her any more than he

could describe his own . . . *viscera.* She lived inside him now.

"I can't do it," he said softly, almost to himself, his voice frayed. "I can't describe you."

He saw the bitter disappointment flood her face. Then watched her struggle to disguise it.

He stood up then, feeling strangely agitated. "How can I possibly describe"—he made an abrupt, sweeping gesture—"everything, Susannah? Because that's what you are. You are . . . everything."

She gazed back at him, stunned.

"Does that satisfy you?" he asked quietly.

He knew it didn't. He was embarrassed by the inadequacy of it. Still, he couldn't bring himself to say the words to her.

"I'll have the coach brought round."

And then he left her, very quickly, as though the enormity of the love he saw in her face and the enormity of all that he felt drove him from the room.

Chapter Nineteen

Kit hallooed for the vicar when they arrived at the Gorringe church, but there was no response. Perhaps the vicar was napping off his noonday wine.

Very well, then. He'd conduct his own tour of the church grounds. He led Susannah and Caroline around back.

The mausoleum was easy enough to find: a somber granite block, glowing white in the sun, guarded by suitably solemn carved seraphim holding trumpets aloft. Kit was amused; it wasn't grand, but the thing was so ostentatious as to be nearly mocking, perhaps more evidence of Lockwood's famously whimsical sense of humor. Or perhaps he really *had* intended to be buried in this mausoleum, and had wanted to do it in style, and add his family members to it, as well, as the years went on.

As Robert Burns had said so well: The best laid plans of mice and men . . .

It was locked. He'd been prepared for this eventuality. He fished about in his pack, came up with a length of wire, poked it in and jiggled it about. He pocketed the lock, as he didn't intend for them to be locked inside, and pushed the door a little. It gave, and the trapped must of years rushed out at him in a cloud of agitated dust.

He coughed and waved his hand.

It was dim inside, despite the brilliant day behind him. He produced a lamp and lit it—Kit was, of course, prepared—allowed the light to pulse into a glow, and he studied the inscrutable interior, which, unlike the door, yielded nothing. He gestured for the women to precede him inside, and they both did so gingerly. And once they were inside, Kit retrieved his pistol from inside his coat, kept it in his hand.

He hesitated to close the mausoleum door behind him, yet he didn't want to call attention to his presence. He compromised by wedging his tinderbox there. He entered, holding his lamp aloft, and waved it around.

The light found it: a box. He gave it a tug from its slot.

Susannah and Caroline leaped back, squeamish.

"It's not a body," he assured them. "No one has ever gone to their eternal rest in this particular mausoleum."

There was a sturdy lock on the strongbox; a few more minutes of fumbling with and swearing at the lock, and it sprang open.

Dust flew out like a genie escaping a bottle, and when it cleared he saw a stack of documents. He settled the lantern on one of the empty spaces above him, and began to leaf through them, his fingers careful; many of them had gone brittle with age.

The first was a letter, sent to a French operative whose name he recognized—they'd apprehended him years ago—in a code he recognized. How on earth had Richard Lockwood acquired this—bribery? Lockwood had indeed been playing a risky game, if he'd undertaken this investigation alone. The next document was a letter in French agreeing to a meeting with Monsieur Morley at an inn near the London docks. Not terribly incriminating, in and of itself, but perhaps useful as part of a story. Another sheet of foolscap below that appeared to be a list of the names of ships. He recognized the names.

There were drawings of guns. And letters describing meetings.

"Sweet Lucifer," he breathed. It was true. It was all true. Morley was a traitor, and in his hands he held enough to hang him.

And then the thick dusty hush of the mausoleum was interrupted by a sound he knew too well, inches behind him: the *click* of a pistol.

And he turned around to discover Caroline Allston pointing one at Susannah's temple.

"Give me the documents, Kit."

He took in the situation with one glance. It would have been a simple thing to snatch that toy from Caroline's delicate little wrist, except—

"This is a dueling pistol, and it'll go off like"—Caroline snapped her fingers—*"that* if you so much as nudge me."

Except for that.

"Then perhaps you hadn't better do"—Susannah snapped her fingers—*"that."* Her voice was shaking, but it sounded more like fury than fear.

"Susannah," Kit said softly. "She's right. Don't move."

Susannah went obediently quiet. Kit could have reached out and crushed Caroline's windpipe between two fingers, such was the force of his fury at the moment. Fury with himself, as well. He'd known Caroline was capricious, and willful, and reckless.

But he'd never for one moment thought of her as violent.

His own prejudice, his own sense of honor, had clouded his judgment here, and now she was aiming a pistol at Susannah's temple.

His voice was a gentle thing. Breeze gentle. "Put the pistol down, Caroline. You don't want to do this."

"No?" She sounded half-amused. "You don't intend to 'help' me, Kit. It's my guess you intend to see me hang. I think I *do* want to do this."

"Why do you think I'd like to see you hang?" Again, gently, gently. So as not to jar her mood any further than necessary.

Caroline all but rolled her eyes at him. "Oh, you needn't speak to me so very *gently*, Kit," Caroline sounded amused again. "I'm not *mad*. Perfectly sane."

"Caroline, if you just hand the gun to me . . ."

She snorted. Held very still. As did Kit. The air itself seemed to congeal.

"She was kind, Susannah," Caroline said slowly. "Your mother."

Susannah's eyes slid to Caroline's face. Kit watched the comprehension begin to dawn there. She was beginning to realize what he'd realized today in the library.

Caroline smiled a little. "So few people really are," she continued. "They pretend to be, because they think that's how they're supposed to be. But your mother was truly kind. And I was a *terrible* maid."

"How do you know my mother?" Susannah said hoarsely.

Caroline's exquisite face registered nothing, but her eyes briefly reflected a boundless, startling sadness. "I *am* sorry," she said.

Susannah choked it out. "It was you that night . . . your hair . . . I remember. It was *you*. It must have been you."

"I was a maid in your home in Gorringe, Susannah. Morley had suspicions about Mr. Lockwood, and he knew that Anna Holt was hiring a staff for her country home in Gorringe, and he arranged for *me* to be part of that staff. And after that, it was a simple thing to just listen, as no one pays any attention to a maid. I might as well have been a flea. Your father told your mother everything. And so . . . I listened, and confirmed Thaddeus's suspicions. I imagine Thaddeus did . . . well, the rest."

The rest, of course, being to arrange for the murder of Richard Lockwood and to blame it on Anna Holt.

Caroline turned to Kit. "And *that's* what makes me think you intend to see me hang, Kit. Because I realized today, when you wouldn't allow me to leave, that you probably already knew all of this. And because you are always loyal to the people you love, so hell-bent on righting wrongs. But you never really loved me; it was all tied up with your bloody sense of honor—the wanting to marry me, the wanting to help me. All tied up in your sense of right and wrong. But you *do* love Susannah. And because of that, letting me walk away today would be wrong."

Kit was silent. *So Caroline was an expert on love, was she?* he thought snidely.

She was, however, altogether correct.

He said it quietly. "You shattered their lives, Caroline. Three little girls. A woman, their father. You were playing at spy with Morley . . . you may have been young, but I think you knew exactly what you were about."

"Well, I suppose I thought of it as an adventure, then . . . I didn't think much of it beyond that. And I *did* say I was sorry, and I am. But that doesn't mean I intend to hang for it, for pity's sake. So kindly hand those documents to me. I intend to burn them."

"Caroline, even if I did hand them to you, even if you do burn them, you'd never really be free of this. I would make bloody certain of it."

Kit could hear Susannah's breathing; it had grown more rapid. Her face, even by the warm lantern light, was pale as the marble walls. He wanted to reach for her, touch, her, comfort her; he didn't dare. He instead looked his love into her eyes, and a faint smile touched her lips. As though she was reassuring *him,* for God's sake. She could teach a few men a thing or two about bravery.

Or perhaps it was just that she put a little too much faith in him. After all, he'd been doing nothing but saving her life for days now.

"And how do you suppose you'll get away?" he asked Caroline, almost conversationally. "You've only the one bullet in that pistol, if it's even loaded. You can't kill the both of us."

"Oh, someone followed us here. A man of Morley's, right scary little man. I imagine he'll be here shortly, and then off we'll go. This will be over sooner if you hand the documents to me now."

There was a faint scuffing noise, and Caroline and Kit swiveled. It was the toe of Susannah's boot moving a fraction of an inch.

"I'm terribly sorry, but I . . . but I think I might faint," Susannah whispered.

Kit felt a rush of concern and then . . .

No. If Susannah hadn't yet fainted—over adders, mad horses, and lunging men with knives—she wasn't about to do it now.

He waited, senses on alert.

Caroline shifted a little uneasily, and Kit watched the gun barrel nuzzle more deeply into Susannah's temple, and he felt it as surely as if it were pressed against his own skin.

"Really," Susannah said, again sounding desperate. "And I think I may very well be sick all ov—"

Caroline took the minutest step back in alarm, and in that instant Kit lashed out and seized Caroline's wrist, yanking it skyward, and the pistol fired into the mausoleum ceiling.

Chips of marble came showering down. Kit swept an arm across Susannah's waist and pushed her aside. He seized the petite Caroline's wrists in his own and twisted them behind her back.

"Susannah . . . pull the string from my knapsack. There's a knife in there . . . use it to cut it free."

For someone who'd just had a pistol pointed at her temple, Susannah managed to do this with admirable dexterity, and Kit bound Caroline's wrists.

"For pointing a gun at Susannah, Caroline . . . I'll see you hang."

The three of them swiveled toward a creak as the door opened fully. A lantern entered. Kit spun, pointing his pistol at the door. "Don't move another inch or—"

"Oh, spare the blustering, Kit, for God's sake. It's only me."

John Carr was holding the lantern, and a pistol, and a knapsack filled with helpful things.

Kit lowered his pistol. "*Now* you arrive, John."

John Carr paused in the doorway, took a look around, the blasted ceiling, the marble fragments on the floor, the broken-open strongbox. "Bloody hell. *Again* you beat me to it, Grantham. How the dev—"

"I'm just better, is all, John."

John shook his head, swearing softly, and Kit laughed.

"Found the documents, then?" John asked. "They do exist? I followed the trail here, at last."

"They're over here," Kit jerked his chin toward the strongbox. "And look who found *me*."

"Hello, John," Caroline said pleasantly. "It's been some time, hasn't it?"

John spun toward her voice. And went utterly, almost eerily, still. Merely regarded Caroline with an expression impossible to decipher.

His stillness was only seconds shy of troubling Kit when John finally spoke again.

"Are the documents what they're purported to be?" John turned away from her, said the words coolly.

"Have a look for yourself." Kit motioned with his hand, and John strode past the bound Caroline and the quiet Susannah, not meeting the eyes of either of them, focused on his goal. He leafed through the documents, skimming the words; his face grew steadily grimmer.

"I came upon a nasty little character named Bob lurking about, knocked him out, tied him up," John said absently, as he read the documents. "I do think he'll be useful when it comes to . . . proving Morley's transgressions.

You may want to send someone for him." He continued reading.

"We've enough there to hang him, I suppose," Kit said. "Morley, that is. With the testimony of Mr. Avery-Finch, if he agrees to testify."

"Yes, it looks that way," John said slowly, as he turned the last of the documents over. "So why don't you let Caroline go?"

Kit wasn't certain he'd heard him correctly. "I beg your pardon?"

"You have enough here to hang Morley," John said calmly. "So let Caroline go."

Kit stared at John's handsome face. The words were disorienting, as though someone else had borrowed John's mouth to speak them. "John . . . are you mad? Tell me you're jesting. She's part of all of this . . . she helped all but destroyed Susannah's family, she helped murder a man, she held a pistol to Susannah's *temple,* in case you're wondering why I've bound her wrists." He gave an incredulous laugh. "She was instrumental in obtaining the very information you're holding there. She's a traitor to England, John, as surely as Morley is."

The traitor to England lifted her delicate brows at this description, but otherwise remained silent.

John said nothing. Merely stared levelly back at Kit.

Then comprehension set in, and Kit's world tilted on its axis.

"You never were investigating *Morley,* were you?" he said softly. "This entire time . . . you were looking for Caroline . . . for yourself, weren't you?"

John kept his gaze level with Kit's, not speaking.

But finally, he squeezed his eyes closed. He opened

them again, and pride and a plea for understanding, were taut in his face.

"I wish I could explain it to you, Kit, but I'm not sure you'd understand. I just . . . never could forget her. I thought of her so often . . . more than I could ever confess to you. I was ashamed of it, if you must know. I knew it was a foolish obsession and yet . . . well, I finally surrendered to the urge to look for her. I began with Morley. I intercepted his mail."

"No one assigned you to do that," Kit said, half-wonderingly.

"No."

"If anyone other than me had learned you were doing that, John . . ." The risk had been extraordinary, the consequences grave, disastrous for John.

"I know." John's mouth twitched ruefully. "Are you beginning to see now? It was a risk I was willing to take. For her."

Kit opened his mouth to speak, and John waited. But no words came.

"And then . . . well, once I began with Morley . . . I started with you, too, Kit. And I don't expect you to forgive me, but I honestly couldn't explain this to you. I didn't think you'd understand. *I* didn't even fully understand. But somehow I knew she would come back to you. Because it was always, always you." He gave a short laugh, a little wondering, a little bitter. The sound of acceptance. "And I thought if I could help her . . . perhaps she would turn to me instead. I just couldn't let the two of you meet again. God, I wanted a chance with her." John looked uncomfortable. "Most of your mail is fairly dull, you know." He tried a joke.

"Sorry to bore you," Kit said dryly.

"But damned if she didn't try to reach you. I was right." John gave a humorless laugh.

"Ah, must be your spy instincts," Kit said. Again, dryly.

"I thought . . . with the information you gave me—the story Makepeace told you—perhaps I would be able to find those documents before you did . . . and if anything among them pointed to Caroline, I would destroy it, and just leave enough to hang Morley. And then . . . perhaps when I found her . . ."

He looked at Caroline now, who was regarding him with utter astonishment. "I'd take her away where no one could ever hurt her again." He said this with quiet, almost deadly, conviction.

John turned to Kit again. "And again . . . she came right back to you, Kit." He sounded half-amused. "Here she is."

"But John . . ." Kit was staggered. "She isn't . . ."

He was about to say, *She isn't worth it.* The very same words John had said to him that morning seventeen years ago, when they'd faced each other over pistols. Bitter words, Kit saw now. Words of self-defense. The loss had somehow been greater for John. Had always been greater for John.

And Kit couldn't bring himself to say those words about any woman.

"I *can't* let you do it, John. I can't let you take her. She helped *murder* a man. Two men, if you include what became of Makepeace. Her actions may have led to the deaths of English soldiers, John. Surely this *matters* to you."

"I don't care, Kit." John sounded weary and bemused and faintly awed by his own confession. "I'm more sorry than I can say, and I know it's all true of her, but when it comes to Caroline . . . God help me, but I don't care."

"John—"

John's voice rose, tense, impassioned now. "Kit, I have only ever truly wanted one thing, so help me. And I don't know whether or not it will make me happy. I'm not sure that I *care* whether it does." He gave a short, wondering laugh. "But I do know that I want Caroline. Know this: I love you as a brother. And if you've ever loved me—and I know what I've done is nigh unforgivable—let me win *just this once*. For God's sake."

Another fragment of marble *chink*ed to the ground. No one moved.

"Don't throw everything away, John," Kit pleaded softly.

John Carr said nothing.

"She doesn't love you, John." Kit could hear the resignation creeping into his own voice. John heard it, too.

A ghost of a smile touched John's face. "Oh, she will, one day. I mean . . . look at me."

Kit smiled faintly, too; he couldn't help it. But his heart was breaking again. He thought again about all the kinds of love there were in the world. Love, it turned out, was a constant surprise, in its mutations and permutations.

Susannah spoke, her voice a soft note in the tense silence. "Kit . . . I think you should let her go."

Kit jerked toward her. "This woman, Susannah . . . what she did to your family . . ."

"I know what she did, but . . . but nothing can undo that now. Hanging her won't bring either my father or James Makepeace back. Mr. Morley . . . isn't he the one truly at fault? Don't we have enough to bring him to justice?"

Kit's sense of justice, his patriotism, his need to put things right, his sense of right and wrong—all were at war here with something that adhered to no laws. He thought of the words of Pascal: *The heart has its reasons which reason knows nothing of.*

"I don't know if it's the right thing to do, Susannah." He said it quietly, almost desperately.

"Perhaps not everything can be either right or wrong. Perhaps you must simply choose."

And so, a moment later, he chose. He did it out of love, and not patriotism, knowing that no matter what he chose, John Carr was lost to him.

Kit turned to Caroline. "Will you go with him?" he said gruffly.

"Hmmm . . ." Caroline looked up toward the ceiling. "Goodness . . . the gallows, or handsome John Carr. Let me think . . . let me think . . ."

Kit sighed, and gestured with his chin toward John, and Caroline went to him. John quickly worked the bonds loose from Caroline's wrists.

"Good knots," he complimented Kit, quietly.

Kit said nothing.

When Caroline was free, she turned to look at John, and he fixed his eyes on her face for a long moment, absorbing her. Neither said a word.

Caroline broke their gaze, finally, and turned to Susannah.

"Your mother . . . well, your parents talked often of Italy. I truly don't know where she might have gone that evening . . . but she might have tried to go there."

Susannah gave a shallow nod of thanks.

Kit looked at his best friend in the world, the man

who'd known him from boyhood, the brother of his heart, his rival. Bloody handsome John Carr.

"You'd better leave, John. Before I change my mind."

John Carr lifted a hand to Kit, smiled crookedly. Then turned and pushed the door to the mausoleum open. And walked away from Kit forever.

Caroline was behind him, but she paused in the doorway. She looked at Kit, uncertain; she appeared to be deciding whether she should speak.

"Thaddeus has . . . a cat," she faltered. "Will you see that someone . . . that someone takes his cat?"

She lifted her chin. Daring Kit to mock her. Still, she kept her eyes fixed on him, waiting for an answer.

And Kit gazed back at her, stunned. *How about that? She does love Morley.*

But Caroline wasn't burdened with a sense of honor; she traveled lightly, burdened only with her own sense of self-preservation, living from moment to moment. It wasn't love the way Kit understood it.

He found himself nodding just once, curtly.

"Good-bye then. Good luck to both of you." Caroline gave an ironic curtsy, turned to leave again.

"Caroline," Kit said sharply.

She stopped and turned, lifted her soft brows inquiringly.

"Endeavor to be worthy of him."

She laughed, as though he'd just said something tremendously witty, and shook her head wryly.

And was gone.

He didn't want to speak during the ride home. Silently, he led Susannah into the house, past the servants, up the stairs, into his chambers, where she'd never before been, and sank down on the edge of his bed. And Susannah could see in his posture that every fiber in his body, in his soul, was achingly weary.

"I'm sorry about John," she said softly.

"Come here," he said softly in return.

She drifted over, and stood between his legs, and he looped his arms around her. He looked up. She could peer right down into the nostrils of his arrogantly arched nose, right into those beautiful blue eyes fringed by those gold tipped lashes.

"I love you, Susannah."

"I know." It didn't seem nearly as important anymore to hear him say the words aloud; she knew he simply lived his love for her every moment.

"But I should have told you before now. When Caroline pointed a pistol at you, I—"

He stopped abruptly, turned his head.

"Hush. . . ," Susannah murmured, and cupped her face in her hands, pressed her lips against the top of his head. "It's all right."

"It's not all right." He sounded irritated. He looked up at her again. "It's just that I—"

"Perhaps you weren't sure you loved me, and needed to be cert—"

"Susannah." He sounded amused and impatient. "Please stop defending me. It wasn't any of that . . . it was . . ." He paused, searching for words to describe an amorphous terror. "It was as though if I'd said the words aloud . . . you'd just disappear. And I couldn't bear it. I couldn't bear the thought of loving you as much as I do . . . I love you so much . . . and then losing you."

He sounded ashamed. As though he thought he wasn't entitled to ever fear.

She didn't know what to say. Probably nothing at all would be best.

"In summary," he concluded wryly, "I was a dreadful coward, and I love you."

"Well, that's quite an astonishing confession." Her voice was husky. "From a man who's been crushed by a horse and stabbed in my defense, and shot at by the French, and God knows what else. But you can stop confessing now. I love you, too."

"I know," he said on a sigh, looking dazed and pleased, and his hands wandered lower, until they were looped beneath her behind. He pulled her into him, held her close.

He was just about eye-level with her breasts, and so he pulled her in closer, and pressed his lips to one, over the soft muslin. And his hands wandered up beneath her dress, lifting it until his fingers found the silky insides of her thighs. He leaned backward onto the bed, bringing her with him.

"Hush, now," he ordered on a whisper. "Lie still."

He tipped her to the bed and then knelt over her, reached behind her back and gently, deftly, unlaced her gown, eased it over her head, placed it carefully aside. Next, he applied himself to her garters, untying them, adding them to the dress, rolled her stockings down, still deftly, while she quietly submitted.

And when she was entirely bare, he sighed, and lay alongside her. He kissed her mouth, softly. His lips found her brows, her temple, the pulse in her throat; his hands pulled the pins from her hair, stroking it out until it fanned over his pillow.

And this is how he made love to her: The overwhelming, aching tenderness, the desire and reverence, in his every touch, more eloquent, more profound, than words could ever hope to be. Susannah closed her eyes and only once murmured his name, floating in the center of a bliss that had edges of flame. His hands, his mouth, seemed everywhere, everywhere, from her shoulders, to her breasts, to the round curve of her belly, relentlessly knowing, sure and delicate, setting slow fire to every cell of her until she arched and rippled beneath his touch, until she was nothing but a creature made to be touched.

And then his mouth moved between her legs, and he parted her knees so he could taste the silkiest, most sensitive part of her. Her fingers gripped the coverlet as his tongue dipped, and circled, and savored, loving her, until her blood roared in her ears, until she was nearly sobbing from the pleasure of it, until she splintered into light and sensation.

Then, at last, off came his clothes, which he did as deftly as he did everything else, and his beautiful body hovered an instant over her. She surrounded him with her thighs, pulled him to her with her arms, took him into her body. This joining always seemed never to last quite long enough to Susannah, because she could never fully be part of him, but the finite nature of it made it all the sweeter. And this was slow, slow, too, and his eyes never left hers; he burned his love into her with his eyes. He moved, inexorably to his own release, which came for him with a sigh of her name.

He kissed her. He turned over gently, with her in his arms. They held each other, face to face.

"*That's* how much I love you, Susannah," he whispered.

* * *

They lolled together, until Kit remembered that Aunt Frances would worry, and so they dressed, somewhat haphazardly and quickly, and made their way down the stairs.

Bullton was hurrying toward him again. This was becoming unnervingly familiar.

"Sir—" he began desperately.

He didn't need to say anything more than that. Because Kit heard the sound of an all-too familiar throat clearing in the portrait parlor.

"Sir, he has . . . he is. . . ," Bullton whispered desperately. Then gave up trying to explain. "Well, perhaps you best go to him, sir," he said resignedly. "And you'll see."

Because, of course, it was the very worst thing Kit could possibly imagine happening, the earl was standing in the middle of the room holding Susannah's sketchbook, which she had of course left in the portrait parlor.

He seemed riveted by a particular page. Frozen in place, in fact, staring down at it.

When at last he slowly lifted his head, his expression was . . . well, indescribable, really.

Though "priceless" did go some way toward describing it.

Kit almost squeezed his eyes closed. One never, never, *never* wants one's father to get a good look at one's face in the aftermath of lovemaking. But that's precisely what that particular sketch afforded.

He glanced at Susannah, whom he'd tried to hide behind him. Her hair was sliding out of the pins on one side. She looked beautiful and, unfortunately, entirely wanton.

A cripplingly awkward moment staggered by, while Kit grappled with what he should say to his father. He mentally packed his trunks for Egypt, hoping Susannah wouldn't be disappointed to find herself living in the desert rather than on Grosvenor Square.

"Is this the artist?" his father asked, eyebrows raised in Susannah's direction.

"Yes," Kit confessed.

A silence as vast and arid as the Egyptian desert yawned while his father stared at the two of them.

"We're going to be married," Kit offered tentatively.

"Good God, I should *think* so," the earl said fervently. "Who is she?"

Kit went mute again.

"Well?" the earl gestured with his brows.

At last Kit found his manners, or some vestiges of them. "Father, allow me to introduce to you to Miss Susannah Makepeace, my fiancée. This is my father, the Earl of Westphall."

Susannah paused, and then—because what else could one do under the circumstances?—she curtsied.

Kit almost laughed.

"Makepeace, eh? James's daughter?"

She hesitated, but apparently decided her real story would have to wait. "Yes, sir." Susannah's voice was remarkably steady.

"And did you make these sketches?"

Her face was a brilliant, flaming, summer-sunset scarlet, but her composure held up admirably. "Yes, sir."

The earl stared at both of them again for some time, clearly struggling with a number of diverse thoughts, among them, judging from the twitch of his features, hilarity and horror.

He cleared his throat. "They're really quite good."

Kit was in awe. The earl had clearly chosen the most benign thing from the myriad things he'd *wanted* to say, or could have said. *My father, the diplomat,* Kit thought. *I really should take lessons.*

"She's very talented," Kit said quickly.

Kit realized too late how this must sound, given the sketch his father had no doubt been reviewing. He nearly slapped his forehead.

The earl just sighed.

"Miss Makepeace, it is a pleasure to meet you. I should like to speak to my son alone now."

Susannah shot Kit a sympathetic look, and looked relieved to be leaving the library. Kit was tempted to pull her back by the elbow.

"I'm sorry about the folio assignment, father," Kit began quickly. "I'll complete it, I promise you. Rather a lot of things . . . came up. That you will find very interesting."

"You were seen in London, Kit."

"By whom?" he said swiftly. *Bloody John!*

"Miss Daisy Jones said a Mr. White had come inquiring. I knew it was you."

"You conducted your *own* inquiry?" Kit asked. So his father *hadn't* thought he was mad when he mentioned Makepeace. It was a little mollifying.

Wait. Or maybe . . . "How do you know Miss Daisy Jones?"

His father just smiled enigmatically. "Did you find what

you were looking for, Kit? What you should *not* have been looking for, I should say?"

"Yes, and it's true, sir. Everything Makepeace said was true. I'll show the documents to you, if you'd like to see them. Correspondence, lists of ships . . . and Morley is mentioned specifically. Lockwood really did gather valid evidence. It looks bad for Morley, sir. I spoke to an antiquities dealer who might be persuaded to testify."

The earl went still. After a moment, his face reflected a deep sadness. "It's a shame. All of it. He wasn't a bad politician, Morley. An intelligent man. A waste. A pity. A murderer."

"And a traitor, sir. He was a traitor."

"It was dangerous, what you did, Kit. Going about this alone. You could have been killed."

"I could have been killed any number of times in my life," Kit said wryly. "There's still time."

"But I *expressly* told you not to go anywhere near London." His father's tone had the ring of pyramids now.

"I swear to you, sir, I'll finish the folio assignment. I . . ." He paused when he realized this was true. "I *want* to finish the assignment."

The earl sighed again. "There was no assignment, Kit."

A silence.

"I beg your pardon?" Kit said flatly.

"There *was* no assignment. It was just . . ." The earl turned away from him and rotated to look about the grand room, stopping to admire the portrait of his family. He smiled softly up at it, perhaps remembering the sittings. "I was worried about you, son. You seemed so . . ." His father paused. "Lost. Wallowing in various pleasures, but finding no *real* pleasure. A little too reckless. Unhappy without realizing it. And it had gone on for too long. It's the sort of thing a father notices."

Kit knew he should have been touched. But—

"And so you threatened me with *Egypt*?"

The earl looked placidly back at Kit. "I thought perhaps you could use a little time away from the *ton* to clear your head. Perhaps even rediscover an earlier, less dangerous passion. And I knew you wouldn't take any time away if I put it quite like *that* . . . and so, I invented an assignment. And . . ." The earl paused again, sounding bemused. "Once more, you've greatly exceeded my expectations. Then again, you never did do anything by halves."

His father gave him one of those sunny but evil smiles. The smiles that said, *I will always be cleverer than you, as long as I'm your father.*

Kit was speechless. His bloody father had *tricked* him.

Kit didn't know whether he wanted to throttle the man, or fall to his knees and thank him abjectly.

But he did know when he'd been bested.

"And it's good work, Christopher. Are your notes as good as these drawings?"

"What do you think?" All arrogance.

His father smiled. "Well, then, you *should* complete the folio. It bears publishing, you know, as good as these drawings are. We'll just . . . exclude a few of them."

"The voles?" Kit suggested innocently.

His father finally laughed. Then he glanced down at the sketchbook, and up at his son again, and shook his head slowly, to and fro. It took every fiber of Kit's self-control not to blush, and he could not remember ever blushing in his entire life.

"What is she like? Susannah?"

Damn. How Kit hated these kinds of questions. Whenever Susannah filled his thoughts, words seemed to flee. He thought of her, and it was just . . .

But his father must have read the answer on his face, and he gave a soft laugh. "Never mind, son. The sketches speak for both of you. And I'm more glad for you than I can say."

Epilogue

She was trimming limp roses from their bushes when the breeze sprang up, a small surprise from the north; she closed her eyes briefly, let it trail around her neck like a damp silk scarf. The moist *sirocco* winds blew across Italy early in the fall, reminding her that she was not a native, would never quite feel like a native, even after seventeen years. The weather inside her was English.

Italy was beautiful, and she had been known safety and anonymity here, but any place that wasn't home would always feel like a prison.

The pain had become an ever-present dull hum over the years; she'd learned to accommodate it the way one did an amputation. She'd known laughter again; she'd even known the faint rush of attraction again; she still turned heads, even as her middle years approached. Her very small circle of acquaintances knew her only as a widow, quietly committed to her mourning.

She'd risked two letters, two selfish letters, in the early years. She hadn't signed them; even still, she knew sending them had been tantamount to aiming a gun at James—or at herself. But the longing and pain had been so fierce then she sometimes thought she would have happily died, happily sacrificed James or anyone else, for one scrap of knowledge of her daughters. James had replied only once: *they are safe.* He was right to discourage her from writing, of course. No doubt it had cost him not to ease her pain. But he'd been protecting them still.

But year after year, hope bloomed and died and bloomed again, like the roses she now pruned to make way for new growth. She would see her daughters again, and the truth would some day be known: this hope kept Anna Holt fiercely alive.

About the Author

Julie Anne Long originally set out to be a rock star when she grew up, and she has the guitars and the questionable wardrobe stuffed in the back of her closet to prove it. But writing was her first love. When playing to indifferent crowds at midnight in dank sticky clubs finally lost its, ahem, *charm*, Julie realized she could incorporate all the best things about being in a band—namely drama, passion, and men with unruly hair—into novels, while also indulging her love of history and research. She made the move from guitar to keyboard (the computer variety) and embarked on a considerably more civilized, if not much more peaceful, career as a novelist.

Julie lives in the San Francisco Bay Area with a fat orange cat (little known fact: they issue you a cat the moment you become a romance novelist). Visit her Web site at www.julieannelong.com, or write to her at Julie@julieannelong.com

Please turn the page
to preview
Julie Anne Long's
next novel

Ways to Be Wicked

Available in mass market
October 2006.

Ironic, Sylvie thought, that the pitching and rolling of that wretched wooden ship should set up a corresponding movement in her stomach, given that motion was more native to her than stillness. She in fact leaped and stretched and pirouetted every day, achieving semi-flight with no ill effects apart from sore muscles and the perversely gratifying jealousy of all of the other dancers in Monsieur Favre's corps de ballet. Sylvie Lamoreux was, in fact, the darling of the Paris Opera, object of desire and envy, the personification of beauty and grace—not accustomed, in other words, to losing the contents of her stomach over the side of a ship.

She supposed it had a little something to do with control: when she danced, *she* commanded her body. Well, and Monsieur Favre had a bit of a say in it, too: "I said like a *butterfly* Sylvie, not a cow. Look at you! I want to moo!" Or "Your arms, Sylvie, they are like timber. Lift them like so—ah yes, that is it, *mon ange,* you are like a dream. I suspected you could dance." Monsieur Favre was a trifle prone to exaggeration, but if she was his best dancer, he had helped make her so, and confidence was marvelous armor against sarcasm.

She'd rather be at Monsieur Favre's mercy any day than that bloody wooden ship, heaving this way and that over the choppy waters of the channel.

He would not be pleased to find her gone.

The letter in her reticule said very little. But what it did say had launched her like a cannonball across the channel to England for the first time in her life. For two weeks, Sylvie had furtively planned her journey, from Paris to Le Havre to Portsmouth, propelled by hurt and fury, poignant hope and a great inner flame of curiosity. She hadn't told a single soul of her plans. This seemed only fitting, given the magnitude of the things that had been kept from her.

Odd to think that a few mere sentences of English could do this. The letter had begun with an apology for bothering Claude yet again. *Yet again*—a little flame of anger licked up every time Sylvie thought of these words. It was not the first such letter sent, in other words. Or even the second, it would appear. And then, in the next sentence, it begged information about a young woman named Sylvie. *For I believe she might be my sister.*

The signature at the bottom said: "Susannah Whitelaw, Lady Grantham."

My sister. Sylvie had never before thought or said those two words together.

To Sylvie the letter meant a past she'd never known, a future she'd never dreamed, and a store of secrets she'd only half-suspected. Her parents were dead, Claude had told her, God rest their souls; Claude had raised Sylvie as her own. And if not for the fact that Claude had decided to holiday in the South as she did every year at this time, with a kiss on both cheeks for Sylvie and instructions to mind her parrot in her absence, Sylvie might never have seen the letter at all.

Sylvie had left the parrot in the care of Claude's housekeeper. He would be in danger of nothing but boredom, as he spoke two more languages than the housekeeper, which was two fewer than Etienne.

Etienne. Sylvie's thoughts immediately flew from him as though scorched. And then flew back again, guiltily.

He was generous, Etienne, with ardor and gifts. He flirted as only one descended from centuries of courtiers could flirt; he moved through the world with the confident magnanimity of someone who had never been denied anything. He made heady promises she hardly dared believe. But his temper . . . Sylvie would never understand it. Her own was a starburst—quick, spectacular, gone. His was cold and patient, implacable. It waited; he planned. And his retaliations always came with chilling finality and a sense of righteousness.

She'd last seen Etienne a week ago in the mauve, predawn light, an arm flung over his head, his bare back turned to her as he slept. She'd placed the letter on her pillow, telling him only that she would see him again soon.

He loved her. But he used the word so easily.

But just as she knew Etienne would have tried to dissuade her from leaving Paris, she knew he would try to find her. And his temper would have been waiting all the while, too.

She did not want to be found until she'd learned what she'd come to learn.

The ship had released the passengers, and now Sylvie's feet pressed against England. She allowed herself a giddy surge of triumph: she'd made it this far, entirely on her own. But she could still feel the sea inside her stomach, and color and movement and noise came at her in waves: Men swarming to unload the ship, sun ricocheting hard between smooth sea and blue sky, gulls wheeling in arcs of silver and white. No clouds floated above to cut the glare or soften the heat. Sylvie took her first deep breath of truly English air: it was hot and clotted with dock odors, and made matters inside her stomach worse instead of better.

She nodded to the man who shouldered her trunk for her, and briskly turned to find the mail coach that would take her to London. She had never before traveled alone, but she had contrived the perfect disguise, her English was passably good, and she was not a child needing coddling or protection from a man. Besides, after Paris, a city as intricate, beautiful and difficult as the ballet itself, no city could intimidate her.

She glanced up then and saw just the back of him, through the crowd, the broad shoulders, the way he stood. The sight of Etienne slammed her hard, sending a cold wave of shock through her confidence. She went motionless against it, uncertain what to do. *It couldn't be. Not yet. Not so soon.*

But it was not a risk she was prepared to take. She swiveled her head, saw the mail coach.

Tom Shaughnessy was alone in the mail coach when a woman flung herself into his lap, wrapped her arms around his neck, and burrowed in, crushing her face against his.

"*What* in the name of—" he hissed. He lifted his arms to try to pry hers from about his neck.

"Hush," she whispered urgently. *"Please."*

A man's head peered into the coach then, jerked back. "I beg your pardon, monsieur, I thought—*pardonnez-moi.*" He jerked his head hurriedly back.

The woman in his lap had gone completely rigid, apart

from her rapid breathing. And for a moment neither of them moved: Tom had an impression of rustling dark fabric, a lithe form, and the scent of spice and vanilla and roses and female.

Startling, granted. But not entirely unpleasant.

Apparently deciding a safe interval had elapsed, she took her arms from about his neck and slid from his lap into the seat a distance away from him.

"And just when I was growing accustomed to you, Madame," he wryly. He touched her arm gently. "Allow me to intro—*ow!*"

He jerked his hand back. What the *devil*—?

His eyes followed a glint to her lap.

Poking up from her neatly folded gloved hands was a . . . was that a *knitting* needle?

It was! She'd jabbed him with a damned *knitting needle*. Not hard enough to wound anything other than his pride. But certainly hard enough to make her . . . er . . . point.

"I regret inserting you, sir, but I cannot permit you to touch me again." Her voice was soft and grave, refined; it trembled just a bit. And absurdly, she did sound genuinely regretful.

Tom glared at her, baffled. "You regret inser—Oh! You mean 'stabbing.' You regret . . . *stabbing* me?"

"Yes!" She said almost gratefully, as though he'd given her a verb she considered useful and fully intended to employ again in the future. "I regret *stabbing* you. I regret sitting upon you, also. But I cannot permit you to touch me again. I am not. . . ." She made a futile gesture with her hand, as if she could snatch the elusive word from the air with it.

She was not . . . what? Sane?

But he could hear it now: She was French. Which accounted for the way her syllables subtly leaped and dipped in the wrong places, not to mention her unusual vocabulary choices, and perhaps even the knitting needle, because God only knew what a Frenchwomen was capable of. And apart from that tremble in her voice he would have assumed she was preternaturally self-possessed. But she was clearly afraid of something.

He looked hard at her, but she kept her head angled slightly away from him. She was wearing mourning; he could see this now that she wasn't precisely on top of him. Her hat and veil revealed only a hint of delicate jaw and gleaming hair, which seemed to be a red shade, though this might perhaps be wishful thinking on his part. Her neck was long; her spine as elegantly erect as a Doric column. She was slim, but the gown she wore gave very little away of the shape of the woman inside it. The gown itself was beautifully made, but it fit her ill. Borrowed, he decided. He was accustomed to judging the fit of female clothing, after all, and this dress was not only too large; it had been made for someone else entirely.

Since he had done nothing but gape for nearly minute, she seemed satisfied he didn't intend to reach for her again; she slid the needle back up into her sleeve. For all the world like a woman tucking a basket of mending under a chair.

"Who is pursuing you, Madame?" he asked softly.

Her shoulders stiffened almost imperceptibly. Interesting. A further ripple in that self-possession.

"Je ne comprende pas, monsieur." Delivered with a pretty little French lift of one shoulder.

Balderdash. She understood him perfectly well.

"*Au contraire,* I believe you do *comprende* my question," he contradicted politely. His own French was actually quite good. All the very best courtesans were French, after all. Many of the dancers who passed through the White Lily were as well, which is why he knew all about the caprices of Frenchwomen.

The veil fluttered; she was breathing a little more quickly now.

"If you tell me, I might be able to help you," he pressed gently. Why he should offer to help someone who'd leaped into his lap and then poked him with a knitting needle eluded him at the moment. Curiosity, he supposed. And that delicate jaw.

The veil fluttered once, twice, as she mulled her next words. "Oh, but you already *have* helped me, monsieur."

And the faint but unmistakable self-deprecating humor and—dare he think it?—*flirtation*—in her words perversely charmed him to his marrow.

He opened his mouth to say something else, but she turned decisively toward the window, and an instant later seemed to have shed her awareness of him as neatly as a shawl or hat.

Damned if he wasn't fascinated.

He wanted desperately to gain her attention again, but if he spoke she would ignore him, he sensed; he suspected that if he so much as brushed the sleeve of her gown his hand would be swiftly 'inserted' as neatly as a naturalist's butterfly to the mail coach seat.

He was watching her so intently he was startled when the coach bucked on its springs, taking on the weight of more passengers: a duenna ushering two young ladies, both pretty and diffident; a young couple glowing with bemusement, as though the institution of marriage was their own marvelous, private discovery; a young man who looked very much like a curate; a plump prosperous merchant of some sort: Tom made his judgments of them by their clothing and the way they held themselves. At one time, each and every one of them, or someone of their ilk, had passed through his life, or he through theirs.

The little French woman might as well have been a shadow of one of the other passengers; with her slight build and dark clothing, she all but vanished against her seat. No one would trouble her or engage her in conversation if she appeared not to welcome it; she was dressed as a widow, and ostensibly still inside a bubble of grief.

Tom doubted it. He knew a costume when he saw one.

More and more people wedged aboard the coach, until it fair burst with heat and a veritable cornucopia of human smells, and the widow finally disappeared completely from Tom's view. When they were full to brimming, the coach lurched forward to London again.

And as Tom was a busy man, his thoughts inevitably lurched toward London along with the coach: How he was going to pay for a new theater was one line of thought; he had just the building in mind. How he was going to break the news to Daisy Jones that she would *not* be playing Venus in the White Lily's latest production was another.

He glanced up; the curate sitting across from him gave him a tentative little smile. Very much like a small dog rolling over to show its belly to a larger, more dazzling dog.

"Exceedingly warm for this time of year," the curate ventured.

"Indeed. And if it's this warm near the sea, imagine how warm it will be in London," Tom answered politely.

Ah, weather. A topic that bridged social classes the world over. Whatever would they do without it?

And so the passengers passed a tolerable few hours sweating and smelling each other and exchanging pleasant banalities as the coach wheels ate up road, and there was seldom a lull in conversation. And for two hours, Tom heard not a single word of French-accented English in the jumble of words around him.

When the curate stopped chatting for a moment, Tom slipped a hand into his pocket and snapped open his watch; in an hour or so, he knew, they would reach a coaching inn on the road to Westerly in time for a bad luncheon; he hoped to be back to London in time for supper, to supervise the latest show at the White Lily, and then perhaps enjoy late night entertainments with a most accommodating wealthy widow.

And then in the lull a pistol shot cracked and echoed, and the coach bucked to a stop, sending passengers tumbling over each other.

Highwaymen. *Bloody hell.*

Tom gently sat the curate back into his seat and brushed off his coat, then brushed off his own.

Brazen coves, these highwaymen were, to stop the coach at midday. But this stretch of road was all but deserted, and they'd been known to stop the occasional mail coach run. A mail coach was essentially fish-in-a-barrel for highwaymen. Which meant there must be many of them, all armed, if they were bold enough to stop a loaded coach.

Tom swiftly tucked his watch into his boot and retrieved a pistol at the same time; he saw the curate's eyes bulge and watched him rear back a little in alarm. *Good god. No man should be afraid to shoot if necessary,* Tom thought with some impatience. He tugged the sleeve of his coat down to cover his weapon; one glimpse of it might inspire a nervous highwayman to waste a bullet on him.

"Take off your rings and put them into your shoes," he ordered the newlyweds quietly. Hands shaking like sheets pinned to a line, they obeyed him, as no one else was issuing orders in this extraordinary situation.

Tom knew he had only a ghost of a chance of doing something to deter the highwaymen, no matter their numbers. Still, it never occurred to him not to try. It wasn't as though Tom had never taken anything; when he was young and living in the rookeries, he'd taken food, handkerchiefs, anything small he could fence. But he had ultimately chosen to work for everything he owned; he found it satisfied a need for permanence, a need for . . . legacy. And damned if he was going to allow someone to take anything he'd earned if he could possibly avoid it. Even if it was only a few pounds and a watch.

"Out, everybody," a graveled voice demanded. "'ands up, now where I can see 'em, now."

And out of the dark coach stumbled the passengers, blinking and pale in the sunlight, one of whom was nearly swooning, if her buckling knees were any indication, and needed to be fanned by her panicking husband.

The air fair shimmered with heat; only a few wan trees interrupted the vista of parched grass and cracked road. Tom took in the group of highwaymen with a glance: five men, armed with muskets and pistols. Clothing dull with grime, kerchiefs covering their faces, hair long and lank and unevenly sawed, as though trimmed with their own daggers. One of them, the one who appeared to be in charge, gripped a knife between his teeth. Tom almost smiled grimly. *A showman.* Excessive, perhaps, but it certainly lent him a dramatic flair the others lacked.

Tom's innate curiosity about any showman made him peer more closely at the man. There was something about him . . .

"Now see here . . ." the merchant blustered indignantly, and promptly had five pistols and a knife turned on him. He blanched, clapped his mouth shut audibly. Clearly new to being robbed at gunpoint, he didn't know that etiquette required one to be quiet, lest one get shot.

And then Tom knew. Almost a decade ago, during a few difficult and unforgettable months of work in a dockside tavern, Tom had spent time with a man who drank the hardest liquor, told the most ribald jokes, tipped most generously, and advised young Tom which whores to avoid and which to court.

"Biggsy?" Tom ventured.

The highwayman swiveled, glowering, and stared at Tom.

Then he reached up and plucked the knife from between teeth brown as aged fence posts, and his face transformed.

"*Tom?* Tommy *Shaughnessy*?"

"'Tis I, in the flesh, Biggs."

"Well, Tommy, as I live and breathe!" Big Biggsy shifted his pistol into his other hand and seized Tom's hand to pump it with genuine enthusiasm. "'avena seen you since those days at Bloody Joe's! Still a pretty bugger, ain't ye?" Biggsy laughed a richly phlegmy laugh and gave Tom a frisky punch on the shoulder. "Ye've gone respectable, 'ave ye, Tommy? Looka tha' fine coat!"

Tom felt the passengers' eyes slide toward them like so many billiard balls rolling toward a pocket, and then slide away again; he could virtually feel them cringing away from him. He wondered if it was because he was on a Christian name basis with an armed highwayman, or because he had "*gone* respectable," implying he had been anything but at one time.

"Respectable might perhaps be overstating it, Biggsy, but yes, you could say I haven't done too badly."

"'avena done 'alf bad meself," Biggsy announced proudly, gesturing at the characters surrounding him as though they were a grand new suite of furniture.

Tom thought it wisest not to disagree or request further clarification. He decided upon nodding sagely.

"'Tis proud I be of ye, Tommy," Biggsy added sentimentally.

"That means the world to me," Tom assured him solemnly.

"And Daisy?" Biggsy prodded. "D'yer see 'er?"

"Oh, yes. She's in fine form, fine form."

"She's a grand woman," the highwayman said mistily.

"She is at that." Grand, and the largest thorn in his side, and no doubt responsible for a good portion of his fortune. Bless the brazen, irritating, glorious Daisy Jones.

Tom gave Biggsy his patented crooked, coaxing grin. "Now, Biggsy, can I persuade you to allow our coach to go on? You've my word of honor not a one shall pursue you."

"Ye've a word of honor now, Tommy?" Biggsy reared back in faux astonishment, then laughed again. Tom, not being a fool, laughed, too, and gave his thigh a little slap for good measure.

Biggsy wiped his eyes and stared at Tom for a moment longer, and took his bottom lip between his teeth to worry it a bit as he mulled the circumstances. And then he sighed and lowered his pistol; and with a jerk of his chin ordered the rest of the armed and mounted men accompanying him to do the same.

"Fer the sake of old times, then, Tommy. Fer the sake of Daisy, and Bloody Joe, rest 'is soul. But I canna leave everythin', you ken 'ow it is—we mun eat, ye ken."

"I ken," Tom repeated commiserating.

"I'll leave the trunks, and jus' 'ave what blunt the lot of ye be carryin' in yer pockets."

"Big of you, Bigsy, big of you," Tom murmured.

"And then I'll 'ave a kiss from one of these young ladies, and we'll be off."

Clunk. Down went the wobbly new missus, dragging her husband down after her; he hadn't time to stop her fall completely. Never a pleasant sound, the sound of a body hitting the ground.

Biggsy eyed them for a moment in mild contempt. Then he looked back at Tom and shook his head slowly, as if to say, *what a pair of ninnies.*

"All right then. Who will it be?" Biggsy asked brightly. He scanned the row of lovely young ladies hopefully.

Tom thought he should have known his own formidable charm would get him only so far with a highwayman.

The crowd who not a moment before had been mentally inching away from him now swiveled their heads beseechingly toward him. Tom wasn't particularly savoring the irony of this at the moment. He wasn't quite sure how to rescue them from this particular request.

"Now, Biggs," Tom tried for a hail-fellow-well-met

cajoling tone, "These are innocent young ladies. If you come to London, I'll introduce you to ladies who'll be happy to—"

"I willna leave without a kiss from one of *these* young ladies." Biggsy insisted stubbornly. "Look a' me, Tom. D'yer think I'm kissed verra often? Let alone by a young thing wi' all of 'er teeth or 'er maidenhe—"

"Biggsy," Tom interjected hurriedly.

"I want a *kiss*."

At the tone, the men behind Biggs put their hands back upon on their pistols, sensing a shift in intent.

Tom's eyes remained locked with Biggsy's, his expression studiedly neutral and pleasant, while his mind did cartwheels. *Bloody, bloody hell. Perhaps I should ask the young ladies to draw straws. Perhaps I should kiss him myself. Perhaps we—*

"I will kiss him."

Everyone, highwaymen included, pivoted, startled, when the little French widow stepped forward. "You will allow the coach to go on if I do?"

Ze coach, Tom thought absently, is what it sounded like when she said it. Her voice was bell-clear and strong and she sounded very nearly impatient, but Tom caught the hint of a tremble in it again, which he found oddly reassuring. If there had been no tremble, he might have worried again about her sanity, and what she might do with a knitting needle.

"My word of honor," Biggsy said almost humbly. He seemed almost taken aback.

Tom was torn between wanting to stop her, and perverse curiosity to see if she intended to go through with it. She hadn't the bearing or voice of a doxie. *I am not . . .*

she had struggled to tell him. She was not someone who suffered the attention of gentlemen lightly, he was certain she meant to say. Not someone who was generally in the habit of leaping into the laps of strangers, unless he had a very good reason to do so.

He hoped, *hoped* she didn't intend to attempt anything foolish with a knitting needle.

Biggsy recovered himself. "I'll take that, shall I?" He reached out and adroitly took her reticule from her. He heard her intake of breath, the beginning of a protest, but wisely stopped herself. Ah, she'd good judgment, too.

Tom saw her shoulders square, as though she was preparing herself for a launch upward. She drew in a deep breath.

And then she stood on her toes, lifted her veil up, and kissed Biggsy Biggens full on the mouth.

And a moment later, Biggsy Biggens looked for all the world as blessed as a bridegroom.

The configuration inside the coach on the way to the coaching inn was this: Tom at one end. A foot of space. All of the other passengers all but knotted together for protection. A foot of space.

And then the widow.

When readers ask me, "Julie Anne, where did you get the idea for your book?" I'm often tempted to be facetious: "In the frozen food aisle at the grocery store. I had a coupon!" But this isn't as far-fetched as it sounds. I've learned over the years that ideas for books are *everywhere*, especially in mundane places you'd never suspect. It's all in how you look at it.

Take **BEAUTY AND THE SPY** (on sale now). I was staring at the blank screen of my computer monitor, sort of ping-ponging between horror (Oh *God*! I have to write a whole *book*!) and elation (Hurrah! I get to write a whole *book*!), when I began to wonder: what if your life is suddenly wiped as blank as the screen facing me? What happens when everything you've always known is taken from you, if the supports of your life as you know it are kicked right out from under you, and not even your own name belongs to you anymore? So that's what I did to heiress Susannah Makepeace. Beginning with the mysterious murder of her father, I yanked the timbers of her charmed life out from under her until she finds herself penniless, jilted, and living in the sleepy town of Barnstable with an aunt she hardly knows.

Once the walls of Susannah's old life are torn down, everything she thought she knew about herself was suddenly cast in a different light, and she's forced to stretch and grow. The first thing she does to test the boundaries of her new life is wander off by herself with her sketchbook, stumble across a naked man swimming—the cheerfully arrogant spy Kit Whitelaw, begrudgingly exiled to Barnstable—and fill a blank page with a drawing of him.

The rest, as we say, is history.

Or historical romance.

Julie Anne Long
http://www.julieannelong.com/

Hi there. This is Angelina Avenger from **Lori Wilde's YOU ONLY LOVE TWICE** (on sale now). No, I'm not the heroine of the book. What I am is a top notch comic book crime fighter, and my creator Marlie Montague—she's the heroine. She loves spilling all my secrets, so I thought why not turn the tables. And no, I'm not dishing just because she barely has time to draw me anymore since that hunky ex–Navy SEAL Joel Hunter moved in next door. <sniff> Here's the tattle on Marlie.

She's the shyest thing on the face of the earth and she rarely goes on dates. And talk about a bookworm. She reads so much it makes *me* cross-eyed.

But to give her credit, when a hit man appears on her doorstep with the business end of a semi-automatic pointed at her, she's smart enough to channel me. Once again, I save the day by getting Marlie out of the house, over the fence, and busting through the kitchen window of the rock-hard action hero next door.

Of course what Marlie doesn't realize is that Navy special agent Joel is on a surveillance gig and Marlie is his target. Now the two of them are fending off more double agents than a Bond flick and having a heck of a lot of fun in the process.

Problem is I'm beginning to wonder where I fit into all this. After all, three is a crowd. And if I'm not mistaken, my little bookworm creator seems to be taking her cues from me and turning into something of a femme fatale.

I'm so proud.

Lori Wilde

Lori Wilde
http://www.loriwilde.com/

Want to know more about romances at
Warner Books and Warner Forever?
Get the scoop online!

WARNER'S ROMANCE HOMEPAGE

Visit us at www.warnerforever.com for all the
latest news, reviews, and chapter excerpts!

NEW AND UPCOMING TITLES

Each month we feature our new titles
and reader favorites.

CONTESTS AND GIVEAWAYS

We give away galleys, autographed copies,
and all kinds of fun stuff.

AUTHOR INFO

You'll find bios, articles, and links to personal
Web sites for all your favorite authors—and
so much more!

THE BUZZ

Sign up for our monthly romance newsletter,
and be the first to read all about it!